HURRICANE HOLE

A NOVEL

D1607841

TODD CAMERON

SHARK ISLAND PRESS

HURRICANE HOLE

SHARK ISLAND PRESS

First Edition Publishing December 2022

SHARK ISLAND PRESS
PO Box 326
Englewood, Florida
34295

Map: Margi Nanney   Author photo: Valerie Vitale

Cover design and interior formatting by:
King's Custom Covers
www.KingsCustomCovers.com

ISBN: 979-8363724145

31 30 29 28 27 26 25 24

For the Cameron sisters—Dale, Corinne, and June.

In loving memory of Bob Anderson and Tom Feehan.

ACKNOWLEDGEMENTS

Although this novel is a work of fiction, Hurricane Charley was a real storm, and the descriptions in this story regarding the hurricane itself—dates, times, locations, impact, and aftermath—are accurate and true. No one could know that eighteen years later, in September 2022, just two months prior to this book's release, another major storm would take a similar path and hit the same location on Florida's Gulf Coast, making landfall again on the barrier island of Cayo Costa.

I must first thank Margi Nanney and her husband Pat for inviting me to stay at their rustic home on Cayo Costa. Their cabin was ground zero for Charley's category 4 landfall on the afternoon of Friday, August 13, 2004. Margi provided me with countless stories and hundreds of photos of Charley's devastation. Fortunately, the cabin stood fast, taking a licking, but faring the storm well. Also a thank you to Kevin Shimp, who joined us out on the island, recounting everyone with wild incidents and photos of Charley's carnage.

I had a couple of fantastic conversations with Annette Nielsen who was the former assistant park manager and biologist at Cayo Costa State Park back in 2004. We spoke of her experiences working on the island through Charley, and I thank her greatly for her revelations and insights. I'd like to thank Jason Foster for taking the time to sit down with me to watch his award-winning documentary *Hurricane Charley* in which he and a handful of other brave storm chasers intercepted and filmed the hurricane's direct assault on Punta

Gorda. As well, Ken Mudge's book *Island in the Sun* proved to be an invaluable resource on Cayo Costa's natural history.

Kudos go to my cousin Finlay MacDonald in Scotland for providing his in-depth knowledge and experience working on large freighter ships. And to Captain J. McLaughlin for his steadfast advisement on all the nautical elements.

Last—but certainly not least—I'd like to extend a huge thank you to my wife Valerie—who again made this second book possible with her continued support and encouragement. Cayo Costa is truly the crown jewel of Florida's state parks. I hope we can all work together to preserve the island's natural beauty for generations to come.

If you think there's good in everybody, you haven't met everybody.

—Gregory Benford

Never mistake her silence for weakness. Remember that sometimes the air stills, before the onset of a hurricane.

—Nikita Gill

In the center of a hurricane there is absolute peace and quiet. There is no safer place than in the center of the will of God.

—Corrie ten Boom

HURRICANE HOLE

PART ONE

GLADES CORRECTIONAL

CHAPTER ONE

August 10, 2004
Belle Glade, Florida

Travis Gahl pushed a button to illuminate his cheap Timex wristwatch—5:41 a.m. Four minutes to the wake-up call for his shift in the laundry. He had purchased the watch at the prison commissary, paying an exorbitant price. A watch certainly wasn't necessary in prison—time went by slow enough without one being reminded constantly—but it was necessary for what Travis had planned this morning. He was working with what could be called a tight window.

Travis had lay awake most of the night, unable to sleep, only dozing through the wee hours. This morning he was fully alert, on his back in his bunk, listening to the familiar early sounds of the cell block. The sun would not be up for another ninety minutes. Travis was planning to be halfway across the state by sunrise.

His cellmate was snoring deeply in the bunk above him. The son of a bitch was snoring like he was sleeping in on vacation at the Four Seasons. Rivas, a fifty-two-year-old Cuban, was riding out a life sentence for the first-degree murder of a charter boat captain in Key West. Travis had been listening to Rivas snore and smelling his farts for three years and one month. To the day.

Today was going to be the last.

To want to escape from prison is human nature. A handful of European countries don't even further penalize the attempt of escape itself, as to be locked in a cell is considered a violation of the right of freedom. Here in the States, Travis would have to be a lot more careful trying to break out. Getting nabbed in the act or after the fact would add serious jail time.

Travis would repeat his mantra to himself daily, going over all he had learned:

What you are trying to do is far from impossible. Thousands of prisoners escape in the U.S. every year from pens of all security levels. Watch closely, observe everybody and everything . . . routines, schedules, transfers. Pay special attention during time spent out of your cell—at work duties, medical appointments, hospitalizations, court hearings. These opportunities present the highest chance of escape. Look for all holes in the security of the facility—guards who are not following procedure, learn how they can be deceived as to your location, or find the ones that are outright corrupt. Guards are human; they get bored easily, fall asleep on the job, and, like you, they can only see in one direction, and they can't see in the dark. Find every possible way to penetrate the containment system complex—weak areas like doors, gates, windows, lights, and ventilation systems—by cutting, breaking, slipping, and squeezing. Sometimes the best deception and method of escape is to look and act like you own the place—and walk straight out the front door.

Their cell block, one of fifty-three buildings on the property, was in the northwest corner of the prison compound. Glades Correctional housed over one thousand male inmates, some of the most disruptive and violent offenders in the state, upon 211 acres on the outskirts of Belle Glade, a farming town forty miles west of Palm Beach. The prison was the state's second oldest, over capacity, understaffed, run down, and antiquated. The correctional institution was surrounded by nothing but muck fields of sugarcane and marshland. Apart from the guards, security was a twelve-foot-high double perimeter fence reinforced with razor wire and an electronic detection system, five armed guard towers, and patrol vehicles.

Travis wiped a greasy sheen of sweat from his forehead with the back of a hand. Even in the early morning hours the summer heat was stifling. Prisons in the state of Florida did not have air-conditioning in the cell blocks—this was not advertised in the brochures. Fans were used to ventilate the masses of packed bodies, and tempers rose alongside the mercury. Three days ago, despite the heat, Travis had traded his fan to Calum, his co-worker in the prison laundry. The exchange was for Calum, a naïve and aboveboard black kid in his early twenties, to arrive ten minutes late for this morning's shift. The offer drew a strange look, but no questions . . . an extra fan in the middle of August in South Florida was a highly coveted item.

Travis was on the first five-hour shift in the laundry—a time slot that was not at all hard to pick up. The laundry facilities for their cell block were in a small outbuilding off the east side of the dormitories. Travis had been working the six to eleven stint for the past three months, quietly observing the routine, and watching everything.

In the hot and dark prison cell Travis checked his watch again and felt his pulse rise more quickly than the dimly lit seconds were ticking down. He took a deep breath, controlling his breathing and slowing his heart rate.

Travis was born in the affluent neighborhood of Alpharetta, Georgia and spent the formative years of his life in the area, until his parents brought him to South Florida in 1989 when he was fourteen. Arriving in Miami, Travis immediately fell in with the wrong group of kids, delinquents—boosting cars, shoplifting. By the time he was eighteen he was selling weed, which quickly progressed to more lucrative drugs, cocaine and MDMA. He never held a real job for more than a few weeks at a time and got through on his street smarts, charm, and looks.

Of German and Scottish descent, Travis was a lean six-foot-tall Southern boy with a face that could double for River Phoenix. With an angular jaw, smooth clear skin, thick and unruly brown hair, and eyes the color of dark chocolate, he had no trouble getting a girl into his bed. During his three-year stint at Belle Glade, he hit the weights regularly, spending a lot of his free time outside in the yard shirtless, and was deeply tanned. He had also picked up some symbolic prison ink along the way. A large clock with no hands covered the entire left side of his chest, his right elbow was an intricate mesh spiderweb, and curving across his lean stomach and right oblique was a large caustic scorpion. Travis had no siblings and was no longer in contact with his parents. The last he heard, they divorced, and his mother moved back up to Georgia. He had no intention of contacting her.

Now twenty-nine, he had been incarcerated since July of 2001, convicted of armed robbery and aggravated assault. In October of 2000, Travis, a small-time dealer in Miami, desperate for cash to cover a debt to a colleague further up the food chain, hit a jewelry store in Wynwood. What was planned to be a quick smash 'n grab job quickly went south, and Travis beat the owner and his wife nearly to death. He fled with a handful of jewelry, gold and diamond rings. Pawning the goods off to a fence two days later, Travis was arrested on the spot. It turned out the fence was a paid informant for Miami-Dade Robbery. The DA bumped the charges up to a first-degree felony as deadly force was involved and Travis had a prior sexual battery charge that had been dropped as the victim—a twenty-one-year-old woman he sold cocaine to—was a no show at his trial. Travis was hit with a hefty sentence of fifteen years. He would be eligible for parole in 2016, at forty-one years of age. A sentence he had no intention of riding out.

Travis had been sure that the Florida Department of Corrections was going to put him in Raiford or Coleman—supermax prisons—or Miami-Dade, a Level 5 maximum security prison out west of Tamiami in the swamp. His prisoner classification score had the FDC drop him in Palm Beach County at Glades Correctional. This was a small relief, as he was going into what was a minor prison under Level 4 security. Security that at more times than naught, was lacking and displayed weaknesses.

Nine years ago, in 1995, six inmates successfully escaped from Glades Correctional by digging a twenty-five yard tunnel from the chapel out under the fence. All were eventually caught, or shot dead, one remaining on the lam for two and a half years before being killed by police during a botched robbery. This led to the addition of radios for all guards, razor wire, and a new electronic detection system on the fence.

But Travis wasn't going anywhere near the fence . . . he was going out the front gate.

Like clockwork, at 5:45 a.m. the guard arrived at the cell door, a dim shadow through the bars. In a cliché fashion he raked his baton along the paint-chipped steel. A small flashlight flicked on, the beam finding Travis's face.

"Alright Gahl, let's go." The guard's voice was a rasping grunt.

Travis rose slowly from his bunk, squinting against the flashlight and feigning fatigue. He noted the guard, their regular wake-up boss, a white man in his early sixties, was looking dog-tired at the tail end of the night shift beat. As the guard unlocked the cell door Travis cast a look back at his bunk and few possessions. He was bringing nothing other than what he would normally carry to a shift in the laundry. He wore the Palm Beach County faded blue scrub prison uniform and beige canvas slip-on shoes. GAHL was stenciled in black block letters on the left breast. Despite the heat, he had on a plain white T-shirt under the loose fitting scrub top. Travis stepped out of the cell and the guard closed and relocked the door. Rivas didn't move, snoring soundly in the top bunk.

Travis walked silently alongside the guard, down the dark cell block. It was still lights out and most of the inmates were sleeping, muffled snores came from behind the line of open-bar cages. The guard did not engage Travis in any talk as he led him to the end of the cell block and out through the main doors. It was no cooler outside, the humidity as thick as syrup. Crickets droned in the surrounding cane fields out beyond the twelve-foot-high perimeter fence, topped with a double twirling of razor wire.

As they approached the laundry outbuilding, Travis looked up to his left and saw the midnight black outline of the north guard tower against the starry sky. He could vaguely make out the shape of the motionless guard inside. As they continued forward the tower disappeared from the line of sight behind the laundry building. Leading, Travis opened the door to a harsh flood of fluorescent light. The guard said nothing as Travis entered the laundry room and did not follow him inside. As expected, the night boss was already headed directly back towards E Dorm, looking forward to his shift ending shortly. The laundry was hot and smelled strongly of detergent and bleach. Until Calum arrived, hopefully purposefully late, as planned, Travis was alone in the laundry outbuilding.

He quickly made his way over to a line of industrial washing machines and dryers. Bags of soiled linens sat in wheeled bins, waiting to be cleaned. It was a Wednesday morning—workers had been in on Monday and Tuesday to service several of the machines, in the process intermittently cutting the power to the laundry outbuilding. For the past two days the CCTV video surveillance of the laundry facilities had been down. The workers were due back again today at eight o'clock.

Travis checked his watch; nine minutes to six. If everything went as planned, he had a full nineteen minutes before Calum would show up—ten minutes late. The guards usually did not come into the laundry room, it was hotter than hell, hotter even than the cell blocks.

Travis moved fast. He cast a wary eye on the dead security camera mounted overhead as he moved around a corner to the far east end of the laundry room. Just above head level, adjacent to a large dryer, a three-foot wide industrial fan in the wall spun loudly, pulling the hot air outside, ventilating the room. On his shift two days ago Travis had observed the repairmen cut the power to service the machines. When the fan stopped spinning it quickly became stifling in the laundry. As the blades had come to a halt, Travis could see outside to the east side of the compound. The east wall of the laundry was in the lee of the line of sight from the north guard tower.

At an electrical panel on a wall opposite the dyers Travis gave the board a look over, hesitating only briefly before flipping a breaker. His heart hammered adrenaline as the entire laundry room was blanketed in darkness.

"Shit!" Travis hissed. He quickly flipped the breaker back on. For an agonizing second nothing happened. The lights flickered once, twice, and finally came back on.

Travis listened intently for a full half-minute. There were no sounds from outside. The lights going out had seemed to not attract any attention. After studying the circuit panel again, he flipped another breaker, this time the correct one. After a few seconds, the ventilation fan began to slow down.

Travis crossed to the dryer units, cast a quick glance back towards the entrance, and knelt in front of the dryer at the far end. He reached a hand back between the dryer and the cinderblock wall, feeling blindly in the dusty and lint-filled space. His hand found what it was seeking. Travis withdrew two objects; a small flat-edged putty knife, lifted from the wood shop, and a straightened wire hanger, lifted from here in the laundry. Travis had planted the items behind the dryer over the past two days.

Hopping on top of the dryer, Travis stood and arduously watched the fan's four thick blades continue to circle slowly, and finally stop. From outside, through the silenced fan chute, the night sounds of chirping insects rose in volume. He glanced back towards the entrance—no sound or sign of anyone. It was 5:56. He needed to hustle.

Setting the putty knife and wire down inside the chute, he grabbed one of the blades, and pulled. The metal was thicker and much stronger than he had anticipated. Using both hands and leaning back with all his weight, it took everything he had to bend the blade back a full ninety degrees, so it was sticking straight out into the laundry room.

He would need to bend at least two of them to get through. Shaking his hands out from where the metal had dug indents into his palms, he grabbed the next blade. Grunting against the strain, fresh sweat breaking out across his face, Travis reefed the metal with every muscle fiber in his back and arms, using his bodyweight to assist, while balancing atop the dryer. The metal torqued, and after tremendous effort, the second blade was finally bent backwards. Travis caught his breath, relieved he would not have to bend out another stubborn blade. He had what looked like just enough room to squeeze himself through and into the chute.

Freedom did not lie outside the laundry outbuilding. He would still be inside the fenced yard. But Travis had been watching . . . watching everything for more than three years. The guards, their shifts and routines, the opening and closing of the gate. He would be outside, unobserved, unchaperoned, under of the cover of darkness, and out of the sight of the north and east guard towers.

6:01.

It was now or never. He brought a knee up and began pulling himself into the opening between the bent fan blades. He was halfway through, up to his waist into the chute, and facing an eight-foot drop to the ground outside, when a voice called out behind him.

"Hey! What the hell do you think you are you doing? Get the fuck down from there."

Travis froze, his blood running ice water. He turned his head to look back through the chute down behind him. He recognized the screw. It was Hill, a Palm Beach County corrections officer in his mid-fifties. White guy, glasses, thirty pounds overweight, a bad back. He carried a baton, handcuffs, radio, and pepper spray.

Travis took a breath, quickly weighing his options. There was only one.

Hill unclipped his baton, eyes locked on the convict. When Travis cut the power to the laundry, Hill, who had been walking from the main gate towards the cell clock saw the building go dark and went over to investigate. He was struck dumb to find an inmate climbing through a ventilation fan at the back of the laundry room.

"Alright, alright . . . fuck it . . ." Travis said, his tone surrendering. He eased one leg back down to the top of the dryer.

Travis settled himself to stand back on top of the machine and slowly turned to face Hill, his body language showing defeat. Hill had taken a few steps closer, baton in one hand, the other unclipping his radio.

"Christ . . . you got me, man." Travis shrugged once and shook his head. He gauged the distance to Hill, who was seconds away from getting on the horn and bringing a handful of screws down on Travis's ass.

Travis readied himself with a breath and sprang.

He leapt at Hill from atop of the dryer, landing directly on the guard. Hill went straight over backwards under Travis's weight, the two of them crashing onto the concrete floor.

The radio skittered away, and Hill had the wind knocked clean out of him. Travis grabbed for the baton as Hill gasped to fill his emptied lungs. Before the guard could draw a breath, Travis pressed the nightstick hard across the man's throat and leaned all his weight on the baton. The force crushed Hill's windpipe and cut off his air. The correctional officer pulled savagely at the baton, his eyes going wide, face reddening. He flailed and bucked wildly under Travis, the heels of his boots scraping across concrete, leaving black trails.

Travis watched blood vessels burst in the whites of Hill's watering, bulging eyes. A half-minute of this, followed by a final lurching effort, and the guard's struggles ceased. His mouth hung slack, tongue protruding to one side, fat and purple. Travis sat up, still straddling Hill, catching his own breath, heart hammering, the realization of what he had done setting in.

Hill was dead.

Travis had done a lot of bad shit in his life, but he had never killed anyone before. He had just murdered a correctional officer. That was automatic life without parole, and depending on the judge, in the state of Florida killing a prison guard was most likely the death penalty. A one-way ticket up to Raiford and getting to decide between lethal injection or Old Sparky. Hell, they might fry him in the same room as Bundy.

Travis had no choice, his plan had to work. It was 6:07. Time to fucking move—*now*.

Eyeing the inert guard under him, Travis saw the small black canister of pepper spray on Hill's belt. He removed the can of pressurized capsicum, leaving the radio and baton. Travis stood and turned, making to scale back atop the dryer.

"Travis?"

Travis immediately recognized the voice. A wave of fresh adrenaline shot through his rattled nerves. He turned to see his laundry co-worker, Calum. He had just come around the corner and was staring wide-eyed at the sight of the prison guard lying on the floor between them.

"What the hell, man?" Calum's tone was high, alarm on his face. "Is he dead?" His doe-eyes flicked up to Travis, blinking twice, uncomprehending. He was only twenty-two but had a long stretch of time at Glades Correctional in front of him. The Palm Beach County DA egregiously leaned harder on darker skin tones.

"I told you ten after!" Travis said, alarmed but keeping his voice lowered. "Where's your guard?"

Calum looked panicked. "Headed back to the dorm. What did you do?"

Travis ignored the question. Making his rounds, Calum's guard would be back to check on them in less than ten minutes.

He would need more time; it was too close. Travis glared at the kid. "Go back—tell them you're sick, that you got the shits—anything."

"I can't, I already—"

"Bullshit! Go back. Get in the can and stay there, stall them like you were supposed to."

"Aw, man. They're gonna come down on me hard for this." Calum was shaking his head, looking close to tears.

"I don't care, stick to our deal. Stall them for as long as you can—go!" Travis moved threateningly forward towards Calum. The kid stepped back, hesitated for only a second, whirled, and disappeared back around the corner.

Travis could only hope the punk would follow through. The time was 6:09. "Christ . . ." he muttered under his breath.

Pepper spray in hand, Travis hurled himself on top of the dryer and heaved his weight up into the gap in the fan. Squeezing his upper body through the blades into the chute, he quickly surveyed the outside. Dark, no movement, the east wall of the laundry was shielded from the lights and guard towers. He tossed the pepper spray out first, onto the grass below, followed by the wire and putty blade. Twisting awkwardly and scraping his hips through the blades, Travis turned his body to pop a leg outside and then another, barking his shin against a metal edge. Grunting, he lowered himself down, the rubber soles of his shoes sliding against the cinderblock wall, and he dropped from a hang two feet to the ground.

Picking up the pepper stray, wire, and blade, Travis stood with his back flat against the wall, studying the large woodworking building straight ahead. The shop was quiet and deserted at this early hour. Adjacent to woodworking was the metal shop, where inmates made state license plates, and between the two was the lumberyard. Travis set out across the lumberyard, moving quickly and cautiously over to the west side of woodworking. Doing his best to stay in the shadows—each building was lit with floodlights at the corners—Travis made his way south, down the lumberyard, staying low, keeping himself pressed against the cinderblocks. Between the wall and stacks of wood pallets, plywood sheets, and beams, Travis approached the south end of woodworking. Ahead was a gravel drive, an access road for the lumberyard. The road veered off to the left, adjoining the driveway coming in from the main gate.

Each morning from 5:45 to 6:15 the gate was left open for arriving and departing employees on the shift changeover.

Employees of Glades Correctional parked outside the fenced compound, before going through security on foot. The only vehicles that entered the compound were service trucks bringing food, supplies, or accessing the lumberyard or metal shop. Everyone else, from the warden to visitors parked outside and walked in, passing through a security gate with a guard shack. On shift changes the twelve-foot-high fenced gate was left open for a full thirty minutes, with only the one guard in the gate shack manning security for the routine coming and going of prison staff on foot. For a maximum security prison this was extremely lax, a weakness in the fenced perimeter. Glades Correctional was on a dwindling shoestring budget, vastly underfunded and ignored by the state.

With the sunrise becoming later each morning as summer drew on, the shift changeover took place under darkness. From where he stood, Travis was just seventy-five feet from the open gate. It looked more like seventy-five miles. The gate area was bathed in bright floodlights.

Travis wicked sweat away from his eyes. The humidity was as thick as mud and the temperature hovering at ninety in the pre-dawn hours. He remained motionless as a group of prison guards approached the gate from within the compound, coming off the night shift. Travis recognized one of them as the boss that escorted him to the laundry. The tired and mute group departed through the gate and made their way out to the parking lot. Engines started, and one by one, four vehicles made their way down Orange Avenue, a gravel road through cane field that was the only approach to the prison.

The woodworking building had shielded Travis from the south guard tower, but it was a wide open line of sight from the tower to where he was crouched at the corner of woodworking across to the front gate. He would have to rely on luck, the piles of lumber for cover, and hopefully a half-asleep guard up in the tower.

Leaning his head out slowly from behind the building Travis eyed the guard tower. The tower stood thirty feet in height, topped with a hexagon-shaped observation platform. Spotlights lit the grounds to the west, casting long shadows. He could not make out the guard in the tower against the glare from the floodlights. Grimacing in frustration he eased his head back behind the corner of woodworking.

Two vehicles approached, coming down Orange Avenue and parking in the lot. Voices carried across the blanket of darkness, rising over the clicking night insects. A small group of people were approaching the gate on foot, employees fresh for the day shift. They had left their vehicles in the shelled parking lot off to the east, a few hundred feet outside the gate. As they neared the guard shack, walking into the pool of light, Travis saw it was three male guards. He heard jesting and scattered laughs and watched as a wave was exchanged with the gate guard.

Covering his watch with a hand Travis checked the time with trepidation: 6:13.

He slunk down and remained motionless as the three prison employees walked past him, not twenty-five feet away,

16

headed for the admin building. Waiting until the trio were out of his sightline, Travis stood, rose on tiptoe and scanned for headlights through the fence down Orange Avenue. The road was dark and deserted. A lull between comings and goings. Peering around the corner again up at the tower he saw nothing had changed, no movement, no sign of the guard. Too dark, too many shadows, too much glare from the floods.

Another time check: 6:14.

Travis stole himself. He was down to the wire. Time to roll the dice, the stakes much higher now that he had killed a prison guard. The death penalty loomed.

Staying low, Travis left the cover of the woodworking building, the can of pepper spray slick in one sweaty hand, wire and putty knife in the other. He sprinted across the field of light towards a pile of lumber. Hitting the wood, he dropped and ducked down against a stack of six-by-six posts. No sound or movement came from the yard. Stealing a look around the end of the posts, he could barely make out the guard in the gate shack. It was impossible to tell which way the guard was even facing. A glance back up at the tower netted the same result, the guard a shadow among shadows.

The front gate was thirty feet away.

Squinting his eyes clear of sweat, heart hammering, Travis took his chance. The clock was running out. The guard could close the front gate any minute now. In a low crouching run he swung out from behind the lumber pile and made a beeline straight for the gate. He did not slow until he was at the rear of the gate shack where he immediately dropped down to a hunkering crouch, back flat against the wall. Travis was pinned now, out in the open, cornered by a surrounding wide pool of light. He would be seen and caught if he hesitated—he needed to keep going. Edging around the corner of the shack he saw the side door was open. Easing forward, he now had eyes on the guard, a uniformed man sitting in a swivel chair, facing a display monitor perpendicular to the doorway. He was not looking in Travis's direction.

Go—now.

Travis went. In a squatting crouch he skirted past the doorway, not even looking at the guard as he sped by. Clearing the door and the shack, he straightened up into a speed walk, out into the full flood lights. Five feet to the gate. Travis broke into an adrenaline fueled sprint that bordered on panic. His vision blurred and time transitioned to slow motion, like running in a dream.

Travis was outside the fenced prison compound.

Expecting to have a spotlight trained on him at any second and the klaxon alarm to start wailing, Travis kept running, heart hammering against his rib cage. He was at an intersection of two dirt roads: Orange Avenue and Poinciana Avenue. The parking lot was to his right, off Poinciana, fields on both sides. Flying across the road, at the far side he slipped, and half fell into a ditch filled with water, losing his footing, and going down in thick bullrushes. He was not used to the slick uneven ground, and almost lost his grip on the wire and putty knife when he fell. Staying low in the tepid stinky swamp he froze. No lights, no alarms, no sounds, no sign he had been spotted.

A car was approaching in the far distance, a pair of headlights coming up Orange Avenue. Travis slunk lower down in the ditch, finding himself in water that came up to his chest. Aware of the strong possibility of a gator in the ditch, Travis pushed thoughts of large hungry reptiles aside. He'd take his chances with a gator over lethal injection. He remained low as the car passed by and turned up Poinciana, and into the parking lot. Another employee arriving for their shift.

The ditch ran along Poinciana Avenue, with the open parking lot behind. A vehicle door opened and closed. Travis waited and watched as a female employee he didn't recognize made her way past him, heading towards and through the gate. He heard more voices, and peered carefully through the reeds, watching two more prison employees coming out the gate, walking towards the lot. Travis settled to his chin in the ditch water, remaining motionless as they passed. From the parking lot came tired voices exchanging partings, vehicle doors opening and closing, engines starting. A sedan and a pick-up passed above him on the dirt road.

There was the whining sound of an electric motor and a clackety grinding. The prison gate was closing. Travis watched it roll across the gap in the fence and latch with a resounding finality.

After a moment he rose slowly and looked back at the guard tower. No one would be looking this way, out past the fence in the shadowy darkness around the parking lot.

Staying in the ditch, Travis made his way through the water, muck, and cattails towards the parking lot. The dirt lot was only lit by two lights, one at each end, illuminating about three dozen vehicles. Reaching the end of the ditch, Travis trudged up the slope, pulling himself out of the water on all fours, reeking of sulfurous swamp gas, covered in slime and muck. Dripping wet, he scanned the length of Orange Avenue and saw only darkness.

Travis rose to his feet and moved towards the parking lot. He approached the line of vehicles, sidling up to the far passenger side of an older mid-nineties model black Ford Taurus station wagon. Travis gave the front gate shack another quick glance before setting the pepper spray on the ground and wedging the putty knife between the top of the passenger window and the door frame. He pried the window out carefully, creating a small gap. Travis slipped the length of wire hanger down into the gap, lowering the end towards the door's armrest. In the low light it was difficult to see, but he could just make out the two power door lock switches. Keeping the window held open he maneuvered the tip of the wire towards the door lock.

Travis has used this technique dozens of times before, boosting cars as a teen in Miami. The end of the wire hovered, held centered over the lock. Travis stabbed the wire down, and the door lock popped open.

A one shot deal.

Unable to contain a grin, Travis extracted the wire, let the window back easy, and opened the door to the Taurus. The interior light came on, a risk he had no choice but to take. He picked up the can of pepper spray and tossed it along with the putty knife and wire onto the passenger seat. He pulled himself into the car, laying across the passenger floor so his head was under the driver's side dash, feet hanging out the open door. He got his fingers under the plastic cover below the steering column and pulled down, ripping it off. In the muted yellow glow from the parking lot light, he could just make out the wiring harness for the ignition switch. He grabbed the switch, twisted it around, and one-by-one, pulled out the three wires running to the back of it: the brown ignition wire, the yellow starter wire, and the red battery wire.

Between his teeth, Travis bit and stripped the casing off the end of each wire in turn, then touched together the bared ignition and battery wires. There was a small spark and the Taurus's ignition and fuel pump turned on. He twisted these wires together, then held the yellow starter wire against the battery wire. Immediately, the car engine started. He let these wires come apart and sat up, pulling himself up and over into the driver's seat, staying low. Grabbing the steering wheel with both hands he turned it and felt it hit a locking point. Using all his muscle and body weight Travis jerked the wheel hard to the right and felt the steering lock break.

Travis looked out the driver's side window at the front gate to the prison. All quiet, no one had noticed a random car start out in the parking lot. Because no one was watching the lot. Flipping on the lights, Travis put the car in Drive and—as normal as possible—pulled out of the parking space. He had not been behind the wheel of a car since his arrest almost four years ago and relished the available freedom and power under his foot. He circled around slowly, rolling down the lot, and out the entrance onto Poinciana Avenue. The gravel crunched under the tires as he accelerated up Poinciana, and made the left turn onto Orange Avenue, directly passing the front gate, the east guard tower now visible in his rearview.

Easy as sliced pie, he was just another prison staffer leaving the long night shift.

The Taurus slipped past the second eastside guard tower, the fenced yard to his right, outside the passenger window. Travis instinctively held his breath. Ahead Orange made a hard ninety-degree turn to the left at the end of the prison compound, and from there it was a straight run out to Belle Glade Road.

It was now that Travis started to feel true tension, he was so close to absolute freedom . . . He made the turn as relaxed as possible, the wheel slick under his sweaty palm. Heading due east now, the car bumped across a set of railroad tracks. Four hundred feet ahead was the T-junction for Belle Glade Road.

As he neared the three-way, another vehicle's headlights approached from the right, lighting the dark intersection. The vehicle's turn signal was blinking to make the left onto Orange.

"Fuck . . ." Travis said under his breath. A wash of anxiety spiked through his body. He tried to slink himself down in the seat. He accelerated a little and hit his indicator to make the right turn ahead. The other vehicle was a midsize SUV, a dark-colored Chevy Tracker. It made the left and as it neared to pass him by, Travis kept his right hand on the wheel and gave a nonchalant wave with his left, coolly covering his face, while looking straight ahead.

He held his breath.

Out of the corner of his eye he caught the driver of the Tracker return his wave. The vehicles passed each other tightly on the narrow gravel road, and Travis's eyes immediately flicked up to watch the taillights of the Tracker in the rearview. The vehicle did not brake. He let out his held breath and inhaled sharply, his tension releasing like a popping balloon. Travis stopped for the stop sign at the T-junction, and made the right turn out onto Belle Glade Road. He was off the prison grounds, on a public road, only a mile outside of town.

The clock on the dash flipped from 6:21 to 6:22.

CHAPTER TWO

Travis drove south, through the town of Belle Glade on Main Street. The small town was still quiet at this hour, only a handful of other vehicles were out on the dark streets. He stayed on Main Street, which curved to the west and became State Road 80, a highway that ran directly across the state between Fort Myers and Palm Beach. Travis was headed for the Gulf Coast. A glance at the fuel gauge showed a reassuring three quarters of a tank.

He felt nothing but elation at his successful escape and newfound freedom. He gripped the wheel, feeling the acceleration and power underfoot. He desperately wanted to go fast, but he watched his speed on the highway. It would be a bad morning to get a ticket. On that thought he reached over for the seat belt and buckled up.

Travis was under no illusion he was home free. Within the next twenty minutes—tops—the jig would be up at the prison, if it wasn't already, and the Palm Beach County Sheriff's Department would be raining hell down on Belle Glade, followed quickly by the Florida Highway Patrol and then the FBI. Travis had read the account of the '95 breakout, and how fast and far the net had been cast. His plan was to put as much distance between himself and the prison and get out of the state.

Since seeing the high possibility for an escape from the laundry last week, Travis had been rethinking what he would do once he got out. Steal a car, head across to the Gulf Coast, swap out for another car, and head north across the state line into Georgia. His planned destination and hideout was a remote cabin in the Chattahoochee National Forest. A childhood haunt, he knew it well, and could find it again easily. He just hoped the cabin was still there after sixteen years. It would provide the perfect refuge to lay low and let the news of his escape cool off and figure out longer term plans. Travis felt they would be looking for him to be back around his old haunts in Miami. No matter what happened from here, he was not going back to prison. He couldn't go back into a cage on death row. This was now a one-way trip: live free or die.

The highway was a smooth cruise westbound. When Travis was halfway across the Florida peninsula the sky in the rearview mirror was starting to lighten, tinting a bright pink. A sign ahead told him he was coming up on the town of LaBelle. The dashboard clock read seven minutes to seven. When Travis got to Fort Myers, he would need to ditch this car in a spot where it would not be found anytime soon and pick up a new ride. Right now, all he needed to do was drive. Travis began to relax into the ride and thought to turn on the car's air conditioning. The cool air was deliciously sweet. Grinning, Travis switched on the radio. A DJ was just announcing a new hit song on the *Billboard* Hot 100: "Heaven" by Los Lonely Boys.

Travis's grin widened into a smile of pure delight at the opening lyrics. The first rays of morning sun reflected in the rearview mirror across his beaming face.

* * * *

The tires on the Ford Taurus squealed to a stop across hot asphalt, leaving twin black strips.

"Christ!" Travis sucked in a fast breath and shook his head.

He had come within an inch of rear ending a garbage truck in front of him that had stopped for a red light. His eye had caught and locked onto a trio of teenage girls walking along the sidewalk. It had been more than three years since Travis had seen the opposite sex out on the street—he had been unable to pull his eyes away from the girls and almost slammed into a Lee County garbage truck. Bad time for a fender bender.

One of the girls, a svelte long-haired brunette, had turned to look towards the sound of the screeching tires. Her brown eyes found Travis's through the windshield.

"Mmm, baby . . ." Travis murmured. He couldn't resist shooting her a dashing smile, but the girl turned away without notice and carried on with her friends, navy blue shirt swirling around her nubile legs.

Travis shook his head again and licked his lips. The first thing he was doing when he had the chance was pick up a girl for some fun.

As the light changed and the traffic pulled ahead, Travis cast a lingering glance at the girls. They were all in uniform, navy blue and mauve, heading to a local high school. It was the first week of classes in Florida. The morning traffic had become heavier as he came into the urban areas of Fort Myers Shores. The day was clear, all blue skies and sunshine—and hot. The time was now 7:23.

Creeping through the stop and go morning commuters, nerves back on edge, Travis finally saw the sign for the I-75 exit ahead and froze.

Two vehicles up, a police car hit its lights and carved a sharp U-turn into the opposite lane, heading back east on 80.

The cop sped directly by and kept going. Travis let out a breath. He needed to drop this car as soon as possible. By now it would have been discovered stolen from the prison lot and

HURRICANE HOLE

there would be a BOLO out. Staying close behind the garbage truck Travis flipped on his indicator. He was going to exit 80 before the interstate and go north on State Road 31. Crossing the dark brown waters of the Caloosahatchee River, Travis saw a sign for Bayshore Road and on impulse he took it, deciding to get off the main roads altogether. This two-lane road was quieter, set back along the north side of the Caloosahatchee. It wound west through a mix of slash pine scrub forest, RV parks, and rural homes. He came upon the interstate, passed under the I-75, and again the traffic thickened, the area becoming increasingly developed as he entered North Fort Myers.

He was approaching another busy intersection, a light for the Tamiami Trail. Travis felt his worry start to border on alarm. It was too risky now to remain in the stolen car in this morning traffic. He started looking for a spot to park and dump the vehicle. He turned the radio down as he neared Tamiami, scanning for a lot to pull into. The northeast corner of Bayshore and Tamiami was a bank and a liquor store. Travis put his indicator on to make the right into the parking lot.

Two police cars sat in the lot, parked in opposite directions, driver side window to window—classic cop car sixty-nine. Travis flicked off his ticker and stared straight ahead, holding his breath. The light went green, and the flow of traffic started moving ahead, crossing Tamiami. Travis's knuckles were white on the wheel, raw nerves of fresh sweat beading his temples. If the police had been alerted and spotted the black Taurus . . . Travis had been ready to peel away through the intersection, and bail from the car on foot if necessary. Then he was across Tamiami Trail. A quick glance back and the two cop cars were still parked side-by-side, no lights, no sirens.

He was still heading west amidst thick morning traffic, passing the usual run of stores, a McDonalds, CVS, Bank of

America, Twistee Treat. As he passed a Wal-Mart, Travis saw that the street he was on had changed from Bayshore Road to Pine Island Road. He was coming upon the city of Cape Coral. He decided to stay with the flow of vehicles on their commute, blending in. Another sign caught his eye: eight miles to Pine Island. Travis had never been out to this part of the state, but he knew about Pine Island, a rural barrier island, tucked behind Captiva and Sanibel. It would be a great spot to dump this car and pick up a new one. If he could make it through the next eight miles to the Matlacha Pass bridge.

After a tense twenty minutes the road started to thin out rapidly, less plazas and businesses, increasing residential and undeveloped land, mostly sand pine scrub. This quickly changed to heavy mangroves bordering either side of the road, and Travis felt ease as the volume of cars on the road dropped away sharply. There was no one behind or in front of him and a car going in the opposite direction passed by only every couple of minutes.

The mangroves ended abruptly as he drove out onto the bridge across Matlacha Pass. The island of Matlacha sat between Pine Island and Cape Coral. Once a small Old Florida fishing village it was now a run of art galleries, island boutiques, and seafood restaurants. Blink and you'll miss it. Before Travis knew it, he was thankfully back amongst the cover of dense mangrove as he crossed onto the island.

Pine Island was about fifteen miles end-to-end, with a rural population of 9000. A quiet, non-touristy farming community hidden behind Sanibel and Captiva. Travis had read about it in a book in prison. He had no intention of the island being part of his escape plan, but it would be an optimal location to exchange vehicles. By the time the Taurus was found way out here, he would be north across the line into Georgia.

HURRICANE HOLE

As Travis came to Stringfellow Road, the single two-lane route that ran north and south up and down Pine Island his instinct was to go south. Making the left at the stop sign, the crossroads only had an Ace Hardware and an Esso gas station. The southbound run of Pine Island was a mix of mango and lychee fruit farming, nature preserves, a KOA campground, and a post office. A dozen minutes from the corner, a sign announced St. James City; he was coming into a small residential waterfront community at the south end of the island.

The Taurus bumped across a little bridge leading onto the finger islands of St. James City. On his right he saw a waterfront roadhouse with the name Ragged Ass Saloon. Behind a line of foxtail palms a police car was parked out front in the shelled lot.

"Fuck me—I don't believe it!" Travis thumped the heel of his palm on the steering wheel.

He twisted around in his seat to look over his shoulder. There was a cop in the driver's seat, a man. It was hard to tell but he looked to be watching the Taurus go by. "Son of a bitch . . . how many cops can be around here?"

Travis turned back to face the road ahead, alarm and dismay spiking. If he was seen and pursued, the road in front was a dead end. The only way off the island was to turn around and go back up Stringfellow Road. He would only be attempting that now with a different vehicle.

Travis continued down Stringfellow Road, one eye glued to the rearview. The police car did not pull out. Feeling the uncomfortable tingling of anxiety abating a little, Travis watched for a place to turn off. There were a few small residential side streets, then a run of townhouses with a wide open exposed lot and few parked cars. No good. Past the townhomes was a church, again an open exposed lot but he could find a spot behind the church to drop the car.

Travis was about to pull into the church lot when he saw the cop car in the rearview.

His anxiety came back in an electric burst. The cop was about a quarter of a mile back. There were no other cars on the road, ahead or behind, and it was wooded on both sides. The cop was driving at what seemed to be a normal speed, not closing on him, no lights or sirens. Travis nervously flipped his left turn indicator, and took the next side street, Fifth Avenue. Once around the corner and out of sight of the police car behind the scrub of pine and palm, Travis tromped on the gas. He took it up to fifty miles per hour down the residential street, flying over another small bridge, the Taurus bouncing wildly.

Whipping past four cross streets—all looking to be dead-end fingers—he braked rapidly at the final street. He could only go right. No sign of the cop in his mirror. Travis jerked a hard right, going south again. To his left was a solid wall of mangrove, and wide residential lots backing onto the water to his right. Large homes, half a million dollars, premium locations . . . he was at the southern end of the island, a terminus.

The road curved to the right ahead, with more spacious waterfront canal homes on his right, and now an open bay to the left, sparkling a deep emerald green under the morning sun. Travis was momentarily overwhelmed by the sheer size and expanse of the bay after three years of steel bars, concrete walls, and a perimeter fence.

He had likely lost the cop in the maze of streets, having made three turns since the police car was last in sight. At the last turn he had caught the street sign: Macadamia Lane. This was a dead end . . . end of the line. He was ditching the car here.

Ahead, he saw a cul-de-sac with a date palm in a landscaped center island, a half dozen homes on expansive waterfront lots. Travis's jaw tightened. There were no cars parked out on the street. Slowing, he pulled over onto the side of the road in the cul-de-sac, near the driveway of an opulent home. The address on the mailbox read 2063 Macadamia Lane.

Casting a wary glance around, Travis reached under the steering column and unwound the ignition and battery wires, and the car engine turned off. Travis took stock. He was about to get out of the car with the wire, putty knife, and pepper spray when he decided to give the glove compartment a quick check. He popped it open and did a double take.

There was a gun in the glove box.

A black pistol was wedged in between insurance paperwork and a sunglass case. Travis didn't move for a moment, not believing his eyes, or his luck. He reached out and touched the smooth steel with a fingertip, sliding his hand around the handgrip, slowly easing the gun out of the glovebox. It was large and heavy, and judging by the weight, fully loaded.

The weapon was a Sig Sauer P365 semiautomatic pistol, matte black. Popping out the extended magazine he confirmed it was indeed fully loaded, with twelve rounds of 9mm ammunition.

"Goddamn . . ." Travis muttered, shaking his head, eyes marveling over the weapon. "It really is my lucky day."

Sliding the magazine back into the well, Travis surmised the gun was the personal piece of one of the guards at the prison. Now it belonged to him—Travis had both a gun and a can of pepper spray. What he needed most was another vehicle, one that all the coppers in South Florida were not looking for.

It was 8:20. The house at 2063 Macadamia Lane had a large 3-car garage separate from the home, off to the right. All the garage doors were closed and there were no cars in the driveway. It was summer, the people who owned these homes were usually riding out Florida's mean season up north.

Travis's eyes flicked to the rearview, sweat trickling down his temple. The AC had been off for a couple of minutes and the heat in the car was building fast. If that cop decided to come down Macadamia Lane and caught him here on this dead end finger, he'd be trapped with nowhere to go but into the goddamned canal. Or, onto a boat . . .

Almost every single one of these homes had a dock out back on the canal with a boat moored up. Travis shifted in his seat to look between the garage and the house. Sure as shit, there was a boat behind the house. Travis began to formulate a new plan. He flicked the safety off on the pistol, set it on the dash, and peeled the scrub prison uniform top over his head, tossing it aside onto the passenger seat. The scrub pants did not have pockets, so he would have to carry the pepper spray and the gun in the open. He decided to leave the wire and putty knife.

Travis stepped out of the car and looked down the street. No cars, and no one was out, just insects droning in the morning heat and the rumble of air conditioners. Travis went straight for the house, cutting across the cul-de-sac under the brief shade of the date palm and up the wide driveway fringed by manicured lawns. He ignored both the house and garage, going right for the gap between the two that led to the dock.

As he got closer, he could make out the vessel better. The boat was moored in the water along a dock that must have stretched forty feet along a seawall. Brilliantly white under the sun the Bayliner Ciera was thirty feet in length from pulpit to stern, with a modified V-hull, open cockpit, and a command bridge. She was powered by a single inboard 310-horsepower MerCruiser. Belowdecks the Bayliner had a compact salon and galley, head, and a small bunk in the bow.

Travis had some experience with boats, taking a few out in Miami in his younger years, and would have no problems piloting the craft out the canal and into the open bay. He would head north, as far as he could—no police or roadblocks—before finding a good place to ditch the boat and pick up another car. With a vessel like this he could possibly get as far north as Sarasota, or maybe even up into Tampa Bay. It would depend on how much fuel was in her tank.

As he slipped past the house, Travis studied the place for any sign of activity. Behind the house was a massive two-story screened-in pool. There was nobody out back. Leaving the driveway and coming out onto the lawn, Travis neared the boat, the gun and pepper spray held down by his thighs. As he neared the dock Travis read the boat's name across the stern transom in black rolling script: *End of Watch*.

Stepping silently down onto the dock in his canvas slip-ons, Travis approached the boat. He cast another wide circling look around—at the house, back through to the street, the neighboring home to the east, and the property across the canal. No sign of anyone. The canal was about fifty feet wide, the water dark green and flat under thick humidity.

The boat was moored with a bow line and a stern line to cleats on the dock. Travis made for the aft cockpit, swinging a leg over the gunwale, and stepping onto the decking. Crossing to the salon door, he paused before stepping into the cabin, eyes adjusting to the shadowed light.

A man was sitting at the salon table. He looked up at Travis.

A full beat of three seconds passed before the man spoke: "Who the hell are you?"

He looked to be in his late sixties, heavier set and burly, with a thick horseshoe mustache. Travis said nothing, still overcoming his rooted surprise at finding someone on the boat. There had been no sign or evidence there was anyone onboard.

The man studied Travis quickly, taking in his clothing,

the gun, the can of pepper spray. He shook his head, almost amused. "No way, buddy," the man said. "Wrong guy, wrong boat." He rose from the table.

A prickle of panic flashed through Travis. Acting on reflex he raised the pistol and fired a single shot. The bullet slammed into the center of the man's chest, and he went back down on the seat a hell of a lot faster than he stood up. The gunshot was deafening in the small cabin. Travis's ears rang from the concussion, and he couldn't hear that the man was making wet wheezing sounds, trying to catch the wind that had been punched out of him.

The bullet had tore through the man's faded pink Margaritaville T-shirt making a fatal mess in his ribcage. A widening crimson pattern spread quickly across his chest. Destroyed lungs flooding, the man unsuccessfully tried to cough, dribbling blood down both pipes of his mustache. Eyes wide, looking straight at Travis, he flailed once, succumbing to the gunshot. He remained sitting upright at the galley table, eyes open, staring blankly at his executioner.

"Holy shit," Travis said, breathing hard, heart pounding. He had killed another person, the second inside of three hours. He felt surprise, and mild disbelief, but no guilt or remorse. Kill or be killed. The guy was in his way. And what the hell . . . a second homicide charge was like a speeding ticket now. Either way it was a cell on death row if he was caught. And Travis wasn't going to get caught.

He turned and stepped back out onto the cockpit into the bright sunlight. The gunshot had been somewhat muffled by the cabin, but the blast had been a hell of a loud retort in the quiet morning. From the three houses in his sight line there was no activity or movement. It looked as if no one had heard the gun discharge, everyone inside behind roaring air conditioners.

HURRICANE HOLE

Travis set the pepper spray down on the cockpit deck, and gun still in one hand, stepped from the boat to unfasten the stern line from the dock cleat. He did the same for the bowline, before stepping back aboard the Bayliner and reentering the salon. The dead man was still sitting upright, leaning almost casually back at the table, staring ahead with wide unseeing eyes.

Travis made his way to the helm on the starboard side of the cabin. He scanned the console and was relieved to see the key in the ignition.

Setting the pistol on the helm, Travis ensured the boat was in neutral and turned the ignition key. Belowdecks the engine rumbled to life. Travis's eyes immediately went to the fuel gauge. The needle was registering just shy of a full tank. Lady luck again.

A lazy slack tide was pulling *End of Watch* off the dock when Travis dropped her into gear and nudged the throttle forward. The Bayliner responded nicely, and he adjusted the wheel, feeling her acknowledge, quickly learning the vessel's feel and handling. Ahead he had to make a sharp ninety-degree turn to port, rounding the rear of the house to exit the canal and enter the bay. Travis looked for any sign of someone observing him through the screened pool enclosure and saw no one.

Travis throttled up and the Bayliner pushed ahead, bow rising. Catching movement in his peripheral vision and hearing a *thump*, he turned quickly. The dead owner of the boat had toppled over and was now laying on his side on the berth at the salon table. Blood dripped from the man's mouth and the gaping wound in his chest. Travis made a face, shook his head, and turned his focus back to the helm and the view through the windscreen. He was leaving the canal and coming into the open bay.

End of Watch was entering Pine Island Aquatic Preserve. A couple of miles ahead was the expanse of Sanibel Island, a long green sweep of low land. There was a compass on the helm, and Travis noted he was heading due south. It was easy to become disoriented quickly out on the water. Looking west he could not see a straight shot to the Gulf of Mexico anywhere. He knew he needed to get around Sanibel and head north, but he did not know these waters at all. Off to the southeast he saw a long bridge spanning across the water . . . the Sanibel Causeway.

Travis spun the wheel to port and aimed the bow towards the causeway. Watching for channel markers he throttled up more, the Bayliner responding and rising to plane across the dark green waters. There were only a few other boats out, and a trickle of cars going across the bridge. Travis began to feel a sense of relief that climbed to pure exhilaration as he piloted *End of Watch* beneath the span of the Sanibel Causeway.

He would round the end of the island and head north hugging the Gulf Coast. Off to starboard the Sanibel Lighthouse was an iron skeleton rising just shy of a hundred feet from the point sands. Travis again could not stop the grin that spread across his face.

Three hours ago, he was locked in a prison cell, a state convict staring down a fifteen-year road. Now he was piloting a cabin cruiser across the emerald waters off Sanibel Island. Lady luck had indeed been both his navigator and co-pilot this morning.

CHAPTER THREE

*E*nd of Watch was only four miles southwest of the Sanibel Lighthouse when the engine coughed, sputtered and died. Travis stared blankly at the console as the bow quickly dropped and the vessel came off plane. The Bayliner wallowed in a long slowing drift. He flicked the ignition key and the engine turned over, started . . . and a few seconds later died.

Travis didn't feel true stabs of alarm until he tried the engine a handful more times with no avail. Taking a break from cranking the key, he accessed the situation. The engine sounded like it was starving for fuel, but the tank was reading almost full. He turned the ignition again, this time giving it some throttle while cranking. The engine caught, ran for a few seconds, and died again.

"Shit!" Travis slammed the palm of his hand against the helm bulkhead. "C'mon, not now." Flustered, he tried again, giving the engine even more fuel while cranking. This netted the same result. "Son of a bitch . . . Why? Not now, dammit."

End of Watch was dead in the water and drifting on an ebb tide. Thwarted, Travis used his index and middle fingers to wick sweat away from his eyes. He had no knowledge of mechanics, other than the absolute basics. Certainly nothing about marine engines. He turned and glared at the vessel's dead owner lying inert on the salon berth.

"All the goddamn boats in Florida and I have to steal this piece of shit. Christ on a bicycle."

Travis tried the key again, with no throttle. This time

the engine barely turned over, making a flat *whirring* sound. Frustration and concern rising, Travis gripped the sides of his mouth with a hand and ran his fingers down his chin. Thinking the situation over, he went out onto the cockpit and did a quick 360, eyeing the surrounding waters. There wasn't another boat in sight on this weekday morning. Looking up to the command bridge Travis went back inside and pulled the key from the ignition. Climbing the stainless steel railed ladder to the flybridge he sat himself in the upper helm seat and slid the key into the ignition.

He got the same result from the engine. Dead and drifting miles offshore. Travis weighed his options. The boat had electric power and a radio. But who was he going to call, the Coast Guard? He had no idea how long it would be before the boat was reported stolen, or the owner missing. They were combing South Florida for him by now. It would not be long, a day at the most, before his photo was released to the public. His best and only real option, for now, was to do nothing and wait and see if another boat came along. Flag one down, possibly take command of another vessel. It occurred to him that if was forced to, cornered, or pushed, he might have to kill more people to maintain his freedom.

The morning sun was blazing hot on the back of his neck. Travis left the flybridge and went below, careful not to misplace the key. On the salon table in front of where the owner had been sitting was an open white binder. Travis spun the binder around, so it was facing him. It was an owner's manual for the Bayliner. Travis noted the boat was a 2001 model, so it was newer, but what concerned him was that the owner had been looking over the pages for the fuel pump on the MerCruiser engine.

Travis skim read a section and pushed the binder away in

frustration. "I can't fix this shit—that's goddamn impossible." He shook his head, becoming quickly overwhelmed.

A repair of this type was well out of his league. He started to look around the salon and found a laminated rolled chart of Sanibel Island and the surrounding waters. After studying it for a minute he set it aside. In the small galley he popped open a mini-fridge and was met with delight. A full twelve-pack bottle case of Busch beer sat on the shelf, the highlight among a few gallon jugs of water, a Gatorade, a jar of peanut butter, and loaf of bread. There was a bag of apples at the back of the fridge that looked like it had been in there since the turn of the millennium.

Travis hauled out the Busch, set the case on the cooktop, tore open the box and pulled out an ice-cold bottle. He cranked off the twist top, the cap spinning away across the salon. He hesitated to savor the moment before taking a massive slug of the beer.

Heaven.

Travis paused to admire the bottle in his hand before taking another long pull. It was only then he realized how thirsty he really was. He had not drunk anything since dinner yesterday. A minute later he had downed the beer and was going for another. The alcohol hit him fast and harder than he had expected. He hadn't had a drink in more than three years. There wasn't much booze floating around Glades Correctional, not even hooch.

Travis took the second beer slower and continued to explore the boat. Forward there was a low cabin with a double berth tucked in the bow. Aft on the starboard side, just before the door to the cockpit was a small head. He went in and used it, belching loudly.

Exiting the head, Travis went back to the helm and tried the ignition three more times. The engine remained dead.

Silently, feeling the pleasant beer buzz curb his worry, he eyed the surrounding waters through the windscreen. There was a sailboat off in the distance, a good three miles out. He was pretty much alone out here. *End of Watch* seemed to be still drifting on the same heading, southwest.

Travis took another sip of the beer before turning to the boat's owner. He approached the salon table, set the bottle on it, and dropped to a knee. The man lay toppled on his right side, his eyes now drooped three-quarters closed. The blood from his chest and mouth was a dark crimson, dripped and spattered across the peach-colored seat cushion. Travis looked him over and saw a square bulge in the back pocket of his khaki shorts. Gingerly, slipping his fingers into the pocket he pinched out the man's wallet. Travis rose, flipped the wallet open, and pulled out a Florida state driver's license. Robert Halliwell, born July 26, 1937. His address matched the house: 2063 Macadamia Lane.

Tossing the license on the table, Travis found three twenties, a five, and a single. Sixty-six bucks, a small score. He found a Visa card, and a blue and white card with Halliwell's photo. The card was a state-issued concealed weapon license. This made Travis raise his eyebrows.

"Two guns are better than one," Travis said, looking down at Halliwell's slack face. He would be sure to scour the boat for a possible weapon.

Behind the concealed firearm license was another card. This one caught Travis's eye as it was crested left and right with the seal of the state of Florida and a police badge. The card identified Robert Halliwell as a retired police officer—a captain with the Lee County Sheriff's Office.

"Aw, fuck me sideways. You gotta be kidding," Travis said, letting out a long moan. He slapped the ID card on the table. He had killed a goddamned police captain. His luck was up and down today. He'd snuffed out a prison guard and a retired police captain inside of three hours. If they pieced these deaths together, pinning both on Travis, they were going to hunt him down hard . . . FBI, U.S. Marshals. This could easily bump him onto a Most Wanted list.

Travis took stock. He had water, some food, the pepper spray, a fully loaded gun. He'd stick to his plan: wait for another boat to go by and flag them down. When they came over to help, he'd board and forcibly take over their vessel at gunpoint. In the meantime, all he had to do was sit tight and wait.

Travis spent the next hour searching *End of Watch* from bow to stern. He found a pair of binoculars and a recent issue of *Hustler*. No gun. Halliwell did not have his weapon onboard as far as Travis could find unless the man had hidden it extremely well. The sun was higher in the morning sky and the day's heat building rapidly. There was a slight breeze out of the north, giving respite from the blazing rays and humidity. Up again on the command bridge, Travis scanned the horizon in all directions with the binoculars. No boats within range to flag down, and he was certainly drifting south, away from Sanibel Island. His Timex read 10:42.

Retreating into the shade of the salon, Travis cracked himself another bottle of Busch. He glanced sullenly at Halliwell.

"Police captain, my ass," Travis lamented, sucking back the dead man's suds. "Thanks for the beers and one shitty boat."

When he acquired another vessel, he would have to try and sink *End of Watch*, along with Halliwell's body. He couldn't toss Halliwell overboard here. The depth finder at the helm was only showing about thirty feet, and he couldn't be more than five or six miles offshore.

Travis slammed back the third beer and grimly crossed over to Halliwell, knowing he had a task to do. Hesitating briefly, he grabbed the man's shirt and pulled the deadweight from the berth. The body tumbled to the deck with a hollow thump. Halliwell was big, the same height as Travis, but a good forty pounds heavier. Travis removed Halliwell's shoes—a pair of white Nikes—and grunted as he dragged the dead man aft, towards the hatch for a compact single bunk compartment belowdecks under the salon. Working on his knees, sweat beading on his forehead, Travis pushed and stuffed the body in. Halliwell barely fit in the bunk, which was the size of a small storage locker. Travis slammed the hatch shut, leaning against it, and latched it against Halliwell's pressing weight. Sitting on the deck, his back against the bulkhead, he caught his breath, forearms draped over his knees.

Halliwell had leaked several pints of blood across the salon deck, leaving a pooled and streaked crimson mess. Shaking his head, Travis pulled himself to his feet and set to work. It took him thirty minutes to clean up the coagulating blood as best he could. He used two beach towels and the sheets from the forward cabin, which he threw overboard when he finished. He covered the maroon-stained cushions of the salon table with a towel from the head and a hoodie. Peeling off his blue scrub prison pants, the knees now completely blood-stained, he tossed them over the side as well. He slipped into a pair of Halliwell's shorts he had found in the forward cabin and the Nikes. The shorts were baggy and loose but fortunately the runners fit decently. It felt good to have on running shoes and shorts after three years of state-issued prison clothing.

After making another scan from the bridge with the binocs and seeing no boats, Travis plunked down at the salon table and popped open another beer. Opening the *Hustler,* he felt a titillating thrill at the glossy pages of naked beauties. There had been a circulation of pornography in prison, but it was expensive and highly contraband. After flipping briefly through the magazine, he set it aside. Now was not the time. He'd save the magazine for later, unless the good Lord above delivered him a yacht full of girls in the meantime.

As the sun passed its noon zenith the heat intensified. The salon was stifling and sweat dripped from Travis's face, his white T-shirt almost soaked through. The litter of empty beer bottles grew, scattered across the table. At periodic intervals Travis would get up and stumble out to the cockpit and scan the horizon with the binocs and urinate over the transom, before returning to the salon to pull out another beer.

* * * *

Travis jerked awake. He was seated at the berth, having passed out lying face down on the salon table. A trail of drool ran across the laminate top. He sat up groggily and wiped a hand across his lips. His mouth felt pasty and dry, his tongue thick. Five empty bottles littered the table around him, a couple still standing, a few knocked over. He squinted at his watch: 5:52 p.m. A little more than two hours until sunset.

Alarmed, Travis rose from the table, wobbly on his feet, and made his way out onto the cockpit. The sun was low in the sky off the starboard bow. Pulling himself up the ladder to the flybridge he could see no land in sight to the north or east. Spinning a full turn, he saw no boats on the water. Using the binocs and looking north, with relief he could see the darker raised line of land on the horizon.

Sanibel Island.

Judging from the position of the sun, he was still drifting in the same direction, approximately southwest. Rough guessing,

Travis judged he was at least a good ten miles offshore now. Possibly more. The easy north breeze and tide had been slowly but steadily pushing him south all day.

Returning to the salon, Travis pulled a gallon jug from the fridge and chugged back a full two pints of the cold water. Wiping his mouth and carrying the jug back out onto the cockpit, he made his way forward along the railed walkway out to the bow.

Looking out over the pulpit at the sinking sun he took another long swallow of water. The sky was cloudless, and already tinging into shades of lavender and burnt orange as twilight approached. Travis swallowed hard and felt a prickling of new concern through the lingering balm of alcohol.

He was going to be out here for the night.

PART TWO

SABRE

CHAPTER FOUR

August 11, 2004
Off the coast of Naples, Florida

The catamaran sat anchored in the bright early morning sun, swinging gently on her line. The multi-hulled Fountaine-Pajot was a majestic craft, less than a year out of the shipyard in France. Running forty-four feet in length, with a wide stable beam of twenty-one feet, her pilothouse, decking, and freeboard shone a brilliant white, her lower hull at the waterline sky blue. The catamaran was topped with an expansive flybridge; the upper helm, dinette table, and surrounding lounges shaded by a sweeping canvas canopy. The pilothouse held the lower helm station, main salon, a large galley, and dining area, all finished in polished teak and chrome steel. Belowdecks were three separate cabins, each with their own full head. She had no mast or sails and ran under power, pushed by twin 300-horsepower engines with a blue water cruising range of 1000 nautical miles.

Her name was *Sabre*.

A breeze from the north twisted the cat lazily on her tether, four miles west of Doctors Pass. *Sabre* was quiet, the only sounds came from the Gulf of Mexico lapping gently at her twin hulls. A single person was visible onboard, a woman, up on the flybridge. She was sitting back, lounging on the large U-shaped cushioned settee surrounding the table, just aft of the helm, reading a paperback novel.

Kim Chambers was twenty-eight, her wavy dirty blonde hair shining gold in the dawn light. Her eyes—running over the lines in the book—were a deep hazel, and her skin lightly tanned, color she had picked up the last few days cruising aboard *Sabre*. She wore a white blouse, open and tied at the waist, over a tank top, and khaki shorts. Her shapely feet were bare, long legs toned and kicked up lengthwise on the settee. She was fully engrossed in her book, *Treasure Coast*, finding the read fantastic, the opening pages pulling her quickly into the story. Kim had picked up the newly released novel shortly before the planned nine-day cruise. *Treasure Coast* had been an immediate New York Times bestseller, and the author John Cannon's debut novel.

Forty pages in, Kim took a second to flip the book over and look at the author photo on the back cover. The man was handsome, with thick wavy dark brown hair and bright blue eyes. He looked to be somewhere in his mid-thirties. Yesterday, in Naples, Kim had got ahold of a copy of the local newspaper and read an interview with the newly published author and his hit book, a Florida noir tale that fell into the adventure-thriller genre.

Kim was thankful for the engaging read, the novel distracting her with some escape and solitude from the events of the past few days. She was on summer vacation—a cruise down the coast, with her boyfriend, Mark, her best friend Andrea, and Chad, a guy that Andrea had recently started seeing. The four of them had taken *Sabre* from Stump Pass Marina in Englewood down to Keewaydin Island. Mark's family owned the catamaran, as well as a large home on the remote south end of Keewaydin. They were on day five of the trip, having spent three nights at the beachfront house, and were already on their way back north. With three days of the trip remaining, the plan was to hit Sanibel Island, Cayo Costa, and Cabbage Key before returning home.

HURRICANE HOLE

Yesterday they had moored for a half-day in Naples, having dinner at The Boathouse, an upscale waterfront seafood restaurant, before pushing back out of Gordons Pass after dark and anchoring for the night.

Kim and Mark Foster had been together for three years, having met through mutual friends. Mark was smitten with Kim instantly, a beautiful blonde in her mid-twenties, and Kim found Mark an attractive, charming fellow, eight years her senior. He was funny, smart, took care of himself, had a nice body, and his family was rich. However, the money was no lure.

Kim was not in love with Mark, and uncertain about the future of their relationship. She had a four-year-old daughter, Kayla, whose father was long out of the picture. Kim worked as a pre-school teacher at Englewood Elementary and rented a small two-bedroom apartment a couple of blocks from the school for $700 a month. She had hesitated at moving in with Mark, despite his repeated requests. He had a four-bedroom waterfront house with a huge pool down in Cape Haze, but she wanted to keep her space and distance. Still, she and Kayla were over at his place every weekend. Mark was good to Kayla and her little girl had taken to him well.

The Foster family was a prominent name in the vicinity of Englewood. They owned Stump Pass Marina and the adjoining Lighthouse Grill, Mark managing both, as well as several other businesses in town. The Fosters were tight with Martin Russell, the owner of Russell Marine in Cape Haze. Money stuck with money. Mark's parents were currently on their own summer vacation up in British Columbia, Canada, which allowed Mark to have use of *Sabre*. Kim and Mark had been planning and looking forward to this trip for months. It was originally to be just the two of them and Andrea. Chad was a more last-minute addition; an invitation from Kim, an offer to bring Andrea's

48

new boyfriend along. Mark was not thrilled with this change in plans, as it had been casually, but seriously, discussed more than a couple of times—usually over copious drinks—that he, Kim, and Andrea were going to engage in a playful threesome on this trip.

Kim was openly bisexual. A few years ago, she had a tryst with the divorced mother of one of her students, and she and Mark had had several ménage à trois encounters. Mark, of course, could not believe his luck.

However, the planned scenario had not come to pass, instead turning into an awkward falling out and rift between Mark and Chad. Last Saturday night at the house on Keewaydin, after a few rounds of potent margaritas, Kim and Andrea had initiated the escapade, much to Chad's initial surprise. He went along at first, but before things got too heated, jealousy reared its ugly head, and he backed out—leaving the three of them hanging. Mark more than a little miffed. He had been longing to have this fling with Andrea for months and was now more so than ever less than thrilled Kim had invited Andrea's new beau along. Chad was a real prude. A wet blanket.

They had all brushed it off in the sober light of morning, continuing with the trip, but there was an undercurrent of tension on the boat. It seemed the forty-four-foot catamaran had shrunk considerably. Kim felt twinges of regret at the situation, as she was the one who had initiated the original idea—but also invited Chad. Both she and Andrea had thought Chad might readily go along with the venture. After the incident Saturday evening the men had not spoken to each other for a couple of days. The scene and mood on *Sabre* were no longer reminiscent of a relaxed vacation, and the incident had put a serious damper on the cruise. The perils and fallout of engaging more than two people in a sexual liaison.

Kim dog-eared her page and set the book down when she

heard someone coming up the spiral stairs to the flybridge. Expecting it to be Mark, it was Andrea who gave Kim a smile as she stepped up onto the upper deck.

Andrea Valencourt was thirty-one, an attractive brunette with sapphire eyes. Her physique was conditioned from regular Pilates classes, and she had an outgoing, bubbly personality. This morning she wore a bright lemon yellow tank top and jean shorts. Originally from Maine, and of French descent, she had been in Florida for six years. Done with the relentless heat and nine-month long summers, she was seriously considering moving back up north. Andrea worked with seniors in Venice and she and Kim had been friends for the better part of five years. The two women met at a coffee shop in Englewood, their friendship becoming quite tight and attached. They kept no secrets, shared and bared all, and came to each other for advice. Kim revealed her bisexuality to Andrea, who was straight; the women remained platonic but intimately close as friends. Kim was the reason Andrea was delaying her move back to Maine, believing she wouldn't find another friend this loyal and non-judgmental.

"You're up early," Andrea said, circling the flybridge and joining Kim on the settee.

"Yeah," replied Kim. "I couldn't sleep."

"Mm-hmm," Andrea shot Kim a knowing look. "You went to bed early—you missed the end of the movie."

Sabre had a fifty-inch TV in her salon, and Mark had brought the DVD of the classic film *Jaws* for them to watch on the trip.

"I know—that wine went straight to my head. And I've seen that movie before. Christ, who hasn't?"

Andrea laughed, pulling her shoulder length hair back from her face, shifting over further to sit under the shade of the

Bimini top. "Well, the guys certainly loved it. They seem to be getting on OK."

Kim folded her arms and looked at Andrea. "That's good. Is Mark up?"

Andrea nodded. "He was just coming into the galley when I came up here. He's putting coffee on. Chad's up too."

Kim said nothing and looked along the stretching coastline of Naples off to the east. They were too far offshore to see anyone out on the beaches on either side of the pass. The wind and current had swung *Sabre* to the south on her bow anchor.

"What's on the agenda for today, anyway?" Andrea asked.

"We're gonna continue to head north. To Sanibel. Mark knows this beach there he wants to take us too." After a minute Kim asked, "How's Chad this morning?"

Andrea shrugged easily. "He's alright." She dropped her voice. "Like I said, the two of them got right into watching *Jaws* together last night—I think any bad blood has finally cleared. They seemed to do some serious male bonding over the movie."

Encouraged, Kim smiled. "I just want us to enjoy the rest of this trip. You know—make the best of it."

"I agree," said Andrea, "although I'm not sure how this is going to go when we get home—"

"Let's not worry that far ahead. We're back on Saturday, three more days. We'll deal with the repercussions—if any—when we're back."

Andrea did her best to read Kim's face, but oddly this time could not glean anything from her friend. Both Mark and Chad were within possible earshot, so she abandoned discussing the topic any further. Andrea could sense a shifted dynamic between Kim and Mark as well since the night on Keewaydin at the beach house.

The women were quiet for a few minutes, listening to the

water slap against *Sabre*'s hulls and taking in the panoramic view from the flybridge. They could hear the men below now, animated talking, followed by the sounds and smells of breakfast being made.

Chad Haney made his appearance, coming up the circular stairs part way until he stood halfway through the access hole in the deck of the flybridge.

"Good morning, ladies," he grinned. Chad was thirty-seven, the oldest of the group by a year over Mark. Standing just shy of six foot, he had a brawny thick physique, carrying just a little extra weight around the middle. His large face was full, youthful, and friendly, under a low forehead and unruly hair. He wore a white rash guard emblazoned with a leaping tarpon, and light blue boardshorts. Chad lived out in the east side of Englewood and worked for a busy car dealership in Port Charlotte. He was another northern transplant, from Ohio, having been in Florida for eight years. Andrea had met him on a new dating website called Plenty of Fish. That was three months ago, and so far, their relationship was going well. Andrea was happy; Chad treated her well, a lot better than some of the other guys she had dated in recent years. She felt lucky to have met him.

"I hope you're both hungry," Chad said, leaning against the handrail, "we're whipping up a real spread this morning."

Andrea looked at Kim and gave her an easy smile. Turning to Chad and standing, Andrea said, "We are. And that coffee smells great." Kim exchanged a quick but pleasant smile with Chad and picking up her book, she rose to join Andrea.

"Then c'mon down—breakfast awaits." Chad spun around on the stairs to make his way back below. The women in turn followed him, circling down the fiberglass stairs to the spacious aft cockpit. The men had been busy setting up a full breakfast:

coffee, orange juice, pancakes, toast, bacon, and scrambled eggs—the teak table was loaded with food and drink.

Mark Foster came through the salon's sliding door as the women took their seats at the table. The man presented a commanding presence; a tall, tanned, and well-built. He had a handsome face with striking blue eyes, rugged jawline, clear skin, and a high prominent forehead topped with thick dark brown hair that was cut short. Mark was the cookie cutter jock, the captain of the football team, the varsity letterman. He wore a beige short sleeve Columbia PFG shirt and navy blue Bermudas.

"Welcome girls, good morning—good morning," Mark greeted jovially, setting down a plateful of sliced pineapple and circling around the table behind Kim. He bent over her from behind and landed a quick kiss on her cheek before taking a seat beside. Kim gave him an undecorated smile.

"This all looks great," said Andrea, sipping a glass of ice-cold OJ. "Thank you both for making breakfast."

"Our treat," Chad said, through a mouthful of bacon. "You missed the end of one hell of a movie last night, Kim."

"Yeah, you did," Andrea said, mocking, giving Kim another smirk.

"I couldn't stay awake," Kim replied, "the last thing I remember was that guy's head popping out of the sunken boat—that was enough for me. I went to bed."

"But you missed the ending, that was the best part," said Mark. "They killed the shark, blew it up with a scuba tank."

"I know," Kim derided lightly, chuckling, "I've seen it before, years ago. When did that movie come out again?"

"June 20, 1975," Mark replied without hesitation. "It's the thirtieth anniversary next year. Can you believe it?"

"I can. How many times have you seen that movie?" Kim asked.

Mark shrugged and laughed. "I've lost count. I can watch *Jaws* anytime."

"I can believe that too," Kim quipped.

"I don't know," said Andrea, grinning slyly, pouring maple syrup onto a pile of pancakes, "there were some great characters and one-liners in there. And a young Richard Dreyfuss with that beard, he was looking cute."

Kim groaned, picking at her eggs.

"Andrea—you're gonna need a bigger boat," Mark gibed, dead pan, quoting a famous line from the film.

"Oh boy," Andrea said, trying to hide a smirk.

"Here's to swimmin' with bow-legged women!" Chad added, goaded on by Mark.

"God, here we go." Kim rolled her eyes and stifled a laugh, exchanging another glance with Andrea. The women were relieved the men had found a shared interest to talk about and were getting on together well. The party ate well, the women patiently listening to Mark and Chad discuss *Jaws* for the next few minutes.

"Alright, what is the plan for the day, Mark? When do we shove off?" Kim finally asked, pushing her plate forward. "We're headed up to Sanibel?"

Mark helped himself to another serving of pancakes and bacon. "Yes, I'd like to take us into Sanibel Island and explore Bowman's Beach. We haven't done any fishing yet either, so we can drop some lines . . . see if we can hook us some dinner."

"I definitely want to see what I can catch," Chad said.

"And I can definitely use some beach time off the boat," Andrea threw in.

"Strongly agreed," added Kim.

"Alright," said Mark, "the north end of Sanibel is our next destination, for some beach time and fishing."

"How far is it?" Andrea asked, downing the last of her coffee.

Mark squinted, looking out at the horizon off to their portside, chewing on a mouthful of pancakes. "I'll check the chart . . . about thirty nautical miles. Say, two and a half, three hours of easy cruising. We'll be there before lunch."

"Sanibel Island," Andrea said the name slowly. "Sounds like an absolute paradise."

"You haven't been?" asked Mark.

Andrea shook her head. "Not yet." She looked to Kim. "Haven't you been there before?"

"Once," Kim replied, "just on a day trip by car, heading up to Captiva. I also camped out on Cayo Costa for a long weekend a few years ago."

"That's the next island to the north?" asked Andrea.

Kim nodded. "Yes, north of Captiva is Cayo Costa, the state park. You can only get to it by boat. There's no bridge."

"Well we've got a boat so we can visit all three islands," said Mark, wiping up maple syrup from his plate with the last piece of forked pancake. "Sanibel, Captiva, and Cayo."

"How did they get those beautiful names?" Andrea asked, looking from Kim to Mark.

"Cayo Costa used to be called La Costa Island," Mark answered, "which simply means 'The Coast'. Sanibel and Captiva have far more interesting histories as to how they acquired their names, especially if you believe the pirate lore."

"Pirate lore?" Andrea said, her interest growing further. "Do tell."

"Well, there's legend that the name Sanibel came from the famed pirate, José Gaspar. His first mate, Lopez . . . Roderigo

Lopez, had to leave behind in Spain his beautiful lover, Sanibel, and asked Captain Gaspar if he would name the island in her honor. As for Captiva, it was apparently also so named by Gaspar himself as this is where he had built a prison, 'Isle de las Captivas', a place he kept captive all the young women he held for ransom, pillaged from passing ships. The captured men, children, and any older, or unattractive women were thrown overboard for the sharks."

"Brutal," murmured Chad.

Andrea made a face. "Is that true?"

"Possibly, some of it, especially for the history of Captiva," replied Mark. "But it's more likely with Sanibel the simplest explanation is that Ponce de Leon, in his search for the Fountain of Youth, named the island for Queen Isabella of Spain. The island is noted on old maps as Santa Isybella, which was modernized to Sanibel."

Kim was secretly surprised. She had just read a similar account of the island's names not an hour ago, in the novel *Treasure Coast*. The book sat with its back cover facing up on the table beside her. Her eyes flicked down again to the photo of the author, John Cannon.

"Hmm, I don't know about all that," Andrea remarked, stretching out her words. "Whatever it may be, I can't wait to see these islands . . . but damn this heat." She wiped a hand across her forehead, skin beaded with sweat. "After I help you guys clean this up, I'm going to take a shower."

"There's plenty of water," said Mark, "I filled the tanks in Naples yesterday."

"Good—because I need a rinse. Thank God for the AC on this boat." Andrea rose and picked up her plate and glass from the table. Chad quickly joined in helping to clear the table.

"Just be thankful you weren't around in the time of pirates,"

Mark jested, "they certainly didn't have air conditioning—or running water onboard their ships."

"Well, I'm damn glad I was born in 1973 and not 1773, or whenever that guy Gaspar was around," said Andrea.

"Good guess. Being born in 1773 would have had you at a prime age to be one of Gaspar's captives," Mark said.

Andrea paused before stepping through the salon door, her hands full of dishes. "So, I wouldn't have been shark bait?"

"Probably not," replied Mark drolly, "just sold to the highest bidder into a life of sexual slavery."

Andrea pulled a sour face at Mark, turned, and retreated gratefully into the cool air of the salon. Chuckling, Chad followed her inside.

"Jesus, Mark." Kim scowled and shook her head but couldn't suppress a mild grin at the teasing. She glanced over to ensure that the salon door was closed tight, their conversation private. "You and Chad have patched things over I see, all buddy-buddy now?"

Mark sat back in his chair. "Whatever. We've both let it go and moved on."

After a beat, Kim said, "Alright."

There was a silent moment.

Then Mark spoke, his voice harsh, "I guess at least one of us got a little something though."

The night of the failed debauchery, before Chad had decided to call the frolic off, it had progressed to the point of Kim luring him in, pulling off her top, teasing, rubbing her hand on his groin, feeling him grow hard beneath his shorts. It was only when Andrea got topless, pert breasts locked in the beam of Mark's ogling eyes, that Chad had quickly decided to bail out.

Kim shook her head, sighing. "Mark, that's cheap. I already

said I know this was entirely my fault. I probably shouldn't have invited Chad on this trip to begin with, and I should have called off the stupid idea of changing it up to try include him. We should have asked him first. Just dropping him into the mix after a few drinks—I had no idea he'd react like that."

Mark let out a frustrated breath. "You know I wanted to—"

"Yeah, so did I, Mark. But Andrea's met this guy, and he seems pretty good. Andrea likes him. A lot." Kim brushed her hair away from her face and glanced at the tinted salon door. She could not see inside through the dark mirrored glass. "There'll be other girls—you're goddamn beyond spoiled as it is."

Mark twisted his mouth to speak but said nothing. He rocked his chair back on two legs, putting his hands behind his head, appearing to study the hazy green tinge of coastline over the rail. It looked like his chances of sleeping with Andrea were off the table, permanently.

Kim was put off by Mark's attitude surrounding the incident three days after the fact. She could hear Andrea and Chad laughing together in the galley. If anything, this incident had brought them closer together. "We've got three days left of this trip . . . let's just enjoy it—and please, get us home on Saturday."

"That's the plan Kim," Mark's voice was a lead balloon. "That's the plan."

* * * *

An hour later the breakfast spread was cleaned up and the mood onboard the catamaran was the best it had been in a few days. The energy between the two couples bounced back unsullied, but there was a lingering pendant between Mark and Kim.

Kim showered in their master stateroom, a large cabin with

an ensuite head, which took up the entire port side of the boat. She came back up on deck wearing a white and pink striped one-piece swimsuit, tying her wet hair back, and joined Andrea forward. *Sabre*'s bow was a wide rectangle of teak decking with four side-by-side navy blue cushioned chaise lounges. Andrea was already lying out on one, soaking up the morning rays, sporting a baby blue bikini with a frilled top.

On the flybridge, Mark fired up the twin diesel inboards, the engines rumbling gently belowdecks. Chad had followed him up onto the fly, sitting back on a large, curved settee adjacent to the helm. Mark nudged the catamaran forward, taking the tension off the rode, and the windlass reeled in the centerline anchor.

Mark pulled down a pair of dark Oakley sunglasses from atop his head to shield his eyes from the sun glinting off the water. He called down to the women below. "Alright ladies, we're off. Next stop: Sanibel Island!"

Andrea let out a whoop and raised a hand. "To Sanibel!"

Mark throttled up. Six hundred horses spun the twin props in the tepid Gulf waters. The catamaran started forward slowly at first and was soon cutting smoothly through the bantam waves at close to fifteen knots.

Chad turned on the lounge to face forward, the humid salt air blowing his hair back, and watched Mark handle the cat with an experienced hand. He had enjoyed this jaunt down the coast aboard *Sabre*. The trip was an unexpected invite from Andrea, and he was glad he had the vacation time to join the last-minute outing. The scenario at the beach house on Keewaydin last weekend was also quite unexpected. Admittedly, the opportunity had excited him at first, and Andrea's friend Kim was a beautiful girl, sexy—and sexual—but he had only been seeing Andrea for a few months, and despite the fact Kim was coming onto him fast and strong, turning him on, he could not get past the visual of Mark with Andrea. He'd balked. Mark at first was clearly put off at him for ending the four-way fling, but things seemed cooled now. Now Chad wondered if an opportunity like this would come up again, or, in the future he'd regret the lucky chance for an unrestrained exploit with two girls. His eyes moved down to Kim on the forward deck, her body lithe in the well-cut swimsuit, and he began to lean more towards regret. He pulled his gaze away from Kim, shaking off his thoughts.

"What could we catch out here?" Chad asked conversationally, raising his voice over the rushing wind.

"Lots. I've got a lot of decent bait—frozen shrimp, pinfish, and a chum bucket. We can drop a couple lines off the island . . . you never know what might bite. Permit, cobia, and pompano are running this time of year, maybe even get a nice snapper or grouper. If we're lucky we'll catch us some dinner."

Chad grinned wide. "Shit, that sounds great."

"It's a perfect day with an easy north wind. I'll drop the hook out just past the sandbar, and the girls can wade in to the beach. Then we'll see what we can get to bite." Mark raised his head and his voice so Kim and Andrea could hear. "Do you girls want to go shelling on the beach while we fish from the boat?"

Andrea tipped her head back to look up at the helm. "Yes! I want to go look for shells—and shark teeth."

"You got it," Mark replied, giving the cat a nudge more power. *Sabre* rode easily at half throttle, moving across the offshore swells at eighteen knots.

Mark watched as Andrea turned and said something to Kim that he couldn't hear over the wind and engines. Kim simply nodded her head in response. She had her sunglasses on, and her nose buried deep in a paperback novel.

CHAPTER FIVE

Thirteen miles southeast of Sanibel Island Lighthouse

Travis awoke slowly, rising in stages from the dark depths of sleep to full consciousness. He found himself in the forward berth on End of Watch. He must have crawled in there at some point late in the night. Bright morning sunlight and blue skies were visible through the skylight in the low overhead of the cramped cabin. A heavy sheen of heavy beaded sweat covered him from head to toe, the bunk mattress under him soaked through. He was shirtless, wearing only Halliwell's shorts. The confined berth was a sweatbox sauna, hotter even than the cell block.

Head pounding, Travis sat up, a wave a nausea rolling through his guts. Rubbing an eye, he glanced at his wristwatch. His heart picked up its tempo when he saw the time. Six minutes after nine. Travis's eyes went wide, and he blinked; he hadn't slept this late in years. The combined sedation of copious alcohol and no wake-up call. He pulled himself onto his knees and crawled out of the berth.

Moving out into the salon, Travis saw the slew of scattered empties on the table, a few bottles had fallen and were rolling lazily on the deck. He had stayed up late last night, drinking the rest of the beer, and gotten himself good and hammered. He popped open the fridge, pulled out the jug of water and chugged back a half dozen swallows. Dropping the container on the counter he stumbled towards the head, wondering if Halliwell had any aspirin or Tylenol onboard. Travis urinated while leaning over the toilet, forehead buried in the crook of his elbow, arm braced against the bulkhead. In a small medicine cabinet, he found a bottle of Advil with four capsules left. He shot them all into his mouth and returned to the galley to wash them down with a large swig of water.

Travis made his way out onto the cockpit. The morning sun was hot on his face and shoulders, and he squinted against the light. He started at unexpected movement. A large brown pelican stood on the transom, staring at him with beady black eyes.

"Go on!" Travis said gruffly, his voice hoarse from a dozen beers. He waved a hand at the seabird. The pelican bobbed its head but stayed put. "Beat it." Travis advanced aggressively towards the bird. The pelican begrudgingly took flight, departing *End of Watch*, swooping away in a wide lazy arc.

Travis had polished off the beer, and his memory of heading to bed was fuzzy, but shortly before midnight he had had the sense to drop the anchor. The hook had gone deep, taking out a lot of rode, but caught the sandy floor and held fast. This kept him from drifting aimlessly on the tide all night.

Travis remembered he'd left the binoculars up on the flybridge. He made his way up the ladder and looked down on the anchor line off the bow. The rode was taught and had held fast through the night. *End of Watch's* stern still pointed southward. Travis picked up the binocs from the helm seat. Sweat beaded and ran down his stubbled cheeks, dripping from his chin, as he peered through the lenses, making a slow and sweeping 360-degree turn. There were no boats visible in any direction, but he could make out the low distant line of green to the north that was Sanibel Island. He was a good ten to fifteen miles offshore.

"Shit," he muttered, lowering the lenses. It was a Wednesday morning; boat traffic was light. Bringing the binocs, Travis dropped down to the cockpit and ducked back into the salon out of the sun. Sitting at the table he assessed his situation again. He had a limited amount of food and water remaining. At some point he was going to have to risk using the radio and call for help. He knew enough to use channel 16 to hail another passing boat. A lot of ears could be listening on the open emergency frequency, and he had no idea how long before Halliwell and *End of Watch* would be reported missing. A BOLO for escaped felon Travis Gahl would have been out for more than twenty-four hours now, his face surely on the news.

He reaffirmed to himself that under no condition was he letting himself be caught. Travis turned, his expression lamentable, to the Sig Sauer pistol sitting on the helm. The gun had eleven rounds. He'd only need one. But would he have the guts? Something told him not.

Head pounding, Travis brushed off morbid endgame thoughts. He rose to his feet and got the Gatorade out of the fridge. Sitting back down at the salon table he sipped the cold lemon-lime drink. He rested for a bit, waiting for the Advil to do its trick and kill his thumper headache. The seat cushion at the table was marked where Halliwell had bled out, the deep maroon looked as black as oil.

It occurred to him that Halliwell had been dead for more than a day. That fucker was gonna start to smell soon in this heat. Travis would need to deep-six the body. He looked at the berth hatch where he had stuffed the retired police captain and wondered if the guy was still a stiff, or if rigor mortis would have released its grip by now. Travis would need something to weigh the body down. Or, if he remembered right, a cadaver would sink—it should only float to the surface after a couple of days, and by then it wouldn't matter if anyone found Halliwell.

Travis put the Gatorade back in the fridge and moved

across the salon to the berth. Pausing for a moment, he popped the hatch. Halliwell was, of course, still stuffed in there, lying on his side, legs pushed up in a fetal position. There was no decomposition odor—yet—but the air in the berth was hot, humid, and cloyingly rank. Sweat, flatulence, and a bitterness that sat heavy in the back of Travis's throat. Where Halliwell's shirt was hiked up the skin of his bloated abdomen was a dark swollen purple.

Travis made a face, grabbed Halliwell's thick ankles and heaved. The bastard felt even heavier than yesterday, and he had broken out in a fresh sweat by the time he got the body out of the berth, across the salon, and onto the cockpit deck. Pushing the cadaver up against the port bulwark, Travis sat and rested on the gunwale, catching his breath. Preparing himself to heave the corpse up and flip it over the side, he looked across the transom to the southern horizon. Dead astern was a boat. A large boat, about a mile distant. Travis squinted against the sun's glare off the water. The boat was underway and heading directly towards him.

Rising quickly, he went into the salon and retrieved the binocs from the table. Back out on the cockpit he stood at the transom, legs spread to balance himself and eyed the boat through the lenses. It was a catamaran. A large power catamaran, well over forty feet in length, with a wide beam and expansive flybridge. There was a man at the helm up on the flybridge piloting the vessel, but what caught Travis's eye was the deluge of exposed, smooth skin—two girls lounged on the bow in bathing suits.

Tearing himself away from the view, Travis dropped to a knee and set the binocs down. He grabbed Halliwell and furiously began hauling the dead weight back into the salon. Working on his knees, Travis pushed and stuffed the body back into the berth compartment. Fighting the pressing weight and finally dogging the hatch, Travis crossed to the helm and grabbed up the pistol. Thinking a moment, he put the gun in the fridge behind the bag of apples. He remembered the pepper spray; it was still out on the cockpit deck. Travis retrieved the canister from where it had rolled into the starboard quarter. He put the pepper spray in the fridge as well, beside the gun.

Back out on the cockpit he judged the catamaran to be a half mile off now. Looking through the lenses again, Travis skipped over the girls and tried to assess the man at the helm in the shade of the sun canopy. He was alone. The count so far: one man, two women.

Travis was going to take the catamaran.

He was down to less than a gallon of water, half a Gatorade, and some shrunken apples. He would have to gamble these people had not yet seen him anywhere on the news. The cat was still coming at *End of Watch* and looked like it would pass a few hundred feet off his port quarter. Travis went into the salon and grabbed his T-shirt from the forward cabin. He leaned against the helm, looking aft through the salon door at the approaching catamaran. Knowing absolutely nothing about marine signals, Travis hit the horn three times quickly and then held it again for another longer blast.

"C'mon girls, let's get your attention," Travis said, moistening his dry lips. He moved back out onto the cockpit and stood again at the transom, waving the T-shirt over his head wildly from side to side. A quarter mile out he saw the cat change heading, coming to starboard, directly towards *End of Watch*.

"Alright, here they come." He spoke to himself under his breath, a nervous but cocky grin on his face, "Come right to Daddy." He readied himself for the encounter, having excellent skills at becoming a chameleon depending on the situation and circumstance. When needed, Travis had an excess of charm, guile, and persuasion and he was going to have to use all three to navigate through this one.

His concern rose sharply when he saw a second man come up on the flybridge. "Dammit . . . two meatheads." Travis cursed again. He hoped this second man was it, and there were only four people on the catamaran. The yacht was a big twin-hulled cruiser, it could have three cabins. There could be six to eight people onboard. Travis felt a stab of alarm that he might have bit off more than he could chew. If they didn't recognize him, and it was too risky, he'd call it off and send them on their way.

A few hundred feet out from *End of Watch* the catamaran slowed up, the engines powering down, and the captain maneuvered the twin-hulled vessel expertly so it would sidle up off Travis's portside. There was little wind and only the easy south current. Travis smiled big and raised a hand, ignoring the women for now, closely studying the two men up on the helm. The catamaran was thrust into reverse to bring her to a rolling stop about fifteen feet abeam of *End of Watch*.

The captain and his mate looked to be in their mid-thirties, the captain tall and muscular, his mate a little shorter and heavier set. Both clean cut, Travis guessed them a little green on the street smarts, but far from dumb, and money, obviously. He wouldn't want to physically mess with the bigger guy, but he had no concerns about the chubby shorter man. Two to one but he had the element of surprise, and he was armed. His eyes skimmed down quickly over the women, a brunette and a blonde, both in their twenties, both real lookers. Travis felt his pulse quicken at the sight of all the bare, soft curves but didn't let his eyes linger. The women and the men all wore sunglasses and so far, he didn't see any sign of anyone else onboard. It looked to be just the four.

"Hey there!" Travis called out, a disarming smile planted firmly on his face, one hand still raised.

"Hey!" replied the captain from the helm, working the wheel to keep the cat aligned nicely. "Heard your signal—what's the problem?"

Travis glanced down at the deck quickly and made an exaggerated shrug. "She's dead. Can't get her to start."

From *Sabre*'s flybridge, Mark looked the Bayliner over. "You got a working radio?"

"No, I think my batteries are dead."

"Where are you out of?" Mark asked.

"Fort Myers. I'm headed north—to Tampa Bay."

"That's a good trip. She just quit on you?"

"Yeah, about an hour ago. Something to do with the fuel line, I think."

Mark hesitated a moment. "Alright, hang on." He turned to Chad, "I'm gonna give this guy a hand for a minute—see if I can get him going or call him in a tow."

"Alright," Chad replied, "what do you need me to do?"

"Nothing."

Chad retook his seat as Mark eased *Sabre* forward, taking up the water she had lost in the current. He brought her halfway past *End of Watch*, the Bayliner's starboard hull just a few feet off their portside. Mark deftly dropped the cat's anchor and drifted astern until the flukes caught the bottom.

On the bow, Kim had put her book down and both she and Andrea were casually eyeing the shirtless man through their sunglasses. As Mark maneuvered the cat the man smiled and waved at the women. Kim returned the smile and raised a hand. He was extremely good-looking, almost leading man material, strong jaw covered in a few days' worth of stubble. His lean physique, tanned and muscular, was glistening in the hot sun.

Mark and Chad had come down off the flybridge, and Kim watched as the man deftly caught a line Mark threw over to him.

"Tie that off and we'll pull you over," said Mark.

Travis fastened the line to his starboard quarter cleat and watched as the captain of the catamaran set out a couple of fenders. The man then used the line to pull *End of Watch* over, so their transoms were lined up stern-to-stern and the Bayliner bounced off the cat's fenders. Mark knelt and tied the two boats together. Kim and Andrea made their way aft to join Mark and Chad at *Sabre*'s cockpit.

Mark stood and leaned across the swim platform extending a hand to Travis. "I'm Mark."

Travis took Mark's hand in an equally firm grip. "Travis. Thank you for stopping to help me out."

Mark got a whiff of beer, stale sweat, and an odd swampy odor from across the gap. "No problem, Travis. Maritime law, it's a legal and moral obligation to help a fellow boater out."

Travis grinned, "Right. It's just like *Waterworld* out here."

"Something like that." Mark smiled at the movie reference and made the introductions. "This is Chad, and his girlfriend Andrea, and my girl, Kim."

"Nice to meet y'all . . . Chad, and you ladies." Travis poured on the smile and kept the charm on high, thankful it was indeed just the four of them onboard. His eyes went quickly up and down the women, seeing only shapely legs and curvy breasts. He settled his sights on Kim, who shot him a smile that made his pulse race. She had flipped her sunglasses up onto her head and her hazel eyes flicked metallic gold in the sunlight, sun-kissed nose and cheeks lightly freckled.

"Let me come onboard and take a look at what might be the

problem," said Mark, "if I can't fix it quick, we'll have to radio a tow in for you."

"Sure," Travis replied, stepping back, giving Mark room to hop down onto the Bayliner's gunwale. Travis could now read the catamaran's name across her transom. *Sabre*. Her port of call was Englewood, Florida. Travis had no idea where Englewood was. "*Sabre*, huh?" he said.

"Yep, she's a big cat," Mark replied, crossing over and stepping down onto *End of Watch*'s cockpit deck.

"Where are you guys heading?" Travis asked.

"To Sanibel," Mark answered. "We've got a few days left of our cruise. We went down to Keewaydin for the weekend."

Travis also had no idea where Keewaydin was. "Where's Englewood? That's north of here?"

"Yeah, just past Boca Grande."

"Y'all live up there?"

Mark nodded. "Kim and Andrea live in town, I'm just south in Cape Haze, and Chad lives over on the far side, Englewood East, out by the Myakka."

Travis did not recognize any of these places and said quickly, "Man, I'm sure glad you guys stopped. I didn't see anyone out here all morning. Just you. You're all staying on the catamaran?"

"Yeah," replied Mark, "she's got enough room, three cabins."

Travis whistled. "Real nice boat you got there."

"Thanks," said Mark, placing his hands on his hips. "Let's see if we can find the issue with yours."

"Sure," Travis nodded once, and led Mark into the Bayliner's salon. "I anchored up, 'cos I was just drifting south. I didn't want to find myself down in the Keys." Travis glanced concernedly to the seat cushions and decking and could still see visible traces of dried blood. The towel and hoodie haphazardly covered the worst of it. "I think it's a fuel line issue."

Mark leaned across the helm, checked the transmission was in neutral and turned the ignition key. The engine turned over but did not fire. He tried twice more to no avail.

"She's starving for fuel—you might be right." Mark turned and made his way back out to the cockpit. Travis followed . . . Mark seemed to not notice the dried blood at all. Chad, Andrea, and Kim were all standing on *Sabre*'s port walkway, watching silently. Mark knelt and popped up a deck cover, exposing the engine below. He looked up at Travis. "Were you messing with the fuel line?"

"Uh, . . . yeah, a bit," Travis answered.

Mark frowned and bent back over the engine. After a half-minute he said, "It looks like your fuel separator is shot. You got water in your fuel line. It's flooded."

"Shit. Any way we can fix it?"

"Not out here. You need a mechanic to look at it, or someone who knows a hell of a lot more than me." Mark stood and brushed his hands together. "Is this your boat?"

"No, it belongs to a friend. I'm supposed to be taking it up to Tampa for him. Honest—I don't know a lot about boats." Travis casually stepped back from Mark, angling for the salon.

Mark said, "Tampa? That's a good run to make without having some experience on the water. We can radio you in a tow and stay with you till it gets out here."

Travis was running several scenarios through his head, stalling now. "How much you think that tow's gonna cost?"

"Not cheap. But hey—it's not your boat, right? Your friend who you are moving it for will pay you back."

Travis grinned and shrugged. "I sure hope so. And I'm not

in a rush, I guess. I was gonna take a couple days to get up there. Make a trip out of it."

"You still can, once you get your fuel separator issue fixed."

Kim, who was leaning over *Sabre*'s siderail, piped up. "If Travis is heading north," she said, "why don't we just bring him with us? We can tow his boat and they can fix it at the marina in Englewood. We got plenty of room—a whole extra cabin—and he'll be halfway to Tampa."

Both Mark and Travis remained silent. This suggestion caught both men equally off guard. Mark had his hackles up. Something wasn't sitting right with him about this man Travis, nor his boat. Travis ran Kim's idea forward and saw it presented a lot of options for him—and an out—if Mark agreed and went for it.

"Ahh," Mark said, stalling, looking hard at Kim, and then quickly at Travis. "I'm not sure. We could tow you into a marina—"

"*Sabre* can tow that Bayliner, no problem," Kim added, pressing, "and the guys at your marina could use the work in the summer slowdown. We're all on vacation and Travis is in no hurry. Help him out."

Mark said nothing for a moment, caught looking like an asshole if he refused. Kim was putting him on the spot in front of Travis, in front of everyone. He felt a flash of anger at her.

"The more, the merrier," Andrea supplied.

Mark, succumbing to pressure and not liking it, turned to Travis. "I've got a marina up in Englewood, they can fix you up and get you going, no problem. We've got a few days easy cruising before we get up there. I can have you in sometime Saturday if you like? Save you and your friend the towing fees."

Travis shook his head once, his expression incredulous. He

massaged the back of his neck with a hand. "Well, damn. Sure. I mean if you're sure—if it's not too much trouble."

"No trouble at all," Mark replied. He shot Kim with a hard icy stare and turned back to Travis. "You like fishing, Travis? We're going to anchor off Sanibel this afternoon and drop some lines."

"I love fishing, I just haven't really had the chance to fish much lately."

"No time for fishing? What have you been doing?" Mark asked.

"Working."

"Well, thanks to Kim, I guess today's your lucky day, Travis. Let's see about getting your boat tethered up to *Sabre*." Mark looked up to Chad. "I'm gonna need your help with this."

"Just tell me what to do," Chad replied.

"You're going to throw Travis a line while I position *Sabre*." Mark turned to Travis. "Get what you need from your boat, we have a full spare cabin you can use."

"Hell—Mark, I really appreciate the generous offer here," Travis said, extending a hand and shaking with Mark again. He looked up at Kim and Andrea. "To all of you."

"No worries," said Kim, smiling, and dropping her sunglasses back down. She caught Travis's eyes pass over and linger for a moment on her breasts in the well-cut swimsuit.

Mark said, "Get your stuff—I've gotta rig a tow line."

Travis watched Mark climb back up and step over onto *Sabre*'s swim platform. His mind was whirling on this new direction and change in plans. They obviously had no idea who he was . . . he would roll with it, go with them and wait for the perfect opportunity to take command of the catamaran. This was the first stroke of luck in a day.

He entered the salon on *End of Watch* and looked around.

HURRICANE HOLE

Travis had seen no sign of a bag or knapsack anywhere, or anything to put the gun or pepper spray into. He was concerned with leaving the weapon on *End of Watch*, but he could not conceal it well enough in the shorts he was wearing. He quickly pulled on his white T-shirt and slipped into the Nikes so it would appear he wasn't going onto their boat too empty-handed. He had little clothing, and no possessions.

Back aft on *Sabre's* cockpit, Mark was busy fastening a double-pronged tow line from the stern cleats. He fixed a glaring eye on Kim. "You really put me on the spot there."

"Mark, it was ultimately your decision," Kim replied sharply. "It's your boat, it's your call. I was just trying to be nice."

Mark said nothing, aggressively reefing and tying a line.

"So, we've got this guy with us for three days?" Chad asked, his tone uncertain.

Mark ignored Chad's question and said to him, "I need you here. I'm going to bring *Sabre* back towards his bow. You're gonna throw him this line. Have him fasten it to his centerline cleat."

Chad nodded. "Alright, no problem."

Without another word Mark took the spiral stairs up to the flybridge. He stood at the helm and saw Travis come out onto *End of Watch's* cockpit. "Head to the bow," Mark called out, "Chad's gonna throw you a line. Tie it off good, then get ready to raise your anchor and jump across."

"Okay." Travis nodded and made his way up *End of Watch's* port walkway, alongside *Sabre*.

Mark weighed the cat's anchor and eased her forward, past the Bayliner. He cut hard over to starboard out in front, and then slowly reversed her back towards *End of Watch's* bow. He stopped reverse thrust and nudged her forward, so the cat settled about ten feet off the Bayliner's pulpit, where Travis was waiting. "Throw him the line!" Mark yelled down from the helm.

With the women observing from the rear of the cockpit, Chad tossed Travis the line and watched as he tied it off to his bow cleat. Mark appeared above, leaning over the rear of the flybridge. "Okay," he ordered, "raise your anchor, and get ready to jump across. Chad, you keep that line tight and clear of the props."

"Got it," Chad acknowledged.

Travis cranked the windless and the anchor freed itself from the sand bottom below. Chad kept the slack out of the lines, and Mark returned to the helm. Looking over the starboard side he reversed *Sabre* until her dual swim platforms were almost under *End of Watch*'s nose. Fortunately, the current was taking the Bayliner south, and not pushing her forward into the cat.

"Alright, get across!" yelled Mark.

Travis ducked under the bow rail, dropped to sit on the side of the pulpit and lowered his legs down towards the cat's swim platform. Chad reached out a hand upwards, Travis took it, and dropped down onto *Sabre*. His left foot skidded off the teak platform, and Travis reeled, losing his balance.

"Whoa!" Chad bellowed, pulling back hard, left arm windmilling, using his weight as a counterbalance.

Travis caught his center of gravity, got his leg back up on the platform, and laughed out loud. "Damn—thanks! We almost went for a swim."

"We sure did," replied Chad, breathing a sigh of relief.

Andrea giggled at the slapstick antics, while Kim just twisted her mouth wryly, slowly shaking her head.

"Okay," Mark's voice came from the helm above, "Chad, let out the slack easy." Mark slowly throttled up and pulled *Sabre* away from *End of Watch*. Chad let the line drop as it pulled out into a wide V-shape, the two lines from the cat joining and forming a single line that ran to the Bayliner's bow cleat. The line reached its end point, tightened, and stretched and bounced once, twice, and *End of Watch* was tugged easily forward. Mark powered up gently and they were underway, towing the Bayliner.

Travis looked back at Halliwell's boat, now a good twenty feet behind, bow cutting into the cat's wake. Going along with their offer was a damn good idea, thanks to this cute blonde Kim. His only regret was not being able to bring the gun and pepper spray onboard *Sabre*. That was not good.

Mark was again back at the rear of the flybridge, checking on the tow set up. "Looks solid. I'm gonna take it a little slower. We're about forty minutes out from the beach on Sanibel. Kim, why don't you show Travis below to his cabin?"

"Aye, aye, skipper," Kim's tone was biting. She watched Mark retreat to the helm and Chad made his way up to the flybridge to join him. She smiled at Travis, looking him up and down for the first time up close. "You travel light."

Travis shrugged. 'Yeah, it was really a last-minute trip."

Kim turned to Andrea, "I'll show Travis below and join you up front again in a couple of minutes."

"Welcome aboard the S.S. *Sabre*," Andrea said with heavy sarcasm, giving first Travis and then Kim a lingering look, before making her way forward.

Kim raised a brow. "It's more like the S.S. *Minnow* around here. Are you sure you're ready for a three-day tour?"

Travis grinned. "It sure beats swimming back."

Kim smiled. "C'mon Travis, let me show you to your cabin."

She moved past him, just inches away, and Travis was hit with her aura, a mixture of vanilla spice and coconut. Her scent was delicious, intoxicating. Travis's on the other hand, was not.

Kim slid open the door to the salon and he followed her inside, his eyes traveling down the contoured lines of her back to her round bottom, perfect swaying curves in the form-fitting swimsuit. Travis felt his heart pump and stir, the beginnings of a swelling in his groin. He quickly redirected his eyes and his thoughts.

As they entered the salon, he was hit again, this time with sweet cool air; the catamaran was air-conditioned. During his stay at Glades Correctional, Travis had only felt AC in the reception and medical areas. He had heard the visitation area had AC, but Travis did not have a single visitor during his three years inside.

Entering the spacious salon, Travis was grateful for the distraction from Kim's backside. The interior of the cat was huge, bright and airy, paneled in dark polished wood. There was a full galley to port, a mix of stainless steel and black Corian countertop, across from a U-shaped dining table and berth seating to starboard, and forward was the lower helm in front of a full beam 180-degree curving windscreen.

Kim's sixth sense radar told her that Travis's eyes were on her ass, and at the helm she turned and caught him. "Down here," she smiled unassumingly, and led Travis down a set of steps to starboard. They entered a small passageway that ran the length of the yacht. "Your cabin is in the bow, and Chad and Andrea have theirs back there, to the rear." Kim nodded aft and went forward to open a door on her right. "You each have your own head with a shower . . . this one is yours."

Travis glanced into a small but full head, with a toilet, sink, and a glass circular walk-in shower. There was a round window in the hull that let in the morning sunlight.

"This is all pretty damn impressive," said Travis. "Do you and Mark own this boat?"

HURRICANE HOLE

"No, Mark's family owns it." Kim continued forward down the passageway and ahead the door was open to a cabin. She stepped inside to give Travis room to enter the berth. The guest cabin on the catamaran was twice the size of his cell, and a hell of lot more luxurious. The bed was a queen, flanked by side tables and reading lights, the walls rich mahogany, with a large wide rectangular window along the exterior bulkhead.

"Very nice," Travis commented, thoroughly impressed with the boat. He was more impressed with Kim, and he shifted from checking out the cabin to her. After three years of not being this close to a woman, Travis could not avert his eyes. His gaze ran the pink and white stripes on her swimsuit from her shapely breasts and down across her stomach. Her thighs were toned and smooth, and he saw well-shaped calves, slim ankles, and pretty feet, expertly pedicured with blue polish.

Kim clearly saw Travis checking her out from head to toe. He had a boyish innocent quality to him, like he was an inexperienced teenager checking out a woman for the first time. She did not feel leered at or threatened. He was difficult to fully figure out . . . just different. Something new, something she could not place. He was attractive in a masculine way, fantastic body, a face almost too perfect with a strong stubbled chin, looking a bit goofy in baggy shorts and shoes a couple sizes too big. He also smelled, badly, of sweat, beer, and . . . was that a faint hint of swamp water?

"Well, this is your cabin. You're welcome to take a shower if you like." Kim almost physically cringed as she said the words aloud.

Travis's eyes went wide, and he scrunched up his face in a disarming smile. "Do I smell like I need one?"

"Well—yes, actually you do."

Travis broke into an embarrassed grin. "Sorry, I've been out on that boat since yesterday."

Kim nodded, catching that Travis had earlier said he went out on *End of Watch* this morning, not yesterday. She let it slide but noted it. "There's a new toothbrush, toothpaste, soap, shampoo, everything you'll need in there. Are those the only shorts you have? No swimsuit?"

Travis looked down. "No, this is it."

Kim twisted her mouth. "I'll see if I can steal a pair of Mark's for you. You two look about the same size. I'll leave them on the bed."

"That's great, thank you. I really appreciate that."

Kim nodded and as she turned for the door, he said, "I think I'll take that shower."

"That's a good idea," Kim gave him a lop-sided grin. "Like I said, there's towels and everything you need in there."

"Thank you, Kim. It was real nice of you to make the offer and effort to bring me along."

"No problem, Travis. Happy to help and have you aboard." Kim smiled warmly, turned, and left the berth.

Travis stood alone in the cabin, reeling from his luck, and the course of his life the past thirty hours. He removed his wristwatch from the prison commissary and set it on the bedside table. Stepping out into the passageway he entered the head and shut the door. The latch did not catch, and the door swung open a few inches. He peeled off Halliwell's shorts and his underwear and kicked them away. Turning on the water in the shower he let it warm up. This was going to be his first shower with privacy in years. He stepped into the hot spray and soaped up in the sunlight streaming in the porthole window. The wide-beamed cat was stable on the water and even underway barely rocked under his feet.

HURRICANE HOLE

Standing in the steaming shower, Travis knew he still had serious problems. There was a state-wide manhunt out for him, and the retired police captain and his boat would eventually be reported missing, with a car stolen from the prison parked on the street in front of his house. It would take the police all of three seconds to connect Travis to the disappearance. At some point soon, he'd need to take control of *Sabre* and ditch *End of Watch*.

Kim returned from the master cabin to the guest cabins with a pair of Mark's teal-colored boardshorts and a fresh black T-shirt in hand. She descended the steps to the passageway, making for Travis's cabin when she saw the door to the head was ajar. She could hear the shower running.

Slowing momentarily, without looking, she carried on past the doorway into the cabin. She placed the shorts and T-shirt on the bed and turned to exit the cabin. As she slipped back down the passageway, she stole a glance into the gap in the open doorway. From this direction and angle, in the mirror over the sink, she caught Travis's reflection in the shower. He had his back to her, the shower glass lightly fogged and beaded with running water droplets.

Kim slowed and came to a stop, pushing back a sharp rising feeling of guilt, and titillation. She watched the shower spray splash off Travis's tanned back, and the sharp contrasting line of white skin below his waist. His smooth buttocks were chiseled alabaster.

Unexpectedly, Travis turned his head and saw her in the mirror. Kim looked up and their eyes met, reflected from mirror through shower glass. Kim felt hot abashment but remained frozen—ducking out of sight now would only make it worse. The corners of Travis's mouth turned up into a devilish smile. He wasn't chagrined with finding Kim peeping, quite the contrary. He turned around fully to face her, and Kim's eyes dropped to his nakedness. Her breath caught in her chest. She was suspended momentarily, before looking up and recapturing his gaze. Their eyes remained locked for a moment, Kim's heart pulsing rapidly.

She shot him a quick risqué smile before continuing down the passageway.

CHAPTER SIX

Sabre arrived off Bowman's Beach—a long stretch of pristine white sand along the northwest side of Sanibel Island— shortly before noon. Mark expertly piloted the big cat into the shallows in a tight turn, sending End of Watch gliding bow first onto the beach. He had Travis anchor the Bayliner up on the sand and dropped Sabre's hook further offshore.

The catamaran drew a four-foot draft, and they descended the swim ladder into crystal clear water with a temp in the high eighties. Mark and Chad waded in, carrying the beach gear held high overhead through the cerulean surf, while the women swam and splashed. As Kim walked over the soft, rippled sand bottom silvery fish darted about and scooted through her legs. She heard Mark call out: "Don't forget to do the stingray shuffle!"

The 'stingray shuffle' was the act of sliding your feet along the bottom instead of walking, to avoid stepping on an unwary stingray and receiving a nasty barb in return. Kim kept her eyes warily peeled for all stinging or biting sea creatures.

The beach was mostly deserted this time of year, many of the homes on the island were used as winter escapes for northerners. There were no houses or hotels on Bowman's Beach, this part of the island looked the way it did for millennia. They had the little piece of paradise pretty much for themselves. The deep blue August sky overhead was peppered with thin strips of cloud.

The day was spent on the sand and in the water, Kim and

Andrea going back and forth between lounging under sun umbrellas, reading, dozing, and hunting for shells. The women would periodically dunk in the sparkling Gulf to cool off. By midday the air temperature was hovering in the high nineties. Floating together in chest deep water, just thirty feet from the beach, Kim and Andrea watched with a mixture of fascination and delight as a large manatee and her calf wallowed up for a curious look at them before continuing their lazy journey.

The men fished from *Sabre*, the conversation slow and relaxed in the heat. Travis fit himself right in, kept on the quiet side, and enjoyed the sport, sipping a cold bottle of Heineken that Mark had offered him. Large towering cauliflower-shaped cumulus clouds built inland to the east, upwelling on rising heat and humidity. Half asleep in the afternoon torridness, Travis was jerked awake by the sound of his rod—the reel took off, spinning madly. Mark and Chad watched with excitement, offering words of encouragement and instruction as Travis spent a solid ten minutes on the fight, pulling in a prize mangrove snapper. The copper-and-red-striped fish was close to five pounds, and Mark proclaimed it would make great eating for dinner. It seemed Travis was earning his keep.

As the afternoon drew on and the heat increased to oppressive levels, the women retreated off the beach to *Sabre*. Mark and Kim, together in their large owner's cabin, took turns showering off the sand, salt, and sweat. Kim could sense Mark was still peeved with her for inviting Travis along. Still wet from a shower, he lay naked on the berth watching her towel off.

"There's something odd about our new friend," Mark said, opening dialogue between them.

Kim bent forward and flipped the towel around her head, wrapping her wet hair. "Oh yeah? What's that?"

"I don't trust him. Something isn't right."

"Like what?" Kim adjusted the towel and began applying moisturizer to her legs. Her skin had picked up a bronzed glow from the day on the beach, and the sun brought out her blonde highlights.

"First off, he knows far too little about boating to be taking that Bayliner from Fort Myers to Tampa on his own. His horn blasts this morning—he was signaling that he as backing up. And I think he might have been in prison—his tattoos, the clock and the spiderweb—they're definitely prison tattoos, jailhouse ink. I saw that on a documentary."

Kim glanced at Mark but said nothing. She continued rubbing in lotion, working over her hips and tummy.

"Also, did you see his legs?" Mark asked.

Kim turned away slightly to conceal a smirk. There wasn't any part of Travis she had not seen.

"They're bone white," he continued, "he's had his shirt off plenty, but he's been wearing only pants for years. His legs haven't seen an hour of sun."

Kim moved to her arms, sliding the coconut-scented lotion across her elbows, forearms, and backs of her hands. "You could be right Mark," she said, "but if he has been in prison, he's not obligated to tell us. We just met him."

She wavered on telling Mark about Travis's slip up this morning. After a moment's hesitation, she said, "This morning when I was showing Travis to his cabin, he switched up about when he left on his boat. He told you he left this morning, but he said to me that he left yesterday."

Mark propped himself up on an elbow. "I knew he was out on that boat longer than just this morning. I think he was out overnight. The boat stank inside—empty beers, sweaty clothes lying around . . ." Mark had smelled another fetid odor too, but he could not place it.

Kim slapped her hands across her belly, wiping off the last of the lotion. "It's obvious he's not telling us the whole truth, but does he have to? He's done nothing wrong."

Mark shook his head. "I'm not so sure."

Kim pulled a pair of white panties out of the dresser and stepped into them. "Well, he's caught us supper, hasn't he?"

Mark scowled and rose from the bed to dress. "That was pure luck."

He had decided he was going to keep an eye on Travis . . . watch him real close.

Sabre sat at anchor in the fading evening light, *End of Watch* pulling easily downwind on the line connecting the vessels. Mark had moved them further offshore and re-anchored in deeper water, letting *End of Watch* swing loose. Warm light came from the catamaran's windows, along with the sounds of conversation and laughter. The party of five sat around the teak dining table on the cockpit, everyone sun-kissed, relaxed, and sipping drinks, all satiated from a large dinner. Mark opened a pinot grigio alongside oven-warmed rolls and butter. They had filleted and grilled the snapper, pairing it with a large citrus arugula salad and shrimp kabobs.

At the sight and smell of the food Travis realized how hungry he was. He was famished and had to control himself to not eat ravenously. The five-star dinner sure beat the hell out of the slop that came out of the Glades Correctional kitchen. He sat at the end of the table, with the couples across from each other. Mark sat to his left, Kim to his right. Her bare leg would bump and rest briefly against his under the table, and he had to resist slipping a hand down to touch her skin. He felt himself immediately aroused at her slightest contact; it was his first connection with female skin in years.

"Somebody was hungry," Kim said, eyes crinkling, looking sideways over the rim of her wine glass at Travis.

Travis sat back and rested a hand on his stomach. "I guess it's been a while since I had a meal like that."

Mark studied their guest, setting down a cloth napkin. "So, Travis, what do you do?"

"Well," Travis stalled for a quick moment, "to be honest, I'm kind of between jobs. I was a bartender in Miami"—Travis had applied for various bartending jobs, but never held one down for more than a week—"but I'm relocating, back up north, to the Panhandle."

Mark asked, "What's in the Panhandle?"

"Family. I'm moving the Bayliner north for a friend in Tampa. I was planning to head up from there."

"Where are you headed in Tampa?" Mark watched Travis closely as he questioned him.

Travis had never been to Tampa, but he had been in the area once before, to Gulfport, near St. Petersburg. A few years back he had driven up from Miami to move an ounce of coke. It had been well worth the drive, he made a nice profit on the blow, and the buyer even tipped, exceptionally. Travis recalled the location now. "To a marina, in Gulfport."

"Pretty ambitious trip for someone who doesn't know a lot about boating," Mark stated.

One corner of Travis's mouth turned up and he cocked his head. "I guess I bit off more than I could chew, that's for sure." He rolled his shoulders. "So, you've got a marina in Englewood that can fix me up, huh?"

Mark nodded. "They can get you on your way in no time."

"So how do y'all know each other?" Travis asked, directing the conversation away from himself, looking back-and-forth between the two couples.

Kim said, "Mark and I met through friends a few years ago. Andrea met Chad just a few months ago."

"Don't tell him how we met," Andrea rolled her eyes.

"How'd you meet?" Travis asked, lifting an eyebrow.

"Plenty of Fish," Kim answered.

"Hey!" Andrea leaned across the table to slap at Kim playfully.

"Plenty of Fish? What's that?" asked Travis.

"A dating website," said Kim.

"Never heard of it."

"It's new," said Andrea, "and there isn't anything wrong with meeting someone online."

"I didn't say there was," Kim replied, her face flashing mock scorn.

Mark stood up. "I'm getting a beer. Anyone want one?"

The consensus around the table was everyone wanted a beer, and Mark stepped away into the salon.

"What about you, Travis," Andrea asked, 'are you seeing anyone, or can we get you on Plenty of Fish?"

Travis looked amused. "No, I'm not seeing anyone right now—the only fish I seem to catch are in the Gulf of Mexico." The women laughed at his jest. "And I'm not sure about meeting people off the internet. Sounds weird . . . sketchy."

Andrea reached across the table and put her hand on Chad's. "They're not all bad. Chad's been a great catch—so far."

"Watch it," Chad quipped with a grin.

"Hey—what's all your signs?" Travis asked.

"I'm a Capricorn," said Andrea, 'Chad, you're a . . .?"

"May. Gemini," Chad supplied.

"What's Mark again?" asked Andrea.

"A Cancer," said Kim.

"And you're?"

"An Aries."

"An Aries?" Travis asked, looking at Kim. "I'm an Aries. What's your day?"

"April nineteenth," said Kim.

"No kidding?" Travis's eyebrows shot up, genuine surprise on his face. He said truthfully, "I'm April the nineteenth too. We're one day shy of Taurus."

"What, are you serious? Get out of here."

Travis nodded as Mark came back out to the cockpit, a full round of Heineken bottles in hand and tucked underarm.

"We got a hit—double birthdays here," said Andrea, accepting a beer from Mark. "Kim and Travis share the same day."

"What year?" asked Kim, an excited sparkle in her eyes.

"Seventy-five," said Travis. "You?"

"Younger—by a year. Seventy-six."

Mark sat and passed out the remaining beers, not exactly thrilled his girl shared a birthday with their unexpected guest. "I think you're the youngest on the boat, Kim," he said.

Kim was looking at Travis. "Where were you born?"

Travis did not hesitate with his lie. "Tallahassee. You?"

"Just north of here. Englewood."

Travis broke Kim's eye contact, and thanked Mark for the beer. Mark's eyes were drilled on his girlfriend. As she accepted her beer, leaning over, Travis felt Kim's leg again touch his. She smelled exquisite, luring island scents of coconut and vanilla pulling him in. Her legs were crossed, right over left, the soft toes of her bare foot periodically brushing his calf muscle.

"What's your background?" Kim asked. Her body language was open and directed towards Travis.

"It's a bit of a mix. Scottish and German."

"What's your last name?" asked Mark.

"Gardner," Travis lied smoothly.

Kim said, "You're a very similar mix to myself; I'm German—Irish—Scottish."

"Same birthdays and backgrounds," said Travis.

"To birthdays and backgrounds," Kim echoed, and tipped her bottle towards Travis. They clinked glass and Travis felt her foot caress his leg again.

Mark had already sucked back half his beer.

All too familiar with Mark's tension and mood, trying to break the chemistry between Kim and their guest, Chad said, "I tell ya' what, you gotta catch us another snapper like that tomorrow. That fish was excellent."

The women both chimed in their agreement. Mark was silent and took another slug of Heineken.

"Beginner's luck," Travis whitewashed, "I don't know much about fishing. Mark here set me up with the rod, the bait, everything."

After a few minutes of fishing banter, Mark got up silently and went into the salon. He returned a minute later with a fresh beer for himself. Kim noted Mark was drinking much faster than usual. They had all killed the bottle of wine over dinner, and Mark was already on his second beer, having pounded through his first. He was clearly less than thrilled to have Travis on his boat, conversing and connecting openly with his girlfriend.

The sun had fully set a half hour ago, but the day's heat had not yet relented. Around the table everyone's skin glistened tan under the cockpit's overhead pocket lighting.

"Why don't we move inside where its cooler guys?" Andrea suggested. More than the others, she was affected by Florida's dog days the most.

"Great idea," added Kim, 'this heat won't quit tonight. At least there's no bugs out here though."

Chad looked at Mark, eyes mischievous, and said, "We should put *Jaws* on for Travis."

"Hell no. Once was enough," Andrea said.

"Have you seen *Jaws*?" Chad asked Travis.

Travis nodded. They had actually shown the movie just last month at the prison for the Fourth of July.

"We'll put something else on later," Mark stated, his tone flat.

Travis sipped his beer and asked, "So what's the plan for tomorrow?"

"We'll play it by ear," Mark answered, "maybe Captiva in the morning and we'll hit Cayo Costa in the afternoon."

"Cayo Costa?" Travis asked. He had not heard that name before.

Kim said, "It's a state park—no houses, no hotels, nothing. Just a ranger station and some cabins . . . and miles and miles of beach."

"You've been there before?"

"Yes, once. I camped out for a couple of nights a few years ago."

"How far is it from here?" Chad asked.

"A short jump, about fifteen miles," replied Mark. "It's just north of Captiva."

Andrea stood and looked across the table to Chad. "I've gotta head inside. Can you help me clean up these dishes?"

"Yeah, sure hun," Chad answered, standing.

Kim rose with them, and they started to clear the table. As Travis made to get up Kim turned to him and said, "No worries, we can tidy up. You're the guest—stay and finish your beer."

Chad helped the women clear the table, and the three of

them went into the salon, leaving Mark and Travis outside, in an inconvenient and strained silence. Travis looked out over the transom to where *End of Watch* swung on her line twenty feet distant. "The boat will be OK tied like that for the night?"

"She'll be fine," Mark replied. "The current and wind will keep her away south."

Travis nodded, and Mark said nothing further. Travis watched the Bayliner shift on the dark water, with the body of retired Lee County police captain Robert Halliwell onboard. The man had been dead a day and a half. Travis wondered when he would start to smell. He was thankful *Sabre* would remain anchored upwind.

* * * *

Travis woke on his berth in the guest cabin. He could just make out the interior of the cabin by moonbeams streaming in the window. Shades of midnight, shadows of black and blue. Clicking on the bedside reading light he squinted against the brightness and picked up his Timex from the night table. It was thirteen minutes past two in the morning. *Sabre* was quiet and lay still on the flat water.

His tongue felt pasty and the taste in his mouth bitter. Mark had pulled out a bottle of Ballantine's shortly after they had retired to the salon—and Travis had had a couple of glasses of the scotch, neat. The five of them had polished off the bottle, the women having theirs with ginger ale, the men straight up. The liquor had further smoothed over Mark's undercurrent of tension, and the evening was relaxed.

Alongside Chad, Mark had drunk most of the scotch and seemed to chill out a bit, and even enjoy himself. There was a very visible stiff wall between Mark and Kim. Travis decided to retreat to his cabin for the night shortly after Chad and Andrea turned in, leaving Kim and Mark alone. He had passed out immediately in the combined comfort of the Ballantine's, two hundred thread count sheets, and an incredible queen-size mattress.

Needing to relieve himself, Travis rose, wearing only Mark's borrowed boardshorts, and made for the head. The interior of the catamaran was cool, the air conditioning running off the yacht's batteries. Travis felt a chill of gooseflesh cross his skin, not used to the cooler temperature. From the aft cabin at the end of the passageway he could hear light snoring. After using the toilet, he exited the head and stepped silently up into the salon. Moon shadows crisscrossed the teak and steel interior, pale light streaming in through the large curving windscreen. Travis moved aft and stepped around the breakfast bar into the galley. He popped open the fridge and drank several large swallows of OJ straight from a carton.

From where he stood, through the sliding glass door out to the cockpit, he could just make out *End of Watch*. The boat was silhouetted against the shimmering Gulf, lit by the radiance of the night sky. The Bayliner was only twenty feet off *Sabre*'s stern, less than a dozen arm lengths of line pulled in. Travis replaced the OJ in the fridge and slowly slid open the salon door. Stepping out onto the cockpit he was engulfed by the heavy humid night air.

He crossed to the transom, eyes following one of the double lines leading down into the black water and up to *End of Watch*'s bow cleat. It would take him less than two minutes to reel the boat over, hop aboard, get the gun, and hide it in—

"Hello there."

Travis nearly jumped out of his skin.

He whirled around at her voice, looking up and behind him.

Kim was on the flybridge, standing at the aft rail, hidden against the starry sky by the dark backdrop of the canvas Bimini top. Travis remained frozen for a moment and slowly relaxed. She had given him a hell of a fright but had not seen him do anything suspicious. If she hadn't called out, she would have witnessed him reeling in and boarding the Bayliner . . . returning to the catamaran with a pistol.

Travis grinned. "Damn Kim—you startled me real good."

"Sorry," she replied with an easy smile. "C'mon up."

Travis made his way up the circular stairs, twisting up to the flybridge deck. Kim had returned to sit back down on the U-shaped settee lounge. She leaned forward and flicked on a battery-powered lamp on the teak dinette table. Travis joined her on the settee. She was wearing only an oversize pink T-shirt and his eye caught a flash of white panties.

"Can't sleep?" Kim asked.

"I was. I woke up . . . wanted to check on my boat." She still smelled of coconut mixed with a blend of tropical spice . . . intoxicating. "Did you go to bed, or are you still up?"

"Still up," Kim replied. "I was reading." She motioned to a paperback book on the table.

Travis picked the novel up, read the title—*Treasure Coast*—and absently skimmed the cover. He flipped the book over. "Any good?"

"It's great, actually."

Travis's eyes moved down to the author photo, lingered there for a moment, and narrowed. He had a flash of recognition. He had seen or met the man in the photo before . . . but for the life of him he could not place when or where. The author's name was John Cannon. The name did nothing to jog his memory, but the face was familiar. He looked up at Kim. "Is this a new book?"

"Yes, it just came out in June."

Travis looked back to the photo. He was not one to forget a face, but this one was not coming to him right now. He set the book back down on the table.

"Somebody who can't sleep has something on their mind," Travis said, watching Kim's expression.

She let out a breath and sat back on the settee. "Yeah, I've got a few things on my mind."

"Like what?"

"Like I'm looking forward to getting back on Saturday."

"Not enjoying your vacation?"

Kim looked down briefly at the table, then back at Travis. "Not entirely."

After a beat Travis said, "Mark?"

Kim raised her eyebrows. "We've had some bumps on this trip, things haven't gone as planned. And obviously Mark isn't exactly over the moon thrilled to have you onboard."

"I've noticed. I'll be out of your hair the day after tomorrow."

Unexpectedly, mostly to herself, Kim leaned forward, reached out and touched Travis's hand. "There's no rushing it. I've really enjoyed your company today."

Her hand was soft and warm, and remained on his. He resisted twisting his hand over and taking her hand in his. He grew quickly aroused at her touch and closeness.

"And I have too," Travis spoke softly, tenuously leaning towards her. "We still have a couple of days together out here, and tonight . . ."

Kim's eyes traveled over his physique in the glow of the lantern. His shoulders, arms, and chest were muscled, his waist tight and lean. The scorpion tattoo moved with his body, wrapping across defined abdominals. She had leaned into Travis as well, catching his masculine musk, seeing that he was obviously aroused.

"I like your tattoos," Kim said, "that scorpion is pretty savage." She raised her hand from his and reached out to gently caress his chest, circling the clock tattoo. "The clock . . . why is it bare? Why no hands?"

Travis hesitated for a moment. "Time standing still. No hands represent doing time."

Kim looked up. "You were in prison?"

Travis nodded once.

"What for?"

"Drugs."

"How long were you in?"

"Three years."

Kim's hand remained on his. "When did you get out?"

"Just recently. A week ago."

Kim said nothing for a minute. Travis watched her face, trying to determine what she was thinking, how she was going to react.

He felt respite when she finally nodded slowly and said, "You're a real bad boy, huh?"

"I think," Travis said, now brazenly turning his hand into hers, palms together, fingers intertwining, "it would be best if you didn't tell Mark I was in prison."

Kim's voice was soft. "I'm not going to tell Mark anything. Trust me."

Travis leaned in and kissed her, and Kim returned his advance, squeezing his hand in hers.

The build-up broke unrestrained as they kissed hungrily. Kim was surprised by his aggressiveness, fully succumbing to it, her own arousal at a peak . . . the heat, the risk, and the animalistic lust. She could feel every day of his three years away from a woman.

Travis's hands slid over her body, up her thighs, under her T-shirt, around her breasts, squeezing, finding hard nipples. He dropped to his knees between her open legs as she lay back on the settee. He grasped her panties, pulling them down, sliding them off, her legs kicking out.

She tasted sweet, and her hands were on the back of his head, pushing his face into her. Kim was lost in ecstasy, reaching orgasm quickly against Travis's deft tongue. She had to keep her face buried in a lounge cushion, stifling her noises . . . the others were just two decks below. And then he was in her, thrusting hard and with an intensity she had not felt in years. It seemed as if they were rocking the entire catamaran, which excited and terrified her. The fear of being caught spiked her arousal, and she came again, even before Travis, having to further restrain her breathing and carnal sounds.

Afterwards, both covered in a fresh gleam of sweat and smelling of sex, they lay entwined together on the settee. Kim felt the first pang of guilt, but it was subtle, and easily pushed aside. She and Mark had not had sex in more than three weeks, closer to a month. They hadn't even fooled around on this trip. There was no question their relationship was on a downslide, and she had contemplated the serious possibility of ending it more than once. As they lay there, she had thankfully not heard any sounds from below. *Sabre* was silent. But she knew she was pushing her luck.

"I'm gonna head down," Kim said quietly. Travis nodded, his face displaying somnolent bliss. He tucked an arm behind his head as she rose and watched contentedly as Kim straightened her T-shirt.

"Don't dare fall asleep up here naked," Kim smirked. "Put

your shorts back on." Thanking the gods she did not forget her panties, she picked them up from the deck and saw they were slick with her wetness and stretched out from Travis ripping them off. Erring on the side of caution, she tossed them over the rail.

"Those would have been a highly prized possession in prison, you know." Travis's expression was dopey as he watched her. "I had fun with you, Kim."

Kim smiled, eager now to get below. "So did I. Have a good night, Travis."

"See you in the morning," he said softly.

Grinning, Travis watched her pad barefoot over to the stairwell and start down to the cockpit in a looping spiral. Before dropping below the flybridge deck she shot him a final parting look that Travis could not fully decipher. She was trusting him with their secret. He had secrets of his own.

Travis lay there for a few minutes before grabbing up Mark's boardshorts from the deck and pulling them on. He still had the musky taste of the man's girlfriend on his mouth. Kim was a nice little piece, and Travis really couldn't believe his luck at this point. He'd just had sex with a hot blonde while her boyfriend slept two decks down. He still had serious hurdles to contend with, but he was on an absolute winning streak. His best bet was to continue to stall and stay out here another day and night with this party and continue heading north. In the meantime, he had it damn good.

Travis looked to the paperback novel Kim had left on the dinette table. He frowned again at trying to place the author's face. The memory hit him like a bolt. Travis sat forward and picked up the book. He flipped the novel back over quickly, eyes going straight to the author photograph. Travis had met this man, John Cannon, once before, a few years back. He had sold him an ounce of cocaine. Travis had just thought of that trip up to Gulfport earlier tonight, at dinner. He'd used Gulfport as a cover for his intended destination. Quite a coincidence. Reading the blurb under the photo, sure enough, the author lived in Gulfport, Florida. Yep, that was him, for sure. Too strange.

"Huh . . . I'll be damned." Travis grunted, tossing the book back on the table. "It's a small world."

He leaned back on the settee and closed his eyes, The catamaran hardly moved at all on her anchor line, the night air stock still. There was only the slightest breeze from the north. In the early morning hours, the temperature had dipped into the high seventies, but the humidity was as thick as thieves.

Travis drifted off listening to the Gulf of Mexico lap gently against *Sabre*'s twin hulls.

* * * *

The grating sound of crackling radio static roused Travis from the depths of sleep. Coming slowly awake, finding himself lying on his back on the flybridge's lounge. It was still dark, but the lamp on the table was on, lighting the upper helm. The continued hissing of an open frequency made Travis sit up. He roused himself quickly. From the helm radio a broadcast began, a man's voice cutting the silent early morning hours.

> *"All stations, all stations. This is United States Coast Guard, St. Petersburg. At five a.m. a hurricane warning has been issued for the Florida Keys from the Dry Tortugas to the Seven Mile Bridge and for the Southwest Florida coast . . ."*

Travis swung himself to his feet and swiftly circled around to the helm. The VHF radio's display screen was backlit a dull amber. He quickly found the volume control and lowered the sound. The broadcast was coming across channel 16.

> ". . . from East Cape Sable to Bonita Beach. A hurricane watch has been issued from north of Bonita Beach to Tarpon Springs. Switch to channel 22 for a detailed update. United States Coast Guard, St. Petersburg out."

Fully awake now, Travis sat himself in the captain's chair. In their current position off Sanibel, they were within the area of the hurricane watch. Travis was unsure if the lower helm radio was on, or if anyone below, sleeping, or awake, would have heard the broadcast. He heard no sounds or movement from the salon. Travis switched the dial to channel 22.

> ". . . center of Hurricane Charley is located 100 miles east-southeast of Grand Cayman. Charley is moving toward the northwest near sixteen miles per hour. A turn to the north-northwest is expected over the next twenty-four hours. Maximum sustained winds are near eighty-five miles per hour with higher gusts. Strengthening is forecast during the next twenty-four hours. Large and dangerous waves and storm surge flooding of two to four feet can be expected in the Florida Keys. Storm surge flooding of six to ten feet is possible along the southwest Florida coast. Rainfall totals of four to eight inches are likely in association with Charley. The next advisory will be issued at eight a.m. United States Coast Guard, St. Petersburg out."

Travis sat still for a minute, listening for any sound from below and fully digesting the implications of the broadcast.

Sabre remained still and quiet.

A goddamned hurricane . . . and they were right smack in the projected path. If Mark learned of the storm, he would likely head them back in a lot sooner, straight away. The hurricane was not an immediate threat, it was still on the other side of Cuba. But it was certainly headed their way.

Travis knew all too well about hurricanes, and not to mess with them. He was seventeen years old when Hurricane Andrew pummeled Miami in August of '92. That was a horrific experience he did not want to repeat. However, this storm could possibly help him. It would hamper search efforts along the Gulf Coast. And it would provide a great cover in which to cut *End of Watch* loose once he got the gun. He needed to get rid of the Bayliner. The corpse onboard would be stinking to high heaven soon. And the Coast Guard likely had received an ABP on the stolen vessel.

Travis decided to gamble. If the others did not know of the storm, he was not going to tell them. And he would delay their finding out for as long as possible. He stood and looked over the helm station. There was an access panel below the wheel. He got the lamp from the table and returning to the helm he dropped to a knee and held the lamp up. He flipped open the panel and saw what he was looking for immediately, a bank of a half dozen fuses. One was marked VHF RADIO. He pulled the fuse and the radio's amber screen immediately went dark.

Satisfied, Travis closed the panel, switched off the lamp, and made his way quietly down the stairs to the cockpit. The interior of the salon was still dark. He slid open the door and stepped silently inside, the conditioned air cool and dry. He carefully closed the door behind him and moved forward without a sound to the main helm. This station was larger, but the radio was in the same location. The screen glowed the same dull amber. He flicked on the lamp, knelt in front of a panel to the left and below of the helm, and popped open the access hatch. There were three times as many fuses as the flybridge panel, but fortunately each was clearly marked. He pulled the fuse for the radio and again the amber screen went dark. He was taking a chance. Mark might try and use the radio and find the fuses missing, but it was a chance he was willing to take. He did not want them learning of the approaching hurricane.

Travis closed the panel, switched off the lamp, set it on the galley counter, and made his way down the starboard stairs to the guest cabins. The sound of soft snoring came from Chad and Andrea's berth. Travis went forward to his cabin. He put the two fuses in the bedside table drawer and lay back on the bunk. It took him a full hour, but he finally drifted off to sleep.

CHAPTER SEVEN

Everyone slept late. It was a slow start to the day on Sabre. The morning drew calm, clear—and impossibly— hotter than the day before. Cloying humidity sat heavy and stagnant across the Gulf of Mexico. Travis woke to bright sunlight streaming in the window of his cabin. He checked the time: 8:44 a.m. It had been almost four hours since the Coast Guard broadcast. And Halliwell had been dead for forty-eight hours. He'd for sure be starting to stink by now.

Travis threw on his T-shirt and went up into the salon, finding it empty. It appeared he was the first one up. Stepping through the salon door into the thick salt air, Travis looked from *Sabre*'s cockpit to *End of Watch* and was surprised to see the green haze of Sanibel Island off their portside. The wind had shifted through the early morning hours, coming from the southeast, but was still just a light breeze. Fortunately *End of Watch* would always remain downwind on her tether.

Forty minutes later Travis was joined by Chad and Andrea, both comatose, still half-asleep, and more than slightly hungover. They had both imbibed heavily on the scotch. Travis was thankful he had restrained himself. The three of them shared a quiet, light breakfast of cereal, toast, coffee, and juice.

As they were finishing up, Kim came out to join them, the lack of sleep showing around her eyes, a mug of coffee in hand. She exchanged a quick and veiled glance with Travis. Any conversation between the party of four was slow and easy. At half-past ten Mark made his appearance, looking like the morning after.

"The captain rises," Chad looked up at Mark. "Boy, you look like I feel."

Mark said nothing and wearily dropped himself down at the table.

"Do you want some breakfast?" Kim asked.

Mark shook his head and crossed his arms on the table, resting his forehead down upon them.

"A lil' too much scotch, me thinks," Chad grinned.

Without raising his head Mark grunted. "I'm fine."

"That bad?" Kim asked, putting a hand on Mark's arm. "I can get you some coffee?"

"No," he said brusquely. A moment later and a little less harsh, he added, "Thank you, I'm good."

"Damn, it's hot," Andrea bemoaned, "Feels hotter than yesterday. I can't handle this heat. There's barely a breeze. If we were under sail we'd have gotten nowhere on this trip."

Chad drained the last of a glass of OJ. "I'd like to do some fishing again. I feel lucky today."

Travis grinned, he sat languidly, an arm hooked over the back of his chair. "That's the spirit. I've been feeling more than a little lucky too, lately." He looked over at Kim, still grinning slyly. "You gotta live lucky."

Kim remained stoic, broke Travis's eye contact, and stood up from the table. "I'm going to get some more coffee, and something to eat. Does anybody want anything?"

Travis and Chad declined, Mark didn't make a sound or move from his head down position. Andrea got to her feet and said, "I'll join you inside—I need to cool off already. This day is gonna be an absolute scorcher."

Mark lifted his head, eyes squinting against the sun and looked to try and make an attempt to get up from the table.

"Are you coming inside?" Kim asked.

Mark shook his head, stood stiffly, and started to weave his way around the table towards the flybridge stairs. "I'm going up top to lay down for a bit. We're in no rush to be anyplace."

Kim watched Mark start up the circular stairs and apprehensively glanced at Travis before heading into the salon with Andrea. His expression was amused, a mischievous twinkle in his eye. Kim gave him a stern look before closing the salon door. Her guilt level was up a few notches this morning.

Chad tipped back in his chair and cocked a foot up on Andrea's vacant seat. "You think you can catch another snapper like the one you got yesterday?"

Travis shrugged. "I can certainly try."

"Yeah, we'll see who can bag the biggest fish today." Out of their party this morning Chad was the most chipper, enthusiastic about the day ahead on the yacht. He was truly enjoying the Gulf cruise with his new girlfriend and the week off work. Chad motioned up to the flybridge and dropped his voice. "I don't think we're going anywhere soon though. Why don't we see what we can catch right here?"

Travis shrugged again. "Sure, why not?"

* * * *

Kim reclined against an oversize pillow on the king-size bed in *Sabre*'s master cabin, paperback in hand. She had showered after breakfast and gone up to the flybridge to get her book and check on Mark. He was passed out cold on the settee that she and Travis had sex on just hours ago. Inwardly, she winced and returned below to the coolness and seclusion of the cabin to read.

She was almost a hundred pages into *Treasure Coast* when

there was a knock on the cabin door. "Come in," Kim said, eyes peering over the novel, praying it wasn't Travis. He wouldn't be that ballsy to come see her in her cabin . . . would he?

The teak round-topped door cracked open, and Andrea poked her head around. "Hey."

"Hey Andrea, c'mon in."

Andrea circled into the cabin and shut the door behind her. She crossed the suite and sat on the side of the bed. Her hair wet, she was freshly showered and dressed. "How's that book?" she asked.

"It's great. I'm glad I picked it up," Kim replied, saving her page, and setting the novel down.

"Yeah? You're going to lend it to me when you're done?"

"Definitely. I think you'll love it. It has the right amount of everything . . . and some of it is set locally, right around here on the Gulf."

"It sounds good," Andrea said. After a moment she continued, her tone more serious: "Look, we haven't had much of a chance to talk privately since Travis joined us. What do you think of him?"

Kim did not answer immediately, and Andrea lowered her voice an octave. "He's damn good-looking. And pretty chill— he seems like a cool guy."

Kim nodded once. "That he is." Her conscience tugged at her, and she was torn. Strangely she felt worse about deceiving Andrea than Mark. After a moment's hesitation, she said, "I'm glad you came to see me, so we have this chance to talk. There's something I want to tell you."

Andrea's eyebrows raised expectantly, and she shifted on the side of the bed. "Do tell."

Kim bit her bottom lip, and decided to spit it out, not beating around the bush. "I slept with Travis last night."

Andrea's eyes widened and mouth dropped open. "You what?"

Kim only nodded in response.

"You slept with him?" Andrea asked. "Where? When?"

"Last night, late. Up on the flybridge."

Andrea stared at her friend. "Christ, you're serious Kim. Aren't you?"

"Yes."

"Wow." Andrea lowered her voice again. "If Mark ever found out he would throw Travis right off the flipping boat."

"I know."

"How'd it happen?"

"You know—it just happened." Kim was quiet for a minute. "Mark and I have been off, off for quite a while. We haven't had sex in three weeks, at least. Then our planned three-way fell apart—"

"I'm sorry about that, about Chad," Andrea interjected.

Kim immediately regretted bringing up the incident. "That wasn't Chad's fault, or yours—it was mine. I wish I could go back and change it. I should have shut that idea down right away when this turned into a party of four."

Andrea's mouth twisted. "Yeah, well now it's a party of five. And it's even more complicated."

Kim gave an exasperated sigh. "Tell me about it. I'm being reckless, making some bad decisions." She paused for a moment, shrugged, and shook her head. "Mark will come around. His male ego is just bruised."

"Well, you better just make sure he doesn't find out about last night."

"Right."

"Can you trust this guy, Travis?"

"Hell, I don't know. I—we, just met him. What's terrible, I think . . . is I don't even feel that bad, or that guilty."

Andrea raised a brow. "You don't have to. It's not a requirement."

"I don't know . . ."

After a minute Andrea grinned, lightening the mood. "Alright, so, Travis . . . how was he?"

Kim rolled her eyes and groaned.

Andrea prodded. "C'mon, he's got a smokin' hot bod."

"That he does."

"Tell me."

"It was hot."

"No, you gotta gimme more . . ."

Kim chuckled. "Well, he sure knows how to go down on a girl."

"Ohh, lucky you," Andrea said, humming softly. "But this was just a one-time, one-night thing with him, right?"

Kim pursed her lips and said nothing.

"Sorry—my fault, I shouldn't pry too much. Just don't overthink it all right now. Enjoy the rest of the trip. You can see where you and Mark go when we are back home and off this boat. We all need space after what happened Saturday. Two more days, and we're back in Englewood."

"Two more days," Kim echoed.

Andrea rose from the bed. "I'm going to go check on the boys. Where is Mark now?"

"Still passed out cold up on the flybridge."

"It's probably a good thing he drank so much last night, huh?" Andrea crossed the cabin for the door and turned back to Kim before leaving. "Don't forget—I want to borrow that book when you're done."

HURRICANE HOLE

* * * *

"Holy shit!"

Travis froze at the sound of Chad's cursing coming from out in the cockpit. Travis was alone, in the galley, looking down at a black Motorola RAZR cellphone sitting on the salon's countertop. The slim phone was Mark's. Travis had come inside to get a couple of cold Gatorades from the fridge and the cell had just started ringing, a loud trilling electronic tone.

He looked through the salon door to Chad standing at the transom. He had a fishing rod gripped in his hands, legs braced wide, and he was canted over backwards, fighting a strong opposing force on the end of the line.

"Shit!" Chad bellowed again. "Travis! Mark! I got something!"

Travis glanced forward through the windscreen. Kim and Andrea had got up from where they were lying out on the bow and were now making their way aft down the starboard side walkway to see what the commotion was. Mark was out of sight, somewhere up on the flybridge.

Travis set the sport drinks down on the counter, picked up the cellphone and quickly looked it over. It trilled again, an ear-grating oscillation. The phone had no keypad that he could see. After a second, he figured out the phone had a front cover that flipped open, revealing a lit-up blue keypad and screen that looked to be displaying the number that was calling. Travis had never seen a modern phone like this. He recognized a red button and pressed it, ending the incoming call. On the side he located and held the power button. As the phone shut down, he glanced again out at Chad. He was still fighting the line, the girls had joined him, and Mark had come down from the flybridge to assist with reeling in the catch.

Travis slipped the cellphone into the pocket of his boardshorts and picked up the bottles of Gatorade. Holding a bottle under one arm he slid open the salon door and stepped outside.

"Whatcha got?" Travis asked, joining the excitement.

"Something big!" Chad bellowed, widening his legs to keep his balance, gripping the pole tightly. "It sure ain't no snapper!"

Andrea was leaning over the starboard rail beside Kim. She raised her sunglasses, looking down into the sparkling clear water. A large dark shape flashed below. "I see it!"

Mark was hovering over Chad, trying not to crowd him. "OK, keep reeling it in—there's not a lotta drag on that line."

Travis set one of the sport drinks down on the table, cracked the other, and took a swallow of the sweet liquid. He leaned back against the side of the table, casually watching the action. Kim and Andrea were both bent over the rail, two bikini-clad backsides, side-by-each, making a sight for his eyes. He grinned stupidly, going back and forth between Chad fighting a denizen of the deep and the women's twin curvy rears. Travis envisioned a fantasy scene with the two girls . . .

A loud thump reverberated against the hull, and a huge spray of water kicked up. Both Kim and Andrea jumped back.

"It's a shark!" Andrea let out a squeal.

"You got a sandbar!" Mark exclaimed, "it's a sandbar shark!" He flipped up his sunglasses to wipe saltwater from his face.

"What do I do?" Chad bellowed.

"Nothing," Mark replied, ducking for the salon, "I gotta cut the line."

"Cut the line?" Chad turned his head to look after Mark but quickly returned his eyes to the prize fish.

HURRICANE HOLE

Travis stepped forward to have a look over the gunwale. A large sleek shark twisted and frothed in the water beside the catamaran, its skin a shimmering light bronze. As it rolled the shark's belly and underside of its pectoral fins were a brilliant snow-white. The animal stretched at least seven feet from nose to tail and had a high triangular dorsal fin. The shark reared out of the water and tugged its head sharply against the hook embedded in its mouth.

A loud snap resounded, and a fine misting shot of water sprayed the cockpit. Chad lost his footing and went over backwards, tumbling hard at Travis's feet.

"Shit!" Chad said, groaning. He was flat on his back on the teak deck, the wind half knocked out of him, rod still in his hands, the monofilament line hanging slack across the gunwale. Travis watched the shark disappear into the blue and looked down at Chad. "You alright?"

"Hell—yeah," Chad grunted, chagrined, short for air.

Travis held out a hand and helped him to his feet.

"The goddamn line snapped." Chad was still catching his breath.

Mark returned to the cockpit, took in the scene, and looked quickly over the side. "Damn. I can't believe the line even held—that's only thirty-pound mono on that reel."

"Hell of a fish you got," Travis cracked.

"I'll say," Chad said, his breathing finally returning to normal, breaking into a sheepish grin. "Got knocked on my goddamn ass. I can't believe I caught a shark."

"A bloody big one too." Andrea said, looking non-plussed. "Did you guys see its teeth? My God, we were just swimming out here yesterday."

"It was a sandbar shark," said Mark, taking the rod from Chad. "Harmless. Would've made a nice catch if there was heavier line on that rod—coulda been one for the books—and some killer photos."

"I'm just glad you didn't kill it," Kim said.

Travis stepped forward and handed Chad the second Gatorade. "Nice catch, Chad," he said, before returning to lean back against the table.

"Thanks," Chad replied, a grin still plastered on his face. "Man, I think I got the bug now."

Travis nodded. "You girls best keep your toes outta the water when Chad has a line dropped."

Andrea chuckled and exchanged a look with Travis, her thoughts returning to Kim's late-night escapade. Travis flashed Andrea his most charming front, and their eyes lingered. A flush crept up Andrea's face and she could not keep the corners of her mouth from turning up at him, before turning away.

Travis's curiosity was piqued. Did Andrea know? Did Kim spill to her? He thought Andrea was a damn good-looking brunette, a little paler and a little taller than Kim, but with killer legs and a near perfect ass in that baby blue bikini. Still, Kim was more his type, but if he had to choose between the two now it would be a tough choice. Breaking his three years of celibacy had opened the floodgates. Travis was hungry, and he had to forcibly remove his eyes from Andrea's breasts in her little frilled top. He had developed a serious new itch for Chad's girl. He would play this out so he could have Andrea as well, whether she was willing or not.

"All right," said Mark, stowing the rod, "I think that's enough fishing for now. It's past one. Time we better make waves and head for Captiva."

Kim, ever observant, had caught the exchange between Andrea and Travis, and she gave him a brief but hard look before turning to head forward. As she settled on the bow lounge, Kim felt a trickle of concern about Travis but brushed it aside and picked up *Treasure Coast*. At least Mark seemed to be recovered from his hangover and they were on the move.

Travis lingered in the cockpit as Chad followed Mark up the stairs to the flybridge. Beneath his feet the twin engines hummed to life. After raising the bow anchor, Mark spun *Sabre* in a full 180-degree turn and powered up, heading them northwest, with Sanibel Island dropping away off their starboard quarter. *End of Watch* followed faithfully, pitching easily in the cat's wake.

Travis stepped to the transom and leaned against the teak wrap-around rail. The wind had shifted around yet again, and was coming out of the southwest, picking up a bit, but still just a moderate breeze. The skies were clear, and the mercury hovered in the low nineties. There was no sign at all of a storm on the southern horizon. At least not yet. But one was out there.

The weather was downright pleasant, save for the heat, a great day to be out on the water. Travis was picturing himself alone on *Sabre* with just Kim and Andrea, reimagining his fervid fantasy again, and how nice it would be to have both girls for himself.

Glancing first up at the flybridge, Travis slipped the cellphone out of his pocket and tossed it into *Sabre*'s roiling wake.

CHAPTER EIGHT

A t half past two that afternoon Sabre was anchored a little more than two miles southwest of Redfish Pass, the strait between Captiva and North Captiva Island. In the master cabin, Kim lay under Mark as he drove himself furiously into her. It was she who had come onto him, partially out of guilt, partially out of genuine desire, and he had reciprocated avariciously.

Mark had stamina, and Kim tried to lose herself in the sex. She did not think of Mark, or Travis, whom she had slept with just twelve hours earlier, but strangely she saw the dace of another man, the author pictured on the back cover of *Treasure Coast*.

John Cannon.

He was handsome, for sure, but that was not it alone, somehow, the man had entered her primal psyche on a deeper level than physical attraction. Maybe because she had spent a few hours of her life reading his written words. The author had got inside her head, and she into his. Kim was not one for wanton unrealistic fantasies and she pushed the odd illusion aside. Mark, oblivious to Kim's inner projections, worked himself into a pent-up frenzied release. Kim did not orgasm.

Travis sat alone in the salon, eating a bowl of sliced papaya. After the shark encounter, both Kim and Andrea had decided to skip swimming off North Captiva's sandspit, so they had dropped anchor offshore. Mark talked about later going through the pass into Pine Island Sound and making their way north up the intracoastal. In the growing afternoon heat, both couples had retreated to their cabins through the hottest part of the day to lie down, leaving Travis by himself.

He forked the last piece of papaya into his mouth and slowly chewed the sweet, soft fruit. The catamaran was quiet save for the hum of the air conditioning . . . and the muffled sounds of sex from below. His curiosity piqued, Travis rose from the salon table and went forward, standing behind the helm. The muted sounds were coming from the portside stairs, resonating up from the owner's cabin. Travis moved closer to the stairway and could make out Kim's suppressed noises. A hot emotion flashed through him, but it wasn't jealousy. More a pure rancor for Mark. And Chad. A resentment that the men were on the boat. A boat that was soon to be his.

Again, Travis saw himself with Kim and Andrea as his own. And both men no longer in the picture. The catamaran did not look all that challenging to pilot and Travis could get a lot further north on *Sabre* than the Bayliner. A plan began to formulate in his mind; retrieve his gun and the pepper spray, cut *End of Watch* loose, lose the men, and head up the Gulf Coast with the girls. The hurricane watch was issued at five o'clock this morning. That was almost ten hours ago now, but the storm, even if it was headed directly this way, was still far to the south. And there was never a guarantee with hurricanes, they had a mind of their own and went were they pleased. The storm could veer due east or west and bypass Florida entirely.

Travis remained still for another minute, listening to the curbed tempest from below, remembering Kim's smell and taste, her subtle notes and velvety softness. He would have her again, soon. And Andrea too. Travis crossed the salon to the starboard stairs, making for his cabin. At the passageway he stopped, another sound catching his ear. He stepped silently aft, towards Chad and Andrea's cabin. The door was closed. It was not the sound of intimacy from the cabin, but bitter voices. The couple were in a heated discussion. Their words were subdued by the teak door, but Travis could clearly hear what they were saying. He stopped a few feet from the door, his back against the passageway bulkhead.

Andrea: "Is this because of what happened last Saturday?"

"No—yes. I just . . ." Chad stumbled on his reply, inflection uncertain.

"Jesus, Chad. Most guys would have jumped at that chance."

"I'm not most guys. And it was unexpected. From you."

"From me? What does that mean? What were you expecting from me?"

"I wasn't expecting us to start swinging—or whatever you want to call it—three months into our relationship. Do you want to have sex with Mark?"

Travis was all ears, his interest in the conversation surging.

"No, that's not it," Andrea replied.

"Well, what then? How does this work?"

"This was something Kim and I had planned awhile back—before you and I met—to have sex together, with Mark."

Travis was frozen in place, his heartbeat picking up its pace inside his chest.

"Are you bisexual?" Chad asked.

"No, I'm not. But Kim is. I'm—it's complicated. It was just going to be a one-time thing. Something for us to try on this trip. I had thought you might be open to it."

There was only silence from Chad.

"I guess it backfired," Andrea continued, "because you're clearly unhappy and we haven't even had sex on this vacation. It was supposed to be fun—"

"It's not fun to be pressured into group sex with some guy—"

"No one pressured you, Chad."

"It kinda felt that way. And it also felt like I let you, and Kim, and especially Mark, down."

"Well, Mark was really looking forward to—"

"To what—fucking you?" That comment from Chad brought a silence from them both. After a moment, Chad said, "Three months is not a long time. I guess I don't really know who you are yet, Andrea. I'm going up to get a drink."

Travis spun an about-face and padded in a light-footed sprint for his cabin. He swung the door closed quickly behind him and closed it gently, leaning against it. He could hear Chad in the passageway, thumping heavily up the stairs to the salon. Travis's heart was beating hard from both the overheard conversation and the dash for his cabin. His mind was buzzing, trying to decipher just what had been afoot before he came onboard . . .

It seemed Chad had dropped the ball on an opportunity to have sex with both women. What a dumb ass. And Kim was into girls? It was like almost nothing but lady luck had been on Travis's side since his escape from Glades Correctional two and a half days ago. He sat back on his berth with sordid wanton visions in his head of himself wrapped up in a triad with Kim and Andrea. Captain and commander of the catamaran *Sabre*, and his two concubines.

* * * *

It was Mark's decision to remain anchored for the night in their current location, two miles out from Redfish Pass. They would depart in the morning for Cayo Costa, taking the intracoastal up Pine Island Sound to stop for lunch at the infamous Cabbage Key. There weren't any complaints heard around, everyone was tired, and it had been a slow lazy day. They ate dinner inside the salon, the air conditioning keeping the intense heat and humidity at bay. The temperature had climbed to ninety-two in the shade, and that was before the heat index, which had it feeling more like several digits over a hundred.

As the early evening drew on and the sun started its descent over the flat expanse of the Gulf, it did little to cool the sweltering temps. Nearing sunset the easy southwest wind died off to an almost non-existent breeze.

By nine o'clock it was dead calm.

The new cold wall between Andrea and Chad was obvious, and Travis used it opportunely. He took advantage of a couple of favorable moments to flirt with Andrea. Andrea's thoughts were still fresh with Kim's recount of her escapade last night, and she was receptive to Travis's beguilement. This casual banter between his girlfriend and Travis pissed Chad off even more and distanced him even further.

When Mark pulled out another bottle of Ballantine's, Travis—with strategy—eagerly accepted the first drink, and then a second, getting the liquor flowing. Kim's forehead furrowed at Mark for jumping into the hard stuff again tonight, but she remained silent. He'd pay for it again in the morning. She and Andrea shared some wine, while the boys dipped hard and fast into the scotch.

Several times Travis made it look as if he had drunk more than it appeared, dumping his drink out in the galley sink, and again while in the head. Whenever he poured another, Mark

117

followed. And Chad was not far behind them both. Pushing ten o'clock Mark and Chad were both lit, while Travis only had a subtle two-drink glow on.

An hour later, Kim looked up from the movie they had all been half watching to where Travis and Andrea were out on the cockpit together. They had both been out there for longer than what would have been socially acceptable. Through the salon door's tinted glass she could see Andrea laughing. Andrea had followed Travis outside and looked to openly be enjoying his company. In the salon, Chad was reclined on the floor, and Mark sat leaning back at the other end of the dinette bench. They were both absorbed in *Jaws 2*. Kim couldn't get into the movie at all, this one, a sequel, was about a bunch of screaming teenagers and another fake shark back at it again. And now she was further distracted by Andrea, outside with Travis. Any assailable trust she had in him was gone.

Unable to restrain herself from intervening, Kim slid out from behind the table and made for the cockpit. Neither Chad nor Mark seemed to notice her depart, both hooked on the film, eyes glazed with alcohol. Sliding open the salon door, Kim first felt the heat and then the incredible stillness. There wasn't so much as a wisp of wind, the heavy air slack and stagnant. The clear night sky was brilliant, a sea of twinkling stars reflected on the mirror-flat Gulf. No moon was visible yet. Travis was leaning back, elbows propped on the teak transom, Andrea by his side, close, her expression and body language open.

Kim slid the door shut behind her. "What's going on out here, you two?"

"Travis is showing me meteors." Andrea said. She wore a lop-sided grin of captivation, her face turned skyward.

"Meteors?" Kim asked. She could see Travis had Andrea

charmed and under his spell. Like her last night. He caught her eye and looked amused, knowing.

"Uh huh," Andrea replied, still looking up.

"It's the Perseid meteor shower," explained Travis, turning from Kim to look up again, "and tonight is the best night to see them—they're at their peak, and it's a good time—with the moon not up yet the sky is dark. We couldn't have a better spot than this to watch them." Travis had seen the Perseid meteors many times as a boy growing up in Georgia, and one of the best shows he experienced was on a boat off Key Biscayne in his teens. He had forgotten all about the summertime meteor shower until he saw the first streak of light across the sky this evening.

Kim looked up and scanned the ceiling of stars, seeing nothing.

"There's not many right now," Travis said, "they get better after midnight, and best right before dawn."

Andrea's eyes went round. "I'm not staying up that late," she said. Looking over to Kim, she asked, "Mark's getting bombed again tonight, huh?"

"Looks that way," Kim replied, "Chad too. They're still watching the movie . . . probably both going to pass out soon."

Andrea nodded at the salon door over Kim's shoulder. "Speak of the devil—here comes the skipper now."

Kim and Travis both turned to see Mark slide open the salon door. "Ladies," he greeted, stumbling out onto the cockpit deck. "What're we all doin' out here?"

"Looking for meteors, apparently," answered Kim.

"Meteors?" Mark repeated, the word coming out slurred.

"Yes," said Andrea, returning her gaze skyward, "just be patient and you'll see one."

Mark crossed the cockpit and stepped down and out onto

the port swim platform. A couple of miles distant a handful of lights burned in the darkness, scattered along Captiva's shoreline. There was a zipper noise in the dark, followed by the sound of a running splash.

"Mark—are you taking a leak?" Kim asked.

Mark turned his head, "It's my boat. I can piss off it if I want to."

Kim rolled her eyes and exchanged a look with Andrea, both women shaking their heads.

Andrea said, "Boys will be boys—"

"Look, there," Travis said, pointing overhead, "and quick—there."

"I saw it!" Andrea exclaimed.

Kim followed Travis's hand and saw a flashing line of light cross the sky. It lasted less than a second, burning bright. "Wow," Kim said, taking a breath, "I saw that one."

Still urinating, Mark looked up and saw nothing but stars. "What? Where?"

"You gotta keep watching," said Andrea.

Mark zipped up, and stepped back onto the cockpit. He leaned back against the transom rail, the four of them all watching the skies.

"I didn't know about the meteor shower," said Kim. "Did you Mark?"

Mark shook his head, studying the heavens. "No."

"Have you checked the forecast for the next couple of days?" Kim asked.

"Yeah," Mark replied, still looking up, distracted, hunting the sky with bleary eyes for any sign of a meteor.

Kim had trouble believing him. "If a storm moves in overnight, you can get us off the Gulf quickly?"

Mark looked down, frowning at Kim. "A storm? The sky

doesn't have a single cloud in it, and there isn't so much as a breeze out here."

Kim's brows drew together. "That's what worries me." She could sense something off, a subtle change in the pressure . . . the stillness, it was too still, like everything around them was a surrealistic painting.

Mark saw Kim's concern and realized he had not checked a marine forecast in days. There had been no need to—it had been day after day of clear skies and sunshine. "If anything moves in, I can have us into Pine Island Sound in a half hour. There's dozens of harbors and holes back in there to take shelter. We're going that way in the morning anyway—straight through Redfish Pass."

Mark looked back up, scanning the night sky with Travis and Andrea. Not seeing anything after a minute he gave up, looking up making him dizzy. "Tomorrow, I'm getting myself a cheeseburger, a cheeseburger in paradise at the Cabbage Key Inn." He turned to Travis. "Did you know that's where Jimmy Buffett got the inspiration to write that song?"

Travis glanced at Mark, shook his head, and answered honestly. "No."

Kim could make out that Travis wasn't nearly as intoxicated as Mark. "Take it easy with the drinking, Mark. You're the captain of this boat."

Mark let out a breath. "I'm fine." He glanced skyward again, his words slurring. "I could sure go for a cheeseburger right now."

"A cheeseburger would be great . . ." Travis commented, "I haven't had a cheeseburger in years."

Mark looked at Travis quizzically. "No shit? What's wrong with you? Well, tomorrow I'm buying."

"You can count me in for that," said Travis.

"Alright, I'm heading back inside—gonna finish the movie. It's hot as the blazes of hell out here," Mark looked to Kim. "Are you comin' in?"

"In a minute," Kim replied.

"I'll join you," said Andrea, moving to follow Mark.

"I'm heading in too. We can come back out again later," said Travis, stepping forward to join them, "there'll be even more meteors later."

Andrea followed the men inside and gave Kim a questioning look as she walked past. Kim nodded, and said quietly, "I'll be in in a minute."

When the salon door closed behind them, Kim crossed to the transom rail, and braced her hands wide, leaning against the polished teak. A streaking line of light caught her eye directly off the stern, slipping across the water. The meteor reflected on the Gulf, a surface that was flat as a mill pond, polished smooth as glass. The night was like none other she had experienced before in Florida. The stillness was eerie . . . no wind, no waves, absolutely no sound at all. Just the periodic radiant meteoroid flashing through the sky above.

The surreal scenario was magical, but it also gave Kim an unsettling sense of foreboding.

PART THREE

CHARLEY

CHAPTER NINE

August 13, 2004
Two miles west of Captiva Island

The rhythmic rocking movement of the catamaran roused Travis. He woke slowly, rising from heavy sleep, eyes squinting against the bright morning light splashing in the cabin window. Sprawled on the berth, he had slept like the dead. Travis reached for his wristwatch on the bedside table and seeing the time came fully awake. It was eleven minutes past ten.

Shocked by how late it was, Travis quickly sat himself up. His first thoughts went to the storm, and he chastised himself for sleeping in. It was his third night out of prison and not on a regimented and strict daily routine and sleep pattern. He was getting disoriented on the unregulated passage of time, and days were sliding into one another. It had been a late night again; they had all stayed up well past two in the morning, going back out repeatedly to watch the meteor shower. Travis had maintained control over his alcohol intake and drunk the least out of everyone. The women together killed a bottle of wine, and Mark and Chad imbibed in even more scotch than the prior evening.

The wind was up this morning, but nothing to cause any alarm. Travis had had a haphazard plan to wake early and pop one of the radio fuses back in to listen for an update on the storm, but he had slept right through that opportunity. At this late hour, everyone was likely already awake. However, the boat was quiet save for the soft whir of the air-conditioning and the Gulf slapping against the hull outside his cabin.

Travis rose from the berth, wearing only the borrowed pair of Mark's boardshorts. He opened the door to his cabin and looking down the passageway saw that the door to Chad and Andrea's cabin was ajar a few inches. Assuming they must be awake, he made his way up to the salon, but found it empty, just the lingering faint air of stale alcohol. Crossing aft to the salon door, he found the table out in the cockpit also vacant. The sky was a hazy mix of fast-moving light cloud filtering under wide patches of blue sky. Sliding open the door, Travis stepped outside. The morning was cooler than last night, but the humidity still thick. The wind was blowing, but of no real concern, still just a moderate breeze. It had shifted through the night however and was coming directly out of the east. Both *Sabre*'s and *End of Watch*'s sterns were pointing due west, away from Captiva.

Puzzled as to where everyone was, he went up the circular stairs to the flybridge and was surprised to find Chad by himself, crashed out on the settee lounge. Travis smirked. He had flirted with Andrea through last night, and she had returned his banter openly. She and Chad had started the evening off badly, and it appeared Travis's brazen cruising had driven them further apart, with Chad spending the night up on the flybridge. Which meant Kim and Mark must still be in their cabin, and Andrea in hers. Or could Andrea be in with Mark and Kim?

Both aroused and jealous at the thought, Travis retraced his steps lightly, backtracking down the stairs and into the salon. He slid the door gently closed behind and made his way forward, back down into the guest cabin passageway. He went aft, ever so silently, towards Chad and Andrea's cabin. The door was still ajar several inches.

Slowly pushing the door open, he saw Andrea. She was asleep on the berth, lying on her side, facing him. The berth in this cabin was positioned across the beam, against the rear bulkhead. Her dark hair spilled in waves across the white pillow, falling off the side of the bunk. In sleep, her sun-kissed face was only pure and innocent. She lay under a single loose white sheet, pulled up and crumpled under her arms. At the base of the bed her bare feet were exposed, sticking out from under the sheet, small pleasing toes pedicured and polished a dark blue.

Travis eased into the cabin quietly, and pushed the door back over behind him, but did not close it. Gingerly, he sat on the side of the bunk, feeling his pulse quicken. Andrea's scent was subdued and delicate but intensely female. He watched her shoulder rise and fall with each breath.

On the innate sense that someone was with her, Andrea awakened. She stirred slowly, Travis coming into focus, sitting on the side of her bed. His presence confused her, but she did not show any immediate surprise or concern. This boldened Travis.

"Hey, you . . ." he whispered. "Good morning."

Andrea blinked twice and covered a yawn. "Good morning," she replied, looking around the cabin and then back at Travis. "What time is it?"

"Not too late."

Andrea eyes narrowed. "What are you doing in my cabin?"

Travis's sheepish grin turned into a charismatic smile, feigning innocence. "I just came to see if you were up."

"I am now," Andrea said. She stifled another yawn, and stretched, propping herself up on an elbow. Travis saw she was wearing a white sports bra as the sheet dropped and repositioned. "Where are the others?"

"Still sleeping," said Travis.

"Where's Chad?"

"He's passed out up on the flybridge."

Andrea felt a shot of guilt, which Travis saw flash over her face.

"Did you guys get in a fight?" he asked.

Andrea furrowed her brow and shook her head once. "Sort of, yeah . . . where are Kim and Mark?"

"Still sleeping." After a beat, Travis asked, "Do you know what today is?"

Andrea shook her head.

"It's Friday the thirteenth."

"Oh . . . An unlucky day?"

Travis's eyebrows rose. "I don't think so. It all depends on how you look at it. I'm not superstitious, are you?"

Andrea shook her head again. "Not really."

Travis let his left hand settle it on her bare ankle. Andrea didn't react and he slid his down over her foot, cupping his fingers under her sole. "Mmm, you have soft feet."

Andrea's face went rose under her tan and a shiver passed up her spine. "Thanks," she said awkwardly. Her usual strong voice was airy, tone uncertain. She recalled Kim's revelations yesterday morning of her tryst with Travis. She couldn't believe this guy was now coming onto *her*, so brazenly, with such high risk of being caught.

"I've been catching some—tension—between the four of you," said Travis. Andrea did not pull her foot away, and he started stroking her instep with his thumb.

"We've had some issues—some things have come up on this trip." Andrea's eyes traversed Travis's tanned and muscled upper body . . . his long lean arm, his hand on her foot. Despite his physical appeal she felt a rising sense of uncomfortableness and indiscretion. If she was discovered by Chad with Travis in her cabin like this . . .

"What kind of things?" Travis asked. His thumb was still stroking her foot.

Andrea's eyes flicked down to a noticeable bulge in Travis's boardshorts. Immediately her flesh prickled, and she battled the urge to recoil. Averting her eyes from his crotch she pulled her foot from his grasp. "It's nothing we should talk about, Travis," she said, "it doesn't concern you."

"Aw, c'mon," said Travis, showing obvious displeasure that she had pulled her leg away. "I'm a friend too. I'm here to listen." When she said nothing, he added, "You're a beautiful girl, Andrea."

She stared at him, not responding to the compliment, feeling the first onset of anger. "Kim told me about you—I thought it was *her* you have the hots for?"

Travis's grin broke and he let out a breath, more than a little surprised Kim had so soon revealed their escapade to her friend. The two were close. His face twisted back into a smirk, and he shook his head. He reached for her ankle, grasping it firmly in his hand this time. "Kim's a fun girl, but it's you I really like, Andrea." She tried to tug her leg away, but he held it fast, his grip hard, hurting.

"Let go of me," Andrea said sharply.

"Hey now, don't be like that," said Travis, sliding towards her on the bunk.

Andrea sat herself up, pushing away from him. "Be like what? Let go of my leg."

Travis leaned towards her, eyes flashing fiendishly. "What if . . . I don't want to?" Dominance and desire for her coursed through him, clouding any thought of repercussions. "It's you I want . . ."

Andrea's anger, now mixed with rising fear, made her react.

She bucked her leg forcibly out of his grip. "Get the hell out of here, Travis!"

Her voice was abrasive, loud. Loud enough to possibly be heard across the catamaran in the master cabin.

Travis looked quickly to the cabin door, then back at Andrea—and lunged at her. He was on top of her before she knew what happened. She felt his weight, his hand going for her mouth, his musky scent filling her nostrils. Andrea froze momentarily, in total shock and disbelief this man was assaulting her. She reacted, her brain going into survival mode, unleashing a burst of adrenaline. She brought her knee up hard for Travis's groin and felt it impact rubbery flesh. He jerked up and away, sucking in a rushing gasp of air. Andrea seized the opportunity, spinning out from under him, rolling beneath the sheet and right off the berth, tumbling onto the floor.

Travis was surprised at her offensive speed and catlike agility. There was a flashing ache and numbness between his legs. Her knee had grazed his balls; a full crushing contact might have temporarily incapacitated him.

Andrea pulled herself to her knees, scrambling forward, making to rise and run for the door. Hopping to her feet, she was about to bolt when Travis grasped a handful of her hair and yanked her forcefully backwards. She reached behind her head with both hands, found and grabbed his wrist, turned her head and sunk her teeth into the back of his left hand.

He didn't let go immediately and she bit down harder, feeling the skin split and warm coppery blood rush into her mouth. His grip on her hair loosened, and with a jerk she was free, falling forward, again on her hands and knees. Gaining her feet in a blur of panic, sensing him recovering, coming fast, Andrea bolted for the door, catching it with her fingers and whipping it open. She was in the passageway, feet slapping the wood panel deck. She caught the side handrail and catapulted herself around the corner and up the stairs into the salon.

His hand throbbing and running blood, Travis was inches behind her, just missing her at the top of the stairs. She sprinted ahead of him, instinctively going aft through the salon towards the cockpit. Andrea had to stop to reef open the sliding door and Travis was on her again. She made to lunge through the open doorway, but he grabbed a fistful of her hair and this time she was hauled backwards off her feet and went down hard on the deck, flat on her back.

Below, in the owner's cabin, Kim woke from the thumping sound of Andrea hitting the deck. She raised her head from the pillow. "Mark, did you hear that?"

There was no response from Mark, just muted snoring. Kim did not hear anything further but was alarmed by the noise. Whatever caused the sound was heavy, and it certainly wasn't a dropped glass or pan in the galley.

Travis stood over Andrea. She lay on her back, sprawled lying half in and half out of the salon doorway. Her lungs wheezed, diaphragm working hard to inhale air. She had the wind knocked fully out of her and was mildly concussed, her head slammed hard into the salon flooring. Blood dripped from Travis's injured hand, spattering the laminate deck beside Andrea's head. He was about to reach down and haul her to her feet when he heard a voice from above.

"What was that?"

Chad. His voice thick and heavy with sleep.

Travis froze, then quickly stepped over Andrea, going out onto the cockpit, coming around the flybridge stairs towards the portside companionway. He tucked himself back against a washdown table at the rear of the pilothouse behind the stairs. Beside his left elbow was a coil of one-inch thick braided white line, neatly looped on a hook. He could not see Chad from where he stood but he could hear him . . . coming slowly and heavily down the stairs. Travis unloosed the line, remaining out of sight behind the stairway enclosure.

Chad immediately saw Andrea lying on the deck at the base of the stairs, her legs sticking out into the cockpit, upper body inside the salon. It took him a moment to process what he was seeing, still half asleep and fully hungover.

"Andrea," he called out in surprise and stepped down to kneel over her. His first thought was that she had slipped and fallen. "Hey, babe, are you OK?"

She looked to have knocked herself cold, and Chad's alarm rose when he saw spattered drops of bright red blood on the floor by her head. There was a smear of fresh blood across her mouth as well. He felt his worry lift some when Andrea stirred, groaning lightly. She slowly moved her head from side to side.

"Andrea, can you hear me?" Chad asked, placing a hand on her cheek.

Travis circled around out from behind the stairwell, directly behind Chad. He held a length of the line taught in each hand and passed it in a blur over Chad's head, pulling it back around his neck. Travis wrapped and twisted the line hard, strangling Chad with the makeshift garrote.

Chad's hands shot up for his neck, and he tumbled away, feeling himself being dragged away, his head pulled viciously backwards. Travis watched Chad's upturned eyes meet his. They bulged and watered, and his mouth twisted wide, but he made no sound. The line had effectively cut off his trachea. Chad's bare feet kicked out, lashing Andrea, who was still only semi-conscious. Travis further dragged Chad back by the cruel garrote. The line dug deep into his neck, cutting off all air to his lungs and blood flow through the carotids. Despite the intense flailing of his body, Chad never once reached for Travis, only trying to free the crushing pressure from his throat in a desperate battle for air. His vision blurred and dimmed, the image of Travis over him fading, and the sound of his labored breathing becoming distant.

Cutting off the blood supply to Chad's brain, it took Travis only seconds to render him unconscious. Chad went slack and lay still; his eyes wide open and shot with broken blood vessels. Travis was sitting on the deck, leaning back against the stairs, arms burning from the exertion, catching his breath. He kept the line tight around Chad's neck, the neatly braided line stained with blood running from his injured hand.

Travis slowly released the tension from the garrote. Chad was dead weight. This was now the third person he had killed, in as many days . . . only a number to Travis, he felt nothing. Simply another speeding ticket at this point. He'd snuffed out Chad as quickly and efficiently as he did the prison guard and Halliwell.

Andrea had come more awake, groggy and sore. She sat up on an elbow, feeling dizzy, eyes focusing, and saw Travis and Chad together. She took in Chad's lifeless face, unseeing eyes, the draped line and dark red contusion around his neck. She blinked, uncomprehending. Travis pushed Chad's lifeless body aside and got to his feet. Andrea's eyes widened upon remembering and realizing the scenario and the threat. Before she could scream or make a sound Travis was over her. She held up her arms defensively and fell back to the deck. Travis straddled and quickly overpowered her, getting his hands around her neck. She clawed vainly at his face, immediately feeling his hands grip her throat. Vision blurring, all sounds muffling, Andrea started repeatedly slamming her feet down hard on the teak decking of the cockpit.

Mark had woken painfully to a blinding headache and nauseous stomach. Kim had prodded him from sleep. He had not heard the noise she was querying about; he would have slept through the apocalypse this morning. At the new sound of Andrea's feet thumping the deck above the cabin overhead Kim jumped out of bed.

"Mark—get up right now," Kim called loudly, heading for the door in a tank top and panties.

"Christ, all right," Mark replied, hearing the pounding above. "What the hell is going on up there?"

Irritably, he dragged himself out of bed, feeling off balance, head throbbing. Wearing a T-shirt and boxer shorts, he followed Kim out of the cabin, cursing under his breath.

Kim took the stairs up to the salon in a single leap and froze behind the helm station when she looked aft through the galley. Travis was on top of Andrea, throttling her.

"Mark! Get up here!" Kim screamed, and rushed forward, stopping short of the entangled duo, unsure immediately what to do. Travis looked up and locked eyes with Kim.

"Get off of her!" Kim yelled. She saw Andrea's face was beet red, eyes wide, wet, and bulging. Kim also saw blood, fresh spatters of it on the salon floor, Travis's hand, and smears across Andrea's lips.

"Mark!" Kim screamed again. Travis didn't react, he just kept strangling Andrea while looking at Kim. Kim was paralyzed with fear, her heart in her throat.

"What is it?" Mark came rushing through the salon, quickly taking in the scenario.

Mark's appearance emboldened Kim and she rushed forward at Travis. Mark saw Kim take off ahead of him for Travis and after a moment's hesitation he joined her. They reached Travis almost at the same time, Kim outright tackling

HURRICANE HOLE

him. Travis released Andrea and toppled over backwards out onto the cockpit deck as Kim crashed into him. In a scrambling melee, his hands were now going for Kim's throat.

"You son of a bitch!" Mark howled, and dove into the mix, falling to his knees to try and separate Kim and Travis. The three of them bowled together into the dinette table, sending it sliding away, toppling chairs. Mark used brute strength to pull Kim free, and with his own anger and confusion boiling, went on the offensive after Travis.

Kim fell back and saw the two men go into a full-on jockeying brawl. She rose to her feet and spun back into the salon, scanning the galley for any kind of weapon. Reefing open a drawer, she pulled out a seven-inch fillet knife. Dashing back out to the cockpit, she saw Mark on top of Travis, both locked in a clashing deathmatch.

Over Mark's shoulder Travis saw Kim coming with the knife—the look on her face told him she meant business with the razor-sharp blade. With a renewed burst he shoved Mark up and to the side, into the dinette table, crashing it right over, sending a chair flying down onto the swim platform and bouncing overboard. Travis pulled himself to his feet and managed to step back as Kim swung the knife inches from his chest. The razor edge sliced a second time, whistling past his face. Travis ducked back and jumped down onto the port swim platform.

Kim didn't slow her advance, fully intending to slash him with the knife. Travis had nowhere to go, if he remained on the platform, she was going to carve him open. Kim swung the blade again, this time forcing Travis right off the platform.

She watched him drop backwards into the water, disappearing under the choppy cerulean surface. The water kicked up over Travis in a thumping, foaming splash, and Kim looked for him to reappear. He did, already a dozen feet distant. The east wind was pushing a swift surface current, and Travis was pulled quickly away from *Sabre*. Kim noted the catamaran's swim ladder was up. Without it down it would be a challenge, if not impossible, to climb back aboard. The freeboard up to the swim platform was close to three feet. Kim's eyes found Travis's, and they locked. He did not call out, just staring back at her, seemingly unconcerned, treading water silently. He was drifting west, nearing *End of Watch*'s bow. It would be a challenge to board that vessel as well, he would need to swim hard across the current for it, but instead he just sculled, bobbing easily in the light swells, looking at her. She could not read his expression, but his drilling look held her transfixed in terror.

"Kim!" Mark's voice pulled her back around. She turned and saw Mark kneeling over Chad.

"He's not breathing," Mark said, looking to her, panicked.

Hurrying, Kim stepped back up onto the cockpit deck. "Does he have a pulse?"

"I don't know."

"Check," Kim snapped, "if you can't find one start CPR." She quickly circled around Chad's inert body to Andrea and knelt beside her. She was breathing, but only semi-conscious. Kim put her hand on Andrea's face, tapping her briskly. "Andrea, can you hear me? Wake up."

Andrea stirred, eyes opening, squinting, trying to focus.

"He's got no pulse." Behind Kim, Mark's voice was stricken with angst.

"Start CPR," Kim ordered, "I'll be there in a second—where's your phone?"

"In the salon—in the galley—I think." Mark was distraught, trembling with dread. "What's first? Breaths or compressions?"

"It doesn't matter—just start now," Kim replied, trying to recall her training. "Two breaths, thirty compressions."

Andrea was coming more awake and trying to sit up when she saw Mark starting CPR on Chad. Already in a shocked and disoriented state this set her off. She made a moaning sound and called out, "Chad!"

"Shh," said Kim, putting her hand on the side of Andrea's face. "He's OK, he's going to be OK. Just rest, lay back down."

Andrea complied and lay her head on the salon floor. "Just breathe for me," Kim said, "I need you to do that. OK?" Andrea nodded weakly. Satisfied for the moment, Kim stood and looked to Mark. He was bent over Chad, performing chest compressions.

"Don't stop. I'm going for the phone," Kim said. Mark only nodded in response. Kim looked out over the transom. There was no sign of Travis. Concerned, she stepped a few paces towards the stern rail and scanned the swim platforms and surrounding water. Nothing. *End of Watch* pitched easily on her tether, but there was no sign or evidence of Travis around that boat either. She could not see the stern of the Bayliner where he might try and board, but for now at least he looked to be nowhere near *Sabre*.

Kim turned and moved past Andrea into the salon. She looked over the galley counter for Mark's cellphone, not seeing it anywhere. She went forward to the helm and saw no sign of the phone there either. Hurrying back to the salon door, she asked, "Where is your phone? I can't find it."

Mark finished giving Chad a resuscitative breath, and wiped sweat from his face on the shoulder of his T-shirt. "I don't know—it should be there. Find it."

"Did you check his pulse?"

Mark nodded. "Nothing."

"Shit." Kim winced and came to kneel beside Mark. "You do compressions, I'll breathe."

Mark started a cycle of compressions on Chad's chest, his hands overlapped on the man's sternum. "Where is Travis?" he asked, "can you see him?"

"No, he's not near us. The current took him away quickly."

"Keep an eye out for him," Mark said, finishing the compressions as Kim adjusted Chad's airway and have him two large breaths. Chad's chest rose and fell with the rescue breaths. They continued, trading compressions for breaths, Kim periodically checking Chad's carotid pulse. She felt nothing. Her own pulse hammering, she kept an eye out across the cockpit to the swim platforms.

Andrea had pushed herself up to a sitting position, leaning against the bulkhead. She sobbed softly and rubbed her tender throat, watching with numbing anxiety as Mark and Kim worked on her boyfriend.

After three straight minutes of CPR and not finding a pulse, Kim's breath began to shake and her soul chilled. Chad's throat was marked with a deep crimson band of broken capillaries from the line. Exhausted, they did another cycle of compressions and breaths and Kim checked Chad's pulse again. His artery lay flat and unmoving under her fingers.

"Anything?" Mark asked.

Kim shook her head. "I need to find that phone—where is it, Mark?"

"Christ, I told you, it's somewhere inside. Last I saw it was on the galley counter." Mark sat back on his haunches, drained from performing CPR. "What do we do? Do we keep going?"

Kim said nothing for a moment, then, crestfallen, shook her head. "I don't think so. We need to get help. Go and find your phone."

Mark got up, fighting stress, fatigue, and the aftereffects of copious alcohol. He was sure he still felt more than a little inebriated from the late night of heavy drinking, which he was thankful for. He made his way past Andrea, avoiding her eyes, into the salon, searching frantically for his cell and finding nothing. Cursing, he went forward to the helm and did not see the phone anywhere up front. Thinking he might have left it in the cabin, he went below to check.

Kim got up from where she was kneeling by Chad and came to sit beside Andrea. The look on Andrea's face was a layered mix of bereavement, confusion, and disbelief. Kim put her arm around her friend, at a loss for the right thing to say. "I'm sorry," she finally said, dully. Andrea broke out into sobs and dropped her face on Kim's shoulder. Kim held her friend tightly, as equally shocked, pained, and confused by the events.

A minute later Mark returned, looking exasperated. "I can't find my goddamn cell anywhere. Did any of you bring a phone?"

Kim shook her head. "You were the only one who had one. Get on the radio, we need some help out here."

Mark didn't respond, biting his lower lip, hesitating. He turned abruptly and wheeled back inside. At the helm he picked up the handset and saw that the VHF radio was powered off, but the switch was in the on position. Frowning he turned the power switch off and back on again. Nothing happened. He turned it off and back on twice more, but the radio remained dead.

"What the hell?" Mark said, agitation rising. A new trepidation occurred to him. He placed the handset down and made an about face, heading straight through the salon and back out to the cockpit.

Kim looked up at his abrupt reemergence. "What is it?" she asked as he hustled by. "Did you get through on the radio?"

Mark did not reply and jogged up the stairs to the flybridge, his head pounding with each step. He could hear Kim's voice calling after him, concerned.

He leaned over the helm, rising wind gusts tousling his hair, and saw the flybridge radio also looked to be dead. With bated breath, fearing the worst, he turned the power switch off and back on. Nothing happened.

"Son of a bitch!" Mark cursed, shaking his head. "I fuckin' knew it." He looked forward out over the helm to Captiva Island two miles distant. He noticed then the wind had really come up, the morning's moderate offshore breeze out of the east was now pushing a strong twenty-five knots. *Sabre* was rocking and jostling on her anchor line. The sky was mostly clear, but heavier lines of layered and swirling cloud were passing by rapidly overhead, blocking the sun intermittently. The horizon to the south was a wall of approaching darkness. A storm front was moving in, fast.

Descending to the cockpit, Mark saw Kim helping Andrea to her feet. He looked down to Chad's body lying sprawled out on his back. The dead man's eyes were wide and unseeing, a cold blank stare. A shiver of repulsion went through Mark.

"What's wrong?" Kim asked.

Mark shook his head. "The radios. They're out."

"Out? What do you mean, out?'

"They're dead."

"Dead? Both of them?"

"Yes—I can't find my phone and both radios are cut off. My guess is our friend Travis has been up to no good." Mark looked to Andrea, expression blazing. "What the hell happened?"

Andrea sniffed, eyes wet, still trembling in Kim's arm. She

shook her head slowly. "He came into my cabin . . . attacked me
. . . I ran—he chased me out here. I . . ."

"It's alright," said Kim, seeing Andrea welling up on a total
breakdown. "Let's get you inside."

Mark first checked over the transom and swim platforms,
seeing no sign of Travis, before following the women inside. He
slid the salon door closed and locked it.

Kim helped Andrea onto the U-shaped bench at the table.
Within the past few minutes, *Sabre* had started yawing much
more roughly on her anchor line.

"We need to head in," Kim stated.

Mark did not respond. His mouth was dry with adrenaline,
unease, and too much booze. He went into the galley and
popped the fridge open, pulling out a bottle of Gatorade,
twisting the top off and taking a long pull.

Kim watched the orange fluid drip down Mark's chin. She
repeated, "We need to head—"

"Christ, Kim—I just need to think for a minute," Mark said,
coughing on the drink. He took another swallow and breathed
deeply.

After a moment Kim spoke again, easing her tone. "We
need to find a marina on Captiva and get in."

Mark set the Gatorade on the galley counter. "No. I'm
taking us home."

"What? To Stump Pass?" Kim asked.

"Yes."

"There's a storm coming—"

"I know, that's why we're heading home. I don't know any
marinas on Captiva, and we don't have a radio to call ahead. I'll
stay in front of the storm. I'll take us into Pine Island Sound
and go up the intracoastal. I can have us back home in a couple
of hours."

Kim looked exasperated. "Chad's dead, Mark. We can't head up the intracoastal with him—"

"It's twenty-four hours to report a body on the water, and as the captain—I've been drinking—a lot. I'm not speaking to the police and explaining this all anytime soon."

"Why'd he do it?" Andrea asked unexpectedly, her face stricken with grief and shock. Both Kim and Mark turned to look at her. "Why'd he have to kill Chad?" Distraught, Andrea sniffed and used the heel of her hand to wipe an eye. "I should have just let him . . . I should have just slept with him too."

Kim felt a rush of dismay at Andrea's wording. "It's not your fault," she countered quickly, covering, "this is not because of anything you did." Awkwardly, Kim looked up to Mark. He was staring blankly at Andrea, digesting the implied scenario. Before he could say anything, Kim said, "Hand me that cloth."

Mark remained motionless for a moment, then glanced at Kim, his eyes flashing foul. He retrieved a dishtowel from the galley, bringing it over to her. Kim reached for the towel, facing Mark's icy stare. "I'm going to take Andrea below," she said, "and we need to get Chad inside."

Mark dropped the dishcloth on the table, jaw clenched, expression hostile. "I'll get him."

"Do you need help?" Kim asked.

"No."

As he unlatched the salon door, Kim said, "Be careful. Watch for Travis." Mark did not acknowledge her comment.

Leaving the salon door open, Mark stepped out onto the cockpit, his eye drawn first to Chad, and then across the transom and swim platforms. There was no sign of Travis. The wind was up even more, blowing at more than thirty knots. The line from *End of Watch*'s bow tugged hard at both of *Sabre*'s port and starboard stern cleats. Mark was tempted to cut the

Bayliner loose. His eyes crisscrossed *End of Watch* for any trace or evidence that Travis might have made it aboard. If he hadn't made it on the boat, there was no way he, or anyone, would be swimming into the beach in this offshore wind. Anyone in the water would be blown and carried west, out into the open Gulf. The waves were piling up on each other, peaking at a foot and a half, spray starting to whip from their tops. Streaks of white foam lined the troughs.

With the radios down, there had been no alert or warning about this fast-approaching storm. Mark hoped it was a light squall that would blow over quickly. He was thankful the system appeared to be approaching from the south and not the north, but the wind was coming strong out of the east. This alarmed him for a couple of reasons, it would be a hard crosswind to fight running home, and it pointed to a larger storm system, moving in the classic counterclockwise rotation of a hurricane.

Brushing aside concerns of the weather, he turned to Chad, and started the grim task of hauling the dead man inside.

* * * *

Chad's body lay on the dinette bench in the salon, covered in a bedsheet that Kim brought up from below. Mark had struggled with the deadweight and was relieved to have the man's lifeless face covered. Neither he nor Kim had the nerve to close Chad's eyes.

They all dressed for the day, Kim assisting Andrea in her cabin. No words were spoken. Andrea was numb and appearing in a state of semi-shock. Otherwise, Kim was relieved to see she was unhurt; the blood had not been hers. It appeared Andrea had injured Travis.

Kim stood in the galley, making coffee, barefoot in a sky blue T-shirt and beige Bermuda shorts. *Sabre*'s deck bounced underfoot, more so than she had ever felt the cat move before at anchor. The twin hulls were causing a double jerking snap roll from a choppy beam sea. Andrea sat up forward in one of the helm chairs, bare feet propped up on the seat, staring blankly at the hazy line of Captiva Island through the windscreen. She had on a yellow halter top and charcoal-gray shorts. Mark knelt beside Andrea, examining the fuse panel. He wore khaki boardshorts and a coral-colored T-shirt with the Stump Pass Marina logo on it.

"Shit," he muttered, scowling, "I knew it."

"What is it?" Kim asked.

"The fuse for the radio—it's missing. Gone." Mark stood up, face reddening, and looked aft through the salon to Kim. "That asshole!" He kicked the panel door shut. "I bet he has my phone too. I bet that prick took my phone."

Kim frowned and turned to look through the salon door out at *End of Watch*. "What do we do with his boat? We can move faster if we cut it loose."

Mark shook his head. "No, we need it. We tow it in. That boat is full of proof and evidence of this guy, Travis Gardner—or whoever he really is—his fingerprints are all over it, possessions, ID . . . but I think that boat is probably stolen."

"I think you might be right," Kim replied, looking back towards the helm. She was still avoiding Mark's eyes. Andrea sat huddled in the chair, quiet and motionless. "We need to get going. This storm has come up quickly and it's getting worse."

Mark came aft to the galley. "We have time. This storm is still far off. Let me have a coffee first and we'll get underway."

Kim poured a mug for Mark and slid it across the counter for him. The steaming black liquid swayed along with *Sabre*.

HURRICANE HOLE

"Don't you think we could head in somewhere here? Sanibel certainly has a marina, or Pine Island? What about Tarpon Lodge?"

Mark picked up the mug and blew on it. "I told you, I don't want to go in here. We're going to need to call the police, and I'd rather deal with the police at home. Our police. In Englewood. I know those guys." He sipped the coffee, hoping the brew would clear his head and help him make sense of the situation. He huffed and spoke with a lowered his voice. "Just what in the bloody hell happened this morning?"

Kim did not respond, only shaking her head. Mark blew on the coffee again, took another sip and pressed his thumb and index fingers to his temple.

"Headache?" Kim asked.

"Fuckin' killer," he replied. He dropped his hand and his eyes locked on Kim's face. "We should never have brought this guy onboard."

"That's pretty obvious. Don't spin this around on me now."

"Well, it was you who was all gung-ho to bring him along."

Kim said nothing and Mark took another cautious sip of the coffee. His forehead furrowed and he glanced quickly back at Andrea. A hot flash of sour jealousy coursed through him. His eyes shifted and bored into Kim. "Did you sleep with him?"

Kim was taken aback at the direct question and went on the defensive. "Now is absolutely not the time to discuss this—and I don't want to be the one held responsible for this entire incident—you could have said no if you didn't want him coming aboard your boat."

"Right. That would have made me the real asshole."

"You can be an asshole, Mark. Finish your coffee and let's get the hell out of here." Kim circled curtly around him, out of the galley, heading towards Andrea at the helm. From Mark there was only silence. Kim knew once they were back, they would have a discussion that would likely be the end of this relationship.

Five minutes of silence passed when a lull in the approaching front settled *Sabre* still in the water. Kim had brought Andrea below, to lay down in her cabin, but now she sat back up in the helm chair. She tried not to dwell on the fact that Chad lay dead, shrouded in a bedsheet, not fifteen feet away. Sensing the new stillness, Mark came up from below, looking peculiarly through the windscreen.

"It stopped," Kim said, glancing to Mark questioningly.

"I know," he replied, making his way aft. "It's just a break between bands, but a good chance to get the anchor up. I'm gonna get us underway."

Kim felt a small weight of tension lift from her shoulders.

Mark slid open the salon door and stepped out onto the cockpit. *End of Watch* sat level in the water, the tethering line slack. The wind had eased back to a light breeze, but the direction had shifted again as well, swirling in from the northwest.

The smell hit Mark like a punch in the gut. He almost retched immediately and put his hand over his face. Drawing himself quickly back to stand just outside the salon door, he was thankful when another breath of wind pushed the foul odor away. The stench was unlike anything Mark had ever experienced, a putrid rank that could be only death. It came from one place: *End of Watch*.

"Christ Almighty," Mark said, a hand still covering his face.

Kim turned from the helm, alarmed, feeling her skin prickle. "What is it?"

'It reeks!"

"What?" Kim rose from her seat.

"It bloody stinks out here," Mark replied, "something on that boat smells—bad."

Kim went aft to stand beside Mark at the salon door. "I don't smell anything."

And a moment later, with another shift in the breeze, the odor hit her nose. Her reaction was identical to Mark's. Kim came close to vomiting.

"Oh my God . . ." she said, backing away, forearm over her face.

Grimacing, Mark studied *End of Watch* across the water. "Wait a minute . . ." he said. "Something's not right." He walked across to the transom and stepped down onto the starboard swim platform. Grabbing the line in his hand he pulled out the slack and leaned back, tugging against the weight. Slowly, *End of Watch* moved forward, towards the catamaran, pitching gently on the foot-high waves.

"What're you doing?" Kim asked. Wrinkling her nose and pressing her lips together against the stench, she stepped through the salon door onto the cockpit, crossing to the transom.

Mark was taking in the line quickly as the Bayliner's momentum built. "Before we tow this boat in, and call the police, I want to find out just what the hell that smell is."

Fear crossed Kim's face. "Mark—no. Travis could be on that boat. He could've got onboard—I didn't see where he went."

Mark said nothing and continued to pull in *End of Watch*, the bow just ten feet off their stern now.

"This is not a good idea," Kim continued, and wheeled about into the galley. She found the same fillet knife she had used to drive Travis off into the water. She quickly returned to the cockpit, closing the salon door behind her, stepping down onto the swim platform by Mark's side. The wind had shifted back out of the east again and they were both grateful to be upwind of the Bayliner.

"If the wind changes and I get a whiff of that smell again I'm going to throw up," Kim said, gripping the knife handle.

As the Bayliner's bow nosed up to *Sabre*'s swim platform Mark held the line for Kim. "Here, take this, keep her close."

Kim grasped the line in her free hand. "This is really, really stupid, Mark. We should just tow it in."

"I'm not bringing that boat into our marina—to the police—without knowing first what is onboard." Mark leaned over, reaching up to grab *End of Watch*'s bowsprit. He pulled back hard, using his bodyweight, angling the Bayliner off *Sabre*'s starboard side, running hand over hand along her gunwale, until the portside cockpit came up alongside their swim platform.

A reeking blast of putrefaction hit their nostrils, and they both turned their heads. Kim coughed and gagged, the stench sticking in the back of her throat. With his mouth clamped shut and lips pursed, Mark brought the Bayliner's hull tight against the rear of *Sabre*'s swim platform. Thankfully, another gust from the east carried the worst of the smell away. The wind was returning, another storm band coming straight at *Sabre*'s bow, building quickly.

"Hold her here for a minute," Mark said, hiking a leg over the Bayliner's rail. Kim grabbed the gunwale, and Mark shifted his weight, planting a foot on *End of Watch*'s deck. "Keep your weight on the line, I'll be less than a minute."

Kim nodded, thankful the wind had cut the smell, but the fast-rising breeze was also going to make it difficult to hold *End of Watch* in place. "Hurry," she said.

Mark crossed over the gunwale to stand aboard the Bayliner, the smaller monohull craft rocking under his weight.

HURRICANE HOLE

The cockpit looked just as he had last seen it. The doorway to the cabin was open. The horrific smell, whatever it was, was coming from inside. Mark peered into the darkened cabin, seeing the small galley to starboard and salon table to port. Forward, the bow berth appeared empty.

Cautiously, Mark stepped inside. The stench was overpowering, and he pulled up the chest of his T-shirt to cover his mouth and nose. He felt a rising gorge. The coffee he had drunk was acrid and bitter in the back of his throat, mixed with the awful permeating odor. A trail of dark semi-dried fluid running across the cabin decking caught Mark's eye. He did not recall seeing it there two days ago. His gaze followed it to the source, coming from beneath a hatch in the port bulkhead. The fluid was a black-brown color and had a viscous consistency.

Kim felt the Bayliner start to pull away from *Sabre* in the strengthening blow. She would not be able to hold the boat much longer. The wind was returning to a sustained strong breeze, pushing broadside against *End of Watch*. The hull was pulling away beyond her reach, the bow yawing out to starboard.

"C'mon Mark," Kim muttered in frustration. The Bayliner's bow was continuing to pivot out, her port quarter grinding against *Sabre*'s swim platform. "Dammit . . ." Kim said, sucking in a breath, feeling the fingers of her left hand start to slip. She still held the fillet knife in her right hand, but now she set it down and reached out to grab *End of Watch* with both hands. Fighting the impossible weight of the nearly five-ton boat drifting away, Kim sat back on her haunches, her fingers straining white.

From the new angle and vantage point, she could see the swim ladder on the Bayliner was down.

With his nose crinkled and gritting his teeth behind sealed lips, Mark reached out and unhooked the bulkhead hatch. It popped open an inch from a weight and pressure behind. He looped a finger over the top and flipped the hatch open.

Mark jumped back in shock, eyes widening, taking in a full gasp of gaseous rotten stench. The three-day-old corpse of Robert Halliwell had expanded, filling and soiling the berth, bloated and swollen. His skin had ballooned and pooled a dark crimson purple. Halliwell's eyeballs bulged from their sockets, lips blown up like an over-injected supermodel. The stained T-shirt he wore was now stretched tight, looking three sizes too small.

Hot bile rose in Mark's throat, and he threw up onto the cabin deck.

Backing away, heart hammering adrenaline, he froze at the blood-curling sound of Kim screaming his name.

"Mark!"

Wiping vomit from his mouth, Mark stumbled and whirled for the cabin door, slipping and stumbling barefooted in the dark greasy sludge on the floor. He wanted only to escape from the dark, hot, rank cabin and its grisly cargo.

Kim lost her grip on the Bayliner, the gunwale slipped from her fingertips. Grabbing up the line in a flurry she looked up to see Mark come out of the cabin, his face paled and aghast, a streak of vomit down his chin.

Behind Mark, Travis stepped out from the cabin.

Kim froze in horror. She watched blankly as Travis raised a handgun in slow-motion, pointing it at the back of Mark's head.

Before she could react, a loud crack crossed the ever-widening space between the boats. A splattering mist of blood and brain painted Kim's face. She blinked through the mess, seeing a hair-covered tuft from the back of Mark's scalp flip up. Kim remained fixed for another second, then she dropped the line, half stepping, half falling back onto *Sabre*'s cockpit.

Her right foot shot out and kicked the fillet knife, sending it spinning across the teak deck. It came to rest an inch from the edge of the swim platform. On instinct, not yet even beginning to process Mark's death, she lunged forward and snatched up the knife, ducking back behind the centerline transom as a second gunshot erupted.

The bullet tore into the fiberglass between the twin hulls, punching through and missing Kim's head by a foot. She looked from the hole in the transom over her head to where the bullet had crossed the cockpit and lodged into the pilothouse bulkhead.

"Hey Kim!" Travis called out, his voice playful and taunting, "it looks like it's just me, you, and Andrea now. A picture perfect threesome!"

Kim remained silent, crouched behind the bulwark, eyes wild. Her adrenaline was coursing out of control, clouding her thoughts, having her on the brink of panic. She remembered; *Sabre* was tethered to *End of Watch*. Travis could pull his way back over to her. She needed to cut the Bayliner loose. Edging slowly over to the starboard side, knife gripped in her hand, Kim could feel the deck under her, rolling and pitching harder. The wind was rising, kicking hard from the east, working in her favor, pushing *End of Watch* swiftly away from the catamaran.

"C'mon Kim," Travis's voice carried over the wind, "I'm not going to shoot you, for Chrissake. Come out from there."

Kim ignored him, reaching up with the knife, and began cutting through the line. The fillet knife was razor sharp and made quick work of the braided rope. The starboard line let go, and she felt *Sabre* shift as the Bayliner's weight transferred to the portside cleat.

Travis saw the line spring free, and *End of Watch* immediately fell away more rapidly from the catamaran with the extra slack.

If she cut the other line, quite simply, he was fucked. Bracing himself against the Bayliner's gunwale, Travis held the gun pointed at where Kim hid behind the cat's transom.

"Kim! Listen to me . . . I'm not going to hurt you or Andrea. I promise. Do not cut that line."

Staying low behind the transom, Kim went on hands and knees to the port cleat and started slicing through the line's fibers, watching them snap and fray apart under the high tension.

"Kim—don't you dare cut that goddamn line! You hear me? I said I'm not going to hurt you."

A few seconds later a bullet slammed into the pilothouse wall directly over her head with a resounding thud. Wincing, eyes watering, she kept sawing fiercely at the line. It let go with a splitting pop. *End of Watch* jerked free from the tether, leaving *Sabre* bobbing in the rising swells.

"You bitch!" Travis bellowed. "You fuckin' bitch!"

Already his voice sounded more distant. The wind, now bordering on a gale, would carry the Bayliner quickly away from the anchored cat. Kim remained low behind the transom as another shot rang out, muffled by the wind. The bullet passed again directly over her head and smacked into the salon door. Kim shielded her face, and lay flat on her stomach on the deck, eyes closed.

On *End of Watch*, Travis had to work to keep his balance in the cockpit, seeing the catamaran fall away. His aim on the pitching and rolling boat and the rapidly widening distance had him not waste another shot. He had already fired three times at the cat, missing Kim with them all. He was smart enough not to use up the remaining rounds. He was going to need them.

His hand throbbed from where Andrea had bit it, still seeping fresh blood.

HURRICANE HOLE

The wind came in gusts, whipping across the Gulf, spraying saltwater and foam over the building peaks and troughs. The sky to the south was an ominous black, and already to the east, past *Sabre*, Captiva Island was disappearing in swirling cloud and mist. He did not need a weather update. It was clear the storm had moved from the Caribbean north into the Gulf of Mexico. Travis was stranded on a dead boat in the direct path of a fast approaching hurricane.

The first drops of rain began to spatter across his face.

CHAPTER TEN

Before she dared move, Kim waited a full three minutes collapsed behind the bulwark, lying prone on the deck. Her breathing had not slowed, she was taking in large gasping lungfuls, hyperventilating. Droplets of rain roused her from slipping into a state of shock. She sat up and peered cautiously around the side of the centerline transom, out over the port swim platform. Under the increasing overcast sky, the water's surface had transitioned to a muted emerald-gray color. End of Watch was already three-quarters of a mile distant. Kim could not make out Travis anywhere onboard. The boat was drifting away bow first, pitching and rolling hard, pushed west into the open expanse of the Gulf of Mexico

Grabbing a cleat to pull herself to her feet, Kim turned for the salon door and wavered a moment. Just above waist height was a perfectly round hole an inch wide, punched through the glass. Kim slid open the door and stepped into the salon, slamming the door shut behind her, latching it tight. She braced herself against the galley counter, taking a few deep breaths of the dry, cool air, working on slowing her breathing. *Sabre's* deck was rocking harder under her feet, and bouncing, the bow fighting against the anchor line.

Kim slowed her thoughts and focused, formulating a step-by-step plan. She needed to get off the open water of the Gulf and head inshore, and find a marina, a harbor, or a hole to escape and ride out this storm. She had little experience with boats and had only piloted *Sabre* a few times with Mark by her side. And that had been only on clear calm days.

Kim made her way forward to the helm, bracing herself off the galley counter and grabrails. As she passed the stairs down to the guest cabins, she called down loudly: "Andrea! Andrea—get up here now!"

Through the windscreen any sign of Captiva had dissolved into a blur of cloud, rain, and blowing spray, foam and froth whipping across choppy waves peaking at three feet in height. Kim scanned the helm controls, recognizing the basics and familiarizing herself with the console. She turned the starboard ignition key and felt encouraged to hear and feel the diesel engine fire up. The port engine followed suit, also rumbling quickly to life, the twin inboards humming confidently underfoot.

Kim turned to see Andrea come up from below, looking grief stricken, bewildered, and confused. "We have a problem. Have a seat," Kim said, nodding to the second helm chair.

Andrea's neck had darkened and blotched a deep red where Travis's hands had strangled her. She slid off-balance into the starboard helm chair and looked at Kim, her face quickly shifting to a darkly disturbed expression. "My God," she asked, "what's on your face?"

Kim lifted a hand to her cheek, felt wetness and pulled it away to see slick bright red blood across her fingertips. Blood, and something else. Horrified, her stomach turning, she quickly wiped her fingers on her shorts.

"What is it? Where's Mark?" Andrea asked.

Kim didn't answer. Her eye had caught that the GPS and radar display to the right of the wheel were both dark. In the center of the LCD monitor was a circular indent, the screen cracked and split in a spiderweb pattern.

"Shit," Kim murmured, staring dully at the screen, comprehending in disbelief. "I don't believe it." The bullet that had gone through the cockpit door had traversed the salon and destroyed the GPS display at the helm.

"What is it? Where is Mark?" Andrea asked again.

Kim looked directly at her friend. "Mark didn't make it. He's dead, Andrea."

Andrea's face twisted into a mask of dread. She shook her head. "Dead? What? How? I thought I heard—were those gunshots? Is Travis here?"

"No. Travis isn't here. He's gone, he can't hurt us. He was on his boat—I cut it loose, he's gone."

Andrea's eyes were staring wide and glistening wet. She turned to look aft, through the salon door. "But—Mark's dead? What happened?"

Kim shook her head. "It doesn't matter right now. We need to get the hell out of here. I want you to just sit tight and hold on. I've got to get us into the sound—behind Captiva. This storm is getting bad very fast."

Andrea peered through the windscreen, seeming to notice the surrounding storm for the first time. Rain and salt spray pelted the glass and Kim flipped on the windscreen wipers. She could not discern any land whatsoever, just a tumultuous sea—shades of gray, white, and green. The compass told her they were facing due east. On that bearing they should hit Captiva directly ahead; they were only a couple of miles offshore.

Kim found the electric windlass switch and flipped it on to raise the anchor. There was a low complaining whine from the bow. The motor was straining to reel in the anchor line, the catamaran held aft by the wind. Kim shifted the engines into gear and nudged the throttle, moving the catamaran forward. She had to give it some power to press ahead into the headwind. The waves were already breaking over the twin bow pulpits.

HURRICANE HOLE

With the tension off the anchor line, she hit the windless again and the line started reeling in. Kim brought the cat forward until she felt the anchor pull free from the sand bottom. Immediately the boat was pushed sideways, yawing to starboard, the wind and waves hitting her broadside. Kim spun the wheel to port and pushed the throttles forward. The cat ploughed ahead, and the bow swung—resisting—back into the headwind. She heard the windless stop and the dull clunk of the anchor raised into the centerline under the bow deck.

They were loose, and at the mercy of the elements, *Sabre* under Kim's command. Eyes flicking between the compass and the invisible horizon, Kim braced her legs wide and rose on tiptoes to keep balance and see better, both hands on the wheel, fighting the driving headwind that tried to throw the bow to either side. Andrea clung to the helm seat with both hands, eyes staring blanky through the windscreen.

After a minute of pushing forward, the bow climbing each swell, stern pitching up as they crossed the peak and fell into the following trough, Andrea asked, "Where are we headed?"

Kim shook her head. "I'm not sure. Onto the other side of Captiva, into Pine Island Sound to start. We can't stay on the Gulf. We'll have to try and find a marina, or somewhere to anchor. We've got no radio or GPS, just the compass. If we keep heading due east, we should see Captiva soon. Help me keep an eye out for the island."

Andrea resigned herself silently, curling up in the helm seat, bracing herself against the console. *Sabre* was starting to pitch viciously, her bow climbing and dropping over growing rollers. Kim's alarm grew at the strength of the wind and size of the coming swells. The offshore waves were topping out at eight feet in height, the crests blown off into spindrift. The surface of the Gulf was streaked with long trails of foam running in line with the wind, the water a slate gray. The rain was coming in slashing torrents, the windscreen wipers barely keeping up now. Visibility was down to a quarter mile.

Kim knew they had been anchored two miles out from Redfish Pass. If she kept their course due east, she might be able to locate the pass and slip through, between Captiva and North Captiva, into the shelter of the sound. In this squall, there was no question Pine Island Sound was going to be kicked up hard as well, and not provide much respite, but it was far better than the open Gulf of Mexico.

The wind was gusting to gale force, now throwing *Sabre*'s bow to port, the compass constantly spinning off to northeast. Kim guessed the wind had shifted slightly, coming more out of the southeast. She had to keep the wheel chocked hard to starboard to keep them from broaching.

"Just where the hell did this come from?" Kim voiced the recurring question in her head aloud. She felt a quick flash of anger at Mark, followed by guilt and sorrow. She pushed the horrific vision of the bullet tearing into the back of Mark's head from her mind, trying to focus only on handling the catamaran.

Sabre rode over a massive swell, the wind pivoting the cat on the crest, again pushing the bow hard to port. Sliding down the backside into the trough Kim felt the cat broach and saw the compass spin due north. Coming atop the next wave the wind was going to be hitting them fully broadside. The catamaran had a wide stable beam, but every vessel had its limits.

As they rode up the front of the next swell, Kim hung onto the wheel, bracing the back of her legs against the helm seat. Andrea had almost been thrown from her chair and slid off the seat to stand, taking a similar position to Kim. She gripped a grabrail above the helm with both hands, knuckles white. *Sabre* crested the towering peak and all but fell down the backside.

HURRICANE HOLE

There was a dull hollow thump from behind them. Both women turned to see Chad's body had been thrown from the dinette bench, landing on the deck under the table. He lay splayed out, half unwrapped from the bedsheet, rolling up against the table stand. His eyes were open, staring . . . Andrea began to let out a low whine, her face a veil of horror.

"Don't look," Kim said, fighting her own revulsion, looking from Chad's staring eyes to her friend. "It's OK. Hey—Andrea—look at me." Andrea's teared, pained, and terrified eyes left her dead boyfriend and found Kim's. "All I need you to do is hang on and keep a watch out the window with me. Can you do that?" Andrea nodded slowly and Kim had to immediately return her concentration to handling the seas.

As *Sabre* came over the next crest Kim felt no control in the wheel and the catamaran continued to rotate. The craft spun, pitched, and came down the backside of the massive swell stern first. When the stern dug into the trough Andrea's feet went out from under her and she fell backwards, glancing off the helm seat, into the starboard bulkhead, hitting the canted deck hard.

Kim was slammed back into the helm chair, and pitched sideways, but kept her footing, both hands letting go of the wheel and hanging onto the overhead grabrail. Seeing Andrea fall out of the corner of her eye, Kim heard her cry out. Terrified, the cat circling wildly, she hammered both throttles full ahead with the wheel hard to starboard, to try and get *Sabre* hove to. The cat was wallowing in the trough of an overtaking sea. *Sabre* rode up the next swell stern first this time, sending Andrea sliding forward into the helm bulkhead. Thrown forward, it took all of Kim's focus and three more sets of swells to get *Sabre* back onto a bow sea, on an easterly heading. Through forced trial and error Kim figured it out, learning to ease off the throttles on the backside of a swell to keep control and not stuff the bow and lose lateral control in the trough. She ignored the repeated *thumps* from the rear of the salon—Chad's body being tossed about. It was several minutes before Kim could look to where Andrea lay on the deck, awkwardly mashed forward against the helm.

"Can you get up?" Kim asked, one eye on her friend, the other on the sets of oncoming waves.

"My ankle—I twisted it—bad," Andrea replied, gasping. Her face clenched in pain, she was bracing herself against the helm panel and starboard bulkhead, one hand grasping her leg above her right ankle.

"Dammit," Kim said. "Alright, just stay there, we'll be at the island soon."

Kim had no idea how much distance they had covered. They should be nearing Captiva anytime now, and the waves would be less severe in the lee of the barrier island. Her arms and legs were burning with the effort of keeping the compass due east while staying balanced on her feet. Every minute or so she would glance down to check on Andrea. Her friend was clearly in pain, gripping her ankle. The strangle marks around Andrea's neck were transitioning to an even deeper maroon. Kim could see where Travis's individual fingers had dug into her throat.

The swells remained a constant barrage, topping at out ten feet, and the wind was increasing in speed, severely lashing the catamaran. Rain came in non-stop driving bands, thick droplets hammering deafeningly loud into the windscreen. Visibility had dropped off to less than a hundred yards, and Kim could not discern any boundary between water and sky. Out beyond the bow was just a gray-white swirling blur of whipping sea spray and blowing foam. There would be no way to find the pass unless she came directly upon it.

HURRICANE HOLE

The wind gusts were terrifying, it seemed as if *Sabre's* pilothouse might be ripped from her decks. The gale howled through the railings and flybridge overhead. Coming over top of another spindrift crest, Kim felt a shaking and rattling from above, followed by the twisting pop of metal snapping. Riding the backside of a swell she turned around to see the entire canvas Bimini top had broken free and was tumbling over the transom, falling, and spinning off into the whitewash behind them. It sounded as if the vessel was being ripped apart at the seams.

"What the hell was that?" Andrea asked, looking wide-eyed at the overhead, her face filled with dread.

"We just lost the Bimini top," Kim replied as calm and coolly as she could. First thoughts began to cross her mind that this tempest was not just a late summer gale or tropical storm that was going to pass over quickly. These winds were damn close to, if not, hurricane force.

Kim was successfully keeping their heading east, but an innate compass told her they were also being pushed north. The cat was steadily being shifted broadside from the incredible wind. Just how much was impossible to tell. The sky was darkening further, off to the south it was charcoal black, the thick clouds taking the appearance of boiling oil. Dead ahead it had taken on a dark bruised purple color—Kim noted, ironically, looking like the coloring on Andrea's throat.

This surreal and terrifying scene changed Kim's mind; she no longer had any intention of trying to locate Redfish Pass and enter Pine Island Sound. At the first sign of land, she was going to beach the catamaran—any port in a storm. She prayed whatever amount of surf break existed it was going to be navigable to get the cat up on the sand, and they could get off the boat safely. If the swells grew any larger there was a serious possibility the catamaran could be capsized. It only occurred to Kim now to think of lifejackets, and she did not even know where they were kept. Again, she silently accursed Mark.

Riding a wash of fear, pain and regret, an object ahead caught her eye. Kim squinted, and the object disappeared as they dropped down the backside of another swell. Throttling up the frontside of the next wave, in frustration, Kim searched the tempest and saw it again—a coconut palm. The resilient tree was bent over in the wind at a forty-five degree angle towards *Sabre*, its fronds whipping violently. Kim felt a massive wash of relief at sighting land and cried out: "I see the island!"

Lying haphazardly on the deck ay Kim's feet, Andrea let out a sob of reprieve, her face white, eyes wet. She had wedged herself between the front of her helm seat and the console, one hand still grasping her ankle, the other around the base of the chair. "Brace yourself and hang on," Kim said, "I'm going to put us in on the beach."

Kim could only guess how far out they were from the sandbar shallows, maybe two or three hundred feet. The palm tree disappeared again behind another swell and riding the top of the next crest Kim could make out the beach, a run of dunes barely visible through the driving rain. Large, rolling, and breaking waves were crashing onto the sand, but they were less than half the size of the open water Gulf swells. The wind was blowing offshore, flattening out the surf break, working in their favor.

Her intention was to drive *Sabre* as high up onto the sand as possible. Kim gritted her teeth, readying herself, unsure how the cat was going to respond upon hitting the beach. After climbing and descending three more rolling sets of swells the waves began to fall off. The pitching subsided as they moved into shallower, calmer water. Kim could now clearly see the backside of breaking waves rolling in and crashing up onto the sand. The surf was rough, but the cat looked to easily be able to power through.

Her mouth set in a hard line, Kim throttled up both engines and aimed *Sabre* directly at the palm tree, using it as a target. The beach was void of any people or structures, just a line of dune backed by thick sea grape and palms. Straining to see through bands of rain, Kim worked the wheel to keep the bow headed at the tree. She felt the bow pitch again as they came upon the first roller, the wave broke under their hull, the momentum now assisting in pushing *Sabre* forward against the wind. A second roller hit the stern, lifting *Sabre* up, giving her a boost. Kim cut the throttles to half, and let the waves do the work, they had plenty of forward speed.

Through wipers wicking away heavy blown foam she watched the line of sand disappear under the bow. Kim stiffened for the impact and called out, "Hang on! We're on the beach!"

First came a grating rushing sound as the hulls slid up onto the sloping pan. This quickly changed to a grinding and vibrating crunch as the twin propellers dug into the sand. *Sabre* was driven high onto the beach, her forward half clear out of the crashing surf. A fountain of roiling water, foam, and sand churned up at her transom as the props chewed into the bottom, and the engines stalled out.

Kim was thrown forward over the wheel, whacking an elbow as the cat came to a complete stop. Righting herself, she looked down to check on Andrea. Her friend had been protected from any forward momentum, secure against the helm bulkhead, save for sustaining a solid bump on the head.

"Are you OK?" Kim asked.

Andrea nodded, wincing, and shaking her head. "Yeah."

"How's your ankle?"

"Not good."

"Do you think you can walk on it? We need to get off the boat and find shelter somewhere."

"I think so . . . do I have a choice?"

Kim gave Andrea a weak but encouraging smile and shook her head.

The incoming waves slapped *Sabre*'s stern and rocked the cat, shifting her around on the pan. Kim powered down the ignition, the wipers stopped, and AC fans quit running. The wind was impossibly louder now, and thundering rain plastered the pilothouse roof. Out the windscreen cascading rainwater dissolved the view to a blurred running wash. Kim looked to where Chad lay on the deck, twisted up and wrapped around the leg of the salon table, still half-covered in a bedsheet. The sheet did not cover his slack blank face. There was nothing they could do for him now; they would have to leave him where he was.

"C'mon," Kim said, bending to help her friend to her feet, "let's get you up." Andrea's ankle was not showing any signs of injury, but it was painful for her to put any weight on it. Kim looped Andrea's right arm around her shoulders and helped get her up off the deck.

Both women were barefoot, and Kim had decided quickly they would not need to bring shoes or much of anything else. Getting off the catamaran and finding shelter was a priority. Both the bow and stern were too dangerous to exit from. The stern was being pummeled with non-stop sets of incoming waves that shifted *Sabre* with each impact. The canted bow rested a good ten feet off the sand. Too high to jump from safely, even with healthy ankles.

"We're going to get off the side," Kim said, assisting Andrea aft through the salon. Andrea could only hop, putting little weight on her sprained ankle. As they passed Chad, Kim felt Andrea look to the body and tense.

"We can't leave Chad here," Andrea said, hesitating. "I know, he's dead, but—"

"There's nothing we can do for him right now," Kim said as gently as she could. "He's alright where he is, Andrea. We'll come back for him."

With Andrea hanging off her shoulder, Kim slid open the salon door to the full brunt of the hurricane. The east wind ran *Sabre* bow to stern, shrieking through her railings, and yowling around the pilothouse. The rain came in billowing blasts, driven at an angle near parallel to the ground.

"Hold onto me," Kim said, squinting her eyes against the gale. Together they stepped out onto the cockpit deck, in the lee of the pilothouse. Kim slid the salon door closed behind them. Before she stepped around the flybridge stairs and into the portside companionway, Kim knew it was going to be bad. When they came out of the lee and into the full onslaught of the storm it was worse than bad—the wind and rain was mixed with sand flayed from the beach, the grains blasting their faces and exposed skin. Barely able to open her eyes, Kim led them forward up the companionway, away from the stern which was being slammed with crashing surf. Kim found a point amidships that looked best to disembark. The deck was still a good five feet above the sand.

Kim went first, stepping up over the rail, feet on the gunwale, turning to face Andrea. She had to shout over the wind. 'Let me get down first, then I'll help you."

Andrea only nodded in reply, half-blinded. Both women could barely see, having to keep their eyes closed against the stinging sand. Kim lowered herself down, sliding a foot against the hull until she could let go of the bottom rail, and drop to the beach. She looked up to Andrea, her voice raised to a shout over the gale. "Now you."

Andrea gingerly crossed over the rail, balancing on the gunwale on the balls of her feet, gusts of wind full of rain and sand rocking her off kilter. Slowly, watching Kim below her, Andrea eased herself down, dangling her bad right ankle, and using her left foot to slide down the hull as Kim had done.

Kim had her arms up, reaching for her friend, guiding her. "Drop and I'll catch you, fall onto your good leg."

Andrea only hesitated a moment before letting go, fully trusting, dropping into her friend's arms. Kim caught Andrea and took her weight. Andrea was able to land on her uninjured foot, favoring her right with Kim's support. They leaned against the hull together for a brief respite.

"Let's get up the beach and into the cover of those trees," Kim said. Sand stuck to her lips, grains in her mouth, grating between the enamel of her teeth. Together, Kim assisting Andrea, they hobbled up the sloping pan, onto the wide open beach. The sand was combed flat by the wind, raked across their shins, stinging. Through scrunched eyes, Kim scanned the beach again and saw no buildings of any kind. She guessed they must be on the north side of Redfish Pass, having landed on North Captiva Island. North Captiva was only accessible by boat and small aircraft, and sparsely inhabited, with only a scattering of remote houses. From vague memory she knew the homes were all concentrated at the north end, and it could be a hike to reach them depending on how far south they had come ashore.

There was also the possibility the island was evacuated in advance of this storm. Kim had no idea what kind of notice people received, any watches or warnings, or what the full scale of this storm was.

HURRICANE HOLE

As they neared the top of the beach the blowing sand abated, the wind cut to some degree by the cover of the trees and foliage. Kim led Andrea up a small dune, covered thick with blowing sea oats, under an overhang of sea grape. They were careful to stay clear of the lashing branches. Here she took a moment to try and clear sand from her eyes and look back at *Sabre*. The catamaran sat high in the waves that broke behind the stern and rushed up along her hulls. She was mostly undamaged and would likely ride out the storm securely on the beach.

"Where do we go now?" asked Andrea, looking wildly up and down the beach. Granules of sand clung to her wet face, her voice strained and shaky. "What do we do? We can't stay here."

Kim jerked her head away from a blowing sea grape branch to look up the beach. To their north about forty feet, stood the large coconut palm she had sighted from the water. Any homes would be to the northern end of the island. "Let's head this way, up the beach. We'll find a house . . . shelter, someone to help us," Kim said. Saying this she knew they were most probably on their own; feeling for sure now any home on North Captiva would likely have been abandoned, in advance of the storm.

With Andrea hobbling beside her, Kim started them along the beach, grateful to be on the leeward side of the dune and the island's interior scrub. Kim kept a wary eye out as they passed the solitary coconut palm, its trunk waving and bending wildly in the gusts. The tree was bare of any fruit; any coconuts had already been ripped loose and carried off by the gale. Behind the palm, an open expanse of sea oats was bent almost flat by the wind, lying across sprawling railroad vine running underfoot down the dune and onto the beach.

Across the span of sea oats on the windward dune slack, a structure caught Kim's eye. Nestled deep in the blowing hammock of live oaks she saw a flash of wood stairs and a screened porch. There was what looked to be a cabin, high in the growth, set back at least a hundred feet from the dune. Immediately Kim started to look for an access path. Any beachfront house would have a trail or boardwalk cut through the sea oats and dune to reach the water. Sure enough, twenty paces ahead there was an opening, a sandy footpath splitting the dune.

"Here," Kim said brusquely, guiding Andrea ahead. "It's a path. I see a house."

Andrea followed Kim's guidance blindly. Her ankle was throbbing with each half step, bruised throat aching, whipped by rain, back-to-back wind gusts nearly toppling her. Grains of sand blasted around their bare legs, leaving skin reddened as they left the lee of the dune and turned up the path through the strand of lashing sea oats. Ahead the hammock was a thick cover of foliage, a closed canopy of cabbage palm and live oak, thrashing wildly in the wind. The trail cut straight into the hammock, bordered by dense ferns, coral bean trees, and wild coffee.

Moving into the interior the wind and daylight were dampened considerably. Covering thirty feet of the trail, they came upon a large twisting gumbo limbo tree, and directly behind it was a stilt structure. The women paused to look up at the construction. It was a large rustic cabin, the framework set high in the surrounding canopy upon massive post beams. In the open space beneath the cabin hung a pair of kayaks and paddles, along with a BBQ, piles of lumber, and an array of tools for woodworking and landscaping. The roof was peaked in the middle, and the entire front was a doublewide screened-in porch. A set of plank handrailed stairs rose to a wood-framed screen door. There were no lights on, or any other sign of anyone being home.

"Let's go," Kim said, starting them forward again. The wind still penetrated and carved through the hammock, tunneling under the structure, tumbling freshly torn leaves and small branches at them. They set out up the stairs, gripping the weathered railing, worn smooth by use and time. The wood steps were wet and slick, and Kim cautioned Andrea to watch her footing, assisting her up the flight. The porch sat high, a good dozen feet above the ground. Reaching the top landing Kim found that the screen door latch was padlocked shut.

"Is anyone here!" Kim called out futilely. "Hello!"

There was no response. Without hesitating more than a few moments, Kim had Andrea support herself against the railing, and she put a foot through the lower screen. The material split open easily. Kim dropped to her knees and quickly tore the gap in the screen apart, ripping open a passage big enough for them to slip through.

Kim looked up to Andrea. "Come on, you first . . . I'll help you."

Andrea carefully knelt herself down and crawled through the opening into the porch. Kim followed suit on Andrea's heels. Inside the porch she stood and helped Andrea to her feet. The porch was large, full of rustic island knick-knacks, tropical decor, and bric-à-brac. At the far end was a high round table and chairs, and the back wall was a row of large windows, looking through to the inside of the cabin. The porch interior was dim, and the cabin through the windows was dark—the overcast conditions and the surrounding hammock left little light.

Kim crossed to the front door and gave the handle a pull. Unlocked, the door swung open easily. Kim peered into the cabin, Andrea hobbling over to join her. In the low light they could make out that the inside was one large single open room, chock full of belongings, but neat and tidy, everything in its place. Along the right wall were two beds, in the rear corner one quite large, and towards the front, against the porch windows was a bunkbed. Both beds were neatly made. The entire left wall was the kitchen; sink, stove, refrigerator, and one long run of countertop. Above the counter homemade shelving was cram-packed with items of every sort: dishes, utensils, shells, carvings, dozens of empty wine and liquor bottles. The rear wall was a bank of large windows, like the front of the cabin. A large kitchen table and six chairs sat in the center of the room. Someone had been residing or coming out here regularly, for years. The place had a lived-in and cared-for feel, and the smell of old cabin, but it was an inviting earth and wood smell, not dank or musty. Yet, Kim got the feeling the people who owned the place had not been here in a while. They had not left recently to flee the storm.

"Let's get you off your feet," Kim said, "and take a look at that ankle."

They stepped into the cabin, feeling an elevated sense of safety and security being off the water and inside a home. Shelter from the storm. Andrea hobbled gingerly to a chair that Kim pulled out for her and sat down. Kim kneeled to look at Andrea's leg. Like her own, Andrea's skin was welted and braised red from the windblown sand. Her ankle was showing some light swelling. That, coupled with the fact she could still put some weight on it, had Kim hopefully guessing it was a mild sprain.

Kim said, "It's doesn't look too bad."

"It hurts like bloody hell," Andrea shot back curtly.

"I'll see if I can find some ice for it, and some water for us to

HURRICANE HOLE

drink. And maybe if we're really lucky, a phone." Kim stood and Andrea reached to grab her hand before she could turn away. Kim looked down at her friend. Andrea said nothing, but her eyes—pained and distraught—told all. She looked to be on the verge of a total breakdown.

"I know," Kim said, her voice quiet, gently squeezing Andrea's hand. "It's going to be alright. We're safe here . . . we're out of the storm. It's going to pass soon now. We're going to sort this all out and get help."

Andrea only nodded, sniffing and wiping her nose, reluctantly letting go of Kim's hand.

Kim scanned the cabin over for a phone . . . the bedside tables, kitchen counter, walls. She could not see one anywhere and wondered if the cabin had a phone line. She crossed to the fridge and was dismayed to find it empty, dark, and warm inside. She tried the kitchen tap and nothing happened. There must be a generator for power. If she could find it and start it up, they'd at least have lights, fans, and running water. And eventually, ice.

The far left corner of the cabin was walled off and opening a door Kim found that she had guessed correctly: it was the bathroom. A clock on the wall outside the bathroom door read quarter after three. Kim was shocked how much time had passed, and how late in the day it was. The storm was still raging outside and had not let up. In fact, it seemed to have strengthened. The windowpanes along the rear of the cabin were rocking in their frames. They faced east, taking the full brunt of the wind head-on. Kim was certain the tempest would start to pass and abate soon.

Looking around some more she saw a calendar tacked to the side of the kitchen shelving. It was for the previous month—July 2004—someone had been here within the past month. She turned to the opposite far wall behind the beds and viewed dozens of photos that looked to be all a large family—smiling sunburnt faces, taking part in fishing, boating, and various island adventures over the years. Some of the photos were dated, going back decades. Kim discerned the main couple, likely the owners of the cabin, and what she guessed was their children, and young grandchildren. Looking from photo to photo, Kim could see the children sprouting up, everyone growing, aging. She could only speculate how upset they might be when they found their tropical island hideaway was broken into.

Remembering Andrea, Kim turned and went into the bathroom. Inside a medicine cabinet she found a half-full bottle of Advil. Grabbing the bottle, she was about to leave the bathroom when she looked upon another framed photo. It was the same couple, a lot younger, together in front of what was clearly this cabin. Hand-painted on the frame were the words: 'Cayo Costa, Summer 1982'.

Frowning curiously and cocking her head, Kim left the bathroom and backtracked swiftly through the cabin, past Andrea. Still seated, Andrea watched Kim pass her by. "What is it?" she asked, alarmed.

Kim did not answer, heading back out onto the front porch. She turned to look up at the wall above the windows. A large dusty hand-painted sign set back high in the rafters had indistinctly caught her eye when they had first entered the porch, but what was inscribed upon it did not fully register. In colorful letters, bookended by palm trees and a sunset, was a painted welcome sign, revealing the cabin's location, along with a pair of latitude and longitude coordinates.

"Kim, what is it?" Andrea called out again, more loudly, concern in her voice. A moment later Kim stepped back inside the front door of the cabin, staring at Andrea with a blank expression.

Kim slowly shook her head and slumped against the doorframe. "We're not on North Captiva. We're on Cayo Costa."

PART FOUR

CAYO COSTA

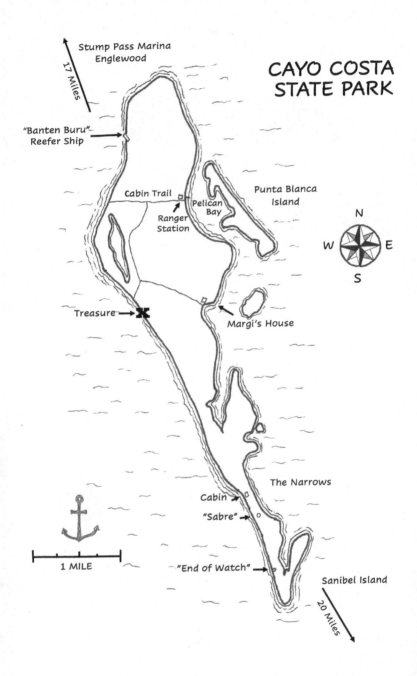

CAYO COSTA
STATE PARK

Stump Pass Marina
Englewood

17 Miles

"Banten Buru"
Reefer Ship

Cabin Trail

Ranger
Station

Pelican
Bay

Punta Blanca
Island

N

W   E

S

Treasure ➝ ✖

Margi's House

The Narrows

Cabin ➝

"Sabre" ➝

"End of Watch" ➝

Sanibel Island

20 Miles

1 MILE

CHAPTER ELEVEN

Kim pulled a bottle of rum down from the kitchen shelf and paused absently to watch a large shiny reddish-brown cockroach scurry away for cover. Back-to-back gusts of wind were rocking the cabin on its stilts. Limbs and leaves from the surrounding hammock thrashed wildly, scraping against the walls. The windows vibrated in their frames and the porch screens rippled savagely. Daylight was falling further away; it was almost as dark as night outside under the thick overcast. Finding a glass, Kim poured a wallop of the dark amber liquor. Shaking four Advil caplets out into a cupped hand, she brought the drink over to Andrea and knelt beside her at the kitchen table.

Kim slid the glass across the table and held out her hand. "Here, take these."

"With rum?" Andrea asked, a hand rubbing gently at her throat.

"It's all we've got—and I think you could use it. The ibuprofen will help keep the swelling down in your ankle."

Kim watched Andrea wash the caplets down and purse her lips, letting out a sharp breath at the heat of the neat rum.

"I'm going to see if I can get the generator started," Kim said, "and maybe we can get some lights and running water."

"What about a phone?"

"I didn't see one anywhere. I don't think Cayo Costa even has phone lines running out here."

"Just where exactly are we?" Andrea asked.

"Well, we missed North Captiva. We must have been pushed by the wind, across Captiva Pass. We're on the next island to the north—Cayo Costa."

"What does that mean?"

"It means, we're probably alone on this island. It's a state park, and there's no bridge from the mainland. There aren't any homes, just some cabins like this one." Kim tried to recall the layout of the island; it had been years since she was out here. "There's a ranger station and docks, but they're up at the north end, and over on the bay side. With this storm, it's likely everyone left the island well in advance. They would have definitely closed the park."

"Whose cabin is this?" Andrea asked, casting another glance around.

Kim looked over her shoulder to the photos on the wall. "I think it belongs to a family. I had heard that a few older properties were grandfathered in when they created the state park. This must be one of them." Kim stood and looked down at her friend. Andrea was still soaked through, hair dripping, skin spattered with wet sand. "I think it's time we got dried off and cleaned up. We might be here for a bit, until this storm passes."

"How long will that be?"

"I'm not sure, but this must be the peak of it now. It's moving across."

Kim went into the bathroom and returned a minute later carrying a couple of towels. She handed one to Andrea. "Wipe off, you're soaked," Kim set the other towel down. "OK, I'm gonna see about getting us some power and lights."

"The storm's getting worse," Andrea said, shaking her head, glancing warily up at the ceiling as she gently toweled her neck. "Are we safe in here?"

"I think so, this cabin's been here for decades. It's been through worse storms than this." Kim started for the door. "Sip that rum—when I get back, I'll join you for one myself. Maybe two." She stopped at the doorway and turned to look back, forcing a smile. "Hey . . . we're gonna be alright." Kim was reassured some when Andrea returned her a faint smile.

The wind was strong enough now that it had knocked over and blown around all trappings on the porch; driftwood, shells, glass bottles, and coconuts lay scattered. A bundle of fishing rods and a net had been strewn across the wood deck, the high breakfast table cleared bare, all four chairs pushed around.

Kim crossed to the front door and ducked through the torn gap in the screen. Squinting against the gale, bracing herself with the handrails, she descended the slick wood steps, careful to not slip in bare feet. Circling around the side of the cabin she was back into the full bore tempest, the wind and blown debris blinding and dangerous. Reaching out a hand to grasp a thick post beam for support, she ducked under the cabin and saw it sat high on nine of these pilings, each a foot thick, embedded deeply in a concrete anchor and limestone gravel base. Someone had constructed this cabin well, to withstand tropical storms like this. At the rear of the structure she spotted a large plywood box with a power cable running up a piling into the flooring overhead. The box had a large, slatted vent to one side.

The generator.

Having to lean against the wind, Kim crossed the length of the cabin, going from piling to piling for balance, passing under the kayaks, and came around to face the front of the generator box. She stumbled, almost knocked off her feet by a gust stronger than any she had felt yet. The blasting squall tore through a barrier of mangroves at the rear of the cabin, ripping away leaves, dozens of branches snapping and letting go one after another, lashing her from behind.

Pushed forward up against the box, Kim fought to lift the lid. Inching it up by a metal handle, the wind caught the underside of the lid, flipping it open violently, ripping it from her hand. The edge of the plywood narrowly missed smashing into her face. Unless the wind abated, it would be impossible to reclose the lid.

Inside the box was a 4000-watt gasoline-powered generator. Kim knew the basics of starting one up. She was going to need to get this thing going—and get back upstairs, fast. The wind was no longer gusting, it was transitioning into one steady ripping blow. The storm was not yet at its peak . . .

Whoever owned the cabin likely used the generator as recently as a month ago. Kim was betting it had fuel in it, and the fuel was good. Flipping the main switch on and closing the choke, Kim grabbed the recoil cord and gave it a yank. It was harder to pull than she had expected. The engine turned once but did not fire. She tried twice more, getting some momentum, but still nothing.

Eyes tearing from the wind, blurring her vision, a melee of rain, leaves, sticks, dirt, shells, and gravel railing and pelting her back and legs, Kim made the quick decision to bail on the generator. She would ride out the storm and try to get them power after it passed.

The sound of the wind grew in volume, deepening. The storm's presence was pressing, heavy and threatening. The spray and spindrift coming though the mangroves off the bay was salty on her lips. A massive resounding crack of splitting wood spurred Kim into action—she dropped the recoil cord and set out back under the cabin, pushed forward by a powerful tail wind. Overhead the kayaks jostled and bumped wildly, as if they were fighting invisible rapids, paddled by ghosts.

The wind was shifting from whining moaning gusts to a howling deafening roar. The gale was so loud it drowned out even the sound of mature live oak limbs snapping like twigs all around. Kim's heart thudded; her chest tight with sharply rising fear. As she came flying out from under the front of the cabin, circling towards the stairs, the surrounding hammock canopy seemed to explode. A concussive blast shot through the trees, seeming to tear every last remaining leaf from the branches in one fell swoop. Kim stumbled forward, an outstretched hand catching the rail kept her from being pushed to the ground. She slipped on the loose wet shell and barked a shin on the bottom stair.

Fighting a force she had never experienced before in her life, Kim hauled herself up the stairs. The wind screamed between the steps around her ankles. Climbing to the lee of the cabin provided little respite now. Kim dove through the bottom of the screen door into the porch. From where she lay on the floor, she turned to look back through the door—the gumbo limbo tree looked to have come alive, limbs akimbo, a scene seeming lifted right from *Poltergeist*.

Kim scrambled to her feet and leapt for the inside door, feeling as if the entire cabin was being sucked into a monstrous vacuum.

Dashing into the cabin she slammed the door shut behind her, making to secure it but found there was no lock. The door rattled in its frame, the glass in the windowpanes reverberating to the point of breaking. Kim backpedaled, rooted at the ferocity of the storm.

An explosion of breaking glass from the rear of the cabin had her reel an immediate about-face. A live oak limb had come through the back windows, shattering the glass, and falling across the bed. Andrea, still seated at the table, let out a shrieking scream. In with the tree came the roaring monsoon—a cyclonic mash of rain, branches, leaves, and broken glass flooded the cabin, pushed and carried by tornado-like winds. Everything inside that wasn't nailed down went airborne. Pictures were torn from the walls, books flew off nightstands, bottles and dishes tumbled from kitchen shelving, decor and knick-knacks were spun into flight, all becoming deadly projectiles.

Kim dropped to her knees and saw Andrea topple from her chair.

True fear knotted her stomach. Living in Florida all her life she had yet to experience a major hurricane. Her hometown of Englewood had been lucky—so far. This beast overhead felt like it was making a direct landfall on Cayo Costa. As Kim crossed the cabin on hands and knees to Andrea, holding up an arm to cover her face against the blinding rain, she couldn't imagine a storm this severe. It was a lucid nightmare, and it was all around them. Dropping an arm around Andera, Kim helped her over against the kitchen counter, both women cowering low. They were pinned in the meager lee of the bathroom.

"What the hell is it?" Andrea cried, terror flashing in her eyes, hands shielding her face.

"A goddamn *hurricane*—and it's right on top of us."

The wind tore through the cabin from back to front, hitting the windows along the porch, creating a blowback maelstrom. The pillows and sheets on the bunkbeds were kicked up and torn from the mattresses, curtains lining the windows danced wildly and were torn loose. A framed chart of Pine Island Sound was plucked from the wall and sent crashing to the floor, glass shattering, shards spinning away crazily. In the center of the rafters overhead a five-bladed ceiling fan had started spinning and was picking up speed, appearing to be under power.

The cyclone was fully rocking the cabin on its stilts. The entire structure shifted ominously under them, and Kim felt a shiver of anxiety slip up her spine. The sound of the wind was as if a freight train was passing directly through the cabin. No, a dozen freight trains.

Clutching Andrea, hunkered against the counter, Kim thought that this must be the storm's peak, it couldn't possibly get any worse . . .

A massive wind thrust inside, feeling three-dimensional, an impetuous wave ripping through the cabin like a subway though a tunnel. It plucked the table and chairs straight up into the air and sent them flying right through the front porch windows. The mattresses on the bunkbed followed suit, taking flight. One went sailing out onto the porch, the other pinned vertically up against the wall. Something struck Kim on the side of the chin, drawing an open gash an inch long, the object spinning away in a streaking peripheral blur. Forced down flat, the women dropped to their stomachs in front of the kitchen cabinets.

Kim scurried forward towards Andrea and shouted into her friend's ear over the screaming gale: "The bathroom! We need to get into the bathroom!"

Andrea must have heard her, because she popped up and started crawling towards the bathroom on hands and knees, hugging the floor, head down and turtled into the wind. Kim followed on Andrea's heels. It took them a half-minute to scramble across the wet wood floor, slugging forward head down blind into the wind, and slip around the corner into the bathroom. Kim pushed the door over behind them, having to lean her back against it and push with both legs, feet propped against the pedestal sink to get it closed against the incoming force. The tempest diminished a fraction to an exterior roar, but the enclosed bathroom cut the wind almost entirely. It whistled fiercely from the gap under the door and howled off the outside corner of the cabin.

The bathroom held a sink, a toilet, and a small tiled walk-in shower. There was one jalousie window, it was closed and—so far—intact. The window was fortunately on the north wall, perpendicular to the wind. Kim eyed the glass slats warily.

Andrea sat across from Kim, on the floor beside the toilet, hugging her knees. "When will it stop?' she shouted, her voice dulled by the jet engine blast.

Kim shook her head and looked from the window to the ceiling, trying to curtail the fear in her voice. "I don't know—but I think we're safe in here." This was an outright lie. Kim thought the entire cabin was about to be ripped free of its pilings and thrown into the Gulf of Mexico.

Both women felt their ears pop as the barometric pressure plummeted. The hurricane grew further in its assault.

The wind became a deafening and constant scream, unrelenting. The cabin rocked and shuddered on its stilt pilings. From behind the bathroom door it sounded like the entire contents of the cabin were being spun about in a massive blender. A sustained wind of 150 miles per hour, brushing the cusp of a Category 5 storm, blasted the barrier island, shearing leaves, branches, and limbs from its canopy. Airborne projectiles slammed into the rear of the cabin, each impact sounding like gunshots, making the woman jump and cringe. Kim slid over to Andrea and the two of them huddled together beside the toilet, their faces down. Andrea clamped her hands over her ears, trying to block out the wailing monster. The hurricane did not relent, for forty minutes it hammered down on them, the angry hand of God. Water came under the door in small torrents and blasted into the bathroom through the crack around the sill.

Over the course of about a minute, the storm had backed off, the wind dropping to almost nothing in comparison to the full-scale assault. As their ears adjusted to the new quiet, they could hear light rain pattering on metal roof, droplets falling straight down, not being whipped sideways in blinding sheets. With water running down her face, gathering and dripping from her chin, Kim finally raised her head, looking around the bathroom, and then at the ceiling, surprised and relieved to see it was still there.

Andrea's face was shellshocked as she looked up, following Kim's gaze upwards. "It's stopped," she said, her own voice sounding distant.

Kim said nothing and continued to study the ceiling, listening to the patter of the rain. The floor of the bathroom was flooded with several inches of water. Water had slowed from a pour to a trickle down the wall from the tiled sill of the jalousie window.

"It's stopped," Andrea repeated. "It's over. Thank God."

Kim remained quiet, uncertain. The storm had stopped extremely fast, cutting off almost immediately, like someone closing a tap or flipping off a switch.

Andrea's eyes turned to Kim, pleading. "Where the hell did this storm come from? A hurricane? Why didn't we know? Why no warning?"

Kim looked to her friend, and licked her lips, tasting salt, and feeling granules of sand on her tongue. Slowly she got to her feet, pulling herself up by the sink, muscles fatigued, joints stiff. "There was no radio on *Sabre* . . . there was no way for us to receive a warning. Travis . . ."

Distracted, through the window's slats she could see the sky was brightening, quickly. Kim turned the handle and eased open the door. Bright daylight was filtering into the cabin. The entire interior was soaked through and absolutely everything strewn about, covered in leaves and branches of every size, from snapped twigs to broken limbs more than a foot in diameter. It looked like the place had been razed. Nothing remained on the walls or shelving and all the windows and screens were completely blown out.

"We'll have to head for the ranger station," Kim said dully, still standing at the bathroom door, transfixed at the damage. "There's a dock there, and that'll be the first place people will come back to the island." She pulled her hair back from her face, gathering her senses, trying to recall the location of the ranger station from her visit to Cayo Costa. "The docks are at the north end, over on the bay side. This island isn't small, it must be a few miles—possibly more—to get up there. It's gonna be a helluva hike, especially with your . . ."

Kim frowned, looking out the back windows of the cabin at the canopy. Most of the leaves had been stripped from the live oaks and mangroves, leaving the branches bare. It had continued to brighten outside, this both encouraging and worrying Kim. The hurricane has ceased far too abruptly.

Kim turned to Andrea; her eyes had a haunted look. "Stay here for a minute."

Before Andrea could reply, Kim exited the bathroom and navigated her way carefully over and around the wreckage to the cabin's front porch. The ambient canopy has been almost entirely denuded of greenery and the gumbo limbo tree showed raw wood where it had sustained damage, losing several limbs. Stepping out the doorway to a porch of tattered screens, she was thankful to see the stairs intact. Looking down upon the trail they had taken up from the beach, she saw it was crisscrossed with fallen branches and debris. Visible through the leaf-cleared hammock was the beach itself. The Gulf was a swirling cauldron of gray-green spray and froth, the crashing storm surge had climbed up the sand to the dunes leaving a line of thick foam.

The wind was only a fresh breeze on her face, coming from the west now. It had shifted a full 180 degrees, blowing in off the Gulf. Looking up she saw a circular column of cloud swirling directly overhead, and in the center—impossibly—blue sky.

They were in the hurricane's eye.

Kim stood transfixed at the surreal scene above. It was impossible to gauge the distance across, but the storm was all around them, a three-dimensional living entity. The hurricane felt alive, an enveloping all-powerful being, and Kim succumbed to it, fully. A trancelike state of submission came over her and she fell into subspace, the threat of the storm itself and the events of the past few days dropping away. A serene calm rose and spread through her body, hypnotic, acting like a powerful opiate. For a half-minute she lingered in the bliss.

What pulled her from the euphoric trance was the renewed crashing of the surf. Shaking herself languidly out of the daze and looking to the beach, she saw the waves were picking up right before her eyes, driven by a new onshore wind. A wind which grew quickly from a light breeze to a strong gust, becoming another sustained gale. Kim squinted into the renewed tempest, her wet dirty blonde hair billowing out behind her. The eye was passing overhead, moving northeast quickly. The hurricane's second half was upon them. Although she had not experienced it, Kim knew the backside of a hurricane's eyewall hit with an abrupt, extreme force and much heavier rains and wind.

They were in trouble.

She took a deep breath of the salty air and made an about-face, returning into the cabin. Reaching the bathroom, she stepped quickly inside, and closed the door behind her.

"What is it?" Andrea asked, looking up hurriedly with rising concern. She had felt the wind building against the cabin's walls. "What now?" She noticed the cut on Kim's chin for the first time, a crimson diagonal slash an inch long. "Hey—your face, you're bleeding. On your chin."

Kim's hand absently went to her chin. She had not felt or noticed the cut. "We're not out of the woods."

A shadow of alarm crossed Andrea's face. "What do you mean?"

"We're in the eye. The center of the hurricane. It's passing right over us—the wind is going to come back; it's going to come back quickly."

Andrea's stomach knotted, and she shook her head. "No . . ."

Kim crossed the bathroom and dropped down beside Andrea, huddling again with her friend. "It will pass us by, we're safe here. We know the cabin can take the storm, and we're halfway through. We'll just have to ride it out again."

Andrea fought back tears, still shaking her head fitfully. "No . . ."

"Shh, we have no choice." Kim gripped Andrea assuredly. "We're going to be OK."

Kim had full sympathy; the hurricane's onslaught was nothing short of terrifying. The rain was no longer resounding gently on the roof, it was again thrashing into the walls. This time the cyclone didn't come in building waves, it took off like a rocket. The eyewall overtook them like a thunderclap, and the cabin shook violently, the wind howling and screaming murder again. From the gap under the bathroom door it whistled, blowing in more water that pooled across the floor. The pilings groaned underneath them, below the floorboards, resisting the incredible force of the wind that now pushed the structure from the opposite direction.

The hurricane was back, a pure unadulterated force of nature.

An incredibly loud bang had them both jump and look up in unison. The noise was followed immediately by a second identical resounding blow, and then another. It was as if someone was hitting the cabin wall with a sledgehammer. The women exchanged a nervous glance, cringing as two more reverberating retorts came from outside the bathroom door.

"What the hell was that?" Andrea yelled. Kim could barely hear her above the gale, and before she could attempt a reply both women jumped again as the slats of the jalousie window over their heads was thrust open, sending shooting streams of wind and water into the bathroom. It was as if someone had backed a pair of jet engines up to the side of the cabin and hit the throttles. Anything not pinned down took flight—magazines, hand towels, toilet paper, decorative shells, framed pictures from the walls—all became parts of an airborne maelstrom.

Kim ducked a flying bar of soap, grabbed Andrea's arm and pulled her across the wet wood floor and into the tiled shower stall. The woman ducked down together, backs to the walls, facing each other with legs intertwined, collapsing head down into each other's arms in the rear corner of the shower. The hurricane lashed and pummeled the cabin as the backing winds moved across Cayo Costa. Cradled together the women didn't move, keeping their heads down, faces buried in each other's shoulders. Kim lost track of time, having no idea how long the storm raged. She kept her eyes closed and held onto Andrea, feeling her friend's fearful grip in return.

After what seemed an eternity, but was only thirty minutes, the winds slowly started to abate. When the gusts dropped back to forty miles an hour—a spring breeze by comparison—Kim lifted her head and looked out of the shower stall. The plastic curtain hung slack by one remaining hook. The bathroom was as if a tornado had touched down, everything was now lying in water on the flooded floor. The gusts were becoming less frequent and rapidly falling in intensity. Kim could feel Andrea shaking in her arms.

"Hey," Kim said gently, "hey, it's over. Andrea, the storm has passed."

Andrea ventured a look up, her lower lip trembling. After a moment she said, "For real this time? It's not going to come back again?"

"No. It's gone. It's moved away. It's not coming back now. I promise." Kim looked around the disheveled bathroom. "Let's get up and see if we can get dry . . . maybe salvage anything."

She got to her feet and helped her friend up. Supporting Andrea, they sloshed through several inches of stormwater, stepping around objects on the flooded floor. Kim opened the door, and they gazed dumbfoundedly out of the bathroom. The cabin looked nothing short of a war zone, total devastation—like a bomb had gone off. The bunkbed lay halfway through the porch window opening, and there was no sign of either mattress. The main bed had been pushed against the back wall, the mattress flipped up and on end in the far corner. Every single item from the walls and shelves had been stripped from its place and tossed throughout the cabin. A collection of board games had been plucked from somewhere and it was as if they had been fired from a cannon—soaked Monopoly money had been circulated throughout. However, aside from the scattered contents and all windows and screens being blown out, the cabin itself remained intact; the roof was still on, walls upright, and the structure stood firm on its pilings.

"Oh my God, look at that. . ." said Andrea, gasping.

Kim followed Andrea's gaze upwards and saw one of the

fan blades had detached and embedded in the wall, just below the ceiling. Immediately she looked to the fan and saw it was a bladeless circular stump. A quick scan found the other four fan blades, all embedded at different points around the cabin's walls. The wind had spun the fan so fast that it threw its blades, turning them into missiles.

"That explains the noises we heard . . ." Kim said, letting out a huff, thankful they were not in the room when the fan lost is blades. She looked around to try and find anything dry, but the cabin was completely soaked through. The front doors of the kitchen cabinets below the sink were all pulled open, and she spied a full ten-gallon jug of spring water.

"Well, we'll have to air dry, but we've got water," Kim said, relieved. She had sensed a rising thirst. Both women were unknowingly edging in on dehydration. Watching for broken glass, careful where she stepped barefoot, Kim righted the kitchen table from where it sat upside down in the far front corner of the cabin, along with a couple of chairs. One was wedged tightly under the bed that took a bit of tugging to free. Kim found two undamaged plastic cups and heaved the jug of water up onto the counter. Straining with the weight, she sloshed each cup full. Sitting at the table both women drank greedily, quenching their thirst with the tepid water, listening to ebbing gusts lick across the cabin. Despite its strength and intensity the hurricane had thankfully passed over quickly.

"How does your ankle feel?" Kim asked, breathing heavily after chugging several large swallows of water.

Andrea looked down at her leg. "I don't know. Not too bad right now, I guess."

"That's good. It looks OK, the swelling is staying down. I wish we had some ice, but that's a long shot right now."

Kim drained her cup and spied a wall clock lying face down

on the floor in the corner by the bathroom door. Rising, she went over and picked it up. The hands were stopped at 4:03. The clock could have died well over hour ago when the hurricane first hit. It was possible that it was after five o'clock now. The sun set shortly after eight. Three hours till nightfall.

"I think we're gonna be here for the night," said Kim, her face grim.

"For the night? Why?" Andrea asked, her expression equally downturned.

Kim crossed back to the kitchen and set the clock on the counter. "It's going to be dark in a few hours, maybe less. If we left for the ranger station now, it would be dark before we got there. We'll never find it at night. I don't recall exactly where it is . . . and I don't think anyone will come out to the island this evening." Kim came to sit back down with Andrea at the table. "This storm was severe—that had to be a Category Four or Five hurricane. I think it came from the southwest . . . moving directly across us . . . so it likely hit the mainland behind us—Cape Coral, Punta Gorda, Port Charlotte. Maybe even Englewood."

"We can't stay out here tonight. We need to reach somebody," Andrea said, distraught, "we need help—we need to call the police and tell them what's happened."

"We will, but not tonight. There's just no way. A lot of people will be without power. Phone lines will be down. Even if we had a working mobile phone the cell towers on Pine Island and Boca Grande would likely be out. We'll be fine here for the night. A little wet, but fine. In the morning, we'll head up the beach for the ranger station. I'm sure the park people will be out here first thing tomorrow to check on the island. There also may be a working radio at the ranger station. We've got water—"

"And rum," Andrea cut in, nodding towards the front door. Kim turned and saw where the bottle of rum had survived the storm, rolled up against a toppled bedside table. She felt small comfort at Andrea's levity, her friend able to jest and find the positive in a horrible situation. Kim was concerned at her own optimism—park rangers returning to Cayo Costa as soon as tomorrow. It could be a day, or two . . .

"That will sure make the night better, won't it?" said Kim, displaying a grin. Andrea gave her a weak smile. "I tell you what," Kim continued, "whoever's place this is has a hell of a mess to clean up, but they got lucky . . . because the person who built this cabin sure did a hell of a fine job."

They rested together at the table for the next hour, slowly drip-drying, listening to the storm move away, watching the sky brighten. The hurricane came on quickly, and was departing just as fast, a short, fast-moving, but intense cyclone. The rain still fell in mixed bands, and the wind returned in weakening gusts, but the intervals between them lengthened rapidly.

Kim retrieved the rum, and they exchanged the water for the more potent liquid, sharing a drink. They didn't speak much, both women grappling with what they had gone through and witnessed, both exhausted, mentally, and physically. Kim thought of her daughter Kayla, who was staying for the week with her aunt in Englewood. Kim was sure she was safe, but worried like any mother would be. Halfway through their second round of rum, Kim started rummaged through the chaos and found two pairs of flip-flops that fit them both well. Plastic drinks cups in hand they made their way out to the front porch. Andrea limped slightly. Her ankle was feeling a lot better with the ibuprofen and the rum.

All the porch's screens were either missing entirely or hanging in shredded tatters. The wind had fallen to the occasional gust, and although it was still overcast and raining lightly, they could see the position of the sun lowering in the western sky. The wet air smelled strongly of sap from thousands of snapped limbs and broken branches. The surrounding hammock canopy was almost fully denuded of foliage, with hundreds of patches of bright raw wood left exposed. A blanket from one of the beds was tangled high in the gumbo limbo tree, and items from the cabin were strewn across the trail all the way down to the beach. With the leaves almost entirely gone from the porch they could see out to the rolling surf. The water had already fallen back to the high tide line, but it had come up over the dunes, leaving thick foam and a heavy line of wrack.

Kim looked to the south, through the bared branches of the canopy, over mangled sea grape and washed out dune, past the solitary coconut palm that guided her into the island. A few hundred feet down the beach she could see *Sabre*. The catamaran was now sitting high on the sand, yawed at a forty-five degree angle to the waterline and canted heavily to her port side.

Andrea saw the catamaran as well, and a shudder passed through her. "Is there any chance?" she asked, her expression hardened.

Kim turned to her. "Any chance of what?"

"Of Travis surviving . . . is there any chance of him being on this island with us?"

Kim was quiet for a moment. "No," she answered firmly. "None. He was adrift, his boat was half the size of ours, and not running. There would be absolutely no way he could have navigated that hurricane and made it here, to Cayo Costa. I had full power in a boat almost twice the size of his and we barely made it. He likely capsized and drowned in the storm."

Reassured, Andrea looked out at the destruction, sipping

her rum. There was no sign or sound of any bird or animal, just the lightly falling rain. "How did all this happen?" she asked, voice barely above a whisper. "I can't believe Chad and Mark are . . . gone. This was supposed to be our vacation . . . how could it go so—so wrong . . .?" Tears rimmed Andrea's eyes, and she sniffed.

Kim moved closer, feeling her own stabs of pain, sorrow, and guilt. She was the one who encouraged Mark to bring Travis along. If she hadn't have pushed for it, Mark would never have let him onboard. Both men she had slept with in the past two days were dead, and her best friend's boyfriend was dead as well, all because she was fleetingly attracted to a stranger. Mark's suspicions of Travis had been accurate. Kim questioned just how much of what Travis told her was a lie, and what he might really have been in prison for. She had not lied to Andrea; she was sure there was zero chance Travis was still alive.

The western sky continued to brighten as the sun settled towards the Gulf. The rain slowed further, and then finally stopped altogether, the wind falling back to a shifting strong breeze. The hurricane had moved off quickly, away over the mainland to the northeast, leaving a trail of mayhem and destruction in its path. Kim could only guess how widespread the storm was, and how badly it had impacted the surrounding populated areas.

They returned silently inside the cabin and Kim set them up a place to rest for the night, righting the large mattress and laying it by the kitchen table. However, they ended up just lying on the wood floor, which proved to be more comfortable than a soaked mattress. They made headrests out of rolled up towels as all the pillows were missing, blown right out the cabin. Kim found a flashlight, but it didn't work, and a bag of soggy Oreos, but they weren't hungry.

HURRICANE HOLE

They had sipped away half the bottle of rum and were both feeling comfortably numbed to the events of the day, the storm, and the coming night.

In the drawing darkness, Andrea spoke softly: "I hope everyone at home is OK."

Kim turned to where Andrea lay beside her. "I'm sure they are. They would all have had plenty of advance warning about the hurricane. We're safe here for the evening. We've got water, alcohol, a roof over our heads, and even a proper toilet. What else could we need?" In the dimming light she saw Andrea give her a boozy smirk, eyes heavy with fatigue and bleary from the drink.

"Tomorrow we're going home," Andrea said, more a confirming statement to herself than a question. Her eyelids drooped; she was fighting to keep them open. "Tomorrow we'll find help and get off this island . . . we're going home."

"Yes," said Kim, her voice barely above a whisper, "tomorrow we'll be back home."

She reached out and brushed her friend's hair from her face. Andrea eyes closed, and Kim listened to her breathing rhythm change as she fell into a deep sleep. Kim lay there for some time but was unable to fall asleep herself. After a few minutes of lying in the dark, the tug of sleep nowhere in sight, she sat up and took a large swallow of rum from the cup beside her makeshift bed, the liquor hot in her throat. She rose quietly and stepped carefully in near total darkness across to the porch. Looking out over the treetops she was surprised to see a swath of starlight. A large strip of the night sky was clear, and stars shimmered overhead. The night was dead quiet, and still, not so much as an insect trilled, just the smooth rhythmic rush of waves down at the beach.

Sliding on a pair of flip-flops she ducked through the

screen door and descended the stairs. The ground in front of the cabin was strewn with branches and storm debris, and in the light of the stars she navigated her way down the path to the beach. One of the bunkbed mattresses was visible, tossed in a thicket of wild coffee. Coming out onto the open beach the stars were bright enough to cast her shadow across the sand, however there was no moon visible. The humid air had a strong freshly churned smell of salt and seaweed and tree sap.

The Gulf was dark, the churned murky surface not reflecting any light from above. High on the beach, just below the dune, Kim walked south, and she could see the trunk and fronds of the coconut palm silhouetted against the sky, and the dark shape of *Sabre* against the sand. She paused ahead, just beneath the palm, the long pinnate leaves rustling gently overhead.

Her head turned sharply upwards at a flash of light. A brilliant streak of greenish white crossed the sky at incredible speed, far out over the water. It lasted a full three seconds, burning incredibly bright, like a phosphorescent flare. The shooting star—a meteor vaporizing in the Earth's atmosphere—burned out as fast as it appeared. Kim blinked, the orb still visible, seared into her retinas. This was not the Perseids they had witnessed last night. This was a large, low, fast meteor that seemed to have pierced the atmosphere to splashdown somewhere out in the Gulf. Eyes readjusting, she continued down the line of dune. *Sabre* was both yawed and canted towards Kim, her portside hull buried deep in compacted wet sand. Only her port stern quarter was still in the water, the hurricane had lifted the catamaran high onto the pan.

Kim paused again, a rift of emotions flooding her as she looked upon *Sabre* under the starlight. Eyes tearing, she was about to turn and head back up the beach when she spotted something in the dune.

It was about ten yards away . . . a person, a body, lying face down.

Kim froze, heart stuttering, chest tightening. It was a man. He lay at a haphazard angle, like the catamaran, half-buried in the sand. In the darkness it was impossible to identify who he was. She was only certain of one thing—he was dead. Her first thoughts were that it might be Chad. The hurricane could have plucked his body from *Sabre* and washed him up here into the dune. It might have been possible, but *Sabre* was still upright, high and dry, and she clearly remembered shutting the salon door.

Could it be Travis?

Heart pounding, Kim moved towards the prone figure. Eyes straining in the darkness, her throat tightened—she recognized the physique, the coral-colored T-shirt, the khaki shorts.

Mark.

Shock and grief twisted Kim's gut. It didn't make sense—she and Andrea had walked right by here after they had beached *Sabre*—about five, maybe six hours ago. Mark's body wasn't here then—he couldn't have been—he must have been washed in later. If Travis had thrown Mark overboard, or his body was pulled from the Bayliner by the storm, the hurricane's wind and waves might have brought him in here. *Sabre* was moved much farther north than Kim had expected, so it was possible the hurricane had done the same to *End of Watch*. Travis's boat might also have been pushed in the same direction, and even beached on Cayo Costa . . .

But there was no way Travis was alive, he was adrift with no power, no engines. That hurricane would have surely tossed and capsized that Bayliner. That was how Mark ended up here. *End of Watch* would have been sunk; Travis drowned. He was shark bait or washed up somewhere half-buried in a dune himself.

Hand over her mouth, Kim tore her eyes from Mark's body. She turned and set out for the cabin, trudging across the heavy wet sand, worry snaking through her like a thief in the night.

CHAPTER TWELVE

K im could not hold her grip any longer. Leaning off Sabre's swim platform, her upper body plunged to the waist in the dark Gulf water, straining to hold her breath, she clung desperately to Mark's outstretched hand with every ounce of strength she had. Mark was looking up at her, fear and panic etched across his twisted face. Below Mark, hanging onto his legs, was Travis. The two men dangled in the watery void, hovering over a bottomless black abyss.

She was looking straight down at Mark, her eyes locked on his, as he swayed over the void. A trail of bubbles escaped his open mouth, flowing upwards in slow motion towards Kim's face. Further below, Travis was thrashing and tugging wildly, pulling on Mark's legs, ever so slowly weighing him down, inching him further into the deep. Mark frantically kicked his legs, trying to shake Travis loose and free himself, his struggled movements appearing at a funeral pace.

Kim felt her hand slip—she looked past Mark to Travis— his dark eyes were wide, a sickly grin across his face, teeth bared. Travis's weight was becoming heavier, impossibly heavy, too much for her to hold. Mark's hand was sliding free from hers; skin slick in the saltwater, she was losing him. Mark's face contorted into a renewed mask of fear and panic, his head twisting around, a fresh burst of bubbles billowing from his gaping mouth as he screamed.

Her own lungs burning for air, Kim saw then that the back of Mark's head was split open, a gaping hole from which inky blood swam, a piece of his hair-covered scalp floating loose. She jerked back in terror—and lost her hold on him. Kim opened her mouth to scream but was unable to, she had no breath, her own lungs empty. Frozen with fright, she watched Mark sink away, his hands vainly clawing the water . . . below him, Travis still grinning and holding tight, pulling them both down into the depths.

Kim jerked awake with a gasp, pulling sweet air into her lungs. She could breathe. Blinking her eyes against harsh morning sunlight, Kim stifled a scream as she was wrenched back to reality. The real nightmare came rushing back all too quickly: Travis, Chad and Mark's deaths, the hurricane, the cabin, finding Mark's body in the dune last night . . . She found herself on the hard floor of the cabin, skin glistening with a heavy sheet of perspiration, T-shirt damp through.

Andrea sat on her own makeshift bed beside Kim, her face awash with concern, having witnessed her friend's sleeping antics. In a beam of sunlight she could see the pulse in Kim's neck fluttering hard.

"Are you OK?" Andrea asked. "You were having a nightmare. A bad one. I tried to wake you."

Kim frowned and brought a hand to her temple, trying to leave the visions of the dark dream behind. She nodded; eyes heavy with fatigue, scrunched tight against the bright light streaming in the rear windows of the cabin. She was going to ask Andrea what time it was but remembered they had no way of knowing. By the sharp angle of the long shadows it still looked early, like the sun had been up for about an hour. Already the heat of the day was building, the cabin stifling, even with all the windows blown out. The island was eerily silent, with absolutely no wind, and even if there was a wind, there were no leaves for it to blow through. No birds chirping, no insects droning. Just a deathly stillness.

"I've been up for a bit," said Andrea. "I let you sleep."

Kim absently rubbed a crusty eye. "Did you sleep OK?"

Andrea nodded. "Yeah . . . alright. The rum sure helped."

Kim sat up slowly, lower back and hips stiff from sleeping on the wood floor. "Damn, it's hot. We need to drink some water."

"I had some already, there's plenty. And it's nice and warm too," Andrea said with heavy sarcasm.

Kim let out a fleeting groan, stretched, and moved her arms and shoulders around, loosening her joints before rising. At the kitchen counter she poured herself some water from the jug, still feeling the emotional aftereffects of the nightmare, her brain working to separate the vision from reality. She could clearly see the image from last night—Mark lying face down in the dune, half-buried in the wet sand—and him standing on *End of Watch* yesterday, the bullet tearing into the back of his skull. Her guts roiled and a haunting shiver went through her. The scenes were forever burned into her visual cortex. Kim sipped the water slowly, forcing it down, knowing she needed the hydration, fighting a gnawing sickness in her empty stomach. The taste of the sickly sweet rum was still strong in her mouth.

She decided not to tell Andrea about finding Mark, or about her fears that whatever forces brought Mark's body to Cayo Costa may have also done the same with *End of Watch*.

"How's your ankle this morning?" Kim asked, swallowing another sip of the tepid water. It had a strong plasticky aftertaste.

"A lot better."

"That's good. Because we have a bit of walking to do today."

"We're heading for that ranger station?'

"Yeah," Kim replied, thankful they were to make their way north, and not south, past Mark's body. Past where *End of Watch* might have come in.

"Shouldn't we maybe just wait here?"

"No. I have no idea when the people who own this place will come back. Especially after this storm. The ranger station—that's the first spot anyone returning to the island will arrive."

"How far is it?"

"I don't know exactly. A few miles, maybe a bit more. We'll head straight up the beach. When we get to the campgrounds, we'll head east, cut across to the bay side. There's a main trail that leads straight across the island."

"Do you think there's anyone else on the island with us? Anyone else who went through the hurricane?"

"I doubt it," said Kim, leaning against the counter. "That thing was a monster, there would have been warnings—they would have surely closed and evacuated the park." Kim was only concerned about the grim possibility of one other person being on the island with them. "We'll need to bring lots of water. We've got a bit of a hike ahead of us. Drink up, and it might be best if you take more Advil. Bring the bottle."

They spent the next twenty minutes preparing for the walk to the ranger station. Kim found a knapsack, and into it put two liquor bottles filled with the spring water. She found an old half-full tube of sunblock that they slathered on, as well as a couple of wide-brimmed hats. Unfortunately she could not find a pair of sunglasses anywhere.

Sliding into the flip-flops, they stood together inside the front porch at the top of the stairs. The silence was omnipresent, even the gentle wash of the small waves coming in on the beach seemed subdued. The canopy was almost entirely denuded by the wind, brown and bare, like it had been hit with a chemical defoliant. The limbs looked like skeletons. Their nostrils were overpowered by the smell of wet vegetation and fresh sap. The sky was mostly clear, and a brilliant blue, only a smattering of clouds passed slowly overhead, the morning sun already strong. Kim guessed the time was somewhere around nine.

Together they descended the stairs, Andrea favoring her tender ankle. They came out onto the front clearing and the path leading to the beach. Here they both paused, to turn and look back up at the cabin. The screens to the front porch were hanging in tatters, but otherwise the structure itself had survived the onslaught well.

"Thank God we found this place," said Andrea.

Looking upon their shelter from the storm, and room for the night, for the first time in over a day Kim felt her spirit lift a little. "We got lucky," she said. "I couldn't imagine having to ride out that hurricane in the open."

Andrea winced. "We would have died."

"Well, we didn't." Kim put her hand on Andrea's shoulder. "We survived. And we'd best get going, it would be a good idea to get to the ranger station as soon as possible, before it gets too hot. I'm hoping the park rangers make to come back early."

They set out through the busted and broken hammock and came into the full beating sun on the open beach. Kim saw Andrea turn, shielding her eyes to look south at *Sabre*.

"We'll have to send someone back . . . for Chad," said Andrea, sorrow tightening her chest.

Kim slowed, but continued making her way up the beach, only glancing quickly back, leading Andrea on. "That will be the first thing we'll do. Let's not dwell here. C'mon, let's keep moving."

They crossed down to the hard-packed pan at the waterline to walk on the flat wet sand. It was far easier to walk barefoot than in loose and blistering sandals that were not the correct size. The beach was raked smooth by the storm's surge, and every hundred yards or so they came upon a dead seabird killed by the powerful winds: a pelican, a snowy egret, an osprey . . . The birds were strewn about at odd impossible angles, wings broken, feathers ruffled and wet, half covered in sand. The dead birds reminded Kim too vividly of Mark's corpse, each one they came across a fresh punch in the gut.

The sun rose quickly in the eastern sky, the rays pounding the sides of their faces. They pulled the sunhats low, pausing to sip water, before continuing up the beach. After a half hour of steady going Andrea's ankle started to complain. They took a break and drank more water. There were no signs of anyone at all on the beach, and no other cabins or houses. The long strip of sand was devoid of anything, even of the usual trash and debris that is washed in after a storm. Just dozens of dead seabirds, an ongoing morbid scene.

As they set off again, Kim started to keep an eye out for anything that might distinguish the camping area. She knew there were a dozen small cabins set back from the dunes, as well as tenting sites, for rent through the state park to campers. Kim judged they should be coming upon them soon. Moving at a slower pace now, with Andrea favoring her ankle, they traversed the seemingly endless stretch of sand.

Ahead, the beach began to thin, the distance between the waterline and the dune decreasing. Here the dune showed massive erosion from storm surge, as if the hurricane had run the backshore berm with a gigantic bulldozer, leaving a five-foot high wall of scarp with hundreds of jutting exposed roots from toppled sea oats. Making their way along the pan, the eroded dune wall got closer and closer as the existing beach disappeared, having been washed out by the storm's powerful wind and waves.

Kim had been eyeing a long low object on the pan ahead, and as she got closer, she saw it was a cabbage palm. The tree had been snapped off at the base by the hurricane and now lay perpendicular to the waterline, almost entirely buried in the hard-packed sand. Only half the trunk and a handful of flattened leaflets were left exposed. The Gulf rushed up and along the trunk's spiky bootjacks as the women stepped over the tree, the blood-warm water swirling around their ankles.

A dozen paces past the tree Kim noticed Andrea had dropped back. She turned to see her friend had stopped and was peering down at the sand. "What is it?" Kim asked. "Your ankle?"

Andrea didn't reply but instead used her toe to nudge at something small in the sand. Kim watched as Andrea bent and picked it up, standing to study it closely.

"What did you find?" Kim asked, starting to head back to Andrea. "This really isn't the time to hunt for shells."

Andrea pinched the small, flat, round object between her thumb and index finger. She slid grains of wet sand from it with her thumb and shook her head. "It's not a shell. I think—I think it's a coin."

Coming back beside her friend, Kim frowned, and Andrea held the piece out for her. Taking it in her hand, Kim saw that it indeed looked like a large coin. It was a type of metal, slate gray, heavily oxidized, and about an inch and a half in diameter. It was not uniformly round, the edges were ragged, and she could see it was stamped with a design that looked like it might have been a cross, but the imprint was worn down, smoothed by centuries of time and difficult to discern. She was not good at judging weight, but it did not feel all that heavy.

"You're right. It's a coin, a real old one," said Kim. "I think it's silver. The hurricane must have washed it in." She held the coin back out to Andrea. "Impressive. Keep it for sure."

Andrea took the coin back, her demeanor brightening some at the lucky find. She studied the coin again for a moment, before carrying on and following Kim. Her ankle had really begun to throb the last half mile, and she was grateful for the rest stop and fortunate distraction of finding the old coin. She kept the silver piece gripped tightly in her palm.

Andrea had not gone five steps when she spied a second coin. The curved half-moon edge was poking up out of the flat pan. She stooped and pinched it out of the wet sand, brushing it clean with a thumb.

"I found another one," Andrea called out, a hint of excitement in her tone.

Kim turned and this time came right back. Andrea held the coin out in her palm for her friend to see. The second coin was about a third larger than the first, the same color and off-circle shape, and was also imprinted with what looked like a cross. The emblem was a bit clearer on this one. It was an equal-armed cross, slightly off center with a design in each quadrant. But this coin was also too worn away to determine exactly what the designs were.

Andrea used the tip of an index finger to flip the coin over and they both peered at the other side. The metal on the opposite face was also stamped, with what looked like squares and rectangles, an odd circular indent, and possibly letters or numerals. The surface was polished almost entirely smooth by hundreds of years of saltwater and sand abrasion, leaving it impossible to read.

Kim said, "Someone who knows a hell of a lot more about coins than me is going to have to figure out what these are, and where they might be from. The storm has definitely kicked them up for you to find. One thing is for sure, they're really old."

"How old?"

"Centuries, at least."

"Huh. Real pirate treasure?" Andrea asked, eyebrows rising.

Kim let out a breath, smirking. "Maybe. I think so. I think you got real lucky." She turned and looked up the beach. "I think we're close to the camp site. Hell, we've gotta be almost there by now. Let's get going. We'll set a slower pace if you need. How's the ankle?"

"I'm alright," Andrea replied, buoyed by her finds, ignoring the throb in her leg. "It's just hot." She wiped sweat from her brow with a forearm, the two coins gripped tightly in her palm. The women set out again side by side, continuing north along the sloping pan. A dozen paces up the beach Andrea stopped again, thrusting her balled fist out across Kim's chest, stopping her abruptly.

"I see another one." Andrea voice was hushed. She slowly removed her fist from Kim's chest and pointed an index finger out front.

It took a few seconds for Kim to spot it. This coin lay a half dozen feet ahead, sitting at an angle at the top of the swash zone. Unbelieving, Kim shook her head, stepping forward up the beach face and retrieved the coin. It was just like the first two, similar in size, shape, and design. Kim walked back to Andrea studying the piece of silver in her hand. "Hmm, you've sure got an eagle eye for finding these. You find any more and—"

"Look at the dune."

The intensity in Andrea's hushed voice drew Kim's full attention. First, she glanced up at her friend, who was staring intently at the line of dunes over Kim's shoulder. Kim turned and looked across the beach.

The length of dune was severely eroded, leaving a vertical wall of sheared sand and exposed roots almost the same height as the two women. At the base lay toppled sea oats and piles of collapsed wet sand. From the scarp jutted tangled roots, and something else . . . a large pocket of long rectangular objects . . . lines too straight for nature, fabricated only by human hand. The hurricane's waves had torn away at the dune, ripping away thousands of pounds of sand, exposing what looked to be a stack of squared logs, or long bricks. Saying nothing, and moving slowly, Kim and Andrea approached the anomaly in the dune face.

Andrea stopped yet again, looking down. "More coins!" she exclaimed, this time pure excitement in her voice.

Kim looked down. Between her feet and all around her were dozens of coins scattered in the sand. Her eyes darted from piece to piece, and she quickly lost count of how many she was seeing. Continuing up towards the dune, she had to step carefully to not walk on them. The silver coins were pieces of eight, ranging in value from one to eight reales of the precious metal.

Watching their footing, the women closed in on the eroded dune, squinting against the morning sun in their faces. The berm of the high beach in front of the dune was littered with a mass of coins, as if they had been spilled out of a chest, which, in fact, they had. The storm surge had ripped hundreds of the coins free from their resting place in the dune, throwing them across the beach. There were so many that as Kim neared the dune, she had no choice but to walk on some.

She eyed the stacks of bricks, and saw they were too large to be bricks, and were of a metal material, not clay or concrete.

HURRICANE HOLE

They looked oxidized like the coins and a similar color, a light whitish gray. Each brick, or bar, was a little more than a foot long, and about five inches high, and a little less in width, maybe four inches. The top was rounded like a baked loaf of bread. There looked to be at least sixty or seventy of them embedded in the scarp. About a dozen had fallen out, tumbling to the sand, lying scattered at odd angles. Kim put her foot on the closest one and pushed. It was solid and heavy, extremely heavy. Well over fifty pounds.

"What are they?" Andrea asked.

"I think," Kim said slowly, "I think these are ingots."

"Ingots?"

"Yeah, bars of metal. Silver bars."

"Jesus . . ." Andrea said under her breath.

The women gazed in disbelief at the horde of silver. One ingot that had fallen out near Andrea was upside down, the bottom flat. Andrea knelt and used a hand to wipe drying sand from the rough surface.

"It's covered in markings," Andrea said, whisking sand away faster, using a fingertip to brush grains out of the grooves. Kim moved in to kneel beside her and they could see etchings and stamps embedded into the silver. Like the coins the metal was worn and oxidized but they could clearly make out block capital letters, imprinted in the center: DCCXLVII. To the left of that in smaller lettering was: P1622. There were also three stampings of the same imprint they saw on the coins, equal-armed crosses with designs in the four quadrants. There were other markings, including what looked like a large fancy capital A on the right side.

Kim studied the Roman numerals. "That's a number in the high hundreds somewhere." She slid her thumb back and forth over the P1622. "And this could be a date. Maybe, the P is for 'produced', and the year, 1622?"

Andrea wasn't listening. She was staring intently at the dune, to the right of the stacked ingots. Set in the slumping wall of sand, near the top of the ingots was a dark pattern of many small gemstones packed together, dozens of them, ranging in size and shape from a pea to a domino. Most were the size of large marbles. Andrea slowly glanced down. In the fallen sand in front of her knees were more scattered gemstones. She had been so focused on the ingots she had almost knelt on a carpet of them. Picking one up, pinched between her index finger and thumb, she held it up to the sunlight coming over the top of the dune.

"I think this is an emerald," said Andrea, her tone matter-of-fact, gazing at the stone in the sunlight.

Kim looked up to the gemstone in her friend's hand. It was the size of a large die, jagged and rough. It did not sparkle, and was opaque, but in the sun, it was unmistakably green, a deep blue-green hue. Andrea turned the gemstone slowly, so they could view it from all sides.

"Yes," Andrea continued, "it's an uncut emerald. There're dozens of them, maybe hundreds."

Kim saw the pocket of emeralds in the face of the dune. Her eyes widened as she realized fully what she was looking at. She watched as Andrea reached out her free hand and touched a larger stone amid the cluster embedded in the scarp. Making to pull it free, both women started as the pocket broke apart and several dozen stones fell loose, falling and rolling into the sand. A few came to rest against Andrea's thighs.

"Holy shit . . ." Kim said quietly, a stunned expression on her face. She tried to guess how many emeralds they were looking at.

"I don't believe this," Andrea murmured, still having trouble comprehending what she was seeing. "Is this buried treasure? Like for real?"

Kim picked up one of the stones, examining it. "I think so. Someone hid—or for whatever reason—left this stuff behind here a long time ago, and our hurricane yesterday unburied it."

Andrea pulled an oblong emerald from the dune, this one the size and shape of a cigarette lighter. As she did a handful of smaller stones surrounding it fell free. "Look at this one," Andrea said, holding the grand gemstone up, "what do you think this one alone is worth?"

Kim shook her head. "I have absolutely no idea." She looked behind them to the surf rolling in just twenty-five feet away. She could only guess how many emeralds and silver coins were washed out into the Gulf by the storm. "This treasure has all gotta be worth millions. Tens of millions."

Andrea looked at Kim, her breath catching. "Wait—can we keep any of this?"

Kim let out a quick chuckle. "That I highly doubt. This find is in a state park. We might get our names attached as the original finders, or salvors, or whatever they might call it, but I don't think they'll let us keep a penny of it."

Andrea was quiet, digesting this. She glanced at the emerald in her hand. "Well, what they don't know about they won't know about. I'm keeping the coins, and this emerald."

Kim cocked her head and grinned. "I promise I won't say anything." She knelt forward and looked more closely at the stack of ingots as Andrea got up and stepped away, looking over the litter of coins. Kim inched closer to the cluster of emeralds. She gently brushed away sand above the far end of the ingots and saw the edges of darker circular shapes, stacked flat. These weren't silver coins; they were much larger. Kim carefully pulled the top one out of the packed sand and shook it clean. It was a disk, shaped almost exactly like a large cookie, just as rough, flat on one side and slightly rounded on the other. The gold bullion disk was easily three times the weight of one of the silver coins.

She brushed sand from the convex surface. It was marked with capital block letters: MCH—the next two letters were blurred out—and then CA. She saw the repeated stamps of a seal but could not discern what it was. The piece was too large to be a coin, but Kim was sure it was gold. She set it down on top of the ingot and gently began brushing sand away from the other disks.

Behind Kim, Andrea had pocketed the three silver coins and the large rectangular chunk of emerald, as well as two smaller emeralds. It crossed her mind that she had discovered what would make a showstopping set of gemstone earrings and matching pendant. She could only guess their value and imagine the look on the jeweler's face when she brought them in to have them mounted.

Kim continued to brush sand away from the face of the dune, clearing around the stack of gold disks. Including the one she had pulled free, there were twelve disks. Someone—a person centuries dead now—had stacked an even dozen. Kim wondered if the emeralds and gold disks were originally stored in a type of wooden chest or cloth bags that had long since rotted away. Yet another article caught Kim's eye. Above the disks was a round object, this one shaped like a ball. Brushing away sand she saw it was a darker metal, and it held a gemstone, an emerald. Kim continued to clear away the packed sand, and saw the metal ball was gold, and intricately designed. At four points around the ball were set four more slightly smaller emeralds. Kim grasped the ball and gently wiggled it. The ball was attached to something longer and larger, buried under the hard-packed sand. She worked it loose and inched it slowly out from the scarp. Behind the ball was a handled grip, a hilt. Wiggling it loose enough to pull free, Kim fully withdrew the piece from the tumbling sand.

Her heart leapt and her mouth fell open.

It was a dagger.

Taking in a sharp breath, she shook the remaining sand from the weapon. The metal blade was six inches long, double-sided with a central ridge, the same luster as the silver coins. The pommel and cross-guard were made of what looked to be gold, and inlayed with dozens of cut and polished gemstones, emeralds and rubies. The twin quillons were ornate, also encrusted with jewels. There were close to thirty stones in total, averaging the size of a large raisin. The largest was the emerald in the pommel, the size of a walnut. The dagger had some weight to it, Kim judged it at more than half a pound, at least, all gold, silver, and gemstones.

"Look at this," Kim finally whispered, finding her voice.

Andrea turned from where she was hunting lost emeralds and coins scattered on the beach. Her eyes bugged when she saw the dagger. "Oh—wow. You've got to be kidding. A knife?"

"It's a dagger," said Kim.

"That's a fancy dagger."

"I found gold as well, twelve disks, there's one there." Kim used the dagger to point to the disk she had set atop the ingot. Andrea just stared incredulously at a loss for words.

"I think," Kim said, "this is what they call finding the Motherlode."

Andrea broke from her reverie. "I need some water."

"Good idea. Me too."

Unslinging the knapsack from her back and pulling out a

rum bottle filled with water, Kim uncapped it and passed it to Andrea. They both took turns drinking heavily, almost draining the remaining contents between them. The heat of the day was building fast, and there was no shade out on the beach. Kim judged they had hiked about three miles up from the cabin. They had been walking for well over an hour, close to an hour and a half, but their pace was slow. Kim wiped water from her mouth and looked at the cabbage palm in the surf behind them, less than a hundred feet to the south. The felled tree made an excellent landmark to find the treasure location again.

"We should get going," Kim said, "we must be close to the trail over to the ranger station now."

"Good. It's getting hot, and my ankle's starting to throb—bad. How far?"

"Maybe a mile, give or take."

Andrea groaned. "I don't think I can go another mile. Maybe I should stay here and guard the treasure?"

Kim snickered, shrugging on the backpack. "No way in hell are we splitting up. They do that in every single stupid movie. This is real life. You can make it. There might even be help already waiting at the ranger station by the time we arrive."

As if on cue, the sound of an engine rose above the surf, the distinctive *whump-whump* of a helicopter. Both women turned to look towards the sound. From the northeast, against the blue sky, an orange U.S. Coast Guard HH-65B Dolphin topped the hammock, heading due west across the island.

Kim felt Andrea tense beside her. "Wait," Kim said, reaching out a hand. "They're too far. Let's see if they come down the beach."

The helicopter was a couple of miles distant, and banked north, circling around in a half loop. The chopper stopped and hovered for a full minute, about a hundred feet above the beach, twin turboshaft engines whining.

"They're looking at something down on the island," Kim said, "something on the beach, around the point, out of sight."

"Why don't they come down here?" Andrea's voice was edging on desperation.

"They might. If they do, don't bother yelling, just wave your arms like mad."

The chopper broke from its hover and swooped to the southeast, accelerating quickly, beelining back across the island. Kim and Andrea began waving their arms wildly, but the rotorcraft did not change its trajectory. It passed them by a full half mile, disappearing briefly against the morning sun, before crossing out over Pine Island Sound.

"Goddamn it," Andrea moaned, her spirits falling.

"It's OK," Kim encouraged. "This is good sign. They saw something, or somebody. They'll be back. There will be people returning to the island today for sure. Let's make our own tracks—it's time for us to move."

The women turned to take a last look at the incredible find in the dune, still in a state of dubiety that they had found real treasure.

"I can't believe we're just going to leave all this here," said Andrea, surveying the horde.

"There's nothing else we can do. It's been right where it is for centuries. We'll notify the right person, a park manager or someone at the ranger station. Let's get going."

They were down to the hardpack sand of the pan when Andrea spoke. "Wait, you're taking the dagger?"

Kim still held the dagger in her hand, hanging loosely down beside her thigh. "Yes."

Andrea slipped her friend a mischievous look. "Nice. I promise I won't say anything."

The corners of Kim's mouth lifted into a half smile. Her motivation to keep the dagger was primarily defense, not profit. It was the first weapon she had come across since abandoning *Sabre*. Kim had not voiced any of her worries to Andrea about Travis, nor breathed a word about finding Mark's body last night. She carried those burdens herself.

* * * *

A quarter of a mile ahead the women saw a side trail cut into the dune. They took it, and left the beach, headed northeast into the island's interior. The trail underfoot was a mixture of sand and crushed shell. They slipped back into the flip-flops and crossed through a coastal strand of sea oats and open grassland. The trail angled to the left and Kim discerned by the morning sun directly to their right that they were again headed due north. As they entered the heavier growth of the hammock the damage from the hurricane became evident—thousands of broken limbs, the canopy bare and brown, trees entirely denuded of leaves. Large Australian pines were toppled over by the dozen, their massive root systems now towering overhead, ripped clean out of the ground. The air was deathly still, heavy, and the sharp smell of tree sap was overpowering.

The trail wound north for a mile through a thick maritime forest of live oaks and cabbage palms. The wind hardy palms fared better against the storm than most other trees, which lay snapped and strewn everywhere. They had to climb over several downed limbs that blocked the route. Andrea's ankle was starting to bark at her with the exertion, and Kim had to take her friend's weight supported on a shoulder to continue. Their pace was slow going. Thirty minutes after they left the treasure site, they came out onto a narrow gravel road that traversed the island from east to west. The Cabin Trail. They stopped in the middle and Kim looked up and down the route.

"This is it," Kim said, still balancing Andrea off a shoulder, "this is the main trail that runs out to the cabins and camping area on the beach. We go east, towards the bay."

"You're sure?"

"One hundred percent. It's not even half a mile to the bay from here. The ranger station and docks are straight ahead."

Andrea nodded once, determinedly, sweat pooling and dripping from her chin.

The women set off with renewed vigor, straight into the morning sun, which was now much higher in the sky. The road was lined on either side with thick impenetrable scrub and overhung with a thick canopy of live oak, which still provided some sweet shade, despite the trees missing most of their foliage. Branches, thickets of Spanish moss, and other canopy debris lay scattered all over the trail. At one point the path was blocked with a massive live oak that had fallen over the road. Kim had to help Andrea over the enormous moss-covered trunk.

It took them twenty minutes to come upon the grounds of the ranger station, which was also a visitor center for the island as well as the ferry docks. The gravel road opened into a clearing of crushed shell right on the bay, and they immediately saw hurricane damage to the structures. The grounds were littered with storm debris—palm fronds, mangroves, sea grape, and cocoplum, all broken and strewn about.

Kim could sense immediately that there was no one here, that no one had returned yet since the storm. The place had an abandoned feel, no sound or sign of human presence. There were three buildings, the ranger station, a mobile home trailer that was converted into the gift shop, and off to one far side, a maintenance shed. The ranger station and trailer had survived mostly intact, but the shed had all but collapsed, ripped apart with large sections blown away, revealing its contents: tools, landscape supplies, and a red four-wheeled ATV.

Down at the waterfront, to one side of a little cove, the docks were badly damaged, either half sunk and jutting out of the water at a haphazard angle, or missing entirely, washed away in the storm. There was also a small restroom building, made of cinderblock that had survived almost entirely scathe-free. In the center of the grounds the bare flagpole still stood, and off to the right near the docks a large sign that read WELCOME TO CAYO COSTA STATE PARK had also remained standing on sturdy six-inch square posts.

A white pickup truck with the Florida State Parks emblem on the doors was parked against a buffer of mangroves beyond the restrooms. It had only sustained a cracked windshield and a handful of scrapes and dents, but trailered behind the pickup, the two passenger trams had been flipped over and torn from their hitch. Inside a little cove adjacent to the docks a midsize center console boat was swamped, the stern and outboard engine completely underwater, the vessel canted to starboard.

There was no sign at all that anyone had been here since the storm. The entire place was eerily quiet, too quiet; not the sound of an insect droning or a bird tweeting. Just barely a hint of a hot breeze, the temperature and humidity rising rapidly. Kim figured the time to be somewhere around eleven or eleven-thirty.

"There's no one here," Andrea stated, her mood crumbling.

"It looks that way," said Kim, "but there will be people here soon. It's still early. This is the first place they'll come back. Let's get out of this sun. I want to see if there might be a working phone or radio. I doubt it, but I want to check."

They made for the ranger station first, Andrea hobbling badly now, her ankle pushed past its limit. The ranger station was a small single-story wood bungalow, set raised on three-foot pilings. Sections of the roof were missing shingles, stripped bare down to the plywood. The windows had been shuttered in preparation for the storm before the park rangers departed the island for safer ground on the mainland. Oddly, the front entrance was not only missing any coverings, but the door was wide, swung open inside. One of the doors storm shutters lay just off the porch. It looked like the wind must have caught the entrance's shutters and tore them away, before blowing the door in.

Andrea hissed at the sharp pain in her ankle as she climbed the steps, Kim again helping by taking her weight. The inside of the ranger's bungalow was simple, sparsely furnished with a counter, a desk, a couple of filing cabinets and chairs, and a bench along one wall. There was a large map of the island on a wall, and trifold pamphlets and smaller maps of the park. Kim flicked the light switch on and off a couple of times and was not surprised when nothing happened. She guided Andrea over to the bench, and they sat, thankful to get off their feet.

Both women were sweat-covered, shirts soaked through, and red-faced from heat and sun. For a few minutes they were silent, resting. Kim set the dagger on the armrest of the bench and sat forward, shrugging off the backpack. She pulled out the second bottle of water and they drank, quenching a heavy thirst.

Kim pulled off the sun hat and stood, exploring the ranger station, circling around the counter. There was both a telephone and radio, but without power neither would work. She picked up the phone and found the line was dead. Andrea was looking at her expectantly. Kim shook her head and said, "I'm going to go look around a bit. See if I can find us some more water." She came back around the counter towards Andrea. "I want you to rest here and stay off that ankle. Take a couple more of the Advil, they're in the backpack. I'll just be a few minutes."

"How long do you think it will be before someone comes?" Andrea asked, her forehead creased, worry and pain in her eyes.

"Very soon now. Rest up, I'll just be a couple of minutes, I'll be right back."

Kim had been dismayed by the damage to the docks and the swamped park boat. If the docks on Pine Island were just as badly damaged, getting a boat over to Cayo Costa would prove difficult anytime soon. She did not voice these concerns to Andrea, nor the grim possibility that they might be stuck on the island for yet another night.

Stepping back outside Kim surveyed the grounds again, the harsh sun hitting her like a blast furnace. The skin on her bare arms, neck, and shoulders were already tinged red from the hike up the beach. She crossed first towards the docks and looked out over Pelican Bay. The hurricane had churned the bay up, dumping heavy rainfall and storm runoff. The normally emerald-green water was a dark brown. Squinting against the sun's glare across the murky water, to the northeast out Pelican Pass she saw a lone boat. The vessel was at least a mile distant, heading south. Kim watched it disappear behind the north point of Punta Blanca.

Disheartened, she turned and decided to make for the gift shop. Traversing a long ramp up to the trailer she saw the gift shop had a Dutch door, and the top section was open. Reaching the door and leaning in she saw the interior had been hit with the hurricane's full force winds, and the entire contents had been both tossed and soaked through. What caught her eye was the plethora of snacks and drinks that had been strewn about the trailer—bags of chips, chocolate bars, granola bars, cans of soda, bottles of water and sports drinks—among sunblock, mosquito repellant, and dozens of other camping supplies.

Kim tried the handle, but the door was locked, and she couldn't figure out how to open it from inside. Hiking herself up on two hands, she popped a leg over the sill and swung over the top of the door's lower half, dropping down into the trailer. The carpeted floor was completely soaked underfoot. Kim bent and scooped up a couple of snack bars and bags of chips, as well as a plastic quart bottle of orange Gatorade and a can of Coke. Shoving the bars into her pockets she spied a freezer full of frozen confectionaries. She didn't need to even slide open the lid to know they were all long melted. Cradling the drinks under an arm and the chips pinch-gripped in her other hand, Kim hauled herself back over the top of the Dutch door. She returned directly to the ranger station cutting across the grounds. From this direction she saw that the far side wall of the park ranger bungalow was a large hand-painted wall mural map of Cayo Costa.

Kim stopped and studied it for a minute. Cayo Costa was a long thin island, running north to south, shaped somewhat like an archer's bow. The curved western shore facing the Gulf of Mexico was sandy beach, and the straighter eastern side on Pine Island Sound was salt mangroves. The location of the ranger station was marked, about four-fifths of the way up the island on the bay. Hand-painted in black lettering off to one side near a compass were some facts about the island.

Cayo Costa was 2426 acres in size, nine miles long and averaged a mile wide. It received 100,000 visitors a year, and two park rangers lived full-time on the island. Kim was sure the park rangers evacuated and did not remain on the island through the hurricane. If so, they would have surely returned to check on the ranger station by now. Kim noted the Cabin Trail which ran straight across the island from the ranger station to the camping area on the beach.

The southern end of the island was called The Narrows, a long thin stretch that looked only a few hundred feet across in parts. Judging from the distance they had walked north, somewhere down there was the cabin in which they had spent the night, and where they had come ashore on *Sabre*. She saw the dashed line for the smaller side trail where they had cut in off the beach. Kim knitted her brows at the map, and roughly guessed the location where they had found the treasure to be. It was about two-thirds of the way up the island, just south of a massive lagoon. Kim extended an index finger and touched the wall mural.

"X marks the spot," she said confidently.

Returning into the ranger station, Kim found Andrea dozing in the late morning heat, lying on her back along the bench. Her friend had taken off the sun hat, and looked exhausted, face flushed and sweaty.

"It's freaking hot," Andrea said, rolling her head lazily to look at Kim.

"I know," Kim replied, coming to kneel beside the bench. "Look what I found though, drinks and some food. We need to eat something." Kim held up the drinks. "Gatorade or Coke? Sorry, they're not cold."

"Coke."

Kim popped open the soda and handed it to Andrea, digging the candy bars out of her pockets. "Here, I got us Snickers, and chips too."

HURRICANE HOLE

"Thank you," Andrea said, sipping the Coke and fanning her face. "Christ, this heat—it's going to kill me."

"It must be coming up on noon," Kim said, "it's gonna get even hotter." She kicked off her flip-flops and sat cross-legged on the floor beside Andrea, pulling open a bag of chips and popping one into her mouth. Kim hadn't thought of food much at all and didn't realize how hungry she was. They hadn't eaten anything since the evening before yesterday.

"The park rangers should be back here soon—they'll for sure be able to get over here today, right?" Andrea asked.

Kim answered through a mouthful of chips. "I think so. I'm positive someone will come to check on this place. But this hurricane must have done some serious damage to Pine Island and Cape Coral as well, or wherever they're coming over from. They've likely got stuff to deal with where they are as well."

"You think the storm hit Englewood real bad too?"

Kim paused putting more chips in her mouth. "I hope not. I don't think it would have reached that far north. We got the brunt of it here, that's for sure; the eye of the hurricane went right over us. I think Englewood would have just got some strong wind."

Andrea was quiet for a moment, and then asked, "How do you know the eye went over us?"

Kim chewed and swallowed a mouthful of chips. Without looking at Andrea she answered tonelessly. "I saw it."

Andrea observed Kim's sober and detached face and decided to remain silent for a few moments. Finally, she stated the obvious. "We're going to have to call the police."

Kim broke from her reverie. "I know. We will. It's the first thing we're going to do."

After a silent couple of minutes, Andrea tore open a Snickers. The chocolate was a melted mess inside the wrapper.

Licking a finger, she asked, "What was Travis's last name? Grainger? I think it started with a G."

"Gardner, if I remember right. He's from Tallahassee. We have a photo of him."

Andrea looked up from her liquefied candy bar. "We do?"

"He's in the picture I took, the day before yesterday. When we were anchored off Redfish Pass, the afternoon Chad caught the shark. I snapped a shot of the four of you together."

Andrea's eyebrows shot up. She nodded, remembering. "Yes . . . that's right."

"The camera is on *Sabre*. We can show the photo to the police."

Andrea was still nodding slowly. "We're going to have to contact Chad and Mark's families . . ."

"Let's not think about that all right now, Andrea."

Kim had brushed aside thoughts of having to call Mark's parents on vacation up in Canada. What would she say to them? How would she explain this? Thinking it through, she didn't even have a number to contact them at . . .

They ate the half-melted candy bars in silence, licking their fingers clean, and sipping the tepid drinks. They waited, dozing as the afternoon temperature built. The skies were mostly clear, just the occasional light cloud passing lazily overhead. The August sun beat down on the quiet hurricane-thrashed island, raising the heat and humidity to oppressive levels.

CHAPTER THIRTEEN

Kim woke again, for the second time today on yet another hard wood floor. She opened her eyes to the dim interior of the ranger station. The air was still, heavy and humid. Her skin was slick with a beaded layer of sweat, and she could feel her clothing damp, almost completely soaked through. It must have been pushing a hundred degrees in the bungalow, a sweatbox sauna with the only ventilation being the open front door. She raised her head and looked up to the bench beside her.

Andrea was not there.

Frowning, Kim sat up stiffly, and yawned. A quick look around revealed Andrea was not inside the ranger station. Judging from the angle of the sunbeams streaming in the doorway some time had passed since she had fallen asleep. Maybe an hour, an hour and a half.

"Andrea?" Kim called out.

No answer.

The island outside the door was dead silent. It would have been comforting to hear the usual insects buzzing and birdcalls, but after a hurricane there were none of these sounds. The violent storm wiped out much of the island's wildlife—crushed, drowned, or blown away. Kim rose and stretched, loosening her tight shoulders and neck. She was still hopeful they would be able to get off the island today, and she could sleep on a dry, soft mattress tonight. A mattress and air conditioning. At least the floor of the bungalow was dry.

The floor was dry . . .

Kim slid her bare foot across the floorboards, grains of sand sliding beneath her sole. She looked up, glancing quickly around the interior of the ranger station. Everything was in order: the pamphlets, brochures, and paperwork behind the counter were not only dry, but they had also not been disturbed by high winds.

Kim's expression hardened, a new trickle of concern snaking up her spine, bringing her fully awake. The front door to the ranger station had been closed during the onslaught of the hurricane. Someone had only opened it later, after the storm had passed. Someone had been here since—there *was* someone on the island with them.

Kim picked up the dagger from the armrest of the bench, gripping the hilt in a sweaty palm. She crossed to the door, glanced over the grounds, and stepped slowly out onto the porch, squinting against the glaring sun. The visitor area vacant and silent, with no sign of Andrea anywhere.

Hesitating only a moment, Kim called out loudly, a hint of concern in her voice. "Andrea!"

A couple of beats passed with no reply.

Kim's concern began to creep its way up to outright alarm.

She heard a faint scratching noise and looked down off the porch to see a large gopher tortoise making its way across the gravel path. The reptile had a dark brown-bronze patterned shell a foot wide, and was moving incredibly slowly, the sound of its claws on the crushed shell loud in the ambient silence. The animal stopped and looked up at Kim, studying her with small black eyes.

The gunshot cut through the quiet afternoon like a hammer, causing both Kim and the tortoise to jump.

Kim froze, eyes wide, heart pumping adrenaline.

The tortoise disappeared into its shell.

HURRICANE HOLE

* * * *

Andrea's bladder had woken her. She came awake on the bench in the ranger station and looked down to where Kim slept on the floor below. They had both dozed off, a siesta through the midday heat. Andrea needed to pee, bad. She got up quietly, so as not to wake Kim, stepping over her sleeping friend, and slipping into the flip-flops. Her ankle had improved somewhat again with the rest and another round of ibuprofen, but still complained loudly when she stood on it.

Fuzzy headed from dozing deeply, both overheated and exhausted, Andrea made her way out of the bungalow and down the front porch steps, hobbling, putting weight gingerly on her injured ankle. She crossed the visitor grounds towards the restrooms. Looking to the docks and scanning the sun-glistened waters of Pelican Bay, she saw no sign of any boats. Despondent, she crossed towards the cinderblock restroom structure. Both entrances were on the far side from the ranger station, facing the bay. Passing the men's entrance she continued to the women's door and pulled on the handle. The door was locked.

"Shit . . ." Andrea muttered under a tired breath, turning and backtracking to try the men's door, expecting to find it locked as well. It was.

Taking a step back, her bladder pressing, she abashedly looked around and saw no one. The grounds were as deserted as when they first arrived. She walked back to the opposite women's end of the restrooms and stepped from the crushed shell path onto grass. She looked around again, feeling awkward, hesitating, then hurriedly dropped her shorts and panties and

226

dropped to a squat. Finishing quickly, Andrea grasped her clothing and stood . . . and caught a rush of movement off to her right. There was a sharp hissing sound.

A spray of cool liquid hit the right side of her face. At first, Andrea thought it was water, but a second later she felt a searing burn. Before she could turn to look at who or what had sprayed her, her eyes, nose, and mouth came afire. Immediately it became impossible to open her eyes. Andrea's hands abandoned buttoning her shorts and went straight to her face. Instinctively she rubbed her eyes, but this only made the burning instantly worse. The noxious bitter liquid burnt her face, searing her lips and was sharply bitter in her mouth. Eyes watering, unable to open them, the pain building, and with her shorts and panties fallen back around her ankles, Andrea was helpless.

Blinded, she stumbled back against the cinderblock wall, her right ankle sending a stabbing jolt to her brain as she put her weight fully upon it. Her face was a tortuous mask of scorching heat, and she gasped to try and breathe through the acrid fumes.

Andrea felt a fist grab her hair and her head was savagely yanked back. A voice hissed in her ear: "You fucking little bitch."

She froze in horror, a blast of realization and fear punching through her gut.

Travis.

He was alive. He was here.

She tried desperately to open her eyes, but they stung like they had been splashed with acid. She could only make out his watery, blurred shape through scrunched eyelids impossible to force open. Andrea wheezed to call out for Kim, but Travis was on her, one hand around her throat, slamming her back against the cinderblock wall.

"Both of you—little sluts," Travis said, his face inches from hers, grinning like a mad hyena with his prize, his fingers brutally crushing her windpipe. The backside of his left hand was deeply pockmarked with a semi-circle of rouge marks from where Andrea had bit him yesterday. "Left me for dead in a goddamn hurricane, huh?"

Travis was barefoot, his salt-matted hair wild and unruly, five days of dark stubble on his face. He shoved the canister of pepper spray back into the side cargo pocket of the shorts, alongside the Sig Sauer.

He held Andrea pinned hard up against the wall, his eyes going down her body. She was naked from the waist down, crumpled shorts and panties around her ankles. Travis hungrily eyed the neatly trimmed strip of brown pubic hair below her toned belly.

"Oh boy, missy, you and I are finally gonna have our fun."

Andrea was straining to open her eyes against the burning capsicum, struggling to gasp air past Travis's hand crushing her trachea. She felt his other hand slip between her legs, and she twisted away, but it backfired—he went with it and rolled her right around, so she was faceup against the wall.

Travis slid his rough chin against the back of her neck, pulling the fistful of hair. He could smell coconut-scented sunblock and her strong female scent, a sweaty heat, oozing pheromones. It had been three days since he had sex with Kim, and more than a day since he tried to come onto Andrea in her cabin. Travis was mad horny, angry, and in pain, having been through his own ordeal to survive the past twenty-four hours.

He had been tumbled inside *End of Watch*'s cabin like a sock inside a spin dryer, badly wrenching his right leg and hip when the boat was thrown up onto the beach. He had pulled himself from the grounded vessel, taking only the gun and the pepper spray, lying flat in the lee of the dunes through the worst of the hurricane. The wind-blown sand had abraded his skin raw, and he nearly drowned in the storm surge. After the cyclone passed, he had tried to get his bearings, hiking north, unhinged and enraged, limping under the stars up the island. He blindly crossing over to the bay side in The Narrows, missing both *Sabre* and the cabin.

Andrea struggled fiercely in his grip, but he leaned his weight against her, tightening his hand again around her throat.

"You know I fucked your friend Kim—now it's your turn sweetie. I'm gonna have you both, just like you and Kim were planning to have Mark and Chad. Yeah, I know about that. Too bad they're dead now." Travis's words and breath were in her ear. One hand at her throat, the other slipped up under her shirt, roughly squeezing a small breast through her bra. "You girls were on my agenda since I first saw you, so I'm quite happy to see you made it through that storm." Travis pulled roughly at the tie cord of his boardshorts. "Where is Kim, anyway? Is she around? Maybe she wants to watch?"

It was all Andrea could do to breathe and fight the burning pain across her face, let alone scream or try and defend herself from the assault. She realized she was totally helpless. Involuntarily she felt her body go slack, and this surprised her, she felt distant and numb, and was overcome with a detachedness from the scenario, fallen over with a tonic immobility.

Travis's mouth was against her ear, breathing labored. There was no sense of the passage of time.

Andrea felt his hand release from around her neck and after a few seconds she felt a rushing return to reality, a harsh jolt as she gasped wildly for air. The pepper spray's burning pain returned horribly, and she could still not open her eyes, nose running, mucus cascading down her face. She spat and leaned forward with a forearm on the wall, eyes squeezed shut, streaming tears.

He stepped back, breathing hard. "Alright, where's Kim?"

Andrea didn't reply. Travis had noticed she was favoring her right ankle. He looked at Andrea's bunched-up shorts and panties around her ankles and saw a small round metal object had fallen from one of her pockets. He did not know at all what to make of it, more concerned with locating Kim. "Where's Kim?" he asked again. "How long have you been here?"

Travis hadn't stuck around the ranger station long upon arriving earlier this morning. He departed soon after breaking into the bungalow and finding nothing useful, missing the gift shop entirely, and taking a long winding path called the Cemetery Trail. Reaching the Quarantine Rocks at the far north end of Cayo Costa and finding nothing there, he had doubled slowly back to the visitor grounds, hobbling on a bad hip. Hot, tired, hungry, and incredibly thirsty, he had been just about to venture up and explore the gift shop trailer when he saw Andrea crossing towards the restrooms and circled around behind her.

Sobbing, Andrea shook her head and turned to lean a shoulder against the wall. She spit again, straining to see Travis through burning, tearing eyes. She bent and felt for her shorts, pulling them up. As she did a second silver piece tumbled out onto the grass, catching Travis's eye. Andrea fumbled with zipping and buttoning her shorts, sniffing back mucus, her cheeks streaked with tears. "You asshole," was all she could murmur, with pure rancor, trying to halt her sobbing.

Travis stepped forward and tromped a foot down hard on Andrea's right ankle. She hissed sharply and lifted her leg, twisting awkwardly, the strained ligament screaming in agony.

"I said where is she?" Travis asked, closing in on her again, threatening. His eyes flicked down to the two metal coins on the grass. His face glowered, having no patience with her. "What're those?"

Andrea could barely see and had no idea what he was talking about. Before she could respond, Kim's voice rang out: "Andrea!"

Travis's hand went immediately for the pistol in his pocket. "Don't you say a fucking thing—keep quiet." His tone was hushed, uneasy. Kim was somewhere around the far side of the restrooms, up near the ranger station. "Don't move," Travis ordered, raising the gun, edging himself towards the side of the restrooms.

Andrea saw Travis's blurred shape move away. In an uncontrolled panic, unaware he had a weapon, she took her chance and bolted. Half-blind, her ankle stabbing pain with each agonizing step, she dodged, going around the opposite side of the restrooms, making for the path back to the ranger station. She had only gone a half-dozen yards when the Sig Sauer erupted behind her. She felt a crushing blow over her right hip that felt like she had been hit by a car.

The 9mm caught her in the right oblique, tearing through the muscle, shredding her kidney in half, and exiting her lower abdomen. The impact sent her flying forward, spinning around, and tumbling to the crushed shell. Andrea's sandals flew off, spinning away, and the third silver piece came out of her pocket, skittering, rolling, and toppling over to stop a few feet out in front of where she lay.

* * * *

HURRICANE HOLE

At the sound of the gunshot Kim dashed from the porch, dagger in hand, towards the restrooms. She saw Andrea straight away, raise her head, eyes scrunched closed. Blood was spreading quickly from her waist, staining her yellow shirt a bright red, seeping through her fingers. Kim slowed up her run quickly, despair twisting her gut, stopping a few yards from Andrea.

Kim looked up from her friend and saw Travis. He was coming around the far side of the restrooms, the pistol pointed directly at her, a twisted mixture of evil and delight in his eyes.

He limped on his right leg, and she saw there was a deep bruise and a cut with crusted and dried blood over his right eye. He had somehow survived the hurricane on a boat with a dead engine and made it onto Cayo Costa—but not without taking a few licks. Kim tried to catch a breath, an awful roll of dread and panic rising in her chest.

Travis held the pistol out, straight at Kim's head. "Nice of you to come out and join the fun," he said, "it's finally just the three of us."

Kim broke her eyes away from Travis and looked down to Andrea. She was groaning, lying flat on her stomach, right hand still clamped over the side of her waist. Andrea squinted down at the slick blood pouring through her fingers. Her breathing was rapid and labored. Kim saw then that Andrea's face was red, her eyes half closed and watering, nose running profusely. That was something other than the gunshot wound.

Kim made a step towards to Andrea.

"Don't move," said Travis, coming forward, angling the pistol threateningly.

Kim hesitated, and decided to ignore him, concern for her friend overpowering fear of Travis. She walked ahead, dropping to a knee beside Andrea. As she did so her eye quickly caught the piece of eight lying on the crushed shell.

Anger rolled through Travis. "I said to not fucking move!"

Not looking at him, Kim leaned over Andrea, trying to determine what to do, for both her friend's wound and the dire predicament they were in. She could see the bullet had gone in and out, through Andrea's waist about two inches above her hip bone. Andrea was lucky it did not hit her spine or a vital organ, but she would need medical help right away.

"You're OK," Kim said. "Keep your hand covering—just keep pressure on it."

Steeling herself, she turned to look up at Travis, facing him directly from where she knelt. "If you're going to kill us, then go ahead and kill us. I need to help Andrea. Whatever you say, or tell me to do, I'm not listening to you. You can fuck off."

Travis was taken aback by Kim's seemingly fearless gall. "Like hell you're not listening to me." He stepped forward repositioning the gun a half dozen feet from her face.

Kim winced and held her position.

"Where's the catamaran?" Travis asked.

Kim paused for a moment and shook her head. "It's high and dry—up on the beach."

"Where?"

"At the south end of the island. A two-hour walk from here. It doesn't matter, forget it. You can't use it—it's grounded."

"Kim . . ." Andrea's voice was faint and thickly layered with pain. She raised her head, straining to open teared eyes. "He raped me."

Kim went rigid, her anger spiking and blood going from simmer to full boil. She saw red. Kim stood slowly, raising the dagger in her hand, holding it out threateningly at Travis. "You bastard."

Travis glanced at the dagger and his brows knitted, the gun wavering. He snickered. "What the hell is that?"

Kim's eyes dropped to the dagger in her hand and glazed for a moment.

Travis laughed again. "Are you kidding me, Kim? You ever hear the one about bringing a knife to a gunfight? Where did you get that from? The gift shop?"

Kim said nothing, she was only thinking, an idea forming. She glanced down at the silver coin that had fallen from Andrea's pocket. She looked back up at Travis. He still held the pistol pointed directly at her face; the weapon's steel matte black in the hot sun.

Kim spoke as confidently and unwavering as she could. "Travis, I'm going to tell you something, and you're going to believe me."

Travis took on an amused expression and cocked his head. "Why the fuck would I believe anything you tell me?"

"Because you're an absolute fool if you don't."

Travis blinked twice and shrugged. "Well, alright, try me. I don't have all day. What is it you want to tell me?"

Kim licked her lips. "We found treasure on the island. Real treasure. Out on the beach. The hurricane uncovered it . . . in the dunes. It's got to be worth millions. This dagger"—Kim teetered the blade in her hand—"is part of what we found. So is this."

Using the toe of her flip-flop she flicked the silver piece on the shell in front of her across to Travis. Suspicious, he looked down at it briefly, recognizing it as the same as the other two pieces that fell from Andrea's shorts. "What's that?" he asked, his eyes already back on Kim.

"That's a silver coin," Kim answered, "there are hundreds of them out on the beach, as well as emeralds. All about a mile from here. I can show you exactly where they are."

Travis's face twisted into a lopsided smile. "What in the Christ are you—"

"I'm not lying, Travis. I'm telling you the truth. I'll show you where it all is. All I want in return is for you to leave Andrea and I alone. Let us go. I will give you a long head start. I won't say anything to the police that will help them find you. You'll have until they figure that out."

Travis shook his head, looking both amused and confused. Amused because he didn't believe her, confused because it sounded like she was telling him the steadfast truth. "Wait. You're telling me you found buried treasure out here? Like buried pirate treasure?"

"Yes. And you've got—maybe—just enough time to gather as much of it up as you can carry and get off the island with it. There's a park ranger boat over in that cove. It looks like it still works." Kim nodded off to her left, bluffing, hoping Travis had not yet seen and would not immediately check the boat. "I will even help you carry it. You can take it all and get away clean, with a running head start, if you hurry. People will be returning to the island, soon now."

Travis said nothing, glancing towards the cove, adjusting his stance, his arm tiring from holding the gun out, his brain digesting Kim's words. Treasure or no treasure he was interested to learn there might be a working boat on the island. "Where's this boat?" he asked.

Kim felt her heart pang. She couldn't be caught in a lie now. She nodded towards the cove. "Right over there."

Travis looked again over towards the cove, then back at Kim. "This all sounds just a bit too unbelievable."

Kim raised the dagger and angled the blade so it faced away from Travis. She slowly dropped to a knee and placed the dagger out in front of her on the ground. She stood and took a few steps back, moving out in front of Andrea. "Take a look for yourself. You tell me if that dagger came from a gift shop."

Travis smirked, looking entertained with this all. His confidence rose further seeing that Kim had relinquished the weapon. Watching Kim closely, he stepped forward, bent, and picked up the coin near his feet. He flipped it over in his hand giving it a quick study. Travis knew nothing about centuries old coins, but to his untrained eye the silver piece looked real. He slipped the coin into his pocket alongside the pepper spray, and stepped forward again, eyes on Kim.

Travis bent and picked up the dagger by the hilt, immediately surprised by the heavy weight and balance. The weapon was real, the six-inch blade steel, and the stones embedded in the pommel and cross-guard looked genuine as well. One thing was for sure, it was no gift shop toy replica. Travis glanced up at Kim, his face twisting in indecision. She said nothing, watching him poker-faced.

Cautiously, Travis turned and walked back to the side of the restrooms. Facing Kim, he knelt, set down the dagger, and picked up the two other coins that had dropped from Andrea's clothing. Examining them briefly, he pocketed them both, before retrieving the dagger. He gave the blade another glance over, stood, and walked back towards Kim.

"Decide now," said Kim, "and choose wisely. That dagger and those coins alone are worth tens of thousands—maybe more, let alone their historical value. But you need to hurry. You need to make up your mind, the clock is ticking, for both you, and Andrea. She dies and the deals off."

Travis grimaced and snickered, resenting that she was putting him under pressure. "What deal? I could just kill you both now and keep what I have."

"Then you'd be walking away from an absolute fortune.

Millions. Settle for just a dagger and three coins? You can carry more than that. There're millions in gold, silver, and stones out there. And the one thing you're going to need most on the run is money—and lots of it. I'm offering you that."

Travis took a breath. "Alright. I'll bite . . . show me this treasure find of yours."

Kim nodded once. "First, I need to see to Andrea, get her back inside, out of the sun. I want to see she is OK—she needs help."

Travis pursed his parched lips and gave Kim a guarded look. "Make it fast."

Andrea was pale and half-conscious, her breathing rapid and shallow. Kim judged she had lost at least two pints of blood, pooled a bright red on the white crushed shell. And more internally. She got Andrea's arm around her, helping her to her feet. Andrea groaned loudly, gasping in short, sharp breaths. "It's OK," said Kim, "I'm gonna get you inside. Keep your hand on your stomach. Keep pressing hard."

Moving as quickly as they could, Travis following a half-dozen feet behind, they crossed the grounds. Kim half dragged Andrea, trying to ignore her moans and hisses as they stumbled up the steps to the ranger station. Kim got her inside, over to the bench and sat her down. Travis stood in the doorway, gun and dagger in hand. Kim had seen a first aid kit on her initial search of the ranger station. She crossed behind the counter and popped the kit open, pulling out rolls of gauze, pads, and tape. She returned to the bench and hastily proceeded to bandage the wounds on Andrea's waist. The entry and exit holes were not huge—the bullet had gone in and come out clean—but they bled profusely. Kim covered the wounds in layers of pads, staunching the bleeding, unspooling and wrapping the gauze tightly around Andrea's waist. Andrea cried out and inhaled sharply with each pass.

"I'm sorry," said Kim, her voice strained. The bandaging had stopped the blood loss for now, but Kim knew Andrea was bleeding internally. She needed medical attention, but they were entirely helpless on the island, even without the threat of Travis. There was no way to call out, and as far as Kim really knew, no working boat.

"Andrea, listen to me," Kim spoke as calmly as she could as she finished taping the gauze wrapping. "I'm going to take him to the treasure. We'll be fast. I'll be right back."

"I'm thirsty," was Andrea's only reply, her voice hoarse and weak. Her eyes were red-rimmed and bloodshot and still only half open, pupils unfocused.

Kim reached for a half-full Gatorade beside the bench, uncapped it, and helped Andrea drink.

"Where did you get the Gatorade?" Travis asked, stepping forward into the bungalow. He had a burning thirst that grew stronger with each passing hour. He'd had nothing to drink for more than a day in the relentless heat.

"I found it in here," Kim lied, not wanting to tell him about the drinks in the gift shop trailer.

"Give me some," Travis demanded.

Kim continued to let Andrea drink most of what was left and reluctantly held the plastic bottle out to Travis. It only had a fifth of the orange-flavored sports drink left. Travis snatched it from her hand and swallowed the remaining contents down in one fast gulp, tossing the empty bottle aside. Kim could see how thirsty he was and guessed he might not have had anything to drink since the evening before yesterday. The more dehydrated he was, the better.

"Is there anymore?" Travis asked.

Kim glanced down at the empty rum bottle to avoid his eyes. "No. We brought some water with us from the boat, but it's gone. We drank it."

Travis scowled at her.

With a look of concern, she turned to Andrea. "I want you to lay down and keep pressure on your stomach." She helped Andrea shift her weight and lean back down, causing her to groan and hiss again. Kim guided her head down to the bench and then got up to retrieve a black hoodie from atop a filing cabinet. She folded it over twice and slid it under Andrea's head.

Andrea turned to Kim, whispering, "Don't trust him. He'll kill you."

"I know," Kim replied, hushed, shifting her eyes to look back at Travis in her peripheral vision. "I have a plan. Don't worry, I'll be back. It will be alright. You rest—don't move, just stay here. Try and keep compression on those bandages."

Andrea's face was a mask of pain and she'd paled considerably under her tan. Kim was extremely worried about her friend, the grievous injury, the shock, the bleeding. There was nothing she could do but lead Travis to the treasure, try and get the upper hand, and return to Andrea as quickly as possible. Maybe the park rangers would arrive in the meantime, or somebody would come to the island . . . anybody. Keeping a show of strength on her face, Kim nodded once at Andrea, picked up the knapsack at the end of the bench and started towards the door.

"Wait," said Travis, "what's in the bag?"

"Nothing. The bag's not for me, it's for you. To carry your spoils. We both need to hurry—let's go."

* * * *

HURRICANE HOLE

Kim led Travis west, along the Cabin Trail, directly across the island for the beach. On a hunch, she decided to pass the intersecting side trail that she and Andrea had come in on, and remained heading west, deciding to go directly to the beach and cut south to the treasure from there.

Travis had the Sig Sauer in one hand and the dagger in the other, both hanging loosely by his side. In the cargo pocket of the boardshorts he had the pepper spray and three silver coins. Kim noted again he was limping off his right leg and he was moving much slower than her, working hard to keep up. She had on the flip-flops, and he was barefoot, injured and dehydrated. She set the pace fast enough to try and wear him down without it being obvious.

"You know exactly where this treasure is?" Travis asked, huffing, working to stay alongside Kim.

"Yes."

"Where is it?"

"I told you."

"Well, what's there, exactly?"

"I told you that too. More coins—lots more coins, emeralds, and gold. You'll be able to carry a fair bit of it. Grab what you can, get yourself back to that boat, and get off the island."

Travis held the dagger up, looking it over again. "You really think this is worth tens of thousands of dollars?"

"Yes, probably more. A hell of a lot more."

Travis grinned. "Maybe you can lift a few pieces for yourself, huh?"

"Maybe. If I were you, I'd focus on yourself."

Travis looked at Kim, his forehead creased and glistened with sweat. "What do you mean, *maybe*? You already grabbed this dagger and Andrea took some coins. And thanks for the advice, but I am focused on myself. I know what I'm doing."

Kim kept up a steady hiking pace while she spoke. "This is a state park. Anything found inside the park of historical value belongs to the state. There's no way you or I or anyone would be allowed to keep anything." She glanced at Travis and saw he was under some strain to keep up. "We need to hurry. I want to get back to Andrea and you need to get off the island as fast as possible, before the park rangers come back."

They carried on for another few hundred yards. The Cabin Trail from the ranger station to the beach was just shy of a mile, a dirt road through a dense maritime hammock of live oak, cabbage palm and tropical scrub. The canopy, although mostly denuded of foliage, provided some shade from the early afternoon sun. The heat was absolutely stifling. Both Kim and Travis were used to Florida's intense summer heat, Travis acclimated even more so, but that aside he was edging on serious dehydration.

"Where did you ride out the storm?" he asked.

"On *Sabre*." Kim lied, and her flesh prickled. After a moment's hesitation, she asked, "Who was the body on your boat?"

Travis snorted. "Ha—if you can believe it, a retired cop. He was in my way. I shot him."

Kim pulled a face and looked briefly at Travis. "You murdered a cop and stole his boat?"

"Yep."

"Killing a police officer—they're going to be looking for you triple time."

Travis snorted again, bragging, all bravado. "Yeah, and I dropped a guard at the prison too. If and when they can get around to connecting any of it after this storm. They need to find me first."

Kim noted concernedly he had a point on the storm,

it would have slowed down and hampered search efforts for Travis. She said, "They can and they will, eventually."

"Bullshit. They've got a hell of a trail to follow, and a hurricane thrown in the mix. I'll be out of the state before they even find that boat—*End of Watch*. And I tossed the stinking cop overboard, he's shark bait. No one will find him."

Kim grimly wondered if Travis threw Mark's body off the boat as well. She had found him . . . The dead cop could wash in somewhere as well.

They came on another downed live oak and had to navigate over it. Kim saw Travis wince as he hauled himself across the trunk. He looked to have an injury to his right hip.

"Is that where you got the gun? From the cop you killed?" Kim asked as they continued across on the other side of the oak.

"No. I found it in a car, outside the prison."

Kim looked over at Travis. "You escaped from a prison?"

"Yeah, from Belle Glade, three—no, four days ago. Hell, I'm losing track of the days out here. Life was a little more structured in the clink." He grinned. "But I'm havin' way more fun out here."

Kim was silent, absorbing this. Travis was certainly spilling all to her now. "What were you in prison for?"

"I told you, drugs."

Kim didn't know whether to believe him, but she didn't question him further. He had no qualms about revealing all this to her. There was no doubt in her mind he had no intention of letting her and Andrea go free. He was going to kill them. As remorselessly as he killed Chad and Mark, but maybe not so quickly . . .

Kim decided then that she wasn't going to take Travis to the treasure.

It took them twenty-five minutes to reach the beach. The trail opened from hammock to coastal strand, winding through clusters of sea grape. They passed the remains of a small camping cabin; it lay collapsed and stripped to pieces on a side trail. The wind had lifted it right off its cinder block pilings. As they approached the backside of the dunes a swath of headless cabbage palm trunks marked the top of the beach. The hurricane had completely sheared off their rounded heads as clean as if they were lopped off with scissors.

Coming out onto the open dune ridges the August sun beat down on them with its full intensity. The heat was incredible. Kim saw Travis's black T-shirt was not that wet, his perspiration had slowed, and his entire back was crusted with a pattern of white dried salt. Walking out onto the sand Kim head straight across the berm, down the beach face towards the water. At the surf she slipped off her flip-flops and carried them, walking north along the cool, wet pan.

Travis set out after her, struggling to keep up, and trying not to let it show. The sunbaked sand was blistering hot on his feet, and he hopped along, hissing. "It's this way?" he asked, flustered, rushing towards the cooler wet sand.

"Yes."

"How far?"

Kim did not slow her walk or turn back. "About a half mile, around the point."

Standing in the ankle-deep surf, the comparatively cool Gulf water relieving the stinging burn to his feet, Travis looked up the beach, past Kim, squinting against the shimmering glare off the sand. He followed her silently for a few minutes, trailing a half-dozen feet behind, before asking, "You came this far north?"

"Yes," Kim replied, lying again. The heat was beginning to

get to her as well; she had a rising thirst and felt heady, light-headed. She had not brought anything to drink, not wanting Travis to be able to hydrate, hoping she could outlast him. "After finding the treasure we realized we were too far north, we had to double back to find the ranger station."

Ahead of them a long white sand spit jutted out into the water, and the beach curved back and fell away to the east. The hurricane-agitated Gulf was a dark greenish brown under the zenith sun.

Solar noon. No shadows.

Kim could sense a hesitation in Travis, and she turned to look back. He trod along, looking hot and in some discomfort. "What happened to your leg?" Kim asked. She didn't care, and hoped it hurt like hell, but she wanted to keep him walking and distracted.

"When the boat beached, it flipped over. Yanked my leg. I bet you thought I drowned, huh?"

"I'd say you got real lucky, surviving the hurricane on that boat."

Travis grunted and glared at Kim. "Lucky enough to come in on the same island as the two of you girls. How much farther?"

Kim ignored the question. "If you play your cards right, you'll get away scot-free and rich. You're gonna need money on the lam, lots of it."

"How much farther?" Travis asked again.

"It's just around the point."

They traversed a wide sandbar and Kim stepped down into a wide tidal pool. The water came to her knees, clear and warm, heated by the sun into the high nineties. Kim saw a large five-armed starfish on the rippled sand bottom. "Where did your boat come in?" she asked.

"What?" Travis asked, stumbling in the water, stepping on something sharp and hissing loudly.

"Where did your boat—*End of Watch*—where did you come in on the island?"

"I don't know. South of here. I walked up the island late last night."

Kim was surprised by this. Travis might have walked right by the cabin, and *Sabre*, but fortunately seemed to have seen either. They did not see *End of Watch*, so if he came in north of them, it was possible the boat was washed back out into the Gulf. Kim stepped up out of the pool and paused, looking back. Travis was struggling to navigate the tidal pool, favoring his leg, arms wavering. If he tripped and lost his balance now, he would plant both the gun and the dagger in the water.

"Where did you spend the night?" Kim asked, attempting to distract him.

Travis looked up at Kim and froze, his eyes immediately focused on something behind her. His face shadowed alarm.

Kim turned quickly—and suppressed a gasp.

A few hundred yards up the beach a massive ship was pushed high on the sand, lying at a thirty degree angle to the waterline. It was a shipping freighter, at least 350 feet in length, with a white hull and towering superstructure. Spaced along her upper deck were four large jib derricks for loading and unloading cargo containers. Her boot stripe was royal blue and the exposed bottom hull a deep copper red. The huge hydrodynamic bow was a bulbous point, and her stern sat resting a hundred feet out into the water. The cargo ship was canted heavily to port, pushed into the shallows and driven high onto the beach by the hurricane's 150-mile-per-hour winds.

In black bold letters amidships on her starboard hull Kim could read ANASTASI SHIPPING LINE and forward on her bow, in smaller black letters, the vessel's name, *Banten Buru*. The freighter was a refrigerated cargo ship, also called a reefer. The red and white flag of Indonesia hung from her stern, hanging loosely in the doldrum afternoon heat. There was no sound coming from the freighter, and no one visible on the decks or bridge. She sat silent, high and dry on the sands of Cayo Costa.

Kim did not react to seeing the freighter, her brain working quickly. She connected that this ship might have been what the Coast Guard helicopter was observing when it was hovering over this area of the island earlier this morning. And that she would have to make it appear to Travis that she had already passed the ship this morning.

Travis was stopped dead in his tracks in the tidal pool, mouth half open, staring at the freighter. Worry knotted the pit of his stomach. "What's this? You knew this ship was here?" he asked, glaring at Kim.

Keeping the surprise at seeing the ship from her face, Kim turned back to Travis. "Yes, it was here this morning. There's no one onboard. It's abandoned."

"Abandoned? Where's the crew?" Travis asked, squinting worriedly up at the windows of the large bridge, looking for any sign of activity.

"I don't know. We called out to them this morning, and no one answered," Kim replied, turning from Travis and starting forward up the beach again.

Travis stepped through the pool. "Wait, why didn't you tell me about the ship?"

Kim did not stop or turn around, her voice harsh. "I fucking forgot, Travis. I've kind of had other things on my mind— like you murdering Mark and Chad, shooting my friend, and threatening our lives."

Travis climbed awkwardly out of the pool and up onto the hardpack sand, trailing after Kim. "Wait—"

"Look, the treasure is just past the ship; we'll be there in a few minutes now. You need to load this knapsack with all it can hold and get back to the boat at the ranger station."

Travis stayed after Kim, looking up nervously at the freighter's forecastle deck and the row of large panel windows across the bridge. True to Kim's words, he saw no one aboard, but was hesitant. Trying to decide what to do, he pushed forward after Kim, his hip pulsing painfully.

Kim was fifty yards from the enormous copper-colored bulb of the bow. She was moving as fast as she dared without further alarming Travis. She was also scanning the decks and bridge windows of the reefer but saw no one. The ship did indeed appear to be abandoned.

Travis felt his worry begin to climb towards anxiety. He didn't like the freighter, and he was starting to suspect Kim was lying to him, leading him on a goose chase, attempting to trap him. She could easily alert any crew onboard the ship, and he would be in serious trouble. He decided quickly he was going to cut out, bail with the dagger and three coins, have her take him to the park ranger boat, and get off this godforsaken island. Looking ahead to Kim he saw she had further widened the gap between them.

"Wait—stop!" Travis called out. "We're going back!" He stumbled to a halt in the sand and raised the pistol.

Kim's eyes desperately searched the reefer's decks for any sign of another human. Seeing no one she glanced back over her shoulder at Travis. He was twenty yards behind and had the gun pointed directly at her. She doubted he would fire it, if he did, he would instantly alert anyone aboard the freighter or within earshot.

HURRICANE HOLE

Riding a wave of adrenaline, chest tightening, Kim turned and bolted for the *Banten Buru*.

PART FIVE

THE REEFER

CHAPTER FOURTEEN

Tearing straight for the reefer ship Kim let the knapsack drop. Sand flew up around her legs as she sprinted across the beach, her flip-flops flying off one after the other. The top layer of sand was baked dry and burning hot as she angled up the sloping backshore directly towards the reefer's mammoth bow. The copper-colored bulbous point was huge, more than twice as tall as Kim. Without looking back at Travis she looped around it, her left shoulder skimming the rough convex wall of plate steel.

Staying close to the port hull, she quickly went aft, the enormous ship canted over her at near to a fifteen-degree angle. The size of the reefer up close was overwhelming. Heading towards the stern, in the lee of the ship from Travis, Kim was moving back towards the water. She was trapped between the ship, the Gulf, and open beach.

Travis would be coming around the bow any moment, only seconds behind her.

Kim traversed the hull, nearing the surf line, stepping across a wide berm of collected large shells, skittering underfoot and rough on her feet. She glanced back towards the bow, heart drumming, mouth dry. No sign of Travis. He was moving slow on a bum leg.

A wall of white steel leaned over Kim, radiating heat in the midday sun. She was nearing the center of the reefer, the name ANASTASI above her in large letters. The deck here was swooped down, a lowered well deck for loading and unloading. The rail of the canted deck was only twenty feet overhead.

Her eye caught sight of a Jacob's ladder hanging down from the fore end of the well deck. It reached almost to the sand due to the ship's roll to port. The ladder was made up of two thick brown braided ropes strung through wood rung slats. She reached out and grabbed one of the ropes—the ladder hung loose but felt anchored firmly above. Hesitating for only a moment, Kim began to climb.

She was more than halfway up when in her peripheral vision she saw Travis come around the bow. Barely slowing her climb, pulse thudding in her ears, she turned to glance over. He was heading down the hull towards her, limping badly, moving slow, favoring his leg. Travis looked enraged, his face snarled and beet red from heat and anger, eyes shooting sparks.

Kim looked up at the edge of the deck and scrambled up the rungs, the rope ladder kicking and twisting under her feet, knocking against the hull. She reached the gap in the railing, bordered by two handhold stanchions. She grabbed one in each hand, hoisting herself up, popping her head over the lip, looking over the tilted expanse of the well deck. *Banten Buru*'s open decking was huge, the refrigerated cargo ship had a beam of sixty feet.

Kim pulled herself up, scrambling onto the deck as Travis reached the base of the ladder. She looked down and saw him grab ahold of a rung. He shoved the gun back in the pocket of his boardshorts, set the dagger blade between his teeth, and began to climb. Christ, was he really coming up after her? The bastard had balls.

Kim cursed—if she had been just a bit faster, she might have been able to pull the ladder up, leaving Travis stranded with no way to board the ship. Too late for that, his upturned eyes were locked on hers, blind with hate, boring into her. His face looked transformed, as it did when he was drifting away from *Sabre*. Gone were his boyish charming looks, his true color and character fully revealed.

In disbelief that he was pursuing her onto the ship, she broke off his acid glare, stumbling backwards, turning and scanning the deck for something—anything she could drop on him. Seeing nothing, Kim looked aft, up to the vacant superstructure and bridge. There *had* to be crew still aboard this ship, they wouldn't totally abandon the freighter here on the beach. Where would they go?

"Help!" Kim cried at the top of her lungs, the shrieking desperation in her voice piercing the afternoon stillness. "Is anyone here? Help! I need help!" She cut from the top of the ladder, moving diagonally across and up the canted deck, heading aft towards the starboard side, feet slapping across the decking. Kim's brain had not yet registered the sun-heated steel burning hot on her bare soles.

She crossed under a derrick, eyes wide, working to control her breathing, daring not look back at the top of the rope ladder. Lining the center of the deck lengthwise were dozens of twenty-foot-long corrugated steel shipping containers, stacked three high and three deep, each one an individual refrigerated unit, painted white. Kim ran alongside the containers, looking for a spot to slip between them. Reaching their end she could see the entire superstructure and bridge above her. The windows of the bridge ran the full beam, fifty feet above the deck, each panel of glass eight feet in height.

"Help me! Somebody!"

No movement, no one visible on the bridge. No one coming rushing out onto the winged observation decks. No one coming to her aid. No one at all . . .

Kim turned and looked back up the deck between the port rail and containers.

Travis was coming up over the side of the freighter. He gripped the stanchions with both hands, the dagger in his mouth, blade still gripped between his teeth, looking like the proverbial pirate. He turned his head and saw her. Kim froze for a half-second, unsure where to go or what to do, watching him kick his feet over the lip and onto the deck.

Panic clawed her gut and she turned and bolted for the superstructure. Approaching the starboard rail she saw a covered passageway ahead. Kim made directly for it and ducked inside the open alcove. To her right, another passageway led back to port across the ship, lined with windows facing fore and doors along the aft wall. To her left, Kim saw another open doorway that was clearly the entrance to a stairwell. She took the stairwell.

Taking the awkwardly canted stairs two at a time, Kim hit the first landing and saw a door marked Boat Deck and kept going up, reasoning that if there was anyone on the ship they would be on or near the bridge. On the third level landing she stopped and looked out a forward facing window. Below, she saw Travis come out from behind the containers, moving with a blundering limp, up the pitched deck. He had the dagger back in one hand and the pistol drawn in the other. She watched him skip and hop, favoring his bad leg, realizing the deck was burning hot on his feet. She had singed the bottom of her feet on the sunbaked steel as well, only just beginning to feel the stinging sensation.

Travis looked nothing short of livid and appeared to have totally come undone. It seemed he was more motivated in hunting her down and killing her than any thoughts of escaping the island or evading capture. Kim guessed if he was confronted by any of the reefer's crew, he would shoot them dead on the spot.

She spun around, passing a door marked Officers' Accommodations and sprinted up the next flight of stairs. Rounding another landing and another identical door marked Captain's Accommodations, she flew up another flight, coming onto a landing with a door marked Bridge.

Kim burst through the door and jerked to a stop, gasping for air. She was immediately dismayed to see a large open bridge, vacant of any captain, officers, or crew. The air was cool, conditioned, and smelled of oil and citrus cleaner.

"Is there anyone here?" Kim called out.

No reply, no movement, no sign of anyone. The reefer seemed totally abandoned, a ghost ship.

"Hello! Somebody—I need help!"

Frustration lining her sweat-streaked face, Kim frantically looked around the bridge. The wheelhouse was expansive. A large U-shaped command center faced the windows, with a helm and twin pilot's chairs in front of a console housing a dozen screens and hundreds of controls. What caught Kim's attention was that the bridge had power, half the screens were on, and the multitude of gauges and switches were lit, several flashing.

She moved towards the helm station; the deck underfoot now canted down away from her. A large GPS and radar screen blinked, and Kim recognized a radio. Hope rising, she made her way over to it, seeing that it was a complex satellite radio-phone system. She picked up what looked like a handset and keyed the transmitter. There was a sharp burst of static.

Quickly realizing that trying to figure out the radio and calling for help was futile, Kim dropped the handset and scanned the wheelhouse for any type of a weapon. She crossed to the port side of the console to what looked to be a chart table. There were several rolled charts as well as one that was spread open, showing the Gulf of Mexico. Turning to the aft wall she pulled open a cabinet door. On metal shelving among more charts, lifejackets, boxes, binoculars, and an air horn she saw a yellow plastic case labelled Marine Emergency Kit. Grasping the handle, Kim pulled the case out and swung it around onto the chart table. Popping the latches and flipping it open she saw a bright orange flare gun and six flares set in black foam. Each flare was the size and shape of a shotgun shell.

Bingo.

Scrambling, Kim withdrew the flare gun and lost precious seconds figuring out how to top break the single shot device and breech load a flare. She snapped the gun shut and snatched the remaining five flares from the case, sliding them into the pockets of her shorts. Flare gun in hand, Kim circled around and ducked down behind the far side of the chart table. She cocked the hammer with a thumb.

For the first time, Kim heard a low electric hum from the bowels of the ship. The reefer had full power throughout. Wherever the crew were, they could not have been gone long, or very far. It was possible they were still on the freighter, but with that Jacob's ladder down, Kim guessed at least some of them had disembarked the ship for the island. Above the center of the command station an analog clock on the bulkhead ticked away the seconds. It was ten after two.

Kim sucked in a breath and held it. She heard the door to the stairwell open, and Travis enter the far side of the bridge. She could discern the sound of him favoring and sliding his foot along the laminate tile of the deck. Hearing him pause for a moment, she wagered he was taking in the vast wheelhouse. Her heart thrummed, blood rushing and pulsing in her ears.

"Kim . . ." Travis stretched her name out, taunting. "I know you're up here. I don't have time for games. You said it yourself; I'm on a clock."

Kim had her back to the chart table, squatting, the flare gun in front of her face. She could hear him advancing further into the bridge. She ran a tongue over parched lips, her mouth dry, hoping her voice didn't crack.

"It looks like we have this ship to ourselves, baby girl . . ." Travis's voice was provoking, "we could find a bunk, have another quickie like the other night?"

Kim found her voice: "Travis, you're insane. You need to stop and think. You need to get off this ship—and this island before—"

The gunshot roared and reverberated in the steel bulkhead of the wheelhouse. The 9mm bullet tore into the chart table, punching through the metal cabinet, and coming out directly beside Kim's head. Ears ringing, she looked down when she felt a warm wetness dripping down the side of her neck. Dark crimson droplets spotted the collar of her blue T-shirt. The bullet had grazed an earlobe.

Travis had shot to kill. There was going to be no dialogue or dealing with him.

Absolute icy fear paralyzed her. She thought of the real possibility of dying, her daughter Kayla growing up alone. She shook her head, pushing away the dark vision, using it to spur her on, to survive.

Controlling her trembling hands, Kim edged to the side of the console. With a quick silent prayer that the flare gun would fire smoothly, she swung out from behind the cabinet. It took her half a second to locate Travis. He was standing to one side of the twin helm chairs. Kim raised the flare gun, put Travis in line with the orange tip on the end of the barrel, and pulled the trigger.

The flare gun went off with a muted pop, sounding nothing like the Sig Sauer moments before. The flare streaked bright across the bridge and hit Travis directly on his left shoulder, bouncing off and flying into the bulkhead behind. It sputtered and fell to the deck, hissing, giving off a white smoke with an acrid odor.

The flare caught Travis totally by surprise. Flinching and dropping, he caught a quick sight of Kim ducking back behind the chart table. Travis looked to his shoulder, seeing the dark smudge of an open burn hole through his shirt, exposed skin reddened. The flare had walloped him hard but did not do any serious injury, a superficial burn.

"You little bitch!" Travis cried out, hissing at the rising sting.

Behind the console, Kim lay flat on her stomach. She reached down to her pocket for another flare, scrambling to reload the gun. There was an exit door behind her, with a large window in it, that looked to lead outside onto the port observation wing.

Two more gunshots erupted, back-to-back, the bullets piercing through the console just above her. Kim squeezed her eyes shut and flattened herself against the deck. As the shots rang off, her hearing dulled. She would not be able to hear him moving clearly. Terror prickled through her body. She had been holding her breath and caught it in a rushing gasp. Over her head the three bullets Travis had fired formed an obtuse triangle in the backside of the chart table, the metal punched outwards.

How many rounds did he have left in that gun? She did a quick count: Travis had likely used one to kill the cop, one for Mark, he had fired three at her on *Sabre*, once at Andrea, and three shots here on the reefer's bridge. Nine shots. How many rounds could that bloody pistol hold? Could he have reloaded it at some point?

HURRICANE HOLE

On the other side of the wheelhouse, Travis had taken cover, dropping to a knee behind the helm chairs. He was doing his own tally. He popped out the Sig Sauer's magazine and saw he only had three rounds left. Not good, he would need to conserve them. He slid the magazine back in, his shoulder throbbing deeply now from the flare's impact.

A tense moment of silence passed, only the sound of the sputtering and dying flare in the far corner of the bridge. The air smelled strongly of sulfur dioxide. Kim slipped a second flare into the breech. She hiked herself up onto her elbows, and slowly and silently wriggled forward to the edge of the console.

This time she peered cautiously around the side of the chart table. The air in the wheelhouse was tainted white by the smoke from the discharged flare. She could see Travis, higher than her on the upward sloped deck, crouched behind the twin helm chairs. He had the far chair swiveled to face her, providing cover for himself behind the backrest.

Rolling silently onto her right side, Kim extended her arm and took aim at him through the hazy smoke. She squeezed the trigger and the rocketing flare shot off. In frustration, before ducking back behind the console, she saw the flare hit the backrest of the helm chair and fall to the seat.

Kim's fear started to shift towards anger. She lay flat on her back on the deck, breathing hard, already reloading another flare into the gun. Travis did not fire back. He was either out of bullets or saving his remaining shots.

"What the hell are you doing, Travis?" Kim called out. "Are you totally fucking mad?"

Travis answered immediately back: "What are *you* doing Kim? I thought you were taking me to this treasure of yours?"

"You're going to get caught. You need to get off this island with what you've got—the dagger and coins."

"No. What I need—and what I want—is you. You're mine. And you're gonna show me exactly where this treasure is. As we agreed. Or, when I'm done with you—I'm going to kill you. You have no choice."

"No, you're gonna get caught. You're going to go back to prison. The crew from this ship, they have to be close by. They will have heard the shots."

"Crew?" Travis said. "What crew? Where? The ship is abandoned. It's just you and I."

The flare on the helm seat had ignited the fabric, the polyester and foam flaming and smoking. A thick black snaking trail of smoke, shot through with a sickly yellow-gray color, billowed up from the seat cushion and was spun through the bridge by the circulating fans.

Kim could smell the strong synthetic odor, burning and heavy on top of the sulfurous flare. The wheelhouse was filling with smoke quickly, the air becoming difficult to breathe. She was trapped, the only exit off the bridge she knew of was past Travis. Precious seconds ticked by. Kim's mind raced, seeking an out . . . she held the gun at the ready. When she finally spoke her tone was curt and earnest: "Alright, I'll tell you where the treasure is."

Travis blinked, eyes watering from the black smoke billowing up from the helm chair in front of him. His anger at Kim had not allowed him to think rationally—he was furious at her. His motivation and plan were to find this treasure—if it existed—and to bring Kim with him when he fled the island. As a hostage, and a plaything. She would pay for crossing him. If he didn't just kill her outright. She looked to be far more trouble than she was worth. Travis hefted the pistol and blinked hard; the smoke was making his eyes sting.

"No," he shot back, "you're not going to tell me where it is. You're going to take me there. Now."

There was another moment of silence. The flare on the helm chair had expired but the seat cushion was burning hungrily, flames licking up the backrest.

Kim was staring up at the smoke-filled overhead, sweat trickling down her temples. She found her confidence and sent out the bait. "Travis, the treasure is just south of here. About a mile down the beach, maybe less. It's up in the dune. There's a palm tree down in the surf—use that as a marker to find it. The treasure is just before the palm. Look to the dune, where the storm ripped out the sand. You can't miss it. It's all there, just like I described it. I swear this to God. Take the knapsack and go. Take what you can and get off the island. All I want to do is get back to Andrea."

Kim lay on the deck, not moving, straining to hear. The smoke in the wheelhouse from the burning helm seat was growing too thick to remain on the bridge much longer. The circulating fans were not clearing it fast enough. After close to half minute and no reply from Travis, her fear returned with a vengeance. Was he advancing silently on her? Kim rolled over and sat herself up, sliding to the end of the console.

Another quarter minute ticked by. Kim's eyes were tearing profusely from the burning pungent smoke, a cloying chemical smell. She would soon not be able to suppress a hacking cough. Where was he? Had he taken her at her word and gone for the treasure?

Cautiously, Kim leaned out from behind the chart table. The bridge was now heavy with dark smoke, the command station barely visible through the opaque haze. The helm chair was a small pyre, the seat's material blackened and melting, dripping in long flaming rivulets to the deck. Kim scanned the starboard side of the bridge but saw no sign of Travis through the smothering murk. It was possible he could be hidden behind the adjacent console, but the smoke was making it too difficult to stay in the wheelhouse much longer, for either of them.

Kim could not hold back a cough, and she hacked, wheezing on the fumes. Her eyes were watering hard, blurring her vision. Staying low, under the heavy cover of the smoke, she backpedaled towards the exterior door behind and leaned on the latch. The door swung open, and Kim stumbled over the lip, out into bright sunlight, gasping in hot, humid—but clean— air. She clung to the downward-tipped railing of the portside observation wing, coughing hard against the acrid fumes . . . catching her breath, clearing her lungs. Thick black smoke billowed out the open doorway behind her.

Blinking her eyes clear, Kim had a flash of vertigo upon seeing she was seventy feet above the beach. She looked down in awe at the massive length of the reefer below her. Kim raised her head slowly, squinting against the harsh sun, taking in the unreal sight. From this vantage point she could see the entire barrier island, the full span of Cayo Costa stretched out from end to end.

CHAPTER FIFTEEN

*L*isa Marie slugged through the dark green waters of Pelican Bay. The twenty-five-foot Sea Ox was a workhorse, used by Florida State Parks to haul fuel and supplies over to Cayo Costa, and garbage out. She was powered with a single 300-horsepower engine, that pushed her slowly but steadily from Pine Island towards the ranger station on Cayo Costa.

The only person on the boat was Teresa Randall. Mid-thirties, shoulder length ash blonde hair, deeply tanned, pale blue eyes covered by dark polarized sunglasses. Teresa wore the sage short-sleeve top and olive drab pants uniform of a state park ranger, with tan leather high-top hikers. She stood confidently at the helm, piloting *Lisa Marie* across the bay.

Teresa was an attractive woman, but her face was lined and hard. She had come to Florida four years ago at thirty-one years of age. Her life back up in Minnesota had not been easy. When she was a junior in high school both her parents had been killed in a car wreck, snuffed out by a drunk driver. She had no siblings and a troubled aunt strung out somewhere in Saint Paul.

On the outskirts of Minneapolis she had shared a rented house with a boyfriend, Kevin, a meat processing worker at Cargill. Coming home from long shifts in the packinghouse Kevin would routinely get blind drunk on Jack Daniel's and find a reason to beat Teresa good. One night, late, in March of 2000, in the middle of a blizzard, her eye blackened, swollen lip bloody, the sharp taste of copper in her mouth again, Teresa had had enough. She had already withdrawn her small savings from waitressing—Teresa liked planning ahead—and with Kevin passed out on the couch she packed up her meager belongings, got in her Hyundai coupe and hit the snow-covered interstate. She headed one direction—south, straight for the Florida border, stopping only twice for gas, and not looking once in the rear view.

Making her way down the Gulf Coast, arriving in Fort Myers, Teresa found a sketchy roach-infested motel, and some work, at Waffle House, and then a second job at Dollar Tree. It took her two years to get the position with the National Park Service, landing a job as a full-time state park ranger on Cayo Costa in 2002.

The assignment was a huge hand up. Teresa enjoyed working on the barrier island, the remote location, nature, and beaches could not be beat, and her co-workers were decent. Still, the pay was a fraction above minimum wage, the hours long, and the work hard. She could barely cover her rent for a rundown one-bedroom bungalow on Pine Island, let alone consider a mortgage for a house of her own.

Just this morning she had returned to her rental place on Pine Island and was relieved to see it and her belongings had survived the hurricane mostly unscathed. Hurricane Charley had been far worse than anyone imagined or prepared for. Yesterday afternoon Charley had made a direct landfall on the south end of Cayo Costa as a Category 4 storm. They had all left the park on Thursday, boarding up the facilities as Charley loomed in the Caribbean, headed for western Cuba. Teresa had left her home early yesterday, evacuating Pine Island to stay in Cape Coral with two other park rangers. After assessing her home this morning, she decided to head up to Bokeelia and see how the park boat had fared. The hurricane's impact and devastation to Pine Island was overwhelming. The power to Southwest Florida was going to out for days, if not weeks. Stringfellow Road up the island was barely passable with downed trees and power lines, and Teresa found the Bokeelia docks had sustained serious damage, but *Lisa Marie* was still moored in her slip, looking seaworthy.

The park rangers all knew that one person had remained out on Cayo Costa through the hurricane. Ninety-one-year-old Margi Pattinson lived alone on the island, with her two cats, on Primo Bay. Margi's husband passed away ten years ago, and she chose to stay on Cayo Costa until it was her time too.

She had been living on the island for close to thirty years, having been through many storms and hurricanes before, and she certainly wasn't leaving for this one. She ignored the park ranger's warnings, remaining at her rustic home, where she lived with no running water, electricity, or air-conditioning and few creature comforts, save for one weakness. At noon each day, Margi would fire up a gasoline generator to power an old Philco television set so she could watch her soap opera *The Young and the Restless*. Once a week a local fishing guide would bring Margi over to Pine Island for groceries, and the park rangers would check in with her daily via radio.

Teresa had come out on *Lisa Marie* to not only check on the ranger station and cabins, but also pay a trip down to Primo Bay and see how Margi had fared. Through the hurricane Teresa and the other park rangers hunkered down in Cape Coral, going through hell with the storm's onslaught, but their thoughts were also with Margi, alone out on the island.

As Teresa piloted the Sea Ox across the bay, she prayed she would not find too grim a scene. Her concern rose sharply when she saw the docks at the ranger station. They were smashed to pieces, with large sections of the slips and boardwalk completely missing, bare pilings jutting out of the water.

Her expression hardened as she slowed *Lisa Marie* and glided in towards the ruined docks. Teresa spun the helm to starboard and brought the port beam easily against a piling with a soft bump. She threw a line over and cut the engine, taking a moment to survey the docks and the grounds of the visitor center, assessing the storm's damage. She glanced at her watch. It was 1:35 p.m.

Teresa's cell phone was not working, but she tried her handheld two-way radio out at the island. Attempting to reach the marina at Bokeelia was futile, she received nothing but static. The repeater towers on both Boca Grande and Pine Island were surely taken down by Charley. There was no way to contact the mainland from Cayo Costa.

Ensuring the Sea Ox was moored safely, Teresa carefully maneuvered her way off the boat and across the length of remaining precariously slanted dock. She jumped clear; onto a newly formed berm of wet sand the storm has collected in the cove.

She saw their twenty-one-foot Mako center console boat that was left behind when they evacuated Cayo Costa. Despite the vessel being secured and sheltered in the cove, the boat's stern was swamped, the 150-horsepower Yamaha completely submerged under the bay waters. The docks were a write-off and the Mako's outboard engine was going to need a complete overhaul.

Teresa's mouth set in a somber twisted line as she head up towards the ranger station, further looking over the damage. The surrounding live oaks had taken a severe lashing, with dozens of split and downed limbs scattered about the grounds. The sultry air was thick, the scent of tree sap heavy. The

HURRICANE HOLE

cinderblock restrooms looked to be in decent shape, and the Cayo Costa park sign and flagpole still stood. Teresa had run down and removed the flag herself, the day before yesterday, in preparation for the storm.

As she crossed the open clearing of crushed shell she frowned when she saw a pair of flip-flops, lying askew about a half dozen feet apart. It looked odd for the storm to deposit the sandals here, together, in the open. The wind should have whisked them away, down into the mangroves.

Passing by the flip-flops, Teresa did not see the pooling of blood just ahead on the shell, her focus on the ranger station as she approached the structure. The bungalow looked to have survived the hurricane well, taking a few licks with armfuls of lost roof shingles and siding. Her forehead creased seeing that the front door was wide open. Teresa had closed and locked the door herself, covering it with storm shutters. The wind must have stripped the storm shutters free—one was lying askew beside the porch—and blown the door in, but the wide open door, coupled with the oddly placed sandals, had her suspicious that someone had been here since the storm. Possibly looters . . .

More cautiously, Teresa took the steps up to the front porch and advanced towards the doorway. With the windows boarded the interior of the ranger station was dim, and she removed her sunglasses.

Stepping inside she glanced around and immediately saw the woman on the bench.

Teresa froze in surprise for a moment, her first thoughts being that the woman was a victim of the hurricane and had found refuge in the ranger's bungalow. At first glance the woman looked to be asleep, in soiled and rumpled clothing, a yellow halter top and gray shorts, lying reclined along the length of the bench. Upon further observation the woman was clearly seriously injured, having bloody bandaging wrapped around her waist, her shirt soiled a dark crimson. The bandages looked to be covering a severe wound to her abdomen. Teresa recognized that her own hooded sweatshirt was balled up under the woman's head.

Moving closer, Teresa saw she looked to be about thirty, a trim and attractive brunette. The right side of her face was bright red, looking like a localized severe sunburn. She was breathing in rapid, shallow breaths.

"Hey," Teresa said, stepping over beside the bench. "Hey, can you hear me?"

There was no response from the woman and Teresa saw her skin was pale and clammy.

"Hey," Teresa said again, "I need you to wake up." She put a hand down on the woman's shoulder.

Andrea stirred, groaned, and half-opened her eyes, her gaze unfocused. "Kim?" Her voice was faint.

Teresa shook her head. "No, I'm not Kim. I'm a park ranger, I'm here to help you. Can you tell me what happened?"

Andrea opened her eyes fully and the woman before her came into clear focus. It took her a moment to piece the woman's words and her uniform together, and a rush of relief passed through Andrea. She tried to sit up and winced, moaning. Her guts throbbed with a swirling paralyzing blend of dull and stabbing pain.

"What happened to you?" Teresa asked.

Andrea's mouth was dry, her tongue thick and heavy as she spoke. "I was shot. He's here . . . on the island . . ."

"Wait," said Teresa, "who's here? Someone shot you?"

Andrea nodded. "Yes. Where is Kim?"

"Who's Kim?"

"My friend. She's with him."

"With who? The person who shot you?"

Andrea nodded again. "Travis. His name is Travis. He's here. He's with Kim. They went for the treasure."

Teresa looked questioningly at the woman, believing she was delirious. "What's your name?"

"Andrea."

"Andrea, I'm going to need to get you help. I have to get you back to my boat—"

"No," Andrea roused herself, balancing her shaky voice, fighting a deep chill and an intense burning thirst. "You need to help my friend. She's with this guy, Travis. They went for the treasure, on the beach. He's got a gun. He killed Mark and Chad."

Teresa's brows drew together. "This man Travis killed two people?"

Andrea nodded. "Yesterday, on our boat. Before the hurricane hit."

Teresa said nothing for a moment, digesting all this.

Andrea rasped, "I'm really thirsty—I need a drink."

Teresa nodded. "I'll get you a drink. Where did Travis and your friend Kim go?"

"I told you—they went to find the treasure."

"Treasure?"

"Yes, we found treasure on the beach—the hurricane unburied it. Pirate treasure—silver coins, emeralds. It's real. Kim took Travis to it. He has a gun. You need to go after them and help her, please."

Teresa studied the woman. Although she was injured and distraught it seemed to Teresa that Andrea was speaking the truth. "Where is this treasure?"

"I'm not exactly sure. Out on the beach, maybe about a mile—a mile and a half south of here. It's in the dune. The hurricane washed it all out. There are coins all over the beach. Silver coins. And—there is a palm tree, down in the surf, right near the treasure. That's where they went—that's how you can find it. You need to help her, please." Andrea closed her eyes and her head rolled to one side on the hoodie, exhausted from the effort of talking.

Teresa was quiet for a moment. It sounded like Kim and this guy Travis had gone in the same direction as Margi's cabin. Teresa could see if she could get the ATV to work, and check both locations, one out on the beach, and one on the bay. "I'm going to get you something to drink, and then I'll go and see if I can find your friend."

"Are you alone?" Andrea asked, words mumbling together, eyes half open.

"Yes."

"Is there any way for you to call for help?"

"No. The towers are down. Cell phones and radios aren't working. There's no way to reach the mainland."

Not having the energy to reply, Andrea closed her eyes again.

"I'll be as quick as I can," said Teresa. "Will you be OK here?"

Andrea nodded slowly. "Just hurry," she said, without opening her eyes.

Leaving Andrea, Teresa quickly backtracked out of the ranger station down to the docks. Carefully navigating the ruined structure and boarding *Lisa Marie* she retrieved three half-liter plastic bottles of water from an ice-filled cooler. Returning to the ranger station, Teresa dropped to her knees beside the bench, set two bottles down and uncapped one. Andrea had her eyes closed and didn't stir at Teresa's return.

"Here, I have water for you," said Teresa, bringing the open bottle to Andrea's lips. Andrea's eyes flicked open, she strained to raise her head and greedily gulped almost the entire bottle of cold water. Immediately, Andrea set her head back down and closed her eyes. Her thirst still burned unquenched.

"There's another bottle here for you, if you want more," Teresa said, putting a second bottle on the bench beside her hand. Andrea nodded her head slowly. "Andrea, I'm going to look for Kim now," Teresa continued, "I'll be as quick as I can. When I get back with her, I'll get you both off the island."

Andrea did not respond. Her breathing was in quick shallow gasps, skin pale and wet. Teresa found Andrea's radial pulse. It was weak, and after a brief count pegged her at well over 100 beats per minute. The woman needed medical help, and for a moment Teresa wrestled with taking Andrea off the island now. But there was another woman who sounded like she needed help, and Teresa wanted to check on Margi as well. She made up her mind—if she took the ATV she could do the loop out to the beach, circle around to Margi's cabin, and be back at the ranger station inside of twenty minutes, twenty-five tops. Teresa checked her watch: 1:57 p.m. Taking the third bottle of water with her, Teresa stood and left the ranger station, moving at a brisk pace.

She found the ATV amidst the ruins of the storage shed and had to pull off and toss aside a half dozen pieces of splintered planking to free the vehicle. The machine started smoothly on the second try. Teresa stowed the water bottle and reversed out. The off-road tires rolled across the shell lot of the visitor center, Teresa navigating deftly around storm debris. She cut behind the ranger station bungalow and head directly west, through the island's interior on the Cabin Trail.

She only made it halfway across the island when she had no choice but to abandon the ATV in the thick of the hammock. A massive live oak lay across the trail, blocking the path. It would be on foot from here. Teresa got off the four-wheeler, took a couple of slugs from the water bottle and slid it back into the holster. She climbed over the downed trunk, setting off at a fast-paced hike. She decided to head straight out to the beach and walk south, to see first if she could locate Kim and this treasure, and then cut back east on the trails to Margi's place.

Moving at a solid clip across the silent island, she reached the camping cabins in less than ten minutes. From what she could see, most of the cabins had survived the storm well, but two were ripped clear from their cinder block pilings and lay scattered in ruins. Hurricanes could be quite choosy at what they destroy and what they spare, sometimes just in the space of a hundred feet. Charley had also effectively ripped out all the Australian pine trees that had encircled the camping area. The towering evergreens had been savagely uprooted, some of the massive trees missing entirely.

Teresa traversed the dune ridgeline, through a beach access trail bordered by thick sea grape. Coming out past dunes covered with sea oats and inkberry that had held fast through the storm, with her experienced eye she immediately saw the erosion to the beach. The shoreline had been drastically altered by Charley, with large swaths of the dune removed. Thousands of tons of sand had been stripped clean away.

Andrea's ramblings, in part, added up. If there was any kind of treasure hidden or long buried in the dune, the hurricane would have certainly exposed it.

Stepping out onto the expanse of beach, the sun drilling down on her, Teresa slipped her sunglasses back on and looked south, down the shoreline. She was about to set off in that direction when she heard a distinctive sound behind her. It was a sharp but muted retort, coming from the opposite direction.

She turned and faced north, squinting, seeing nothing but the long run of beach to where the shoreline banked away to the east.

The sound came again, this time twice in a row, back-to-back. The dual cracking pops were loud and clear over the low rush of surf. There was no question as to what made the noise.

Gunshots.

She quickly abandoned any plans of heading south and started north up the beach.

* * * *

Teresa had only been walking for a couple of minutes when a long lazy trail of black smoke caught her eye. The smoke billowed across the blue sky, drifting away towards the east, coming from over a run of cabbage palms that ran along the coastal scrub.

Gunshots and smoke. And where there was smoke there was fire.

Clenching her jaw, Teresa picked up her pace. Imprinted clearly in the smooth wind-combed sand she saw two pairs of tracks, also heading north, two people, one barefoot, one in sandals. The sizing looked to be a man and a woman. Possibly the Kim and Travis that Andrea had spoken about? But why were they headed north? Andrea had said they went south. Or were there other people on the island? Teresa followed the tracks as they trailed down to the pan and disappeared in the swash.

Continuing quickly north along the beach, her hiking boots leaving their own bold imprints, Teresa warily eyed the wafting smoke trail. It seemed to be coming from somewhere directly on the beach ahead, around the point of a sand spit and large tidal pool. She navigated onto the higher beach, circling around the pool, trudging through the soft sand, trying to locate the tracks again.

As she moved up the beach, coming around the point of coastal hammock, Teresa glanced up and blinked, not believing what she was seeing. Her eyes widened, and she came to a halt, taking in the full sight of the reefer ship.

"I'll be damned," Teresa whispered.

The reefer's white superstructure shone brightly under the sun, reflected in Teresa's dark polarized lenses. The ship looked intact, and was resting grounded high on the beach, sitting off angle to the waterline, and canted to port. The smoke was coming from the far side of the bridge, wafting out from an open door on the observation wing, carried across the beach and over the island on the passive afternoon breeze.

After a moment's hesitation Teresa set out again, headed straight for the ship. She caught the sets of tracks again, on the far shore of the tidal pool, the people who made them clearly headed for the reefer. Reading the name on the hull, Teresa was familiar with the Anastasi Shipping Line, a large American company based out of Port Everglades on the East Coast. Anastasi reefers regularly traversed the Gulf of Mexico and could be seen offshore of Cayo Costa as they accessed the ports in Tampa Bay. Teresa was surprised to see the hurricane had managed to beach such a large freighter, that the captain and company could be caught unaware. A reefer of this size would have a crew of at least a dozen, possibly more. The ship looked vacant, there were no signs of the crew anywhere.

Andrea's story, the tracks in the sand, the gunshots, the smoke, and the grounded ship all spelled trouble. None of this was sitting right.

HURRICANE HOLE

Teresa approached the ship guardedly. She saw a knapsack and another pair of flip-flops on the sand, lying askew. Whoever owned the sandals had broken into a run, their tracks widening from a walk to a sprint, and they had dropped the knapsack. Teresa was a sworn state law enforcement officer, but the park rangers on Cayo Costa did not carry firearms. In her two years of working at the park, Hurricane Charley and events of today were her strangest yet, and she wished she was armed.

She rounded the massive bow, debating whether to call out, when she saw the Jacob's ladder hanging down against the port hull. At some point, before or after the storm and the beaching, a crewmember had deployed the ladder, and one or more—or all—crew may have left the ship. The tracks in the sand erased as they traversed onto a wash of hard shell. It appeared whoever had made the tracks had possibly made to gain entry to the ship via the Jacob's ladder.

Teresa looked up at the deck tilted over her and again debated calling out. Did she want to alert anyone as to her presence? There must be crew onboard, and they might also have battery power and a functioning radio. The ship's radar and antennae above the bridge looked entirely undamaged. And there might also be a doctor and medical supplies onboard to help Andrea. But the reefer was deathly silent, the only sound were the waves rushing up along the steel hull.

Erring on the side of caution, Teresa remained silent and approached the rope ladder. She grabbed a rung and hoisted herself up, scaling the wood rungs easily and popped her head above the lip of the hull, surveying the empty well deck. No sign of anyone, just towering derricks and rows of corrugated steel shipping containers. Heat shimmered off the sun-scorched steel deck. Looking up to the bridge she saw that the smoke coming from the observation deck was slowly abating.

Gripping the stanchions, Teresa pulled herself up and onto the deck. She was well acclimated to the climate and working outdoors but the hike and afternoon heat on the reefer's steel decking was intense. Sweat covered her brow and trickled down her back. She wished she had remembered to grab her hat from *Lisa Marie*. And it would have been a good idea to bring that bottle of water from the ATV.

Scanning the deck, Teresa decided to head aft, almost following exactly in Kim's footsteps, less than twenty minutes before. The bridge window panels above her were vacant, and the fact that she had boarded the ship unseen, nor had anyone seen her, was extremely unsettling. The trio of gunshots had most certainly come from the ship. And what caused the fire on the bridge?

Glancing at her watch, she saw it was 2:29 p.m. Teresa decided she was going to spend a total of five minutes searching the ship, hopefully locating a crewperson, a doctor, and a radio, before heading directly back to Andrea and taking her off the island. Teresa would have to come back to check on Margi and Kim.

Coming to the front of the superstructure, Teresa saw an open entrance to a passageway on the starboard side. She crossed over to it and saw the stairwell. Hesitating for only a moment to decide, she entered the stairwell and removed her sunglasses, starting up the awkwardly slanted steps. Lightly jogging the flights, Teresa began to wonder how such a large ship could get caught and beached by a hurricane. Would the captain not have been alerted well in advance as to the approaching storm? And where did the crew go? Did they all depart the ship for the island? Strange things were afoot, and there was something inherently spooky about an abandoned ship.

She climbed the flights in succession, until she reached the uppermost landing and the door marked Bridge. Her heart and breathing had only picked up a tad from the exertion. Teresa was in excellent physical condition from the park ranger job, daily exercise, and she didn't smoke.

She pushed open the door and was greeted with a film of acrid smoke. The haze had cleared considerably, but still clouded the bridge. Entering from the high side of the pitched command center with a hand over her mouth and nose, and squinting against the fumes, Teresa surveyed the burned helm chair, still flickering with small flames, and the open door on the far portside, venting out the remaining smoke.

Teresa looked to the consoles, and saw the ship had power. The massive diesel engines were shut down, but a generator was running belowdecks. Bewildered to find the bridge empty, Teresa walked around the communication console to see if there was a functioning radio. An open binder caught her eye. It appeared to be the ship's log or manifest, and an itinerary, in English. She reached out and slid it closer for a better look. The vessel was the *Banten Buru*, indeed an American-owned Anastasi Shipping Line reefer. Teresa's eye skimmed down the print . . . the ship was registered out of Surabaya, Indonesia. A customs manifest revealed her cargo was fruit: frozen mangosteen and durian and refrigerated bananas. The *Banten Buru* had a crew of eleven, and departed the Port of Moín, Costa Rica, four days ago, destined for Port Manatee, Florida.

Teresa's eyes moved over to the bank of complex communications equipment. She was bent over the console, trying to locate a radio when a hissing and blinding light shot past her face.

She did not have time to duck, feeling a flash of heat against her cheek. Teresa winced and jerked her head back, but the flare had already zipped by and slammed into the starboard bulkhead behind her. Spinning to confront her attacker, Teresa caught the quick sight of a woman ducking back behind the far side of the U-shaped console. A blonde woman, holding a bright orange flare gun, eyes wide and panicked, with fresh blood streaked down the side of her face and neck. Teresa saw she had a decent cut on her chin, and she was not wearing the uniform of a ship's crewperson—the woman wore a soiled blue T-shirt and shorts.

Staying low in case another flare came her way, Teresa called out between adrenaline-pumped breaths: "Kim?"

There was no response for a couple of beats, just the sound of the flare sputtering on the floor behind her.

Then the woman's voice: "Who are you? Are you one of the crew?"

Teresa shook her head, even though the woman could not see her. "No. I'm a park ranger. My name is Teresa. Teresa Randall. Please don't shoot another flare at me. Are you Kim?"

There was another short pause.

"Yes," Kim answered from behind the console. "How the hell do you know who I am?"

"Andrea told me to come look for you."

Silence again and Teresa saw Kim get to her feet, slowly coming into view. She held the flare gun up and ready, but not aimed at Teresa.

"You saw Andrea?" Kim asked, fully taking in Teresa in her state park uniform.

"Yes, back at the ranger station."

"How is she?"

"Not good. She needs medical attention right away. We need to get back and get her off the island as quickly as possible. Are you hurt badly?"

Kim shook her head. "No. But there's a man after me. He's here, on the ship. He has a gun."

"Do you know where he went?"

Kim shook her head. "No. But he was here just a few minutes ago."

"Who is he?"

Kim closed her eyes for a moment and took a breath. "His name is Travis. We picked him up on our boat—a few days ago—before the storm. He killed two people . . ."

"Mark and Chad?"

Kim looked at the park ranger questioningly.

"Andrea told me," Teresa explained.

"Mark was my boyfriend, and Chad was Andrea's." Kim felt a weight settle on her chest; her body leaden, fatigue starting to grip her.

Teresa nodded, unsure what to say. "Have you seen any of the crew from the ship?"

Kim shook her head again. "No. It's a ghost ship."

Unsettled, Teresa said, "I think we should get going, right now."

Kim came around the console and Teresa saw she was barefoot. The discarded flip-flops . . .

"How many flares do you have left?" Teresa asked.

Kim dug three 12-guage orange flares from the pocket of her shorts and held them out. "Three."

"Is that gun reloaded?"

"No."

"Load a flare and let's go."

The woman made their way towards the stairwell, and as they descended the first flight, Kim chambered the gun with another flare.

"Where are the crew from this ship?" Kim asked.

"I have no idea. I haven't seen anyone myself," Teresa replied. They tread lightly on the steps but moved quickly, heading down the flights.

"Where did you pick this guy Travis up?" Teresa asked. "And what do you know about him?"

"We found him adrift off Sanibel and we brought him onboard our catamaran. Everything was fine for a couple of days . . ." Kim felt a wave of guilt and shame that cut through her fatigue and fear. "He told me that he escaped from prison, and that he also killed a prison guard, and a cop. He stole the cop's boat. It's washed in somewhere at the south end of the island, near our catamaran. It's called *End of Watch*. He won't hesitate to kill us . . . he's gone right off the deep end."

Teresa thought the boat name was eerily fitting, and that she did not want to encounter or mess with guy Travis. They rounded another landing, continuing cautiously down. "Where were you when the hurricane hit?" Teresa asked.

"We found a cabin and got inside, right as the storm came down on us. The hurricane went right over us, directly overhead. I . . . I saw inside its eye. From the front porch of the cabin. I've never seen anything like it." Kim's face shrouded over with reverence as she recalled the unearthly scenario.

Teresa could only imagine, she had been barricaded inside a house in Cape Coral, not stranded out on a barrier island. Again her thoughts went to Margi, and how the older woman might have fared. "You're lucky, to both experience that, and survive. Hurricane Charley made landfall on Cayo Costa. Before we lost power the radar track showed it going right across The Narrows, at the south end of the island."

"Hurricane Charley?" Kim asked.

Teresa paused at the next landing and turned to Kim. "You didn't even know the storm's name?"

Kim blinked, looking perplexed. "No. There was no way for us to know, but I think Travis did. He cut off our radios on the boat . . . stole the fuses."

Teresa's expression sobered. "This guy sounds like one bad seed. Andrea told me you guys found some sort of treasure?"

Kim remained quiet for a moment, not moving. She had forgotten about the horde—and the dagger. Andrea had spilled the news to a state park ranger. The cat was out of the bag on their find. Kim nodded once. "We did. The hurricane uncovered what looks like—well, buried pirate treasure."

Kim saw Teresa studying her face closely, trying to determine if she was crazy, delirious, lying, or all three. Kim continued, "It's in the dune, about a mile south of the Cabin Trail. Nearby there's a large palm tree down in the surf, it won't be hard to locate."

"What exactly did you find?" Teresa asked.

Kim felt an unabashed percolation of excitement. "Silver coins and ingots, emeralds, and gold—gold discs. I also found a dagger, which Travis now has. I gave it to him, to prove the treasure was real. I tried to barter with it for our lives. It didn't work out too well."

Teresa saw the shifting in Kim's moods. "It doesn't matter now. Let's keep moving."

Kim reached out and held Teresa's arm. "I told Travis exactly where the treasure is. I think that is where he might be, he might have gone after it."

"Then we don't have to worry about him right now," Teresa replied.

Descending the last set of the stairs to the main deck they came out of the stairwell into the passageway. Staying together they went forward, side by side, walking out onto the open deck, into the hot afternoon sunlight.

The bullet entered and exited cleanly through Teresa's right shoulder, missing her neck by inches.

The sound of the shot ripped across the metal deck, the bullet careening down the passageway behind them. Teresa stumbled back and over, against Kim, crimson blood spreading like spilled ink across the arm cuff of her sage uniform. Kim caught her and kept their backwards momentum, falling behind the cover of the passageway. Before they could gather their senses a second bullet clanged off the overhead in a sparking ricochet that made both their ears ring. The women ducked and stumbled aft, retreating past the stairwell entrance. Teresa had her left hand clamped over her injured shoulder, the fresh wound wet and slick under her fingers.

"Shit—I didn't even see him!" Teresa said, sucking breath through clenched teeth, twisting her head to look at her shoulder. "Dammit!"

Kim held the park ranger, flare gun still gripped in one hand, as they leaned against the bulkhead. They would need to exit the passageway before Travis crossed the deck and had a clear line of fire. There was a steel door further aft, about twenty feet down the starboard passage. They both saw it at the same time.

"Go for the door," Teresa said, praying it would be unlocked. They hustled down the passageway, Teresa trying to both assess the injury to her shoulder and watch for Travis.

"Get inside, quick," Teresa ordered when they reached the door. Kim needed no hurrying; she heaved on the exterior latch and the steel door swung open inwards. The women stumbled through into a dimly lit, cool companionway. There was another door inside marked as a stairwell, and Teresa said, "Take the stairs," before Kim even pushed the passageway door closed behind them. The hatchway had a simple rotating deadbolt and Kim dogged it.

Catching her breath, Teresa turned and followed Kim through into the stairwell. The flights of stairs went both up and down. Signage on the bulkhead indicated the next level up was: Upper Deck/Ramps. Next level down: No. 4 Aft Hold.

"Which way?" Kim asked.

"Down, go down," Teresa replied.

The metal stairs were beaded with diagonal bumps, the edges lined with black and yellow non-slip tape. Kim tread down on bare feet, Teresa in her hiking boots. They descended two dim landings with no marked exits, and the air temperature dropped a handful of degrees.

"Where are we headed?" Kim asked, heart drumming her chest, worried about becoming lost and cornered in the bowels of the ship.

Teresa's shoulder was beginning to ache, the pain level climbing exponentially. She had paled a few shades behind her tan. "Stop here a minute," she said. The women paused in a shadowy landing with a hatchway labelled No. 4 Aft Hold.

Teresa gritted her teeth and hissed as she looked again more closely at her shoulder. The 9mm had punched a neat hole through her medial deltoid. Moving her arm even slightly was extremely painful, and the wound looked nasty, but she wasn't going to succumb to blood loss anytime soon. The entry and exit holes were relatively small.

"I think," Teresa said, between sharp breaths, "from the hold, we may be able to move forward and find access back up to the main deck."

"Have you ever been on a ship like this?"

"No."

"Then how do you know—"

"I don't."

Both women looked back up the flight of stairs at the sound of a metallic reverberation echoing down.

"He's through the door," Kim whispered, her face painted with fear.

"Let's go," Teresa said, and without hesitation they made for the hatch. Teresa dropped the latch down with her good arm and pushed open the door to a large, cavernous dark hold. The air inside was even chillier than the stairwell and scented with a sugary sweetness. The hold was close to eighty feet in length with a thirty foot overhead, and only lit with four small lights, positioned high at each far corner. Dozens of white twenty-foot corrugated steel shipping containers lined the hold, stacked three high, seven across the beam, with three containers butted end-to-end lengthwise. Each container hummed with its own generator-powered freezer unit. Massive double bay doors were high overhead, for loading and unloading the containers, each door marked No. 4 Aft Hold Hatch.

"C'mon," said Teresa. The women entered the ominous, vast hold and working left-handed Teresa relatched the bulkhead door behind them. She led Kim along the starboard hull, towards the first row of containers. They paused at the end of a long shipping container, where a large, enclosed fan hummed, blowing air. Teresa glanced at a lit LCD display; the container's temperature was set to -18 degrees Celsius. Having spent winters in Minnesota, Teresa knew that was damn cold, around zero Fahrenheit.

"This way," said Teresa, acting quickly, leading Kim around the right side of the container. They traversed the tight gap between the starboard hull and the twenty-foot container. In the faint light Teresa could make out that the side of the container was painted with the name Anastasi Shipping Line in black block letters. There was some warmth emanating from the metal hull, baked on the other side by the tropical sun. Reaching the spaced junction at next container in line, Teresa held up a hand, and they paused.

There was no mistaking the distinctive grating sound of the hold's bulkhead door swinging open. Teresa felt Kim shiver beside her.

"He's inside," whispered Kim.

"Be ready to use that flare gun," Teresa said under her breath, "I have an idea—let's move down to the next container—quickly."

They carried on forward in the gap, their voices and movements covered by dozens of whirring generators. Advancing between the side of container and the hull they reached the next junction; one last container before the end of the line—the forward wall of the hold. Teresa spun around and approached the double doors at the end of the container they had just traversed. Two steel latch handles, both just above knee height, held the doors closed. The right door overlapped the left and needed to be opened first. Grimacing, Teresa unlatched the pivot locks on both handles, and then grasping the first handle with her left arm, she pulled it back. The handle pried open slowly until reaching a stopping point at ninety-degrees. She grasped and pried the second handle back, using her thigh and body weight to assist. There was a subtle pop and the sound of rushing air as the seal on the door broke, like opening a refrigerator.

Gripping the handle Teresa leaned back, swinging the eight-foot-high door wide open. Frigid heavy air and condensed fog rolled out, enveloping the women, pooling around their legs and across the deck. The container was dark inside, but Teresa could make out cardboard boxes stacked on pallets. Several near the door had toppled over. The boxes were labelled Frozen Durian in green ink and there was a stamped print of what looked like a large spiky fruit.

"What are you doing?" Kim asked. She had the flare gun raised and was angling her head out to look back down the gap between container and hull.

"Just wait—stay behind the container."

"We can't hide in there, it's too cold—"

"We're not going inside," Teresa replied. She bent and flipped open one of the boxes. Inside were a dozen durians, a yellowish-green tropical fruit, roughly the size of a large cantaloupe. The fruits were covered in a rind of sharp thorn-covered spikes, and each fruit was enclosed in yellow plastic mesh bag with a long handle for carrying them safely, without getting stabbed. Teresa lifted one out by the stretchy mesh handle, feeling the weight. The frozen fruit weighed at least eight pounds.

"He's coming," Kim whispered sharply and pulled back from the side of the container. "He's at the next container down."

"Get behind me—don't make a sound but be ready to shoot—only when I say." Teresa wrapped the plastic handle securely around her left hand, twirling the hefty fruit, bouncing it in its stretchy mesh sack.

The women stood with their shoulders against the closed left door of the container, facing the hull, Teresa in front of Kim. Their bare skin prickled with gooseflesh from the blanketing cold air. Kim didn't know if she was shivering from the cold or fear, or both. She almost jumped out of her skin when Travis called out her name.

"Hey Kim!" His voice was loud but muted by the vast hold and humming fans. "Who's your new friend?"

Teresa felt Kim start behind her, and—shoulder smarting— put her right hand back on Kim's hip to steady her. Kim was debating calling out, unsure what to do. Feeling Teresa's hand she bit her tongue.

"Is she one of the crew?" Travis asked. There was a long strained minute of silence . . . Travis waiting for an answer. Receiving none he called out again. "Time to come out, Kim. I'm not playing hide and seek. It's time for us to get off this ship. All of us. You need to get back to Andrea."

The women didn't move and another few seconds of silence passed. Travis continued, "This is your fault you know; we had a deal—you show me where the treasure is, and I let you and Andrea go. Remember that? What happened?"

Teresa tensed; an ice cold drip of sweat ran slowly down her temple. She could just make out the sound of Travis moving, approaching cautiously down the gap. Her stomach knotted and she could hear Kim's breath shaky behind her. She quickly second-guessed her plan, her offensive stance faltering, wondering if they shouldn't fall back between the rows of containers for the port hull and try and circle around the hold. Fight or flight? It was too late; he was too close. Teresa boldened herself and chose to fight. Standing her ground she inched forward to the corner of the container, keeping the durian hanging loose.

Travis was close, but how close Teresa didn't know. She strained to hear his feet on the deck, trying to judge how far down the gap he was. She glanced at the durian in its elastic mesh, weighing it in her hand again, estimating how far it would stretch out when swung.

She needed Travis within the arcing range of the fruit. He would need to be close. Very close. Inside of three feet. Teresa remained rigid, starting to shiver briskly in the cold from the freezer, her shoulder throbbing. She ignored the pain and tried to stay loose, ready.

She saw Travis's faint shadow pass across the deck in front of her, cast long from the aft lighting. Teresa watched his shadow jog left and right across the decking as he moved forward. She could hear him breathing now—saw his breath condense on the air in front of her.

Now.

Teresa swung the durian in a wide clockwise circle around the side of the container. She swung high and hard, using the fruit like a medieval ball-and-chain flail. She prayed she would not hear the durian miss and smash into the side of the container.

Teresa's judgement and aim were true. The durian caught Travis directly on the right temple, a handful of the thorny spikes impaling through to his skull. The impact knocked him cold, and he dropped like a sack of potatoes, tumbling to the deck. The mesh sack handle was pulled out of Teresa's hand by the thorns embedded in the side of Travis's head when he collapsed. Both women jumped, hearing Travis, the Sig Sauer and the dagger hit the steel deck.

Teresa took a breath and stepped out around the edge of the container.

Travis was lying face down, unmoving. The durian lay beside his head.

Teresa quickly took him in. He looked to be around thirty, wearing only boardshorts and a black T-shirt. Like Kim, he also barefoot. Her eyes flicked to the gun lying by his waist, and she knelt quickly and scooped up the weapon. Instinctively, she stepped back and aimed it at Travis's head. If he so much as moved, she was fully intent on pulling the trigger. No hesitation. No bullshit.

Her eyes flicked again, and she saw the dagger. Even in the dim light of the cargo hold the stones set in the pommel and quillons glittered. Teresa's brow wrinkled as she studied the gilded blade in both surprise and curiosity.

Kim stepped out, coming around beside the park ranger and saw Travis prone on the steel deck. His head was turned to the right, showing his temple and cheek deeply pockmarked and bloodied where the durian's thorns had impaled him. He was breathing deeply in low snuffled grunts.

"He's out," said Teresa, the gun still aimed at Travis's head. "For now."

Kim said nothing. She bent and picked up the dagger, the blade rasping across the decking.

Teresa glanced briefly at the dagger. "Is that . . .?"

"Yes," Kim answered, still staring at Travis. After a moment, she asked, "What are we going to do with him?"

Teresa glowered, and nodded once, slowly. Her voice was rock steady. "We're going to lock him in the container."

Without looking away from Travis or missing a beat, Kim replied, "Yes."

Teresa looked at Kim. "He could die in there."

Kim's tone was severe, unflinching. "Freeze him."

"Alright," Teresa said, "we need to hurry; I don't know how long he's gonna be out for. Grab a wrist—be careful."

Teresa used her left arm, holding the Sig Sauer tenderly in her right. Kim set the flare gun down but kept the dagger in her left hand. Together they each grabbed Travis by a wrist and unceremoniously dragged him around the corner of the container. Teresa put her hip on the door and swung it wide. The cold air seemed to rouse Travis, he snorted loudly, breath condensing in a billowing cloud.

"Hurry," Teresa urged.

They hauled his shoulders up over the container's six-inch lip. There was just enough space by the doors to squeeze

Travis inside. Teresa heaved, stepping up and backing into the container, leaning against stacks of cardboard boxes. Kim repositioned to pick up Travis's ankles, lifting and swinging his legs, working with Teresa to get his hips up and over the lip, twisting and pushing him inside. Teresa quickly hopped down out of the container, over Travis, who was making his way slowly back to consciousness. The women grabbed and leaned on the heavy freezer door, slowly swinging it over.

Travis let out a groan from inside the container.

Working together they closed the door with a resounding thud. Teresa quickly swung both latch handles over, pushing against them with her hip and thigh, sealing the door.

There was muffled movement and a bump against the inside of the door.

Teresa scrambled to close a pivot lock on the latch with her left hand, and Kim went for the other. Together they clamped them both tight. With the locks secure, Travis was locked and sealed inside the freezer unit.

Both women were breathing heavily, trickling cold sweat, their arms and legs covered in prickled gooseflesh. An intense pulsing throb ebbed through Teresa's injured shoulder from the effort, and blood ran down her slack arm in fresh rivulets.

"Can he get out?" Kim asked.

Teresa shook her head, wincing and wiping sweat from her forehead. "I don't think so. I don't think there's an inside latch—I didn't see one."

Kim scowled through her exhaustion and relief. "I hope he freezes. That bastard killed two of my friends—and he's a rapist pig."

Teresa looked at Kim, taken aback, but said nothing.

"He was going to kill us both." Kim looked to the gun in

289

Teresa's hand. "I'd like to open the door back up and shoot him myself, right now."

Teresa was silent for a moment. "No. I wouldn't take the risk, and you really wouldn't want that on your conscience. We'll leave the son of a bitch in there. Let the cold do its work." She raised the Sig Sauer and looked the gun over. She had some experience with handguns, both in Minnesota and having fired a pistol at a range in Fort Myers as part of her park ranger training. She pulled back the slide and saw the glint of a brass 9mm round in the ejection port. Returning the slide forward, she thumbed the magazine release button and the mag slipped into her hand. It was empty.

"He only had one shot left," Teresa said, popping the magazine back into the well.

Kim bent and picked up the flare gun from the deck. "Let's head back—I'm ready to get off this goddamn boat."

"You and me both."

* * * *

They backtracked out of the hold, up the stairs, squinting against the afternoon sunlight coming out into the starboard passageway. There was still no sign of any of the crew on the reefer. Making their way forward across the open deck, Kim went down the Jacob's ladder first, eager to be off the sun-heated steel deck. The tide had come in since Kim first boarded the ship, and she dropped from the ladder into knee deep surf that felt deliciously cool on her feet.

Teresa flipped the pistol's safety on and tucked it into the cargo pocket of her uniform pants. Working one-handed, she struggled on the tricky descent to the sand, favoring her injured shoulder, letting out a hissing breath and gnashing her teeth as her arm jerked at each rung. Kim helped Teresa down the last few steps, the park ranger struggling to keep her right arm immobilized. Traversing up the port hull they rounded the bow up onto the sand, following the three sets of tracks back down the beach. Smoke had almost entirely ceased coming from the reefer's bridge.

Within minutes of being back in the sun and humidity their chill from being in the hold quickly tempered. Teresa spied the knapsack and flip-flops lying awry on the beach. She pointed. "Your sandals?"

"Yes. Sort of . . . I took them from the cabin we spent the night at." Kim walked over to the flip-flops and slid them on, ignoring the knapsack.

"Where is this cabin?" Teresa asked as they resumed the hike.

"At the south end of the island, at least a good three miles from here. It's on stilts, set back in the trees. I almost didn't see it."

"I know the place," Teresa said. "It belongs to a nice couple. They come and stay often; they've had the place for years, decades. Since the seventies. I'm sure they'll be back to check on it soon."

"They'll find it mostly intact, but it's a bloody mess. It's gonna need a shitload of new windows and screens. And we drank all their rum."

Teresa grinned. "Now that they might not be too happy about. I tell you one thing—I'm having a drink—or three, tonight."

"I think I'll join you."

Teresa checked her watch: 3:05 p.m. She looked up and down the beach. "It's getting late. We'd better keep moving."

HURRICANE HOLE

The women traversed the sand, saying little, focusing their energies on the hike. They cut off the beach through the dunes at the cabins and head east on the Cabin Trail. The island was still preternaturally silent, void of the sounds of any insects or birdsong. Ahead was the blocked trail and Kim saw the parked ATV.

"We can ride from here," Teresa said.

Stepping over the downed live oak, they shared the rest of the water from Teresa's bottle, gulping it down before climbing on the ATV.

Teresa drove them back to the visitor grounds, a short ride on the four-wheeler, pulling up in front of the ranger station, tires crunching on the shell. The area and docks were as abandoned and quiet as when she had left. Kim's thoughts were solely on Andrea, she got off the ATV first and went quickly up the steps and into the ranger station.

Teresa was surprised to see she had been gone for almost ninety minutes. Still seated on the ATV, she shut off the engine to all-encompassing silence and scanned Pelican Bay. There were no boats at all in sight out on the viridian waters. *Lisa Marie* still sat moored to the damaged docks.

Her plan was to get the two women back over to Bokeelia as fast as possible, get medical help for Andrea, and contact the police immediately. Margi was going to have to wait for checking upon. Teresa prayed the older woman was not in need of any help herself. It had been almost a full twenty-four hours since the hurricane had hit.

The Sig Sauer was heavy against her thigh. Teresa's conscience began to creep up on her, and she started to rethink leaving Travis locked inside the freezer container. He would surely die from hypothermia. She doubted he would survive until later this evening, let alone tomorrow, or whenever it was she would be able to lead the police back out to the reefer ship. It might take some time, almost the entire state had its hands full with recovering from Charley. One thing was for sure, she was not going back to that ship without the police or other serious backup. If Travis did die, there would be no repercussions on either her or Kim. The bastard had tried to kill them. Locking him in the freezer was purely self-defense. Teresa did not directly kill him, but the cold would. She would feel no remorse or guilt over his death. But what was right? Should he perish in the freezer or face a judge and jury?

Teresa placed her left hand lightly on her upper arm below the injury. She looked down at the bullet wound in the sunlight filtering through a pocket of cabbage palms. The bleeding had slowed, almost stopped, but the sleeve of her shirt was soiled through and crusted a dark maroon, the blood streaked and coagulating on her arm. The 9mm had punched a small, neat hole straight through her deltoid muscle. The pain seemed to come and go in waves, and the waves were rising in height as her adrenaline wore off. Piloting *Lisa Marie* six miles back across the sound and through Jug Creek to Bokeelia was going to be a real challenge.

Teresa caught movement on the porch of the ranger station and looked over to see Kim had come back outside. Her skin had gone pallid, head and shoulders bowed, body language beaten.

She looked up at Teresa, her expression heartsick. "Andrea's dead."

CHAPTER SIXTEEN

Teresa stepped past Kim, entering the ranger station, pausing just inside the door. The air was hot and stuffy, smelling of sweat and a sour bitterness. Andrea still lay on her back on the bench, her head resting on the hoodie, face tipped to one side, facing Teresa. Her skin was blanched white, eyes closed, one arm hung loosely down to the floor. Blood had seeped heavily through the bandaging on her waist, absorbed and spread further into her yellow halter top. The blood had dripped down the front of the bench, at least two pints pooled on the floor below.

Teresa grimaced and crossed to kneel beside the bench. She placed two fingers on the side of Andrea's neck, feeling for the carotid pulse.

Nothing.

Andrea's skin was still warm, but looking at her face, Teresa could see the woman was dead. Her features were slack, sunken and lifeless beyond sleep or unconsciousness.

Teresa shook her head slowly and stood. After a minute, she stepped back outside to stand on the porch beside Kim.

"I'm sorry," Teresa said quietly. The words felt simple and meaningless, but it was all she could think to say.

Kim did not reply. She shook on her feet. Teresa could feel the intense emotion welling inside the woman. Staring out at Pelican Bay with wet eyes, Kim finally spoke. "He's killed three of my friends . . . Andrea was my best friend." She turned to Teresa, her expression ruthless. "I hope he freezes to death."

Teresa said nothing. She observed Kim closely for the first time. Her blonde hair was dirty and tangled, T-shirt soiled, knees and elbows blackened with oil and grime, calves chafed red. Blood coated one side of her neck from a torn earlobe, and there was a nasty gash on her chin. She still gripped the dagger in her hand, the tip pointed loosely down at the wood planking of the porch.

Seeing the dagger again, Teresa frowned curiously. She had momentarily forgotten about the antique weapon, and the treasure. The gold and jeweled blade looked quite striking, an artifact pulled straight from another century. If it was authentic, Teresa couldn't begin to imagine its worth.

"Can I take a look at that?" Teresa asked, nodding at the dagger.

Kim looked expressionlessly down at the blade in her hand and held it out to Teresa without hesitation, seeming to almost be wanting to part with it. Teresa took the dagger by the hilt, first feeling its weight. She judged it at half a pound, maybe a little more. The stones looked like rubies and emeralds, inlaid in an ornate gold cross-guard and pommel. The tapered blade was a flat gray steel, possibly silver, with a fine point and central ridge.

"Are we going back now?" Kim asked. "You can take us off the island on your boat?"

Teresa was still looking at the dagger. She nodded. "Yes, but there's someone I'd like to check on first."

"Who? There's someone else on the island?"

"Yes. An older lady, she lives alone in her cabin. Not far from here." Teresa looked up at Kim. "Where exactly did you say you found this again?"

Kim took a breath and sighed, pure exhaustion and grief having drained her entirely. "South, down the beach, in the dune. A mile from here."

HURRICANE HOLE

Teresa recalled Andrea's earlier ramblings, describing the location. She had said there was a palm tree down in the surf, marking the spot. It shouldn't be hard to locate. If there was a treasure find on Cayo Costa now was Teresa's only chance to see it herself, alone, before state officials and the police moved in on the island. By this time tomorrow Cayo Costa was going to be swarming with cops, and, if what she held in her hand was real, and what Andrea and Kim described existed, there would also be plenty of officials from the state archeological departments. This island was a state park. Any significant find of historical or monetary value was going to be swooped down upon by the Florida Department of State.

Teresa's curiosity rose further, as did her interest in seeing this treasure firsthand, before the authorities.

"I want you to stay here and rest," Teresa said, "I'm going to check on this lady, Margi. You're safe now. There's nobody who can hurt you. When I get back, we're getting off the island, right away. All of us. I'll take us over to Bokeelia on Pine Island, and we'll contact the police."

Dulled concern crossed Kim's face; her emotions diluted by fatigue. "How long will you be gone?"

"Not long at all. Twenty minutes. I'm going to take the ATV. Stay here . . . I'll get you some cold water from the boat before I go."

Dagger in hand, ignoring the pounding throb in her shoulder with a renewed effort, Teresa crossed over to the docks and boarded *Lisa Marie*. Crouching at a cooler in the cockpit, she drank a full half-liter bottle of water and grabbed three more from the ice. She picked up the dagger from where she had set it down on the fiberglass deck, and turned it over in her hand, examining it more closely. The afternoon sunlight shot through the red and green stones, sparkling and refracting across the deck.

Standing, she carefully slid the dagger into the left cargo pocket of her pants leg, sucking in a breath against the pulsing ache in her shoulder. She had the gun with its single remaining round in one pocket, and the dagger in the other. Returning to the ranger station, she found Kim sitting on the bench on the front porch, her feet hiked up, arms hugging her knees. Her head hung hangdog, blonde hair matted over her face, the fight all but gone out of her.

Teresa set two of the bottles down for Kim, keeping a third for herself. With little energy or motivation other than to quell a burning thirst, Kim picked up a bottle, uncapped it, and drank heavily through parched lips. Water dripping down her chin, mixing and diluting with blood from the gash on her face, she looked up at Teresa.

"This was all my fault," Kim said, her face slack, eyes glazed. "From the very beginning. I should never have encouraged Mark to bring Travis onboard. They would all still be alive. This is all on me."

"Shh," Teresa consoled, trying to find the right words. "This is not your fault, or anyone's fault but Travis. You had a run-in with a certifiable psycho. And right now he's locked inside a deep freezer. Getting his just desserts."

Kim said nothing for a moment, then her eyes focused and found the park ranger's. "Don't be gone long."

Teresa nodded once. "I'll be right back. Stay put and rest." She turned and stepped off the porch, climbing on the ATV, stowing the water bottle. She keyed the ignition and checked her watch: 3:44 p.m. She had plenty of time . . . as far as she knew, no one was coming out to the island today.

Pulling a tight U-turn, Teresa traversed the Cabin Trail back west for a hundred yards before she cut off to the south, following an unmarked side trail. As she penetrated the storm-ravaged oak and palm hammock, Teresa hoped the trail ahead would remain passable on the ATV.

The knobby offroad tires navigated downed debris, and Teresa had to slow and maneuver across large limbs and trunks, but the trail was manageable. She used her left arm dominantly to steer, favoring her right arm.

Coming upon a T-junction she went right, heading west, now paralleling the Cabin Trail. At another junction she veered south, running down the backside of the dunes. She planned to come out onto the beach just over a mile south of the camping cabins, and due west of Margi's cabin. She would run the beach and see if she could locate this treasure find, and then loop back to Margi's place on Primo Bay. On the ATV it should be about a quick twenty-minute ride. If Margi had remained in her cabin through the passing of the hurricane—and her cabin had held up—the older woman should be alright.

Teresa rode out onto the beach on the same path through the dunes that Kim and Andrea had exited the beach from earlier this morning. Coming out onto the backshore and riding over a berm, Teresa immediately saw the heavy erosion to the dunes along this section of beach. From their directions, the treasure should be close. Within a third of a mile.

Teresa rode down to the pan, the ATV's tires leaving twin tracks in wet sand. The beach was deserted. She rolled south at a slower pace, both scanning the dune above her and watching for a palm tree down in the surf. The flood tide had come in fully and the water was up at the high tide line.

She saw the palm tree, submerged out in the swash. It was cabbage palm, under two feet of water, washed over with light breaking waves. As she neared it, Teresa slowed further and head directly up the beach face towards the dune scarp. She did her best to ignore the pain in her shoulder, feeling a sharp stab every time she used her right arm.

Running her eyes up and down the eroded wall of sand, she saw endless tangles of exposed sea oat roots. Approaching the dune she went north first, backtracking, planning to turn and sweep the dune face southbound until she found what the two women claimed to have discovered here.

Teresa saw the stacked ingots first, her eye drawn quickly to the human-made lines. Slowing, she squinted, not sure entirely yet what she was seeing. She rolled to a stop adjacent to the anomaly in the eroded scarp, studying the ingots for a moment before shutting off the engine and stepping from the ATV. She approached the dune slowly, her eyes zigzagging back and forth over the stacked rows of silver ingots, dropping down across the dozen toppled out onto the sand in front of her.

Her heart rate picked up by a ten count, beating hard inside her chest.

She saw the coins, scattered pieces of eight, a shiny carpet under her feet. Bending to pick one up, she studied it for a minute, and looked back to see that she must have driven the ATV across at least a handful of silver pieces on her approach. She had not seen the coins on the sand as she rolled up to the dune.

Teresa brushed sand from the coin and flipped it between her thumb and forefinger, examining the worn markings. Turning back to the ingots she mimicked Kim's actions earlier this morning, placing a hiking boot on the closest ingot in the sand, rocking it, feeling the weight. Resting atop the ingot was the gold bullion disk that Kim had left there. To Teresa it looked just like it did to Kim, the size and shape of a large chocolate chip cookie.

Her eye was then drawn up towards the dark pocket to the upper right of the ingots. The late afternoon sun was now shining directly on the face of the scarp, rays striking the pocket of emeralds. The stones were a mob of blue green against the dry cream-colored sand. She saw how dozens of the oddly shaped rough stones had spilled out, falling into the dune swale amidst sea oat roots.

Taking her foot from the ingot and dropping to a knee in front of the scarp, Teresa dropped the coin and lifted a rough emerald the size of a sewing thimble from the sand, studying the stone closely. There was no doubt in her mind that what she was seeing was authentic.

Hurricane Charley had unearthed a treasure trove.

Teresa's heart sped up further at the significance of the find, and the possible value. There were certainly millions of dollars in front of her, buried in the sand. Gold, silver, precious gemstones. And the dagger—so far, the showpiece of this incredible find. How long had this horde remained hidden in the dune? Three hundred years? Four hundred? A bona fide cache of buried treasure. How many times in the past two years had she driven and walked by this very spot?

An unabashed shiver of childlike excitement tingled up Teresa's spine, evoked by nostalgic memories of *The Goonies*. Pirate treasure, the *Inferno,* One-Eyed Willy.

Aside from Kim and Andrea, Teresa was the only other person to set eyes on this trove. Her thoughts returned bitterly to the reality of what would happen. Police would shut down the park, state department officials would claim the find, and neither Teresa, nor Kim, would get any legal claim to the treasure or see a penny from it.

Like billions of other people, Teresa had hopes and dreams. One of her dreams was to one day own a boat of her own. That was, before she first got a mortgage and a home of course. Priorities. Working for Florida State Parks, her salary in her second year was $11 an hour, which equated to roughly

$22,000 a year, plus benefits. The truth was, on her income she was living paycheck to paycheck—barely making her rent for the place on Pine Island. She was pinned down to the forty plus hours a week, looking at years before she would qualify for the first paltry pay bump. Being able to afford a house, let alone a boat, was a decade or more off. If ever.

Teresa felt the weight of the dagger against her thigh and looked down at the outline of the hilt and blade inside her cargo pocket. She could only imagine the value of the relic. The beginnings of an idea began to form in her mind, and she felt the rising—and strongly divided—pull of a decision. The choice between right and wrong. For a full minute she wrestled with her conscience, before making a firm ruling.

Teresa was going to keep the dagger.

An idea quickly became a plan. She let the emerald drop silently to the sand at the base of the scarp. Her focus was only the dagger, and to check on Margi. The older lady's cabin was due east, directly across the island. If the connecting trail was clear, it was a five-minute haul on the ATV. Then back to the ranger station. Get Kim, get aboard *Lisa Marie* and head for home.

Teresa brushed her hands on her thighs and stood, making to turn for the four-wheeler.

From the dune above her she sensed movement—a rushing blur.

Travis hit Teresa with his full bodyweight, leaping from atop the dune, tackling her from above, taking her backwards, clean off her feet. He landed on the park ranger just like he had landed on the corrections officer in the laundry room at Belle Glade. The two collided with brute force and tumbled to the sand.

Teresa lay flat on her back on the beach, her shoulder a

burning white-hot agony. She felt her lungs vacuum, the wind knocked out of her, and she wheezed, desperately trying to suck in a breath.

* * * *

A burst of adrenaline brought everything into a focused slow motion blur. Teresa needed to breathe, and she felt Travis's hands go directly for her throat. His fingers were like icicles as they circled her throat, his digits ice cold. His dark eyes were inches from hers, impossibly hard and cold, void of any mercy, only hate-filled. Travis's face was streaked with blood, the right side patterned with red divots from the durian. She could feel the ambient cold from the freezer still falling from him, enveloping her. He was still half-frozen.

Teresa's shoulder screamed murder—she had no choice but to use her right arm to fight off his attack.

Her diaphragm relaxed from its spasm, and she managed to suck in a partial breath through Travis's hands crushing her windpipe. He smelled terrible, cold stale sweat and foul breath. She brought up a knee hard, to try and catch him in the groin but he twisted away before she made contact. His chilled fingers dug into her throat, fully cutting off her airway.

Eyes bulging and watering, Teresa let go of his wrist with her left hand and dug down into the cargo pocket of her pants, blindly grasping for the dagger. Her hand wrapped around the hilt. She struggled to withdraw the blade, the cross-guard agonizingly catching twice on the inner pocket. The dagger finally slipped free, and she angled it pointed towards his torso and drove it in with every ounce of strength she had. The six-inch blade sunk to the hilt into the right side of Travis's abdomen.

His eyes went immediately wide, he gasped, and his grip relaxed on her throat.

Teresa clutched the hilt and twisted it as hard as she could with her forearm muscles, rotating the dagger counterclockwise.

Travis let out a hissing grunt and jerked upright, removing his hands from her throat. Teresa took a deep breath of sweet air, followed quickly by another. Travis was kneeling, straddling her hips, looking down in wild confusion at the jewel-encrusted hilt sticking out of his waist. The blade had slipped in over Travis's iliac crest, plunging into his large intestine. Teresa had ripped open the organ when she torqued the blade.

She took advantage of his shock; in one motion she withdrew the dagger, bucked her hips and rolled to her right, out from under him. Her shoulder felt like it was jabbed with a red hot poker as she leaned weight on her elbow, getting to her knees. She fell back against the side of the ATV, using it for balance, catching her breath, wincing in pain.

Travis's face contorted in agony and rage. "You fuckin' bitch . . ." He looked up at her and then back down at the blood seeping profusely from the wound in his side. "I'm gonna fuckin' kill you—whoever the fuck you are."

Travis struggled to get to his feet, hissing and groaning.

Teresa raised the dagger, the blade coated slick with blood. She had no idea how he had escaped from the container—an inside latch? Or maybe the *Banten Buru* was indeed a ghost ship. Maybe it let Travis out, like the Overlook Hotel let Jack Torrance out of the pantry in *The Shining*—but no matter how, he had gotten out and followed Kim's directions to the treasure. The injury to his abdomen was severe, and fatal without medical attention, but he still posed a danger. She remembered—the gun.

Teresa pulled the Sig Sauer out of her pocket, her shoulder

burning fire, and aimed it directly at Travis. She was trembling, her right arm wavering.

Travis struggled to his feet; his right hand pinned against his side, covering the gushing wound. He let out a laugh when he saw Teresa had the gun on him. He shook his head, grinning. "Guess what? No bullets. I fired the last one on the ship. At you. That gun is empty."

Teresa knew he was bluffing.

"No it's not," she said, carefully getting to her feet, keeping the pistol trained on Travis's chest. "There's one shot left."

Travis was chagrined but remained unmoved. The woman must have checked the chamber and magazine. His eye passed over her uniform, and he caught the scatter of coins across the sand at her feet. Frowning, he ran his eyes over the silver pieces running up the beach. Slowly, his face pained, he turned to look behind. For the first time Travis saw the treasure horde. His jaw went slack as he surveyed the stacked ingots, emeralds, and gold bullion, unsure what to make of it all.

Travis cocked his head. "I'll be goddamned." He was taking sharp breaths around the pain in his gut. "This is it, isn't it? And I thought Kim was lying. Christ."

Teresa's finger was wrapped tight on the trigger, she could not stop the tip of the pistol from shaking. Travis was less than ten feet from her, standing in front of the dune, still taking in the unearthed cache.

He turned from the trove to look at Teresa. "Who are you? A park ranger?"

Teresa said nothing, doing her best to keep the gun steady, her shoulder in absolute agony. She saw blood was seeping heavily through the fingers of Travis's hand, running down, darkening the hip of his blue boardshorts.

Travis's expression changed, the hardness magically erasing

from his face. He angled around to face her directly, his voice softening. "This has all got to be worth a fortune." He paused, assessing Teresa. "Look . . . let's call a truce, you and I. I shot you, you knifed me good." He let out a grunt and glanced down at his side. "Real good. We're even there. I ain't gonna lie—there is one round left in that gun. You know it and I know it. Why don't we save it?"

"Save it for what?" Teresa asked.

"In case we need it. You came back here to see the treasure for yourself, didn't you?" Travis nodded, encouraged. "I say let's grab what we can and get out of here. Just you and me, right now. What do you say?"

Teresa said nothing and Travis asked, "Did you come alone?"

Teresa's face transformed into total disbelief, and she slowly shook her head. "You've got to be kidding. The only thing you should be concerned with is staying alive at this point. You're bleeding out, fast."

Travis glanced down at the injury to his abdomen, and back at Teresa. "We can load that quad and get out of here, the two of us, take what we can, and go." He cracked a smile, laying on his Southern charm. "C'mon, I can see you thinking about it. I know your type. You've got it in you. That's why you came here before leaving the island . . . you left Kim and Teresa along up there . . . you had to see it for yourself." He paused to look down briefly again at the blood running out of guts. He would need to make this quick. "What's your name?"

Teresa said nothing.

"Hell, lady. I am bleeding here. We need to hurry . . . what do you say, are you in with me?"

Teresa stalled, her eyes dropping to the blood coming out of Travis. It had totally soiled the right leg of his shorts. "How did you get out of that freezer?"

Travis grinned boyishly. "I'll tell you over drinks one night. So, do we have a plan here?"

Resolved, Teresa asked, "Your name is Travis, right?"

"That's right. And I don't have the pleasure of yours?"

Teresa shook her head slowly, eyes darkening. "I'm sorry, Travis. Stealing this dagger is my plan—but you're just not part of it."

She held the gun as steady as she could, aimed center mass at Travis's chest and pulled the trigger.

There was only a grating sound from within the weapon. The single-stage trigger had no travel.

The pit of Teresa's stomach fell, and panic surged through her. She pulled the trigger again with the same result. A gritty noise.

Travis had tensed, but now he visibly relaxed. His face was brash, tone arrogant. "It's the sand—it makes the trigger stick."

Teresa's eyes widened, looking to the gun in her hand. The matte black pistol was peppered with granules of the coarse beach sand. In a desperate attempt she pulled the trigger again, feeling and hearing the abrasive rasp in her hand. With an unexpected jerk the trigger snapped back under her index finger.

The gun fired, a whip-like cracking sonic boom.

As Teresa recovered from the blast, the pistol kicking her hand with a solid five pounds of recoil, a fear grew that she had fired blindly and missed Travis. Her vision focused through the haze of white smoke.

The bullet had caught Travis in the forehead above his left eye, penetrating his skull at more than 1100 feet per second, killing him instantly. Teresa saw his head kick back, and he fell straight backwards, his head slamming off the side of a silver ingot. He lay motionless in the sand at the base of the scarp, in front of the treasure horde.

Taking sharp breaths Teresa stepped forward; the empty gun still trained on Travis's inert form. As she came alongside him, she saw the extent of the injury to his head and knew for certain he was dead. Travis's blood was pumping from the back of his head in thick rivulets onto the sand. Teresa forced down a rising sickness. She had never killed anyone, although she had envisioned shooting her ex many times. But this was the real thing.

She glanced up and down the beach, seeing no one, and let the gun drop beside Travis. Taking a moment to compose herself and gather her thoughts, with a left-handed struggle she put the blood-slick dagger back into the cargo pocket of her pants.

Crossing to the ATV, she retrieved and uncapped the water bottle and with a shaky hand drank the entire half-liter down. The second round of adrenaline burning off rapidly, she breathed deeply, leaning on the handlebars, looking out across the expansive Gulf, watching the waves crest and break on the sand. After a few minutes of blankly observing the late afternoon sun sparkle and play on the water she looked down at her watch: 4:33 p.m.

Change in plans. Teresa would again skip checking on Margi, and head directly back to the ranger station. Margi had been living on Cayo Costa for almost three decades, the past ten years out here alone. If she made it through the hurricane, another few hours longer weren't going to matter now . . . the police would be out to the island this evening.

Teresa climbed on the ATV and thumbed the engine start. She cast another repulsed look at Travis, her eyes leaving him to again cross the treasure horde in the scarp, before torquing the throttle and heading up the beach.

It took her eight minutes to traverse the mile and a half

back to the ranger station, retracing her path through the dunes and taking the side trail north. As Teresa approached the visitor grounds, she slowed the ATV to an idling roll. A hundred yards west of the bungalow she braked to a stop and killed the engine. Dismounting the four-wheeler, Teresa approached the bungalow on foot and skirted around to the rear, cutting across the grounds, passing behind the gift shop trailer, heading straight for the ruined storage shed. It took her only a half-minute of hunting through the storm wreckage to find what she as looking for: a short round nose shovel.

From the shed Teresa stuck to the far side of the grounds, rounding her way west to the bay, staying on the perimeter, circling and ducking behind the restrooms. Peering out from behind the cinderblock wall, from this vantage point she could see the front porch of the ranger's bungalow.

There was no sign of Kim. She had moved from where Teresa had left her sitting on the bench. Teresa guessed she must have gone inside the bungalow. Squinting against the sun she scanned the rest of the visitor area. No sign of anyone, no one had arrived while she was gone. Looking over her shoulder she saw there were no boats out on the bay, only *Lisa Marie* moored faithfully at the docks.

Teresa set the shovel down, wiped sweat from her eyes on the sleeve of her good shoulder. She looked again up to the bungalow, and still seeing no one, she picked up the shovel and left the cover of the restrooms, crossing the clearing at a brisk pace. She was headed towards covered benches, rows of seating for day-trip tourists and campers arriving and departing the island on the ferry. Continuing past the benches, Teresa made for the Welcome to Cayo Costa State Park sign. Nearing the sign she was no longer in a direct line of sight from the ranger station, concealed behind a shoreline bramble of cocoplum and sea grape.

Casting another furtive look around, Teresa circled around behind the sign, and placed the tip of the shovel on the shell and limestone gravel a foot out from the center post. Favoring her right arm and gritting her teeth against renewed jolts of pain, she began to dig. Despite the injury to her shoulder it was quick work to dig out a rectangular hole in the loose sandy soil. After only a couple of minutes she had shoveled out a hole a foot by foot and a half wide and a foot deep

Crouching, Teresa removed the dagger from her cargo pocket and placed it lightly in the bottom of the hole. The blade was still greased with Travis's blood. She gave the seventeenth century weapon a brief but studied look before rising, picking up the shovel and covering the relic over. She carefully took the time to return the shelled limestone to an undisturbed state, erasing all signs that the ground was recently dug up.

Satisfied, a fresh sheen of sweat broken out across her brow and back, Teresa crossed to the waterfront at the far end of the visitor benches. Still out of sight of the ranger's bungalow, using her left arm she wound up and flung the shovel out as far as she could into the bay.

Checking the time again she saw it was seven minutes past five. Sundown in three hours. She needed to find Kim, get on *Lisa Marie*, and get back over to Bokeelia. Taking a breath to compose herself, Teresa turned and head straight back for the ranger station. She was halfway there, passing Andrea's discarded sandals—

"Hello . . ."

A woman's voice calling out, ten yards off to the left.

Teresa froze in her tracks, nearly jumping out of her skin, adrenal glands jolting her system with a spiking rush of adrenaline.

Heart thrumming, she looked over to see Margi Pattinson.

HURRICANE HOLE

The older lady was standing in the center of the Cabin Trail, looking at Teresa in mild surprise.

Margi was already more than a year past ninety, but her long white hair was tied back in a ponytail that fell out from under a wide-brimmed straw hat. She had on khaki shorts and a cream-colored long sleeve rash guard that had seen some years of wear. Around her neck and tied under her chin was a loose black scarf, used as a gaiter, shielding against both insects and sun. Margi's face was friendly and wizened, pale blue eyes rheumy, skin marked and creased from decades under the Florida sun. She carried a four-foot switch of wax myrtle, randomly whipping the branch through the humid air at an imagined mosquito.

"Gave you quite a fright I see," Margi said. "What's got you so jumpy, Teresa?"

Teresa forced a smile, relief washing over her, and she let out a breath. "Hi, Margi. I'm glad to see you came through the storm OK. We've had a few problems on the island with the hurricane."

Margo swatted her branch. "I don't right remember much of the storm. I went to bed early . . . I must have slept through most of it, that part I can remember. I told you all that I didn't need to leave. See—here I am, all together still, in one piece. Wasn't the first hurricane . . . won't be the last." She swatted again at another unseen insect.

"Your cabin held up alright?" asked Teresa, relaxing further. It seemed Margi had not witnessed her bury the dagger or toss the shovel into the bay.

"Seems that it did, I guess. Might have lost a shingle or two." Margi paused to look around. "There ain't any skeeters this evening. No birds neither. The hurricane blew them all away, I suppose. They'll come back soon enough, 'specially the skeeters. What kind of problems you havin'?"

Teresa didn't want to drop too much on Margi, she tread lightly. "We've had some damage to the grounds and docks. And there's a woman here who was stranded on the island through the storm, she needs help. I need to get her over to Pine Island right away."

The older woman frowned. "What all happened?"

Teresa's face turned hard. "There's been trouble, Margi. We've had a couple of deaths on the island."

Margi drew a sharp breath. "Oh my . . ."

"I'd like you to come back with us over to Bokeelia. I need to contact the police as soon as we get over there. I'm sure you'll be able to return home later this evening, but if not, you can stay with me for the night at my place."

"The police? You need the police?"

Teresa nodded and said nothing.

Margi was silent for a moment, considering, and then nodded. "If you think it's best. But I'd really like to be back home this evening. I've got the cats, you know."

"We'll see what we can do. The police will be out here this evening for certain, and we'll likely be able to come back over with them."

Margi nodded, clearly nettled. "Alright then."

"You head on down to the dock. I'm going to get this woman and we'll be off right away." Teresa started past the older woman, headed for the ranger station.

"My Lord, wait—what happened to your shoulder?" Margi asked, bringing a hand to her chest, peering forward at the park ranger.

Teresa remained stoic. "It's a long story—I had a bit of an accident."

"You're hurt, girl. Hurt badly."

"I'm OK. You head on down to the boat now. Wait for me

to board, the docks are broken up quite a bit from the storm. We'll be right there."

Not wanting to field any more questions Teresa left Margi and approached the silent bungalow. There had been no sign of Kim, and Teresa was again becoming concerned. Taking the front steps two at a time, she stepped across the porch, hesitating only a second at the door, and walked into the cabin. The light inside was dimming quickly in the late afternoon light.

Kim was lying on her side on the floor, beside the bench. Her legs were curled up, head resting on an extended arm. She had come back inside to lay beside her friend. Andrea's blood, dark and congealed now, was pooled near Kim's outstretched hand.

Teresa crossed to Kim and knelt, putting a hand lightly on her shoulder. She whispered, "Hey, hey Kim—"

Kim jerked awake, eyes going wide in alarm, raising her head and sucking in a panicked breath. She saw Teresa and blinked, relaxing some. "What is it?"

"It's OK," Teresa said gently, "everything's OK. You were sleeping."

Kim had prominent lines between her eyebrows, her face a wash of anxiety and fatigue, eyes red-rimmed and dark. With an arm around her, Teresa helped her to sit up. Together, they both looked to where Andrea lay on the bench. Her skin was pallid, and still covered in a sheen of sweat that gave her the appearance of life. Her head was tilted peacefully, resting on Teresa's hoodie, a trickle of blood run down her cheek from her mouth, absorbed into the sweatshirt. It occurred to Teresa that she was never going to wear that hoodie again.

Kim kneaded the back of her neck and looked to the park ranger. "Where were you? You were gone a lot longer than I expected."

Teresa faced Kim, her expression resolute. "He's dead."

Kim's eyebrows drew together, eyes questioning.

"He's dead," Teresa said again. "I killed him. Out where you found the treasure. He attacked me—somehow, he got out. I don't know how but he got out of the freezer. I . . . shot him. He's dead."

Kim said nothing, her face glazing, darkening. "How the hell did he get out of that container?"

Teresa shook her head imperceptibly. "I have no idea. I double latched it from the outside." She brushed away thoughts of ghost ships with doors that unlocked themselves. "It doesn't matter—he's dead now."

They had less than two and a half hours until sunset. And the boat ride back to Pine Island would eat up at least forty minutes. From Bokeelia, Teresa would need to find a location where her cell phone could pick up reception to call the police. She might likely have to drive all the way over into Cape Coral. A long, late night still lay ahead.

"Time to go," Teresa said, gently squeezing Kim's shoulder. "The older lady, Margi, she's here, waiting."

Kim's eyes found Teresa's, focusing, coming back to the present. "She made it through the hurricane?"

"She did. She's waiting for us at the docks."

Kim's voice was resolute: "Let's get off this godforsaken island, once and for all."

* * * *

Teresa stood at the helm of *Lisa Marie*, working the wheel with her left arm. Behind her, in the cockpit, Kim sat beside Margi, the two women quiet, watching Teresa pilot the boat. The sun was low, directly off their stern, hot on Teresa's back. The heat felt good. Her shoulder ached, but the pain was dulling some, a numbness settling in, both physically and mental.

She turned and glanced back at the women, separated in age by more than sixty years. Kim looked drained and disheveled, beaten with grief and trauma. Margi sat upright, still holding her switch, black scarf blowing in the wind. She appeared to be enjoying the boat ride. Catching Teresa's eye the older lady glanced over at Kim for a moment and then back at Teresa, giving her a critical and judgmental look, before turning to gaze back at her beloved island. Margi was nonplussed to be unexpectedly leaving her home and her cats. Teresa followed Margi's watch. The sun was dropping over Cayo Costa, falling atop the bare and beaten hurricane-thrashed hammock of live oak and cabbage palms.

The tranquil barrier island was going to be soon invaded and swarmed over by police, news reporters, and numerous archeological departments. Cayo Costa would be closed to visitors, combed over, the treasure exhumed, and Margi's peaceful life of solitude disrupted for a while.

Teresa's life had been forever changed in a few hours today; she had both been shot by and killed another human. A vision and experience she would never forget. She had stolen and hidden a priceless artifact from the state. And this day was far from over. She would have to lead police back to the island, to Andrea's body, to the mysterious abandoned reefer ship *Banten Buru*, to Travis, and to the treasure. There would be many questions, and she did not have all the answers.

But she did have one secret.

PART SIX

THE DAGGER

CHAPTER SEVENTEEN

October 30, 2004
Key West, Florida

S aturday evening in the country's southernmost city, subtropical Old Town thick in the throes of Fantasy Fest. The fall air was as florid as the rollicking atmosphere; the Masquerade March street parade was in full swing—a mosaic of elaborate floats, risqué costumes, and flowing cocktails. The moving dance party that rivalled Mardi Gras flocked west through town, towards the infamous Duval Street. The late October sun hung low over the Gulf of Mexico and sundown was going to be spectacular; the sky was cloudless and already tinting a burnt orange.

Teresa Randall watched the passing revelers in their merrymaking from Mallory Square. She had arrived in Key West this morning, driving down from Fort Myers in her '97 Jeep Wrangler, checking into The Westin Resort & Marina for two nights. It was her first time in Key West, and the raucous carousal was overwhelming. Teressa was not used to the bustling crowds, a far cry from the stillness of Cayo Costa, and she was already in a heightened state, frayed nerves on edge.

Teresa set out through the dancing crowds of bacchants, making her way towards Front Street. She wore a white button-up blouse, khaki capris, and navy blue canvas deck shoes.

The dagger was in a black Nautica crossbody handbag.

Against her better judgement, at a waterfront tiki bar Teresa had had one drink to calm her anxiousness. She wanted to keep a clear head, and strictly limited herself to a single rum daiquiri. Finishing her drink, Teresa left the bustling square as the evening's sunset celebrations were beginning to ramp up. She cut quickly south on Front Street, back towards The Westin. Teresa had a meeting to keep. She had brief but explicit instructions to ask at the front desk for a man named Mr. Dumas at half past five.

Nearing her hotel, she looked across the street to the Mel Fisher Maritime Museum and could not help but shake her head for the third time again since checking in yesterday at the irony. The museum founders would be quite interested to learn what Teresa had hidden in her handbag. The building was originally a naval storehouse, but now held sunken treasure and shipwreck artifacts on display for the public. Most famously, finds from the Spanish galleons *Nuestra Señora de Atocha* and *Santa Margarita*, wrecked off Key West in 1622.

It had been a tense whirlwind trail since Hurricane Charley back in August that had led Teresa to Key West the day before Halloween.

The 2004 hurricane season turned out to be a banner year; in September three more back-to-back hurricanes hit Florida—Frances, Ivan, and Jeanne, but none with the intensity of Charley. Charley had fortunately been a fast-moving storm with a six-mile-wide pinhole eye, however it brought windspeeds raging on the cusp of Category 5. Charley also did not behave, thwarting the models and predictions that he was going to come ashore near Tampa Bay, instead turning unexpectedly and turning early, making a direct and devastating landfall on the Gulf Coast barrier island of Cayo Costa. The surrounding towns of Boca Grande, Port Charlotte, and Punta Gorda sustained catastrophic damage. Charley brought $14 billion in damages to the Sunshine State and ripped a new pass in North Captiva Island dubbed Charley's Cut.

HURRICANE HOLE

The news broke immediately of escaped felon Travis Gahl, and the treasure. There was a statewide five-day manhunt on for Travis, that was severely hampered and overshadowed by Charley. It ended abruptly when Teresa found reception on Pine Island and got through to the police. Teresa and Kim were interviewed by Charlotte, Lee and Palm Beach County detectives, as well as local and national news reporters hungry for the story—a felon on the lam, a murdered correctional officer and retired Fort Myers detective, multiple homicides inside a state park, and the discovery of riches from the seventeenth century. Teresa kept it as brief as possible, not enjoying any part of the limelight or role as the savior park ranger. She was clear in stating that it was Kim and Andrea who were the first to find the treasure trove on Cayo Costa.

Teresa spent a single night in the hospital. She was lucky, the bullet had missed major arteries and bone in her shoulder, punching neatly through muscle. She was given a cat scan, IV antibiotics, six stitches, and a ten day supply of Vicodin. In a sling for a couple of weeks, her shoulder still ached day-to-day and smarted when she raised her arm.

As the state picked up the wreckage and started to recover from Charley there was extensive coverage on the connected incidents: the Belle Glade prison break, the murders of Palm Beach County correctional officer Warren Hill and retired Fort Myers detective Robert Halliwell, as well as the triple homicides on Cayo Costa, which rocked the town of Englewood and riled the prominent Foster family. Investigators pieced it all together quickly. The vessels *Sabre* and *End of Watch* were both found beached at the south end of Cayo Costa, less than a half mile apart, each with a dead body onboard. Chad Haney was found on the catamaran, and the badly decomposed detective Halliwell on his stolen Bayliner. Mark's body was in the dune right where Kim told authorities it would be. Teresa read the obituaries for Mark Foster, Andrea Valencourt, and Chad Haney in the *Englewood Sun*. She did not visit or speak with Kim Chambers again after that day, but Teresa did not forget her either.

As predicted, Cayo Costa was combed end to end by the Florida Department of State, with swarms of archaeologists from the Division of Historical Resources, as well as teams from FSU's Department of Anthropology. The park was closed to the public for a full month as the treasure was excavated and catalogued. The find appeared to have been linked to and been a part of the *Atocha* galleon fleet. Some of the horde, somehow, ended up buried on Cayo Costa, almost 150 miles due north of the 1622 wreck site off Marquesas Key. A real mystery that had archeologists baffled.

Teresa did feel guilt at taking the dagger. She had stolen what was the highlight showpiece of the find. The dagger would be missing from the roster and cataloguing, separated and lost from the cache, the majority of which looked like it was headed to the Florida Museum of Natural History in Gainesville, and the remainder split between both Mel Fisher Museum locations, the one in Key West and the other on Florida's east coast in Sebastian. She had removed a part of past for her private personal gain. The public would never see the dagger, and the history records had been forever altered.

Any remorse or guilt—that arose like waves throughout the day—left as quickly as it came once she thought it all through again. Teresa was motivated by money, period. She had made her decision that evening on the island. And it held firm.

The news also covered the treasure find in-depth, but what Teresa found perplexing was the lack of coverage and information on the grounded reefer ship *Banten Buru*. Officials from the Anastasi Shipping Line were fast to recover their freighter. Two days after the storm a trio of powerful tugs dragged the ship back into the Gulf at high tide, but there was no sign or talk of the crew. A few wild rumors floated around of a possible mutiny and abandoning, or food poisoning. Teresa did get word that some of the crew had indeed left the reefer and were found up near the Quarantine Rocks at the north end of Cayo Costa. But Teresa never laid eyes on any of them, and Anastasi Shipping Line departed the island quickly and quietly, without ever even speaking with her.

The three coins that fell from Andrea's pockets on the visitor grounds were found, as well as the three emeralds still in the pocket of her shorts. Both Kim and Teresa were asked directly by state officials if they took any of the treasure. Kim said she did not keep anything but was honest in revealing that Andrea took a few silver pieces and stones. Kim also told FSU's archeologists about the dagger.

Under questioning, Teresa held her composure and story well—and lied. She omitted telling investigators she stabbed Gahl, only that she shot him with the gun. They did not ask her about the wound to his side. When asked about a dagger she said she had not seen any sign of an artifact like that. And that was the end of it. They did not press her further, nor request to search her person or home on Pine Island. She was a state park ranger, and a hero, having both been shot by, and having killed, an escaped felon.

Teresa carried on at her job as normal, for another month, completing hurricane recovery and repairs, until the middle of September. Then she resigned, telling her supervisor she was planning on returning north to Minnesota. She worked her final two weeks, giving notice at her rental bungalow on Pine Island. The night of October 3, a Sunday, she waited until two in the morning before driving up to Bokeelia and taking *Lisa Marie* across the black sound on a moonless night towards Cayo Costa.

Heart hammering, nerve up, moving across the grounds in the dark by memory and feel, long shadows cast by a single light up at the ranger station, Teresa found the dagger exactly where she had left it. No one of course would think to scour and search for artifacts where the ground had been already dug up previously when the park sign was installed. Kneeling behind the signpost in near total darkness, she pulled the dagger free from the sandy soil and could still faintly make out the dried smears of blood on the blade.

The next day she left Pine Island for good, driving down to Fort Myers and renting a small efficiency apartment right on the Tamiami Trail. Teresa had spent the past six weeks planning what to do once she had the dagger in her possession, doing some preliminary research, poking around online. She had no idea as to the ornate dagger's exact value but judging from other antiquities she had come across in her searching, and more recently in the Mel Fisher Museum, coupled with the fact the dagger was four centuries old and looked to be attached to the *Atocha* motherlode . . . it was worth a small fortune. Teresa was hoping to net upwards of $200,000 for the dagger from a wealthy private collector.

Searching the web for sales of rare and valuable antiquities, Teresa learned of the active black markets. The online illegal artifact trade was big business, alongside drugs, guns, prostitution, and child pornography. A lot of the online trade seemed to be done in a new cryptic digital currency. These markets were all located on a deep sub-level of the internet not easily accessed. Here, literally and figuratively, Teresa hit a wall, finding herself out of her depth and wading in murky waters she knew nothing about. She had previously only used her laptop to send emails and casually surf the web.

Teresa had noticed a skinny kid in his early twenties regularly hanging out at a beat-up picnic table under the shade of a jacaranda tree at the rear of the apartment complex. He was always wearing baggy shorts and a T-shirt three sizes too large. Sporting pale skin, pimples, and unwashed hair, he was constantly on his mobile phone or hunched over a white Apple laptop. One afternoon, in the slightly cooler temperatures of early fall, Teresa ambled over nonchalantly to speak with him. Exchanging a few words, she learned his name was Kevin. He was twenty-one, lived in the complex with his mother, and seemed friendly enough. He was logged onto something called a LAN, meaning 'local area network'. A wireless connection to the internet.

Learning he was tech-savvy, Teresa asked, "I think you may be able to help me with something . . . can you show me how to access the deep web?"

Kevin looked up at her, squinting against the afternoon sun, eyes mischievous. "You mean like illegal stuff?"

Teresa tried to ignore the whitehead on his greasy nose. "I'll give you fifty bucks if you can show me how it all works."

He simply stared up at her and shrugged. "OK, sure."

Up in Teresa's apartment, Kevin downloaded a Tor browser onto her laptop and used it to gain access to hidden overlay networks. This software covered both Teresa's identity and her tracks online and opened doors leading into the newsgroups—what was the early beginnings of the darknet markets.

"Alright, you're in," Kevin said, expertly clicking off a key and looking up over his shoulder at her. "What exactly are you looking for?"

"Black market trading and sale of antiquities," Teresa

replied. Kevin's expression was unimpressed. She guessed he was expecting or hoping for something more exciting.

"Alright," he said, bemused, punching keys, "antiquities . . . trading forums . . . buying or selling?"

"Selling."

Kevin nudged the touchpad and hit a key. "Here you go. It's up. All you need to do is make an account and create a listing."

Teresa nodded. "That I can do."

He turned to look up at her again and she saw his eyes linger across her breasts. "What is it you are selling?"

Teresa said nothing and pulled two twenties and a ten from the pocket of her shorts.

Kevin looked from the cash again to Tereasa's breasts, and back up to her face. "You're pretty hot for an older chick. Instead of the money, how about a blowjob?"

Teresa's stare was arctic as she held out the money. "How about you take the cash and get the fuck out of my apartment?"

Quickly browbeaten, Kevin diffidently took the bills and departed without ushering another word.

Teresa spent the next couple of hours surfing and learning the deep web trading forums after creating an account. She went out and bought a Sony Cybershot digital camera and photographed the dagger from a half-dozen angles. Under the handle 'OneEyedWilly2004' she posted the dagger—six photos and a short description: "Authentic gold and silver dagger from the August 2004 treasure find on Cayo Costa, Florida. Dated approx. 1622. Total length is 11 inches, blade is 6", handle is 5". Weighs about 1/2 pound. Inlaid with 28 rubies and emeralds."

For three days there was no response to the posting, and Teresa began to worry increasingly with each passing day. She might have to try and sell the dagger via another route. After leaving her park ranger job, cashing out after just two years, she only had enough funds to carry herself for one, maybe two months if she was extremely careful. Coming in from an evening walk on the fourth day since posting the dagger for sale she logged in yet again, her fifth time checking the inbox that day. This time there was a message waiting, from an ambiguous numeric handle.

She clicked on it, finding a brief inquiry: "How did you come across this piece from the Cayo Costa find?"

Teresa thought for a moment, shrugged, shook her head once and typed truthfully: "I was on the island shortly after the hurricane and saw the treasure. I took the dagger." She hit send, trusting the Tor software was going to keep her identity concealed.

Ten minutes later there was a reply: "Interested. I'd like to see the piece firsthand before discussing a price. I will be in Key West the last four days of the month. Can you meet there during this time?"

Teresa typed in response: "Yes. When and where?"

Three minutes later: "On Saturday, October 30 at 5:30pm ask for Mr. Dumas at the front desk of The Westin Resort & Marina."

After a moment thinking this through, Teresa typed back: "OK. I will be there."

She sat back and watched her laptop screen for a reply, but none came. A handful of questions and concerns quickly came to mind—namely, she should have requested that she wanted to be paid in cash. How could she trust an anonymous person on the internet buying illegal goods? Could this be a sting by the feds sweeping the darknet? Was she going to be arrested, abducted or murdered in Key West . . .?

Having no choice but to trust this online connection and move forward, she found the number for The Westin and booked two nights on her credit card, October 30 and 31. She cringed at the price; it was $419 for the two-night booking. The dagger had better pay off, bigtime. She had nineteen days to kill before heading down to the Keys.

All of Teresa's worries arose renewed and swirled through her mind as she entered the lobby of The Westin the night before Halloween. Devil's Night. The daiquiri had done little to calm her jaded nerves. There was a handful of people coming through the lobby, a boisterous gathering, a group from a wedding at the hotel earlier today.

Teresa had heard the scuttlebutt, there was a party staying at the hotel for the Key West wedding, and one of the attendees was the new best-selling author, John Cannon. He had made some headlines recently with his debut novel *Treasure Coast*. Teresa slid herself inconspicuously into a lounge chair off to one far side of the lobby, noting that it was twenty-four minutes past five. She observed the passing wedding party, the bride and groom, an attractive couple in their early thirties, surrounded by friends and family.

She recognized John Cannon in the group immediately from his photos in the papers. Tall, handsome, with an engaging and charismatic smile under a full head of thick and unruly dark brown hair. He had a lot of traits for the leading man, but Cannon was more rugged, hard and rougher around the edges, deeply tanned and fit. He looked like he spent far more time outdoors than at a desk writing books. Everyone in the group was tan, dressed to the nines, and in a celebratory mood. A barrel-chested man with a shaved head somewhere in his mid-forties trailed the company. He caught Teresa's gaze with charming steel gray eyes and winked at her. Teresa compelled a quick smile, and she watched the party exit the hotel, overhearing their banter and laughs. They were headed to dinner at a popular seafood restaurant.

The minutes ticked by. At 5:29 p.m. Teresa stood and crossed the lobby to the front desk. She was steps from the counter when a voice behind her spoke her name, deep and baritone.

"Teresa Randall?"

Teresa inhaled a quick sharp breath, stopped, and turned. A large man stood behind her, towering a half foot overhead. He was in his early-fifties, well-dressed in tan button-up shirt and chambray trousers, huskily built, carrying a bit of weight around the middle, solid weight. He had a large head, with a high sloping forehead and thin black hair, cut short and gelled flat. His eyes were heavy-lidded and dark brown.

Teresa's heart hammered behind her ribcage—she instantly regretted this entire idea. How the hell did this man know her full name? He looked certainly to be an FBI agent or an undercover cop.

He turned out to be neither.

"I'm Mr. Dumas," the man said in his low, resonant voice. There was a hint of a European accent, but Teresa could not place it.

A measure of tension dropped from Teresa's composure. She glanced around quickly; this Mr. Dumas looked to be alone. Before she could speak, he asked, "Do you have the piece on you?"

Teresa hesitated for a moment, unsure, the reply catching in her throat. She finally got the word out. "Yes."

"Would you come with me, please?"

Teresa paused again, but for only a second. "Where to?"

"Through to the rear of the hotel, out to the marina."

Teresa had seen the waterfront boardwalk, shops, and yacht

basin with dozens of moorings for private vessels behind The Westin. Each morning, a massive cruise ship would come in, closing off the basin entirely, unloading passengers for the day to explore the city before departing to clear the view, two hours before sunset. The boardwalk would be chock full of people at this hour, all preparing to watch the sunset.

"Alright," Teresa agreed, again scanning the lobby. There were only a handful of people milling around, and no one was paying them any attention. She followed Dumas past the front desk and down the hotel's main hallway. He said nothing as they walked by the elevators and entered a wide arcade hallway that extended towards the back of the hotel. The bustling arcade was lined on both sides with shops and boutiques catering to the daily flood of guests and tourists.

Teresa's chest tightened as they moved outside into the late-day heat. The sun was even lower in the sky, about an hour left before it disappeared behind the Gulf. The boardwalk was busy, and filling quickly in anticipation of sundown. She stayed with Dumas as he wordlessly set the pace through the mixed crowd: wealthy retired, young honeymooners, families with wailing toddlers, all exhausted, hungry, and hot. The vacationing masses, trying to enjoy their few short days, an expensive escape from the nine to five drudgeries further north.

They left the boardwalk, stepping down a short set of stairs to the dock that ran up and down the basin, passing a half dozen moored boats—liveaboard trawlers, flybridge yacht cruisers, sleek V-hull sport fishers. At the far end of the basin laying alongside the cruise ship pier was a massive superyacht. The Oceanco-built vessel was 200 feet in length with a 35-foot beam. Her white hull and superstructure glinted under the paling autumnal sunlight. It dawned slowly on Teresa as

HURRICANE HOLE

Dumas led her out onto the pier that they were headed straight for the superyacht.

She read the name high on the side of the bridge, above black mirrored windows, raised bronze letters backlit with gold light: *Tigre.*

They walked the full length of the ship, from the bow to the stern, along the ship's starboard side. Dumas remained silent, leading her along at a proper pace. The superyacht reminded Teresa some of the reefer ship. Although not quite as large as the *Banten Buru*, up close *Tigre* was equally overwhelming. And a far more opulent pleasure craft. At the rounded stern, a roped rail and short gangway led to an expansive teak aft deck.

Dumas paused, unclipping the rope, stepping aside and motioned for Teresa to board. "Watch your step," he said, raising a polite and escorting hand to guide the way.

Teresa nodded once and stepped past Dumas, crossing the gangway, onto the superyacht's deck. She waited as Dumas joined her, looking around the rear of the yacht. Forward, twin staircases port and starboard led up to a second level deck. And set stepped above that deck was a third. The yacht's name again, in even larger backlit bronzed relief lettering was set along the overhead stern bulkhead, with the hailing port below: Saint-Tropez.

"This way," said Dumas, leading her forward, towards the starboard set of stairs. Teresa followed him up to the second deck and was fully overwhelmed with the opulence. The wide deck was surrounded by a cushioned settee to the stern, chaise lounges with plush pillows, and in the center a large jacuzzi spa bubbled invitingly. The yacht's accents were all polished chrome steel, glass, and teak. Teresa saw no sign of anyone else, yet. They went forward again, under the open air covered third level owner's deck, passing a massive mahogany dining table and chairs that could seat a dozen. Ahead were two large dark glass double doors. Dumas opened one, stepping aside again for Teresa to enter. She nodded courteously and stepped forward apprehensively into the main deck's salon lounge.

The salon was overwhelming; spacious, bright, cool, and luxuriously appointed, no expense spared. Sheen dark woods and chrome steels, recessed lighting overhead, thick pile cream carpet underfoot. To starboard was a table and four chairs, and a full-size and fully stocked bar. To port was a wide plush sofa, with two contemporary swivel chairs, and between, a large mahogany coffee table polished to a mirror surface.

Crossing towards the sofa, Dumas motioned for Teresa to sit. "Please, make yourself comfortable. We'll be with you momentarily."

Teresa smiled cordially and sat in one of the deep swivel chairs, placing the handbag on her lap. She watched Dumas exit the lounge through a forward door, leaving her alone. She chewed on her bottom lip, watching the crowds gather along the boardwalk across the basin through the tinted salon windows. The sun was dipping off *Tigre*'s stern, the sky a transitioning palette of burnt orange, fuchsia, and lavender.

Three minutes after Dumas departed, he returned, opening the door to the salon for a tall striking man. Teresa turned to take him in; he was taller even than Dumas, six foot five at least, handsome, with a strong angular face and square jaw, clean shaven, skin incredible clear and lightly tanned. He had jet black hair, steel gray eyes, and was about thirty years of age—much younger than Teresa had expected—his physique athletic and well-appointed in a tailored blue dress shirt with the sleeves rolled up, tucked into belted steel gray slacks. He wore a large, blue-faced steel wristwatch, his forearms long and well-muscled. It seemed he took Teresa in much more quickly

329

than she did him. He smiled at her as he approached, an ice-breaking smile, but sincere, warm around the eyes.

"Teresa—welcome aboard *Tigre*. My name is Maximilien." He spoke with a French accent, but in perfect English, while extending a hand to Teresa. She made to stand, and he said, "Please—no need to get up." She remained sitting and took his hand, his grip firm, skin dry and soft. He smelled fresh and strongly masculine. He continued to smile at her, eye contact and charm and pheromones emanating, all working on her effectively. Maximilien released her hand and sat smoothly at the end of the sofa, adjacent to her, all grace and polish.

"Would you like something to drink?" he asked.

"Yes, please," Teresa replied, answering too quickly, nervous and not wanting to be rude. "Just some water would be fine." She immediately regretted accepting the offer. She would not drink anything he offered her.

Maximilien looked over to Dumas who stood by the doorway and said, "Two ice waters." Dumas nodded and crossed efficiently over to the bar, setting about getting the drinks.

Teresa refrained from watching Dumas, and looked Maximilien squarely in the face, composing herself. "I'd like to know how you know my name?"

Maximilien smiled again and leaned back, adjusting himself on the couch. "It was not hard to figure that out, Teresa. A park ranger who walks out on her job shortly after discovering one of the largest treasure finds in the Americas. I followed the news stories on the find closely, of course, and saw you interviewed. There is also your photo on the Florida State Parks website. Well, there was . . . they've since removed it—due to your change in careers. Mr. Dumas laid eyes on you arriving at your hotel earlier today."

Teresa stiffened slightly, and glanced over at Dumas, but he did not look up from the bar.

"You can relax," said Maximilien. "Any of your secrets are safe with me. As, I hope, mine are with you. If you have what you claim to have, you have taken quite a piece. It is possible certain people may be keeping tabs on you as well, but we haven't seen any sign of you being followed to Key West."

Teresa said nothing, digesting all this, her heart rate elevating. A light sheen of sweat broke out up and down her back, damp against the $2200 microfiber camel leather chair.

"I heard you had some other nasty business on the island to contend with. There were some deaths, murders?"

Teresa nodded. "Yes."

"I'm glad to see you fared well. How is your shoulder?"

Teresa was taken aback again by Maximilien's insight. "It's OK."

Dumas crossed the salon and efficiently set down two tall glasses of water wrapped in napkins on the table in front of them, ice tinkling. He returned silently to stand obediently again by the doorway. Teresa, nervously again rethinking accepting the offer of a drink, did not touch her glass. Maximilien reached for his glass and took a healthy swallow. Cutting through her hesitation and trying not to appear awkward, Teresa picked up her glass and took a tentative small sip. The water tasted clean and pure and was velvety smooth on her tongue.

"It's Fijian," said Maximilien. "The water comes from an artesian aquifer in Viti Levu."

"Very nice," Teresa replied, setting the glass back down and cocking her head to glance around the salon. "As is your yacht. Impressive."

"Thank you. *Tigre* is indeed a beauty. She gets me around— for now. I have plans in the works for another yacht, something a little bigger . . . something a little different. More of a floating island, actually."

"Sounds expensive."

"It will be, by the time it is complete." Maximilien said, setting his glass down. He sat forward, not able to conceal his eagerness. "Now, I'd really love to see what you have."

"Yes, of course," Teresa said. She unzipped her handbag and without any fanfare withdrew the dagger. Maximilien's eyes widened at the sight of the relic, and he sat up, placing a hand under his chin, resting his elbow on the opposite forearm. Watching his reaction, Teresa used her left hand to turn the weapon, reversing her grip, and held the dagger out by the blade, hilt towards Maximilien. Not able to cover a modest surprise at her casualness, he smiled and accepted the dagger, grasping it gingerly by the extended hilt. He spent a full minute looking over the 400-year-old weapon from all angles, weighing it in his hand and studying it closely before speaking.

"Fantastic," he said softly. "What an incredible find." He looked up at Dumas and nodded once. Dumas immediately turned and left the salon.

Teresa looked back to Maximilien after nervously watching Dumas depart. She said, "The State of Florida has the remainder of the find, everything except this piece."

Maximilien nodded slowly, still enthralled with the dagger. He looked up at her. "No one else knows you have this?"

"No."

Maximilien gazed silently upon the dagger for another minute. Dumas returned; this time accompanied by a short, heavyset man appearing in his late sixties. The man was nearly completely bald, ruddy faced, and wore small glasses. Dumas positioned himself back at the bar, an obedient sentinel. The older man ignored Teresa completely as he approached the lounge area and sat in the swivel chair adjacent to Maximilien. He unrolled a small white cloth about eighteen inches square and set it out on the coffee table. Inside were three small items, which he removed and placed on the table beside the cloth. Wordlessly, Maximilien handed the man the dagger. The man studied the dagger closely for a moment, then lay the blade across as open palm. He raised and lowered the dagger three times, hefting it gently, judging the weight, feeling the balance. Without saying anything he placed it in the center of the cloth.

Teresa swallowed hard and watched in silence. Her mouth had gone dry, and she wanted to take another sip of the water but did not.

Moving with the practiced efforts of a professional, the man measured the dagger from pommel to point and across the quillons with a soft measuring tape. Then he placed what looked like a small magnet on both the blade and hilt. Nodding once, he set the magnet device aside and put a pair of yellow-lensed goggles on over his glasses. He switched on a small penlight that shone a bright blue light, which he passed slowly over the dagger. He picked the weapon up and aimed the light at the multitude of embedded stones, green and red beams refracting brilliantly across the polished table. Nodding again, he set the dagger back down on the cloth, switched off the light and removed the goggles, setting them aside, and retrieved the final object, a small glass dropper bottle.

Teresa watched curiously, and somewhat hesitantly, as the man let fall a single drop of clear liquid from the dropper on both the silver blade and gold hilt. He set the dropper down, leaned forward and observed the dagger closely for a full half minute. Teresa watched closely as well, and she saw nothing out of the ordinary happen. No reaction. The drops just sat still, remaining inert on the metal.

Seemingly satisfied, the man sat up and turned to look at Maximilien. "*C'est vrais, authentique.*"

Maximilien nodded. "*Merci.*"

The man silently collected up his items, leaving the dagger on the table, stood and departed the salon as quickly and quietly as he had arrived.

Maximilien sat back on the couch, steepled his index fingers and looked over them at Teresa. "How much would you like for this piece?"

Teresa sucked quickly on her teeth. Hesitating, she ran a lock of her hair behind an ear. "To be honest, I'm not quite sure what it is worth."

Maximilien said nothing, observing Teresa closely for a few moments. He lowered his hands and spoke succinctly. "I'll pay you one million dollars for both the dagger and your silence. One million dollars, and you erase the dagger from your mind, completely. This transaction never happened, and we never met. Do we have a deal?"

Teresa sat completely still, in shock and sheer disbelief over the offered sum. She did not reply immediately, with both surprise and a growing unease that the incredible offer was a ruse. She glanced quickly over at Dumas, who now leaned more casually against the bar. His face was unreadable. Teresa returned her focus to Maximilien. There was nothing in his attitude that suggested this was a feint or bogus offer. And he certainly appeared like a person who could drop a million dollars on an antique.

Teresa ran a tongue over her lips. She spoke slowly, "OK, we have a deal."

Maximilien grinned. "Fantastic. I'm going to pay you $250,000 in cash, right now, and I will also"—Maximilien nodded at Dumas—"transfer $750,000 into an account for you at the National Bank in Grand Cayman."

Teresa was still reeling and overwhelmed with the figures of the deal. She nodded, just along for the ride now. The offered sum was five times what she hoped to get for the dagger. She saw Dumas retrieve something from behind the bar. He approached the coffee table and upon it set down a laptop and a light gray attaché case. Dumas also took a small notepad and pen from his pocket and placed it on the table, before returning to his position beside the bar.

Maximilien flipped the laptop open and began typing, fast, his long manicured fingers flicking expertly over the keys. After a minute, he spun the laptop so that the screen was visible to both himself and Teresa. She saw an online banking account on the screen, much like her own. The balance on the account was indeed $750,000 in U.S. currency.

Maximilien said, "I've transferred the money into a numbered account. This account cannot be traced, accessed, or connected to either of us. The bank is physically located in George Town, Grand Cayman. You can access the funds from anywhere globally with your DAN—that is, your depositor account number, and your unique SWIFT code." Maximilien picked up the pen and wrote briefly on the pad, copying numbers from the screen. He tore off the sheet and handed it to Teresa. "Here are both."

Teresa took the slip of notepaper and read the two lines of neatly printed alphanumeric codes. They meant nothing to her, she only understood the basics, but the process seemed simple enough. She had no real choice but to trust Maximilien. From what she had seen and experienced since the beginning she had no reason to distrust him.

Maximilien flipped up the double latches on the attaché

case, opened the lid and turned it towards Teresa. "Some walking around cash, to get you going," he said.

Teresa's eyes zig-zagged over the twenty-five bundles of hundred dollar bills, each mustard yellow paper band marked $10,000. Her heart thrummed with excitement at the sight of the hard currency. Even if she was taken for a ride for the remaining three-quarters, with this cash sum alone she still would net more for the dagger than she had hoped.

She looked up at Maximilien. "Alright, this will work."

"I hope so. It's been a pleasure doing business with you, Teresa. Dumas will show you off."

Teresa closed and relatched the attaché case, folded the slip of notepaper over once and put it in her pocket. She got to her feet and Maximilien stood with her. He extended an arm, and they shook hands, brief but firm. Teresa slung the empty Nautica bag over her shoulder and picked up the attaché case. It weighed about five pounds, give or take. Dumas again held out an arm, leading her back aft. She stepped away, but as she neared the salon door, Maximilien spoke again.

"Teresa . . ."

She paused to look back to where he stood behind the coffee table.

"I like you," Maximilien continued, his eyes crinkling at the corners, "please don't forget our deal. Keep your head down and make that money last. We don't want any . . . trouble." His steel gray eyes bored into her, his expression sincere and tone cordial, but his implication deadly serious. Possibly a veiled threat?

She said nothing, but nodded firmly, returning his look; their trust and agreement were mutual. Without a word Teresa turned and followed Dumas outside and down the stairs to the aft deck. The sun was lower in the sky again, almost about to set, and the heat less intense, but the evening air was still incredibly warm. From across the city came the sounds of the festivities, ramping up now, combined with the building excitement for the coming sunset. Dumas crossed the gangway, unclipped the barrier rope, and waited for Teresa to follow. She stepped across and down from the superyacht, and Dumas only gave her a courteous nod, before reclipping the rope and departing across the deck.

As Teresa turned and walked the length of the pier to the boardwalk, she felt a giddiness take her over. A mixed wash of relief, disbelief, and excitement. The attaché case felt both light and heavy in her hand. So little weight for so much monetary power. A quarter of a million dollars. The moment and experience felt unreal. She edged her way into the crowd and onto the packed boardwalk, blending into the people gathering to watch the sun sink behind the Gulf. The sun shot shimmering waves of golden light across the water.

As she neared the rear entrance of the hotel, she caught sight of one of the marina staff—a man in his early twenties—coiling a line from a large sport fisher over his shoulder. Teresa changed her path, angling across the boardwalk towards him. She caught his eye, and said, "Hey—I have a question for you."

The sunburnt young deckhand looked at her, continuing to wrap the heavy spring line. "Shoot, and I'll see if I have an answer for you."

Teresa glanced back at *Tigre* across the far side of the basin. "That yacht there, do you know who owns that one?"

"Yeah, I sure do—it belongs to the French billionaire, Maximilien Barre. He came in two days ago."

"What's a yacht like that cost?" she asked casually.

"Hell—a superyacht like that? That'll run you about thirty or forty million, maybe more. I'd sure love to see inside her."

Teresa smiled. "So would I. Thank you."

Heady and euphoric, she made her way towards the hotel, the last rays of the days sun hot on her back and shoulders.

CHAPTER EIGHTEEN

December 31, 2004
Bimini, Bahamas

The Sea Ray Sundancer cut the late afternoon swells easily, the thirty-five-foot vessel's lines sleek and balanced. She had a single cabin forward, in a long bow, with an open helm and cockpit. The fast-setting winter sun glinted off the darkening turquoise water and the boat's crisp white hull as the Sundancer circled about and came to a rolling stop. The name across her transom above the swim platform was *Scot-Free*.

Teresa stood at the wheel, eyes skimming back and forth across the sparkling horizon. The Bimini sun had bronzed her even more deeply the past two months. She wore a light coral-colored sun wrap that flapped loosely in the breeze, over a lemon-yellow one-piece swimsuit, her bare feet planted wide, firm on the deck.

Teresa purchased the Sundancer, only a year old, in a fast and smooth cash sale from a seller at a marina in Alice Town. This was only a week after she bought a two-bedroom condo at the Bimini Bay Resort for $128,000. The 1,100 square foot condo was only eighteen grand more than the Sundancer and came with a slip for the boat. Teresa had no problems accessing the funds in the Caymanian account from a bank in Bimini, where she also made a healthy deposit of what was left of the $250,000 in cash.

She had left Key West on October 31, the day after the meet with Maximilien, driving back up to Fort Myers and checking out of her efficiency apartment. Teresa then drove directly north a little over an hour to the town of Englewood and checked into a small motel for the night. She had been having recurring thoughts of Kim Chambers over the past couple of months. Kim had survived multiple assaults from a psychopathic felon, lost her boyfriend and two friends, and despite being the one who first discovered the treasure trove on Cayo Costa, had been all but snubbed by the Florida Department of State.

An idea had first formed early on in Teresa's mind, soon after the incident on the island, and grew in design after she successfully sold the dagger. An idea partially motivated by guilt, to offset any bad karma, and do what she felt was right, deserved and just.

Teresa had already done some background checking on Kim. Kim worked as a pre-school teacher at Englewood Elementary and walked the two blocks to work from her apartment on Orange Street. She was a single mom and had a four-year-old daughter named Kayla. Near sunset on Halloween night, having parked her Jeep in the small neighborhood park at the north end of Orange Street, Teresa had waited in the rising dusk, until she caught sight of Kim and her young daughter heading out together, trick-or-treating. The preschool-age girl was dressed as a bumblebee. Hand in hand, they walked a couple of blocks down to the town's main street where the shops were open late, handing out candy.

Once they were out of sight Teresa moved quickly. She exited her Jeep and crossed the parking lot, approaching the short driveway to a row of small bungalow apartments adjacent to the park. She held a small, sealed manila envelope in her hand. On the front, Teresa had written: Kim Chambers. Inside was $50,000 cash. Five banded bundles of hundreds, and a short note, also handwritten:

Kim,

*This is for you, you earned it. Use it as cash, do
not put it in the bank, and keep your head down.*

A friend

Teresa put the envelope in the mailbox, walked briskly back
to her Jeep, and drove straight through into the falling night for
three and a half hours to Fort Lauderdale, where she checked
into a hotel. The next morning she found a dealership and sold
her seven-year-old Jeep, practically giving it away to ensure
a fast cash sale. She booked the afternoon ferry from Port
Everglades to Fisherman's Village on North Bimini. The only
risk here was entering The Bahamas with close to $200,000 in
cash in her possession. Disembarking the ferry two hours later
she slipped into the country without a problem.

The money—used carefully—padded out a prime lifestyle.
Teresa was living well beyond her highest hopes. As far as she
knew, no one was after her, and even if they were, they wouldn't
know where to begin looking. Her ex-employer, Florida State
Parks, believed she had gone back north. They'd probably start
in Minnesota. Of course it wouldn't be too difficult to trace
her, but why would anyone be even looking? They would have
a hard time proving she did anything wrong, or at least she
thought. As Maximilien had advised her, and Teresa herself
had advised Kim, she kept her head down, laying low. In a few
months she would contact Bahamian Immigration and extend
her stay, having invested in real estate, vessel ownership, and
banking on the island nation.

Scot-Free settled nicely in the offshore swells, sitting in
about twenty feet of water. Teresa dropped the hook with the
electric windlass from the helm, felt it set nicely in the sand
bottom, and powered down the Sundancer's twin engines. She

341

HURRICANE HOLE

went below into the galley and pulled a chilled stainless-steel tumbler from the compact freezer. She had mixed herself a perfect margarita, shaken with crushed ice, heavy on tequila.

The cold steel condensing in her hand, Teresa made her way out onto the extended bow. The Sea Ray pitched gently, pointed into an easy southwest breeze coming across the straits from Florida. Two days after purchasing the vessel she had the boat renamed—a full and proper christening ceremony, safe from the wrath of Poseidon—from the cliché and asinine *Nauti Girl* to *Scot-Free*.

Teresa sipped her margarita and watched the final sunset of 2004, contemplating the day's events. She had had no problems since arriving in the Bahamas—until this morning.

Shortly after waking on the last day of the year, settling onto her balcony overlooking the boat slips with a coffee, Teresa had logged into her email, a new account she had made just five weeks ago. There was a message waiting. The sender and subject immediately caught her eye, and hesitating for only a moment, she clicked on it:

> from: Max <oneeyedwilly_1632@hotmail.com>
> to: biminiblue_1968@hotmail.com
> date: December 31, 2004, 9:08 AM
> subject: Scot-Free
>
> Teresa,
>
> I am checking in to see how you are faring at your newly acquired condo on Bimini. A choice location, and the Sea Ray is a worthy craft as well. I do love the new name you chose for the boat, quite fitting. I think it would be

best if you did not return to the States anytime soon. If you ever need assistance, you can contact me via this email.

Happy New Year.

M

Teresa read the email a second time, and then a third, her heart rate elevating further with each read through. Maximilien Barre knew where she was, what she was doing, and had managed to somehow obtain her newly created email address. She had not used the address publicly anywhere; in fact she had hardly used it at all. The billionaire had a far greater reach and power than she could even imagine. The message was friendly, non-threatening, offered her what must be sage advice, and even help. Maximilien's experience and knowledge was far greater than hers. It was advice she would follow.

She had to smile wanly at his email address, obviously newly created as well, and the message likely sent from an untraceable Tor browser and VPN. Bringing up Google she typed in "Maximilien Barre" and spent a few minutes skim-reading a handful of articles about the French billionaire. He was born July 6, 1975 in Marseilles, France, and it looked like most of his wealth came from real estate interests, as well as publishing and spirits.

The magnate owned a publishing house in London, several distilleries in Scotland, and was the founder CEO of Barre & Company, a real estate venture dealing exclusively in multimillion-dollar listings around the world with offices in Paris, New York, and Miami. Barre also owned several personal properties, a main seafront villa residence in Saint-Tropez, an island in the Exumas, and a large estate in the Coconut Grove neighborhood of Miami on Biscayne Bay—interestingly, less than sixty miles from Bimini. Teresa read an interview with Barre and his future plans to design and construct a floating island mega yacht with the German shipyard Lürssen in Bremen.

After thinking for a minute, returning to her email account, she had sent back a short reply:

> **M,**
>
> **Thank you for reaching out, and for both the advice and your offer.**
>
> **Happy New Year to you as well.**
>
> **T**

From *Scot-Free*'s bow, as Teresa looked upon the setting sun, now half obscured below the horizon, reflecting again on Maximilien's email, she felt both unsettled and guarded. Their exchange, like the face-to-face meeting in Key West, was a mutual understanding and agreement. They had a deal, but she had not been planning on him observing her every move.

She watched the top of the sun dip below *Scot-Free*'s bow rail, only a slice of the molten-gold orb remaining, before finally disappearing behind the Atlantic. A brilliant flash of emerald-green light unexpectedly topped the fading crescent.

Teresa inhaled sharply, her mouth falling open, blinking once, and it was gone. She knew what she had witnessed, a rare and elusive sunset phenomenon—the green flash. It was a once in a lifetime sighting. She had watched for a green flash many evenings off Cayo Costa but had yet to ever see one.

Until now . . . alone, on her own boat, off the island of Bimini, on the last sunset of the year. Teresa accepted the remarkable sighting for the mythos behind it: a sign of good luck.

At least that is what she chose to believe.

ADDENDUM

I was in the final stages of preparing this novel for publication when Hurricane Ian formed in the Caribbean and looked to be headed straight for Florida. Unbelievably, Ian not only followed a similar path to Hurricane Charley in 2004 but made landfall in the same place—on the barrier island of Cayo Costa—ironically, at almost the same time of day. Ian was a Category 4 hurricane with 155 mile-per-hour sustained winds when it made landfall on September 28, 2022. Ian was much larger than Charley, more powerful, slower moving, with a massive eye, and struck at high tide—a deadly aggregation of worst-case scenarios.

The day before the hurricane's arrival my wife and I made the difficult decision to leave our home and evacuate from the town of Englewood, out of the storm's path. The day after Ian passed, we learned—miraculously—that our home withstood more than five hours of Cat 4 winds with minimal damage. Many others in town, even on the same street, were not nearly as lucky. Englewood took a severe beating with widespread damage. We were quite fortunate to dodge several bullets with the storm; evacuating early, escaping serious damage, and having a place to stay on the East Coast during the aftermath. In the U.S. Ian caused an estimated $67 billion in damages, and in Florida took the lives of 130 people, knocking out power to more than 2.4 million homes and businesses.

In researching *Hurricane Hole* I was able to stay at a remote cabin on Cayo Costa belonging to Margi Nanney. That cabin is a setting in this story and was indeed hit by Hurricane Charley in August of 2004. Eighteen years later the cabin would be directly hammered again, even harder, by Hurricane Ian—coincidentally just two months prior to the release of this novel. A couple of days after Ian I came across newly updated NOAA satellite photos showing the storm's destruction, and the first place I zoomed in on was the cabin. I couldn't believe to see it was still there.

I immediately called Margi and she was overwhelmingly relieved to learn that her cabin, which sits directly on the state park's beachfront, had survived. Margi had been in tears for two straight days, almost certain that with the size, strength, and landfall of Ian that their island home was lost. The cabin was constructed in 1974 specifically to withstand hurricane-force winds by U.S. Air Force lieutenant colonel Phil Rasmussen—the distinguished World War II "pajama pilot" of Pearl Harbor—and successfully bore the brunt of both Charley and Ian. These hurricanes weren't the first, and they certainly won't be the last, but the cabin will likely remain standing long after we are gone.

Todd Cameron
Englewood, Florida
October 11, 2022

AUTHOR'S NOTE

Thank you for reading my novel *Hurricane Hole*. I hope you enjoyed the book, and if you did, I thank you again for taking just a minute to leave a review on Amazon. As an independently published author reviews from readers are crucial. You can also support me by recommending and sharing this book with family, friends, and book clubs, and following me online. I love to hear from my readers, so please feel free to reach out via the CONTACT page on my website. Thanks again, and I'll see you inside another story soon!

To receive news and updates on upcoming novels you can sign up for my newsletter here and you will also receive a free ebook of my novella *Midnight Pass:* www.toddcameron. net/newsletter

Find my books on Amazon: www.amazon.com/Todd-Cameron/e/B0979CKVP4

Connect on Facebook: www.facebook.com/toddcameronauthor

Follow on Instagram: @toddcameronauthor

ABOUT THE AUTHOR

Todd Cameron was born in Canada in 1974 and raised in small town rural Ontario. His early pursuits were athletic before an injury finally settled him down to focus on writing—a passion he has had since childhood. Todd has owned and operated a shark diving venture, and is a certified ocean lifeguard, scuba diver, swim coach, and former elite athlete. He completed a 1430-mile (2300 km) swim distance challenge to raise awareness for sharks, swimming the same length as the Great Barrier Reef. He competed successfully in open water swimming in the U.S., Canada, Australia, and the Caribbean with sponsorships from Arena Swimwear and Orca Wetsuits. Todd enjoys reading, movies, fitness, travel, shark diving, and being out on the water. He lives in South Florida.

WWW.TODDCAMERON.NET
FB & IG: @TODDCAMERONAUTHOR